WATCH OVER ME II:
A CHRISTMAS TALE

AJAY BELL

Copyright © 2025 Ajay Bell

All rights reserved.

Contributions by Trinity Bell

First Edition: 2025

No part of this publication may be reproduced, distributed, or transmitted in any form or by any means, including photocopying, recording, or other electronic or mechanical methods, without the prior written permission of the publisher, except as permitted by U.S. copyright law or through quotations in a book review.

References to historical events, persons, or places are used fictitiously. Names, characters, and locations are all products of the author's imagination, and any resemblance to actual events, persons, or places is entirely coincidental.

ISBN (Hardcover): 979-8-9985652-2-9
ISBN (Paperback): 979-8-9985652-3-6

In memory of

Mary Nichols

Beloved and compassionate soul, supporter of this series, and a radiant force of kindness

1953-2025

Contents

I.	Summer's End	01
II.	Home	06
III.	Welcome to Bedfordshire	17
IV.	All Hallows Eve, Part II	28
V.	Life After	35
VI.	Yuletide	49
VII.	Lord of Misrule	64
VIII.	Sojourn	80
IX.	Solivagant	97
X.	The First Day of Christmas	113
XI.	And So It Begins, Once More	124
XII.	A Watery Grave	133
XIII.	Recidivism	143
XIV.	Lull	156
XV.	Memento Mori	174
XVI.	Hysteria	191
XVII.	Tranquility	212
XVIII.	Face to Face with Evil	227
XIX.	Homecoming	243
XX.	The Plan	261
XXI.	Trapped	275
XXII.	This Mortal Coil	293
XXIII.	Watch Over Me, Part II	302
XXIV.	This Side of the Grave	315
XXV.	Up in Flames	336
XXVI.	Deliver Us	357
XXVII.	A Christmas Tale	373
XXVIII.	Purpose	388

Preface

Emelie and her companions seek refuge in a distant port village after surviving the witch trials in Warren Hollow. This settlement is untouched by witchcraft and could allow the survivors to start anew. But in the wake of disaster, healing is much easier said than done. Part II in the *Watch Over Me* series portrays the lasting effects of trauma, manifested through the eyes of victims in colonial America who were fortunate enough to survive this persecution throughout history.

1

Summer's End

The cell feels familiar whilst the door locks behind us. It's as though I am home, reliving the vivid memory that has haunted me each night since our departure. 'Tis a strange feeling to be back in confinement because I never truly escaped the prison of my mind. Dusk brings sleepless nights and echoes of the bitter cold, screams, death, and paralyzing fear until dawn. No matter how far we span from Warren Hollow, its wicked grasp may never be broken. This was not the outcome that any of us could have anticipated.

"Emelie, you must devise an escape! Just as you have before," Thomasin pleads.

I turn, meeting her gaze and offering a despairing reply. "I'm afraid it would be impossible. We shall be trapped until our execution."

None of us were truly prepared for the journey that followed our departure from Rose's home. Samuel, Henry, Thomasin, and I bid farewell to Warren Hollow on that beautiful spring morning without a care in the world. Henry held a general sense of direction from the beginning, but the months of losing our way cannot be ignored. Oftentimes our path was undeviating while we passed landmarks that validated correct movements. Then there were the weeks of traveling in a circle, backtracking and spending day after day trying to make sense of our surroundings. This often led to bickering and exhaustion amongst us, though the thought of returning to The Hollow never crossed our minds.

    Nonetheless, I would not change a single facet of our journey. Even the instances of doubt, starvation, sadness, or those minor disputes. When traversing with nothing more than the company of others, 'tis hard to deny that tempers will rise and friendships can momentarily falter. But the most prevalent factor of our expedition was the pure happiness that we shared. None of us ever traveled beyond the limits of Warren Hollow, aside from Henry in his infancy. This was something we longed for since the days of our birth. A shared desire to reach the faraway village of our dreams or perhaps anywhere outside of The Hollow. We never anticipated that the journey would be a destination in itself.

    Then why do you hold so tightly to those feelings of guilt, shame, and sadness that you refuse to release? Did you not bid farewell to the Emelie of old on that day months ago?

    It would be foolish to think that each of us does not conceal troubles from our past. Perhaps it was unwise to believe that we could move forward from such a tragedy with ease. We spoke little of it on our journey but there is a mutual sentiment surrounding us, and we thought that distance would leave the struggles behind.

    Though unspoken, Samuel still fights to free himself from the guilt of that night in the courthouse. Henry and I's relationship has flourished, yet I feel moments of distance when he experiences his own shame for removing my hand and the troubles that followed. And Thomasin, my best friend and sister at heart, believed she was to be murdered at my own betrayal.

Sometimes I sense her fear when we are alone, or perhaps it is but a projection of my own guilt. I too struggle with what we endured and taking Reverend Thomas's life has cursed me with endless anguish. Although he was a wicked man who deserved to meet his end, my actions still haunt me. Nightmares of being trapped in the prison occur each night when we rest and bouts of panic unravel at the slightest indication of our past. No matter how much I try to hide my shaking hand or my heavy breath, I suspect the others are surely wise to it.

    As time passes, I accept the realization that I may never move on and have yet to fully try. Beneath all the hardship, under the months of torture and witchcraft troubles, there is some good that must be preserved. A single thought burns in my mind each day, my dear brother, John. 'Tis difficult to put my past life to rest because this would also disperse the memories of my brother. His presence has been felt at my side since the beginning of our journey, as I often find myself whispering to him or envisioning the life we could have had. I also ponder on the current state of The Hollow, and how Reverend Gregory would have reacted to Rose's writings. Are the others safe? Does all of Warren Hollow understand that witchcraft was merely a cloak for injustice? Perhaps I shall never know the answers to such questions.

    To my own fault, I have yet to inform the others of the truth behind our torture. Fear often prevents me from relaying the fact that Reverend Thomas used witchcraft accusations to conceal his own sin.

'Tis not of your own doing so you must speak the truth and let them understand. You need not be afraid. They will not leave you and return to The Hollow, will they?

I struggle to reveal that our torture was meaningless or that each of us did not play a part in ridding The Hollow of witchcraft. 'Tis frightening to relay that witchcraft was never the issue and that we were imprisoned under no fault of our own. Our innocence was something we held from the very beginning, but for Reverend Thomas to also know that we were innocent is truly heavy to bear. When the right moment presents itself, I shall reveal it to the fullest extent. However, such an opportunity did not arise on our trek.

But my words should not come across as deceitful, for we had a wonderful journey over the spring and summer season. Our bond is an unbreakable one. An alliance that shall hold until we are no longer breathing. We traveled far and wide together; passing through valleys and climbing mountains, spending nights with strangers that we met along the way, trading and holding company until we needed to advance, and gaining tremendous knowledge.

Endless communities, families, and plantations welcomed us on our travels. Not once did we ever feel danger as we walked through the walls of villages or even when we attended a day of thanks in a farming village struggling worse than The Hollow. We saw the world and fulfilled the desire we shared since infancy. I was fortunate enough to meet a blacksmith in a recent village, and he forged a makeshift steel hand in exchange for one of Rose's recipe scrolls. While it does not function as a full replacement, this has tremendously restored my confidence.

Another restoration that none of us can deny is faith. I made a vow in the prison that I would never turn my back to God again if my survival was granted. While it feels strange at times, we often start and end our days with a subtle prayer. 'Tis not to the same regard as a Reverend's teachings, but we make an effort out of principle. We attended service on numerous occasions while moving from village to village, listening to the unique interpretations and meeting members of the church with no resemblance to Reverend Thomas.

    There be not enough words to fully explain our journey, as the fine details could surpass the length of each and every one of Rose's writings. The fact is that we survived because of each other and finally reached our destination at the tail of summer. With these wonderful companions by my side, I put all my faith into achieving a better future. And while we are uncertain of what lies ahead, my desire is to become nothing more than a commoner in this faraway land.

II

Home

Afall of the leaf and a chill in the air indicates that autumn is upon us. Farming shall soon receive its well-deserved rest as the harvest approaches. 'Twas precisely this time last year when our lives were forever changed. Witchcraft was looming over our village until it broke through the walls on All Hallows Eve. This was the day that altered the course of our lives, so I approach such a recurrence with extra precaution.

"You need not fear such a frivolous day, for the village revels in such a celebration and so does this farm," Henry's uncle, Nicholas, reminds me.

It has been with tremendous difficulty to recapture the magic of All Hallows Eve. We fear showing any signs of celebration and kept our rebellious believes at bay on our travels. However, I must remind myself that life is not the same here as it was in The Hollow.

Our expedition finally came to an end when we reached the Miller family's homestead. And true to the words of Henry, it was a magnificent sight. Their property spans further than any area in Warren Hollow and sits secluded without any neighbors. The home itself is surrounded by vast fields of crops and trees.

Watch Over Me: A Christmas Tale

We arrived in the late hours of the night to this mysterious land but a month ago. Carefully we crept along the outskirts of the nearby village until locating the largest surrounding structure. Henry ensured that his memory was valid and knocked at the door while Samuel, Thomasin, and I stayed a few steps from the porch. I was unsure of what to expect, nervous that our company would not be welcomed by his family or in the nearby village. Both Henry's Uncle Nicholas and Aunt Amelia opened the door, soon recognizing Henry in a state of disbelief while pulling him in for a solid embrace. The rest of us felt immediate relief at the realization that our journey had finally concluded. No more nights of sleeping under the stars or scrounging for a meal.

They talked under the light of lanterns for a few minutes until Henry turned and signaled for the rest of us to approach. One by one we exchanged greetings and friendly introductions. I felt a sense of comfort, as Nicholas and Amelia reminded me of Mother and Father in the days of old. They appeared a bit older in age than I anticipated, but Amelia was beautiful with long brown hair and a perfect smile, and there is quite the resemblance between Henry and his uncle. He has a similar stature, likely from years of farming, and is significantly taller than any of us with a maintained beard. Their presence was welcoming and charming.

"Henry says we have much to discuss," Amelia explained, "but that shall wait until the sun rises. You all need a good night's rest!"

Without further discussion of our situation, they invited us inside for the night. Once more we were amazed by the magnitude of such a structure, unable to make a fair comparison to our homes in The Hollow. Henry told no lies when recalling the wealth and regard that had fallen upon his family. Although it was earned through difficult years of farming and working tirelessly. They gave us a brief tour of the home and showed us rooms that we could occupy for the night. We were all exhausted and ready to collapse so we quickly situated ourselves. I was taken aback by the presence of a nearby mirror, and my rugged appearance halted my steps. Nobody in The Hollow could afford such a possession, so I moved closer in wondrous awe. For reasons unknown it felt strange to look myself in the eyes, perhaps even shameful, so I quickly looked away and vowed to maintain a distance from this item until our departure. Though I knew that it was not the dirt or torn clothes that bothered me, for it was the remnants of the person underneath.

It felt a bit strange to separate from the others for the first time since our days in the prison. Nonetheless, we said our farewells while Samuel and Thomasin entered their chamber for the night. Henry and I found our space down the hall, thanking his relatives once again before disappearing behind a closed door.

"Thank thee for bringing us to such a place, Henry. This home is incredible, and your aunt and uncle are lovely," I said.

"Aye, we finally made it. I spoke quickly of our journey, but perhaps there is someone who can provide the details better than anyone else," Henry replied in a suggestive manner.

I laughed at his words. "And who may that be?"

Henry looked around the room before pointing at me. "Our leader, of course," he declared. For a moment my playfulness dispersed, as I had not been regarded in such a manner for quite some time. Everything was in equal standing on our journey, and I was no longer the leader or the one guiding us.

Such a position was something I hoped to leave in the past, although I doubt it is a reputation I could ever fully outrun.

You cannot deny the enjoyment you felt from that power. It was stressful and frightening at times, but they believed you were the one who could rise above and make a change. And in truth, you knew so as well.

Familiar thoughts often clawed their way from the past when I closed my eyes to rest or when I found any sense of solitude on our trip. And while I wished to shake this regard, I felt that this simple request was one that I must grant Henry. He took great risk in bringing us to a land that banished his father, and I made a promise to tell Rose's story. I often find myself whispering to Rose, for I miss her deeply and want nothing more than to share one final conversation. Within moments I was sleeping soundly on a luxurious mattress for the first time in months.

Just as soon as I drifted off to sleep that night, the sun crept through the window to announce the beginning of the next day. But we were no longer traveling into unknown lands, walking for hours and hoping to obtain rations. Rather, this was the first day in our new home.

Realizing that Henry was not by my side, I quickly prepared myself for the morning and went to wake Thomasin and Samuel. Their chamber was also empty at my arrival. Sounds of discussion on the bottom floor indicated that everyone was awake, so I took a few moments for myself before joining them. I studied the layout of each room, admiring the beautiful decorations and architecture. Each window provided a glorious view of the vegetation and farming areas. And near the end of the property, I caught a glimpse of the village that we crept along in the previous night; a place I certainly wished to explore. I pondered on how my life could have looked if I inherited such wealth or was born into a respectable family.

Everyone cheered at my arrival when I descended the stairs as if they were waiting for me. Thomasin rushed to give me food, and I took a seat next to Amelia at their large table. It brought me joy to see everyone so relaxed and welcomed, and especially for Henry to have reunited with his proper family. It was hard to deny that I was nervous, and I was even shaking at the table. The others failed to notice, or perhaps they chose to keep their attention elsewhere. This was one of the first instances that indicated a deeper-rooted issue, yet I chose to live in the moment and ignore my internal plea.

"They speak so highly of you," Amelia whispered, "Henry especially."

At this moment I understood that our relationships were known and accepted. This brought concern on our journey, as such behavior was unacceptable back in The Hollow. I smiled at Henry who met my gaze and returned a smile of his own from across the table. His reaction was genuine and displayed pure happiness. My heartbeat began to calm, and I felt the tension fading.

Henry saw my presence as a signal to nervously stand and set our discussion in motion. "I offer many thanks for welcoming us last night, Aunt Amelia and Uncle Henry. We had a long journey, traveling through the spring and now to the end of summer," he explained.

"And what has brought you all to our home, or should I say, your home in fact? Has thy father caused more burden on you?" Nicholas asked with concern.

Henry hesitated at his uncle's reply and looked in my direction, so I understood this was my time to interject. It was time to explain the truth and depart if they were frightened.

But which version of the truth did you tell?

I joined Henry at his side, taking a few steps back from the table so everyone could see me. Subtly I smirked at such a situation and realized that I would never escape the eyes of others.

"Around this time last year, just as the farming season began to slow, a tragedy befell our village of Warren Hollow. Reverend Nicholas passed of natural causes so a new Reverend, Thomas, was appointed to our church," I explained. The mentioning of Thomas made me anxious, so I slowly began to pace the floor as my anxiety returned. "Thomas did away with all of Nicholas's teachings and led our village into darkness. Us younger adults were banned from service and prohibited from leaving the village."

"Why would they do such a thing?" Amelia asked in disbelief.

"Crops began to die, farming was quite poor throughout the season, children got sick, and other grievances began to suddenly arise." I realized that there was no reason to further delay revealing the cause. "And witchcraft was to blame. Our apothecary, Rose, was accused of bewitching the village and bringing this evil to our homes."

Amelia and Nicholas looked at each other in shock. "Witchcraft," Nicholas began, "that was nothing more than a passing concern but seasons ago. We heard tales of nearby communities suffering, yet I supposed we were spared."

"We should have been as well," I replied, "although things continued to worsen. Our friend, Rose, was an innocent woman, put to death like an animal in the center of our village for all to see. That was after all the children were detained for sneaking from the village and celebrating All Hallows Eve. In the months that followed, we were held captive in the basement of the prison."

They could not believe my words, and in fairness, perhaps I would not believe such a situation if I did not live through it.

"We suffered through the winter, watching as our friends died from starvation or at the hands of Thomas. He knew we were innocent but used witchcraft to enact his reign. The court, and even our parents, did nothing as we suffered."

This was the perfect opportunity to tell the truth to your friends, yet you did not.

"And I assume you found an escape on one of those nights? Will they come looking for you?" Amelia asked anxiously, and reasonably so.

"Aye, Thomas made a mistake in revealing his plans. Come the end of winter, he was going to execute those who were not already dead. During an act of ignorance he made a mistake, and we were able to free ourselves. We hid behind the snowfall, making our way from the village to Rose's home deep in the forest. That is where we waited for the winter to pass. Then came spring and the new Reverend found us. He traveled to our shelter, letting us know that Thomas's rule was over and that he was a friend who would work to restore order in Warren Hollow. He gave us the choice to return home and clear our names. But we did not feel that there was any life left for us there," I explained, taking my seat with fatigue.

For the next few moments we sat in silence, and I understood that our story was one of tragedy and disbelief. I made it a point to leave out a few instances, hoping that I needed not to provide details of murdering the Reverend, or about my brother.

And just as the thoughts passed through my mind, Nicholas asked, "Why was a third Reverend appointed to Warren Hollow?"

Perhaps I made my rendition too specific. I look to my friends, nearly begging for someone else to devise a tale of a sudden illness or Reverend Thomas's arrest.

"Thomas died," Thomasin added. I shot her a striking gaze, then understood that it would be unfair to conceal such a truth. Before she could provide any further details, I knew that I must do so myself.

"I killed him," I claim without raising my eyes from my lap. Suddenly I held up my arm, loosening the straps and dropping the makeshift hand to the table. I steadied my arm high to show them what occurred. "He mutilated us, killed our friends, used faith to manipulate our parents, and made me watch as my infant brother drew his final breaths. But I managed to deceive him and gain an advantage during one of his attacks. I plunged an icicle through his neck and broke free. Samuel took the blame, staying behind as we all escaped to the forest. Then in the months that followed, the new Reverend, Gregory, saved Samuel and slowly restored order. But we could not return home, we simply could not," I said with tears gently rolling down my face.

The truth was revealed, and I was fearful for their response. Perhaps they would ask us to leave, not wanting to house a murderer and runaways. But regardless of the outcome, it would not be justified to conceal such secrets if they were to welcome us with good will. They looked at each other and quickly rushed to comfort us. Nicholas hugged his nephew as Amelia pulled my head to her chest. She began to recite a prayer, which comforted me at that moment.

"I am sorry for the troubles you faced, and I promise that this is a safe place. So long as you are on this farm, or in this village, you need not to worry for witchcraft or Reverends going mad," Amelia assured.

Perhaps the others believed her words, and I wanted to as well. Our past was revealed, and we were still there. We were not thrown back in prison or accused of being evil. Henry's family welcomed us, and if the village did as well, then this could be our new home. Such kindness was unfamiliar to me, and I found it puzzling.

And with that conversation the next few days came and went. Then the next few weeks. Nicholas and Amelia allowed us to stay on the farm for the time being, assuring that it was no burden and our past was not worth conviction. We settled in properly as the days passed while keeping ourselves busy and making contributions. Henry and Samuel helped Nicholas in preparing the farm for the coming winter while Thomasin and I would assist Amelia with cleaning and tending to the home. I told Amelia about my brother and endless stories of Rose each day. She took quite an interest in Rose's writings and recipes, never judging her as wicked or sinful. And while Amelia and Nicholas did not live as strictly by faith as those back in The

Hollow, they were still engulfed in religion, often traveling to the nearby village for service. We had yet to join them or explore the village, but the time drew near.

Something I often wondered about was Henry's father. I knew him as nothing more than a drunken fool in The Hollow, and it seemed that his banishing was justified from this farm. He was mentioned more than once in conversation, and Nicholas was appalled to know that his brother did nothing to stop Henry's imprisonment. While they felt no remorse for removing Henry's father from their home, I sensed that guilt and regret burned within them for stripping Henry of such a life as a result. So they are pleased to see Henry back home with companions at his side. Nicholas and Amelia never had children of their own, and perhaps the overwhelming hospitality is an act to justify the dispute that removed their only family from this land.

Henry was back where he belonged, and for the first time, the rest of us finally felt at home as well. All Hallows Eve was but a day away and Nicholas thought it was a great idea for us to finally introduce ourselves to the members of the village. The homestead was large enough that we saw no reason to venture any further, or perhaps we were frightened to do so. He waited for this day specifically, wanting to prove that no trouble would fall upon us for celebrating or revealing our presence.

"We shall leave at first light," Nicholas instructed as we departed to our chambers for the night.

Although I was eager to explore the village since the moment we arrived, it was hard to deny the growing fear with All Hallows Eve approaching. This was once a sacred day that now caused pain and misery. The idea of ever celebrating its arrival again was idiotic to us, and I even forced myself to develop a hatred for it as well. Our plan was to let it pass without any acknowledgement, and we never discussed last year's bonfire on our journey. But now, I prayed that Nicholas was accurate and that we would not be marching to our deaths come sunrise. Though if we were to make a grand entrance in this village, then this be the most fitting day for a vagrant group of sinners, witches, and a murderer to make a proper entrance.

III

Welcome to Bedfordshire

And now we stand in the present, moments from leaving the farm and venturing into the nearby village on this beautiful autumn morning. The weeks since our arrival served me well in adjusting and learning to trust Nicholas and Amelia. They are wonderful people, and they would take no such action to cause us harm. Today's venture triggered another bout of panic in the late hours last night and I feel embarrassed that I awakened the entire farm in my despair. 'Tis difficult to look anyone in the eye this morning, though they surround me with care and act as if nothing happened. I must confirm that this village is also a safe place for us, and if so, then today shall finally be the day that I call this place my home.

"What is the plan for today, Uncle Nicholas?" Henry asks nervously.

"None of you need to worry," Nicholas assures with a laugh, "for this village will welcome you. We will attend our service in the meetinghouse, then you can explore the many places and meet our neighbors until you grow tired and return home. Then we can celebrate."

We anxiously prepare to join Nicholas and Amelia on today's journey into the village. I approach this day with caution, hesitant to meet anyone else or make our presence known. While I wish to rekindle excitement for All Hallows Eve, I have no intention of celebrating this year as Nicholas suggests. It would surely bring great risk to their farm. So I remain silent, fixing my hair and putting together an elegant outfit for the many introductions that await.

When the time to depart finally arrives, we gather on the porch with a shared tension. Amelia takes a moment to adjust Thomasin and I's attire, and we are on our way. We start down the narrow path that leads directly to the village. While the sun still shines in the sky, the sting of winter is quite prevalent in the air. Just like the year of last, All Hallows Eve will bring the start of another harsh winter. It be a challenge not to think of the days spent sitting on the frozen ground of the prison as the winter weather came in through the window. Yet, I try to suppress such awful memories and remain optimistic for today's visit.

Our brief venture begins in silence, so I take a moment to admire the beauty of this homestead and the surrounding land. Henry's family truly has a wonderful farm. The leaves are changing colors and falling from the trees while scents of cider and pies from the village pass in the wind. It feels as though we are walking towards the All Hallows Eve we could only try to replicate at our bonfires or in our childhood tales. With such an atmosphere, I imagine myself in one of the bedtime stories I would tell John when All Hallows Eve grew close. Beneath all the fear and remorse, the desire to celebrate is still burning.

Amelia breaks the intensity of our silence with pleasant details of what awaits. "Pastor Noah is a lovely man; he shall take great interest in your journey. He hath been with us for many, many years."

I smile at her remarks, nervous to meet a member of the church but faithful that Amelia speaks no lies.

"I spent some time as a member of the Church in Warren Hollow," Samuel begins, "although I did so out of guilt. Perhaps I can reestablish such a role with honesty if they would allow it."

"Be sure to speak with Pastor Noah after service. I am certain he would revel in such a request," Nicholas happily replies.

As we draw closer, I notice that Nicholas and Amelia have yet to tell us the history of the village, or even its name. For weeks none of us have thought to ask, perhaps intentionally.

"Does this village have a name?" I ask with a bit of angst.

Nicholas and Amelia look at each other and laugh, almost surprised that neither of them elaborated on the finer details of the village.

"My apologies to each of you, we were so focused on your adjustment to the farm that we forgot entirely," Nicholas replies, we all laugh at such an oversight of information. They traveled to the village many times since we arrived and spoke of its many members and structures but never thought to share its history. "This place is known as Bedfordshire and has grown quite lively in the years of recent. New members often travel from far and wide because everyone is welcome in the community. We are home to a massive port, so fishing guides our way of life here."

A settlement with thriving farmlands and fishing ports is quite impressive. Warren Hollow lacked the stability of either method of survival. Structures collapsed around us and a harsh winter would offset the farming, which was our only means of prosperity. I grow eager to explore such a place and notice scents of the sea.

Nicholas and Amelia continue sharing information, from the early days of Bedfordshire to how Henry's family operated one of the grandest farms in all of New England since the founding days of this land. To approach such a thriving plantation is a shock to all of us.

After a few moments we stand just outside of the village. I recognize Bedfordshire to be much larger than The Hollow, with many more areas and structures. Families gather outside of their homes in preparation of the coming service. They dress much fancier than back in The Hollow, which makes me feel a bit out of place.

Do not panic, for you venture alongside one of the most respected families in this village. Nobody will pay any mind to the flaws in your attire.

It is reassuring that the others will know nothing about us until introductions. We can present ourselves as whoever we choose to be. I shift the attention to my surroundings as we continue along the main path into the village. Nicholas and Amelia bid good morning to the families that pass us, all appearing joyful and eager for today's service.

"Emelie, look," Thomasin instructs as she points to the nearby homes.

Our surroundings appear to be decorated for All Hallows Eve. Pumpkins, small ornaments, and other decorative objects are placed outside of nearby homes and shops. I stare in awe and cannot fathom such an open display back in The Hollow.

"I am beginning to like this place, Emelie," Thomasin admits with a smile.

"And I as well," I declare with an even larger grin. Perhaps Nicholas was truthful in his claim that celebrations are not sinful in Bedfordshire.

To see such acknowledgement for this day is not something any of us anticipated. I was prepared to let All Hallows Eve pass without any attention, and yet, this village clearly does not share such fears. This also enlightens me on the balance of religion and court; the separation that failed in The Hollow.

Bedfordshire is properly structured and thriving in comparison. There is an undeniable feeling of comfort as we pass through the main sections of the village and locate the port in the distance. Just as Nicholas described, the edge of the village is open water as far as I can see. 'Tis overwhelming because I have only heard tales of the ocean. The smell of fire also fills the air, which is a scent that I have always loved. Smoke rises from chimneys and bonfires in front yards on our way to the church. A tavern sits nestled near the water, erupting with life and cheers as we draw closer. A cemetery also catches my attention as we continue on the path.

Finally we reach the church, and like the rest of Bedfordshire, it is a magnificent structure. The woodwork appears strong and well-kept, and the outside is a solid shade of white. Glass windows line all sides with fine craftsmanship and care.

"This is our meetinghouse," Nicholas explains, "where all service and most legal matters are conducted."

I cannot find words to describe the beauty of such a place. As we enter, my breath is taken away at what I am witnessing. Back in Warren Hollow our church could hold no more than twenty, maybe thirty people at most. This place is massive in scale, with rows of pews that could easily fit more than one entire village. The pulpit is raised off the ground to allow the Reverend a clear view all the way to the back.

"Would you like to sit on the floor or in the gallery?" Nicholas asks.

We do not understand his question, so he smiles and points above us to the walls on each side. Additional seating above overlooks our current position. In order to blend in, I simply wish to remain in the middle of the floor among the common attendees, although the additional upper level is impressive. Nicholas and Amelia begin to mingle around the room so Henry, Thomasin, Samuel, and I find seating in a pew closer to the front.

"Now," Thomasin whispers, "try not to let them know that we are witches this time."

I gently push her shoulder at such a remark, and we engage in a playful scuffle. 'Tis certain that each of us is feeling the emotions of being back in service, and moments away from having to introduce ourselves. Guests continue to arrive until nearly all the pews are lined shoulder to shoulder. The sun beams through the windows and I start to feel excitement for the sermon to begin. Samuel is also quite eager for such an experience. He whispers to Thomasin of how he would love to get involved and someday hold a position of regard in the church.

"How do you feel about this place?" I ask Henry.

"This church, or meetinghouse as they call it, is truly a wonderful structure," Henry replies.

"I meant Bedfordshire itself, and being back with your family. Is it as you remember?"

"I was quite young when we left so my memory is a bit unclear. Although, I am thankful to be back with my aunt and uncle, and to have you by my side. We can all make a home for ourselves here; this place is perfect."

Yes, perhaps too perfect.

While I have not felt any indications of misfortune, 'tis hard to banish the thought from my mind. Everything is in order and practically a fantasy compared to life in Warren Hollow. Rose taught me that there is always more than meets the eye, so I must stay vigilant and aware. Our conversation draws to an end as service is set in motion. An older man, who must be Pastor Noah, makes his way to the pulpit and ascends to his position. He stands much smaller and fragile than the likes of Reverend Thomas. Noah offers a few greetings and smiles, which immediately reminds me of the late Reverend Nicholas in The Hollow. Memories of him and Reverend Gregory reassure that Thomas was not a clear representation of the church. It took me quite some time to understand this when I lost my faith in the prison.

Everyone rises from the pews, so we follow the exact same motions to blend in. Pastor Noah takes his position at the pulpit and signals for all to be seated. "Hello to each of you here today. Your presence brings you closer to God and strengthens your faith," he declares.

Pastor Noah ends his introduction with a prayer and a moment of silence. He then discusses births and deaths in Bedfordshire, which leads into the reading of scripture. Throughout this service our knowledge of the community and current events tremendously improves. Aside from some illness and the expected intensity of the winter ahead, things are relatively well in Bedfordshire.

This service lasts much longer than what we initially expected but it is full of wisdom and prayer. It is refreshing to strengthen my faith and to feel accepted in a holy place. There are no disputes, nobody screaming or accusing each other of wrongdoing. And to witness members decorating their homes for All Hallows Eve before sitting together in service is remarkable.

As the service draws to a close, Pastor Noah begins to scan the pews before him. "It has come to my attention that we must welcome new members to our community before we depart. Would you be so kind as to make yourselves known?" Pastor Noah asks kindly.

The four of us nervously look at each other and obediently rise from the pews. "Yes," Noah conveys with a smile, "I bid each of you a kind welcome to Bedfordshire. Could you introduce thyself before me?"

Without hesitation, we make our way out to the aisle and move forward. All eyes land upon us, though I sense no hostility. Henry is the first to reach the pulpit, so Pastor Noah descends and respectfully shakes his hand.

"I believe you hold relation to Nicholas and Amelia?" Pastor Noah asks.

"I do, sir. My name is Henry Miller, and I am the proud nephew of Nicholas and Amelia. My father departed from Bedfordshire many years ago, for he was banished on the basis of intemperance. But I can assure you that we will be respectable members in this wonderful community, and I am nothing like my father," Henry explains. I notice his unease, as conversations regarding his father are often avoided by Henry at all costs.

"We are delighted at your return. And you, what might your name be?" Pastor Noah asks as he draws his attention to Thomasin. Henry is visibly relieved at the realization that he shall discuss his father no further. 'Tis troublesome to know of the burden that Henry held throughout his childhood because of his father. He said it himself that he simply stayed away and wished not to trouble any of us with his presence. Though I suspect reuniting with his aunt and uncle has restored his family name in his eyes, and he shall carry it with pride moving forward.

"I am Thomasin Roberts. A good friend of Henry's and a troublemaker at times," she replies, pulling some laughs from the crowd and a smile from The Pastor.

"And I am Samuel, Samuel Hawthorne," Samuel begins abruptly, unable to contain his excitement. He shakes Pastor Noah's hand and continues his introduction. "I served alongside our Reverend back home and would love the opportunity to do so here!"

"Very well, Samuel, it is great to meet you. Perhaps we can further discuss your involvement in the near future," Pastor Noah replies.

The others step off to the side and I am the last to make my introduction. I smile at The Pastor as soon as his gaze finds me. Thoughtlessly I reach out to shake his hand in greeting, forgetting that I have presented my makeshift hand. Noah reaches out and is surprised to make contact with something other than skin. While he draws no attention to it, I notice a subtle shift in his emotions. Perhaps it is at this moment that he realizes we come with a tragic tale. Nervously I pull away and begin my introduction. "It is an honor to meet you, Pastor Noah. My name is Emelie Williams, and I too am a friend of Henry's. We all come from the village of Warren Hollow," I explain.

"Such a far distance from your home, what brings you to Bedfordshire?" Noah asks.

I must formulate my answer with great caution. The hospitality could soon vanish if they discover the events of our past. Yet, The Pastor is aware of my injury so anything but the truth could raise suspicion.

"Well," I begin cautiously, "Warren Hollow encountered some misfortune as of recent. Like other nearby plantations, witchcraft tore apart our home." Some gasps are evident from the crowd, and now the attention is drawn closely to my words. "Our Reverend, Nicholas, lost his life due to illness. And then Reverend Thomas soon took his place. But Thomas was an evil man, using witchcraft accusations to imprison all the children and destroy our home. We sat in the prison through the winter, watching as Thomas tortured and murdered his way through Warren Hollow. Then came the spring, and another Reverend was sent to restore order. We were released from the prison with our innocence. But we could no longer live within those walls. So, we set out to find a better life, and if you would give us welcome, we wish that to be in Bedfordshire," I announce.

Everyone in attendance begins to talk amongst themselves, surveying the room and eagerly waiting for a response from Pastor Noah. Offering a subtle smile, The Pastor takes another glance at the contraption on my arm. He gently pulls it into his hand and immediately recites another prayer. The meetinghouse falls silent while members bow their heads in observance. This brings me peace and safety.

Noah takes a few steps across the pulpit for the entire audience to hear his words. "Bedfordshire is a place of reason and order. While faith is the purpose for being, it shall not become intertwined with injustice and accusation. In my old age, I can assure that I will not begin a murderous rampage. I welcome each of you to our home!"

Relief overcomes me and it's as though I can finally breathe for the first time since our departure. Henry's family welcomed us, The Pastor welcomed us, and Bedfordshire welcomed us. We smile at each other, proceeding back to our pew for the remainder of the service. Some members of the village offer us greetings as we pass, impressed by our history and eager to build relationships. I drop to my seat and let out a long exhale after that intense introduction.

Was I shaking through my words? Did my voice falter? My explanation was bold, but did I give Pastor Noah the proper respect?

I recount each of my words with hopes that I did not make a fool of myself. Under my breath I mutter thoughts of stupidity at the fact that I presented my absent hand. Though service has officially concluded so most families disperse and carry on with their day while paying us no mind. Amelia and Nicholas approach and they speak of our courage and honesty. Nicholas was confident that our arrival would not be an issue, and I must admit that his prediction was accurate. Bedfordshire is now the place we can officially call our home.

IV

All Hallows Eve, Part II

Nicholas and Amelia venture around the meetinghouse, greeting others and remaining joyful as always. They are practically viewed as royalty in Bedfordshire, and it has been an honor to stand alongside them since our arrival.

"I understand this to be a day that you enjoy," Nicholas tells us as he returns, "so I suggest exploring the village before coming home. You will quickly see that you are not the only ones who plan to celebrate."

"Perhaps I shall stay here for a little while longer. I wish to speak further with Pastor Noah about involvement in the church," Samuel says.

Thomasin embraces Samuel, encouraging his discussion but ensuring that we shall see him later at the homestead.

"And I must depart to find some needed supplies for the farm. I would like to help my uncle prepare for the coming winter, if you do not mind of course," Henry explains, Thomasin and I nodding while playfully sending him away.

Thomasin and I are now alone as Henry and Samuel embark on their own tasks for the day. 'Tis a strange feeling when the four of us are separated, but something that we must normalize now that we are safe. The two of us leave the meetinghouse while recounting the events with an eagerness to explore this village.

"I must admit, that was frightening for a few moments," Thomasin claims.

"Aye, 'tis shocking that they are all so welcoming in this place. They care not for our past and pay no mind to such foolishness. Though this must be common when there is order in a community. Do you remember when life was like this back in The Hollow?" I ask.

"Much simpler times, Emelie, but I find comfort knowing that this place can be our new home. There be no indications of corruption in the court or the church, as The Pastor said it himself. Perhaps we shall find everything that we dreamed of."

We traverse through the many paths of Bedfordshire, passing homes and countless shops on the way. More decorations are noticed on the paths and porches, and it appears that occupants of the village are starting their celebrations. Fires rage outside of homes while people dance and consume ale together. A large bonfire begins to shine in the center of the village, and its size draws us closer. For months we viewed our All Hallows Eve gathering as the reason behind the chaos, yet I understand now that our fate was destined regardless of the day.

I held onto that memory with fear and sadness through the winter, which is why I knew that we needed to have another bonfire on our final night at Rose's home. I think back to that night often; time spent with our friends who decided to stay in The Hollow and closure for months of torture in the same way it began.

Some attendees offer greetings as we approach this bonfire, and provide what appears to be cider while crowding around us.

"We welcome you to Bedfordshire, Emelie and Thomasin. I be Abigail, and this is my sister, Rachel. Then this little one here is Chrystopher," the girl explains with a friendly greeting alongside her companions. She stares attentively while studying my appearance with a smile.

These sisters appear to be our age, though Chrystopher is noticeably much younger. Abigail is quite tall, which is intimidating as we stand so close. She has long blonde hair and a striking resemblance to her sister. I look back and forth at Abigail and Rachel, realizing they are undoubtedly twins who share prominent features of beauty.

They remind me of Mary and Edith back in The Hollow. I hope those young children are doing well.

"It is wonderful to meet you all," I begin, "for we are most excited to join your community."

"So, you and your friends practiced witchcraft?" Chrystopher blatantly asks.

Thomasin and I look at each other, understanding we must remain cautious with our answer. "I'm afraid we were accused of such wickedness, as was nearly everyone in our village. Our Reverend went mad and used witchcraft to tear apart our home," Thomasin replies. She maintains her composure, recognizing that she is talking to a harmless, curious child.

Rachel hits Chrystopher on the arm and pushes him aside. "I apologize for his behavior. This must be a troubling occurrence to discuss," she adds with embarrassment.

Abigail nudges her way to the front, cutting off her sister's words and offering her own input. "But we would like to hear tales of your travels and learn more about witchcraft. Please find us the next time you come into the village!"

We smile at them and offer words of departure before continuing our adventure, although it would be joyous to spend the day conversing by the fire, listening to the cheers and jest of the other members who begin to face intoxication. By now the All Hallows Eve celebration is in full effect, so it seems fitting to return home and celebrate with Amelia and Nicholas. It was relieving to share a somewhat normal conversation with other people our age for the first time in recent memory. Perhaps we shall find a group of friends rather quickly in Bedfordshire. Abigail, Rachel, and Chrystopher seemed pleasant from our brief interaction, though it will take some time to tell the sisters apart from one another and tolerate their questions of our past.

Thomasin spots a merchant giving away pumpkins so we each take one to decorate the homestead. I recall when The Hollow used to be this lively, long before everything declined. Faith became a guiding force out of desperation and all the happiness vanished as a result. The mere mention of All Hallows Eve would leave someone stricken with prayer for hours on end. It appears that Bedfordshire knows not the hardship of such tragedies. Fishing is thriving and it was a successful farming year, as Nicholas repeats day after day with pride. Nobody will starve through the winter or succumb to a mysterious illness. But times of prosperity are when misfortune can suddenly arise. This is a thought that constantly fills my mind. While today certainly helped to ease our concern, I shall remain alert for whatever comes our way.

We reach the edge of the village and walk the path back to Amelia and Nicholas's home. The sun lowers in the sky and a chill grows in the air. I watch as leaves continue to blow past us in the wind with all the smells of autumn. Smoke from the fires, dying vegetation, and all the foods from the village are still as prevalent as this morning. 'Tis truly the most wonderful time of year.

"Those sisters and thy friend are a bit odd," Thomasin claims.

"I felt the same, yet they were friendly enough. They are accustomed to structure and comfort so surely our presence brings much interest. If mysterious travelers came to The Hollow with tales of surviving a witch hunt, then we would have acted but the same," I reply optimistically. "We do hold enough tales for a lifetime. And how do you feel about our situation, Thomasin?" I ask as we walk down the path.

"I think that this place is good for us. Henry's family welcomed us to a beautiful home, and even Pastor Noah gave acceptance after hearing of our past; well, most of our past. Samuel will likely find his place in the church and Henry seems delighted. His love for you cannot be denied, Emelie. The way he looks at you and speaks of you to his aunt and uncle is unlike anything I have ever seen. But what do you think of this place?" Thomasin replies with the same question.

I smile at her words of kindness for Henry before responding. "It cannot be denied that this place is lovely. The people are kind, and the village itself is magnificent. This is the place that we longed for, the place I promised John that we would find. I think of him often, along with Rose and all the others who did not survive. Such thoughts keep me awake through all hours of the night, but I wish to someday free myself from such guilt," I explain.

Perhaps I was too honest in my response, but Thomasin is the only one who has ever fully understood me. She must be concerned if she felt the need to ask, so honesty is deserved.

"The past still haunts me, Emelie, just as it does Henry and Samuel. We suffered for months, and you nearly lost your life. It would not be easy for anyone to move on, but I think that this place will allow us to do so," Thomasin declares.

I agree with her words, though I feel awkward discussing something that none of us has acknowledged for months. We all suffer and leave our troubles unspoken. It brings me peace to know that I am not alone in my struggles, and that through all the banter and jest, Thomasin and I still hold this deep connection. Bedfordshire is a place that may allow us to heal and properly move forward. If trouble arises then surely each of us will be ready for it. But this conversation revealed that I am living in fear, and it is not my wish to continue doing so. The Pastor is supportive of our presence, and we already made new friends in the village. Today was a massive step forward in acclimating to Bedfordshire.

We finally reach the farm and place our pumpkins near the small fire pit out back before going inside. Samuel and Henry also returned so we convene and recount our experiences over the massive feast that Amelia put together. Nicholas calls for a fire so that we can carry out the night in celebration after our meal. Henry mentions how Amelia and Nicholas must have hurried home to decorate for All Hallows Eve, which is a wonderful gesture. This day is nothing more than a harmless occurrence and I am thankful that the people of Bedfordshire view it as such. It seems that they revel in any excuse to drink ale and celebrate. Henry talks with Nicholas of how to best prepare the farm for winter and Samuel explains that he will become an apprentice under Pastor Noah. I find happiness for them and feel certain that Thomasin and I shall find our purpose as well.

Hours pass as we finish our meal and move outside to continue the celebration under the light of the moon. The fire rages while we recapture our love for this holiday. Farming season reached its end so while Amelia and Nicholas do not fully understand our love for All Hallows Eve, they have their own accomplishments to celebrate on this wonderful night. They share stories of the supposed spirits who haunt the land, and we further discuss our own mischievous traditions. I scoff at the realization that we sat by the fire for a great deal of time without so much as a thought of the attack on last year's All Hallows Eve. Thomasin, Samuel, and Henry could not be happier, and I recognize this very moment to be everything I ever desired.

Perhaps that All Hallows Eve night was a fitting end to our journey. We settled into Bedfordshire, gained approval from The Pastor, and made new friends. The people welcomed us and provided sympathy for our past. Our future began taking shape. And to my surprise, All Hallows Eve was celebrated across the entire village. Life was seemingly perfect in Bedfordshire.

Maybe we became naive, never anticipating that such horrors awaited us in this place. I kept myself on alert for misfortune when we arrived, but this defense began to falter through all the happiness and love around us. The trials in Warren Hollow were but a feeble occurrence in comparison to what befell Bedfordshire that winter.

V

Life After

All Hallows Eve has come to pass. We celebrated through the night, bonding by the fire and officially putting any doubts to rest. That was a significant day of acclimation to Bedfordshire. We faced no issues or poor judgement from any who witnessed our introduction in the meetinghouse. I held fear that our past would forever define us, especially when entering another church. But Pastor Noah was kind and so were all the people we met in the village. For the first time, it felt as though we finally belonged.

Over a month has passed since All Hallows Eve, and life is wonderful. Samuel spends most of his time in the church while Henry assists his uncle on the farm. Thomasin and I aid Amelia with preparing the home for the coming winter, although Thomasin struggles with a lingering illness that began shortly after All Hallows Eve. Some days are far worse than others, but she handles it well and assumes the cold weather to be the culprit. We often travel into Bedfordshire when her health is stable, spending our days making friends and trading for supplies. Memories of Warren Hollow still cause me distress, but the comfort of Bedfordshire improved my vitality and well-being. While this new life has been exceptional, not a day passes without thoughts of my brother. John would have loved such a place.

"Where are you now?" Thomasin asks.

"Walking through the forest with the witch of Warren Hollow," I reply in jest.

"'Tis not what I meant," Thomasin clarifies as she playfully assaults me.

"I know," I mumble with a sigh. "I was lost in a memory of John. For I miss him so."

Thomasin understands my sadness and shares a similar torture on most days. She always knew when I was captive in my mind and could bring me peace on those sleepless nights in the prison. Walking the longer route into the village often leads to reminiscence on the days of old back home. Memories of John and I in the forest are cherished, and the foliage around us is a constant reminder.

"Do you think the others are well in The Hollow? I often ponder on the moment they walked back through that gate," Thomasin says.

"Perhaps we shall never know for certain, but I like to believe that things are well back there. Even Samuel would have stayed if we did not stop him, and he would never lie to us. But that was not the life I wanted," I declare.

These talks that Thomasin and I share while traveling into Bedfordshire are quite healing. 'Tis comforting to know that we finally found a way to address our pain. And while Henry and Samuel speak less of the past, I know they struggle as well. It is difficult for any of us to vocalize our ongoing worries or even mention what we endured. Thomasin and I try to be honest with each other, though it is certainly with restraint.

Watch Over Me: A Christmas Tale

Winter grows prevalent with each passing day, and I shiver through my coverings as we walk the narrow path. Most of the vegetation will die in the coming days and a long winter shall soon be upon us. Nicholas speaks of the bitter cold and snowfall on the horizon, and heavy winds from the sea make it seem as though it is already the dead of winter.

"We have some time before we are needed back at the farm, what shall we do once we arrive?" Thomasin asks. Our task for the day is to retrieve fish for Amelia at the port, but we have plenty of time to do so.

"The twins shall likely find us before we reach the merchant, perhaps they will provide us with some excitement for the day," I reply.

"If by excitement you mean annoyance," Thomasin mutters with a laugh.

We have grown closer with Abigail and Rachel since our first meeting on All Hallows Eve, though not necessarily by choice. There are not many other young adults in Bedfordshire so our friendships are quite limited. Things were relatively well at first with the sisters, but there has been a constant focus when we are together. They care only for our stories of the events in Warren Hollow, so our gatherings usually turn to Thomasin and I discussing witchcraft. Sometimes Abigail and Rachel's questions become uncomfortable or agonizing, yet I understand that they are simply curious. I doubt that anyone in Bedfordshire could ever fathom what unraveled in that prison, but it would be favorable to visit friends without reliving the past.

Even so, I depart the farm each day with an open mind. 'Tis exciting to meet new people and further adjust to our new home. Although, there are a few other people that Nicholas and

Amelia have warned us about. A notorious troublemaker and violent drinker in Bedfordshire is Barnabas Wilfred. He often spends his days fumbling the paths of the village when he is not jailed for breaking regulations or harassing Solomon, the owner of the tavern. Barnabas is currently prohibited from attending service in the meetinghouse after trying to assault Pastor Noah prior to our arrival. And then there is Griffin Osmund, a name we hear whispered over fireside tales or when anything is awry. This stems from a tragedy in Bedfordshire, as Griffin supposedly murdered his wife and her secret lover upon finding them together in his barn. They say his farm hands bore witness, so he murdered them as well before setting the barn ablaze and fleeing. Older children tease their siblings of Griffin's return, and it is a common myth that Griffin stalks among the shadows when anyone travels alone at night.

With these few stains on the greatness of Bedfordshire, I know to exercise caution with our interactions. It is no surprise that this village has bouts of darkness in its past, as nearly all of New England shares a troubled history. Though tall tales and a few ecstatic drunkards could never give us a negative view of this place.

"I bid good morning to you both," Phillip, an elderly member of Bedfordshire, calls out with a wave as we pass his home. Phillip is quite rugged in his old age, and we learned that like many members of this village, he has drunk more than he has bled throughout his life. Bedfordshire does not shy away from its share of beer, rum, ale, or anything that leads to intoxication for that matter. The old man struggles to carry a bundle of logs to his home, so Thomasin provides him assistance while rolling her eyes.

"You are to hurt yourself one of these days, Phillip," Thomasin informs him as she places the logs on his porch.

"Not as long as I have you wonderful children around," He replies through slurred speech, chugging the last of his drink. Phillip thanks Thomasin and pathetically waves as we continue our journey. I laugh at his reference to us as children, although I do not take offense to these words. The elders often refer to anyone younger than them as children. These harmless interactions are quite common as we traverse through Bedfordshire each day. Of all the people we encountered so far, we have yet to face any judgment or cruelness. Everyone has accepted us as though we are Bedfordshire natives since our introduction in the church.

"You are so kind," I playfully tell Thomasin as we continue. "Just as you were when he needed assistance with his vegetables or while cleaning his hearth last week. Perhaps you are destined to be Bedfordshire's servant to the drunken lot."

"If I am to be a servant, then you are to be the apothecary. And we all know what happened to the last apothecary," Thomasin replies as she grabs my neck.

My mouth hangs open in awe until we laugh at such an inappropriate remark. We forever speak in jest and take nothing as a serious matter, something I know for certain that Rose would appreciate.

"Perhaps that is actually a good idea, Emelie. The role of an apothecary would suit you quite well. We all must make something of ourselves in this village," Thomasin claims, gathering a more serious tone.

"I know not the first thing of such a profession," I reply, doubtful of my abilities.

"That is a lie," Thomasin shoots back, "not a day passes without you reading those journals. You know every word from Rose's lifetime of knowledge. And before the witch trials, Rose taught us for many years. You must put thought into it."

'Tis hard to deny the accuracy of Thomasin's words. Until this very moment, the idea of entering such a practice never crossed my mind. The urge to find my calling in Bedfordshire has grown in recent weeks so perhaps that could be a logical path forward. Yet I understand that this regard would not come without danger. Thomasin still believes that Rose was executed for her apothecary practices, while this was merely a veil to hide Thomas and Rose's relations.

Perhaps this would be a good time to inform Thomasin of the truth. Why do you continue to hide such a reality?

I have yet to inform Henry, Samuel, or Thomasin of the nature behind our torture. When an opportunity presents itself, I simply cannot follow through. Often I ask myself why, unsure of what prevents me from revealing this truth. A momentary silence justifies keeping this concealed for the time being as we make our way past the cemetery.

The burial grounds are eerie at this hour, as the fog from the water drifts through the gravestones and trees. But the merchant of the port lies just beyond the cemetery, so we have little choice in our route. We walk with a brisk pace because anywhere near the water has become frigid in recent weeks.

"Emelie!" A voice calls out, nearly scaring me and Thomasin to death. Abigail and her sister playfully reveal themselves from behind a gravestone. Before I can react, Abigail rushes forward and pulls me in for a deep embrace. She places kisses upon my cheek playfully as I struggle to break free. It takes me a few moments to regain composure, as my heart is racing and my hand is shaking after such a scare. Sudden excitement never bothered me in my younger years but after everything we have gone through, I find that it is not necessarily an easy experience. I am vividly taken back to the moment when Reverend Thomas entered the prison and began shouting my name.

"Emelie! Reveal yourself at once!"

"Hello to you both. What an unexpected greeting!" I reply, trying to overcome my distress. Thomasin is angered by their actions and recognizes my anguish. She prepares to lash out and scold them for such inappropriate behavior. Yet, I stop her words before they begin, understanding that Abigail and Rachel are only seeking amusement. This is likely something that Thomasin and I have done in our younger years to many people in Warren Hollow. Although I do find their behavior to be odd, Abigail especially, as they are no more than a year removed in age from us. Their childlike antics can certainly cause concern at times, and the tension is swelling with each encounter.

"Where are you going on this frigid morning?" Abigail asks, offering no apology for her lack of maturity.

"To the port, we must retrieve fish for tonight's dinner. What brings the two of you out to this burial ground in the early hours of the day?" I reply, which appears to catch the sisters by surprise.

"We ... are doing but the same! Everyone knows that now is the best time to visit the port," Rachel nervously answers.

Thomasin offers me a quick glance to signal doubt for their reply. We continue walking down the path with the twins at our side.

"Chrystopher does not join you on today's adventures?" I ask.

"Nie, he is stricken to a day of chores after his father caught him sneaking from their home last night. Though we are not sure why he cares, for his father is but a useless drunk who leaves home for weeks on end," Abigail explains.

Thomasin offers her own remarks. "We used to do but the same back in our village. 'Tis quite important not to get caught. Chores would have been mercy in comparison to the punishment we faced."

The girls listen eagerly to her every word, nearly jumping out of their skin to hear more details. They beg for tales of our past to the point of near obsession. I understand their desire for knowledge because I held a similar longing in my younger years. Without Rose and her teachings, I would have likely gone mad in that awful village. Yet we are not speaking to children.

"So, was anyone back in your village powerful enough to obtain flight or read the thoughts of others?" Abigail asks in a serious tone.

I try my hardest to contain my laughter while Thomasin fails to do so. "There were never any witches in Warren Hollow. 'Twas nothing more than fear and hysteria, just as we explained last week and the week prior. Everyone panicked and thought it better to call us witches than to confront their own sins and failures," I express.

"Well then," Abigail begins, "perhaps you were not trying hard enough. Maybe if thou believed in the rituals and did not give up, then you would have achieved something magnificent."

Anger swells in Thomasin as she attempts to provide a rational answer. "We never desired to be witches, for we knew not what witchcraft was until our friends started dying. Our apothecary, Rose, was nothing more than a healer. Let it be known that witches are but a fantasy!" Thomasin shouts.

We walk for the next few moments in an awkward silence. I can sense the burning urge within Abigail and her sister to continue their interrogation. Perhaps they notice our impatience, so they decide to remain quiet. Abigail and Rachel believe us to be real witches, capable of casting spells and conducting rituals.

"You would be a fine apothecary, Emelie. And I would do anything to learn from you," Abigail declares, breaking the silence and putting a stop to our movement.

Thomasin is no longer capable of enduring their remarks. She takes a small but aggressive step towards Abigail. Rachel notices the building aggression and begins to pull her sister away. "You two have been following us, and for what reason?" Thomasin asks with little compassion.

"Like I said, we were only looking to retrieve fish." Rachel begins to nervously search through her clothing. "Well, it appears that we have forgotten our payment, so we have no grounds to barter. Farewell to you both," Rachel explains as she hastily rushes from the path. Abigail takes a step forward as though she is to embrace me once more, but she hesitates at Thomasin's demeanor and finally breaks her gaze before running off.

Within a few moments Thomasin and I are alone once more. She is irritated and starts to move forward at a faster pace. "They were following us, Emelie. For who knows how long, or to what end. And they think us to be real witches from the tales and children's stories. We should look for other friends in this village who do not assume we have mastered flight," Thomasin mutters.

I understand her concern. Perhaps I am too friendly and welcoming of such behavior. 'Tis hard to deny that I see much of myself in Abigail and her yearning for freedom or desires beyond an invariable life. Yet, knowing that they were following us and listening to our words makes me uneasy.

"I think they are harmless, Thomasin. A bit odd, but harmless," I reply.

Thomasin sees right through my doubt and takes a few glances behind us. The sisters are no longer in sight so I can finally relax. Everything about that encounter was strange. It may be best to avoid further talks of witchcraft and Warren Hollow with those sisters.

"To be following us at such an hour is not harmless behavior, Emelie. They are not infant children like Mary and Edith, though it seems they share their level of intelligence. Be sure to keep a close eye on them, but Abigail especially." Thomasin looks forward with a smirk as her mood suddenly lightens. She begins to laugh, and I am puzzled by her sudden reaction. "I think that she fancies you."

Her words cause the both of us to laugh aloud. I look at Thomasin and she nods with continued laughter. "She fancies me?" I ask with jest.

"I cannot say for certain, though my suspicion grows with each encounter. Do you fail to notice the way she looks at you or how she revels in your arms? For she just placed a flurry of kisses on thy face, Emelie!"

"They wish to be close to us because of their obsession with witchcraft. And it is true that they are strange, but that is simply it! Though I think you scared them away, perhaps for good," I reply.

"If you so say. Though I believe Abigail has a deeper desire, by the name of Emelie Williams!" Thomasin shouts.

I roll my eyes at her claims and wish to no longer ponder on such intentions. Though Thomasin is accurate in her words of Abigail being overly favorable of me. Until this moment I put no thought into her strange fondness and forced embraces, as these actions are the least of my worries when words of witchcraft fly from their mouths.

We finally pass the last of the gravestones and reach the port. The sun remains hidden by the heavy clouds above as it struggles to rise in the sky. Today is set to be cold and dreary, which is a normal occurrence in a village so close to the water.

A few men attempt to catch fish at the nearby dock and the sound of sailboats swaying in the waves brings me peace. The cemetery is intimidating, although it would be a fine place to sit and watch the ocean come spring. We walk over the wooden planks, listening as they crack and creek below us with every step while breathing in the air of the sea. Upon reaching the door to the mercantile of the port, we push our way inside and are fascinated by our surroundings.

"Look at this, Emelie," Thomasin says as we explore the structure. While there are a few general shops in Bedfordshire, this one is fully dedicated to fishing. The walls are lined with nets, ropes, hooks, and all other components of this profession that Thomasin and I know little of. We share a similar desire of riding on one of the fishing vessels in the future. Thomasin hands me a paddle so I look closely over its features and struggle to hold it properly.

"One day we shall use this on the open water," I claim, rowing with the paddle.

Our commotion has alerted the merchant, who stumbles in our direction. I look at Thomasin and we roll our eyes in unison, realizing that this man is also lost to alcohol. His face is bright red, indicating that he is deep into his intoxication.

"Are you Simon?" Thomasin asks.

The man smiles, slowly rocking side to side as though he is aboard a vessel on the water. "I believe I am, and what can I do for thee?" he replies.

"We are here to retrieve a bundle of fish for Amelia and Nicholas. I am Emelie, and this is Thomasin."

"Ah yes," Simon replies as he struggles to maintain his balance, "I shall return."

Simon disappears around the corner as Thomasin and I continue searching the shop.

"It's as though everyone in this town cares only for drinking. 'Tis of surprise that conflict never arises," I mutter.

"At least none that we have seen, that is," Thomasin remarks.

Although we have spent a great deal of time in Bedfordshire, I am still baffled by daily life in this place. I find it odd that nearly no conflicts or disputes ever occur, and everyone lives a happy life. People like Abigail and Rachel can leave their home as they please, and nobody ever questions our intentions as we pass by. Instead, we are greeted with cheers and harmless drunken behavior. While The Hollow was likely worse off than most plantations, Bedfordshire still feels like a fantasy land.

"Here you go," Simon calls out as he approaches with a net full of fish. We take the net and provide the payment in exchange. Thomasin hoists the large net over her shoulder, and we prepare to make our way back to the farm.

"Simon, do you know of those sisters, Abigail and Rachel?" I ask curiously.

He begins to scratch his head, trying his hardest to recall whom I speak of.

"Ah yes," Simon begins, "those girls live with their grandmother, Clara. She raised them after illness took their parents a few years back. Poor Clara, they give her much grief in her old age. I caught them stealing from this port more times than not, so they are forbidden from stepping foot in here!"

Thomasin and I are not surprised that Abigail and Rachel are viewed as troublemakers to some members of Bedfordshire. Surely they find it amusing to torment the drunken folks who have no means of defense to their jest. Though in truth, this is undoubtedly something that Ezekiel, Robert, or any of us would have done if alcohol was this prevalent in The Hollow.

"Thank you, Simon. It was great to meet you officially, though I suspect you may not remember it," Thomasin replies as we make our exit.

With a friendly goodbye to an intoxicated Simon, we pass through the door to the frigid conditions outside. Nicholas claims that today could bring the first snowfall of the season, and I do not doubt his words. I pull my coverings up to my chin as we begin to make our way back home. Though unspoken, I know that Thomasin shares the same believe of no longer wanting to spend time in the village.

"Perhaps we should repay those sisters with some torment of our own. Then we shall see how they like to be frightened," I reply to break the tension.

"Yes, I have the perfect idea of how to do so," Thomasin replies, swinging her fists with a vicious attack.

I laugh while holding no doubt that Thomasin sees violence as a reasonable solution. A thickening fog causes us to end our mischief and move closer to each other. We pass the cemetery and struggle to follow the path ahead. Every so often I subtly look over my shoulder, not wanting Thomasin to know how unnerved I truly am from our earlier encounter.

VI

Yuletide

We push our way through the front door to escape the bitter cold on the outside. A gust of smoke greets us as a fire burns in the hearth. Amelia smiles at our successful fish retrieval and takes the rations to Nicholas in the kitchen. They immediately begin preparations for another wonderful supper. Thomasin and I wish to relax after such an eventful morning, so I make my way to Henry and I's chamber.

After all our time on this farm, I still fail to wrap my mind around its impressive scale. Climbing the few stairs back home with Mother and Father makes no comparison to the ascent in this homestead. Nicholas and Amelia worked tirelessly over the years to become one of the wealthiest inhabitants in all of the colony. It pains me to know the poor reputation that Henry inherited from his father, because he could have grown up in luxury rather than peasantry. I was not fully wise to their esteem until our regular visits to the village. Bedfordshire claims the Miller family to be their highest power in farming, and any mention of Nicholas or Amelia brings a smile to the faces of all. Some even exaggerate their kindness or act as though we are all royalty, which can be overwhelming at times.

I enter through our chamber door and am surprised to see Henry lying in our bed. At a glance he seems to be stricken with illness. "Hello, Henry, is all well?" I ask.

Henry pulls himself to a seated position on the mattress and smiles. "Of course, Emelie," he verifies with a cough as he pulls me in for an embrace, "although the weather troubles me at the moment. The cold is quite harsh in this place already, and I should have used the proper coverings when assisting my uncle these past few days. Today I took an absence from the chores but will dress accordingly and return to Nicholas's side tomorrow."

We've had little time to ourselves since arriving in Bedfordshire, so I cherish these unexpected moments. Rather than rushing to my planned activities, I gently lie next to Henry on the bed to continue our conversation.

"How was your trip to the village?" Henry asks, gently clearing his throat.

"It was fine, but Thomasin and I had some interesting encounters while making our way to the merchant. I shall explain more over supper, but how do you truly feel about this place?" I reply with a shift to a serious topic.

"Things have been quite well. Reconnecting with my family is something I would have never thought possible. Yet here I am, and here we are, in this place where we can make something of ourselves."

I offer a brief chuckle at his words. "Thomasin spoke in jest earlier of what is to become of me. She thinks it be wise to pursue apothecary practices. Hath she gone mad?"

Henry listens to my words and formulates a response. "Well, perhaps that is not as poor of an idea as you think. Rose believed in you, and you are the only one who understands her teachings. The rest of us try but it's as though you and Rose share a bond through her writings that none of us can configure. And besides, you read those scrolls into the late hours of the night so you must have learned all there is to know by now."

"You sound just as she," I reply, laughing at Henry and Thomasin's near-identical reasoning. An opportunity to disclose the truth about Thomas and Rose seems to be presenting itself once more. Fear clouds my mind as I try my hardest not to show Henry any turmoil.

"I am sorry if I have offended you, Emelie," Henry explains in response to my faltering emotions.

"No, Henry, 'tis not your words that burden me. For I have a struggle of my own that eats at me. Troubles from the past that I fight to carry in secrecy."

Henry fixes his posture and leans in my direction. He grabs my hand and pulls it into his. "Tell me, Emelie, whatever it is that troubles you."

I take a deep breath, realizing that I must finally disclose our past. This is a hindrance that prevents me from properly moving forward. 'Tis much easier to converse with Henry, as I am puzzled by the hardship in explaining this with Thomasin. I believe that her suffering was worse than mine and such a revelation will trouble her.

That is but a lie. Do not act as though you withhold this secret for her protection. You hide this knowledge out of the selfish fear that she will despise you. Speak it, you must tell him now.

"On the day that we left Rose's home," I begin shakily, "I made an immense discovery."

"You can tell me," Henry reassures as I pause in distress. He pulls me closer until I nearly whisper the words in his ear.

"I was gathering the scrolls I wished to take with us from her bochord. But I found something new; a journal that I failed to notice until that day. Rose was documenting the moments leading up to All Hallows Eve. She wrote extensively on how witchcraft was making its way to The Hollow. And then, she wrote of something else."

I stop once more, hesitating to reveal the secret that has burned within me since the moment our journey began. Henry awaits my words, and I try to remain composed while continuing.

"Witchcraft was never the issue in The Hollow. It was but a means to conceal the sins of Reverend Thomas, for he and Rose held a relationship in secrecy. They grew fond of each other in those months following his arrival, though this came to an end just as abruptly as it began. She claimed him to be an unhinged and wicked force that would corrupt Warren Hollow. And then Rose carried a child. Thomas did not take such a revelation well, and her plans to inform the court were interrupted when he imprisoned her. Witchcraft was the perfect way to send his secret to the grave. But then our All Hallows Eve celebration forced Thomas to act without restraint," I explain through tears.

Henry listens respectfully to my explanation, never interrupting or judging me. "So," Henry begins, "do you think that if we stayed home that night, Rose would have been the only one to lose her life?"

"We shall never know for certain. Out of guilt I tell myself that our evaluation in the church would have been the end of it. Thomas would have murdered Rose, damning his sins to the grave and ending witchcraft right then and there. But perhaps our parents became too attentive to his words and accusations, giving him no other choice than to proceed as though witchcraft truly was the disruption they saw in us and their community."

To my surprise, Henry has not moved or shown any indication of anger. He takes in my words, thinking them over in his mind upon discovering that our torture was rooted in lies.

"Well, it be just as we said from the start. All of us were innocent so that does not change. As we knew, witchcraft was never based in truth. But Rose's death was real, our torture was real, your brother's bravery and the sacrifices of the others were real, and you saving us was real. Regardless of Thomas's deeper intentions, we did not leave our home because of our own wrongdoing. But why did you hold such knowledge alone? Why have you not informed me until now?" Henry asks.

"I was afraid. On the day we left Rose's home I gave Robert the journal. He assured me that Reverend Gregory would receive the writing and that the truth would be known. Everyone back in The Hollow surely knows, but I feared telling you all. Our torture could not be for nothing. But in truth I did not want to lose any of you."

Henry pulls me into his arms as I cry. "I shall never leave you, and I know for certain that Samuel and Thomasin would not go anywhere either. They should know, Emelie. You have nothing to fear."

I worried for months that this truth would destroy our bond. And to my surprise, Henry is not angry at me for keeping such a secret. It was my intention to inform them earlier, but I did not wish for our sacrifices, bravery, and journey to falter. But in the words of Henry, everything we went through was real. While the reasons were unjust from the beginning, we survived through a tragedy, regardless of the cause.

"You must already be aware, but the past troubles me as well," Henry says with a subtle, nervous laugh. I pull away until we are face to face, wishing for Henry to express his inner struggles as well. He directs his attention around the room until focusing on the window. "I was nothing in Warren Hollow because of my father. Most people treated me as though I was a dog, and I pretended not to notice their looks of disgust when I would pass by. It was hard to blame them, for I looked at my father the same way. I knew that our family name was one that brought repulsion."

I listen carefully to this painful explanation that Henry provides. He has not spoken to me in such a broken tone and never truly mentioned these details of his past. This is something that has burdened Henry, likely his entire life.

"My father awakened me in the night just before All Hallows Eve. I knew not what was happening before he was on top of me. He tried to strangle me while shouting of witchcraft in a blind rage," Henry explains.

"I am so sorry, Henry," I whisper.

"He was drunk, as usual, and had no idea what he was doing. Thomas warped his mind further than the years of alcohol already had. And this was not the first time my father attacked me. But on that night, I could stand for it no longer. I fought back and struck my father hard. 'Tis difficult to remember how everything happened, but his blood was on my hands and clothes after our struggle. For years I wished to fight back, to kill him even, and the night finally arrived."

"What did you do next, Henry?"

"I wished to kill him at that moment, but I stopped myself. In a panic I fled to our crumbling barn. It was more of a toolshed, and that is where I spent the next two nights before All Hallows Eve."

I fight tears at the torture that Henry endured in his own home. Though my life was dull, I once had a loving mother, father, and a brother to bring me comfort. Torture is all that Henry has ever known. This helps me to understand why Henry is so overly caring and hard on himself, as he carries the burden of his father's wrongdoings. And before he explains his actions on the farm, I already understand his reasoning, or obligation to do so.

"This place gives me a chance to start over. Our name brought nothing but shame upon me my entire life, but the very mention of the Miller family in Bedfordshire is that of greatness. It is strange to me, but I must do my part to show that I am worthy of this family name, the one I hated for so long, and worthy of living on this farm."

"Henry," I begin while holding his face, "thy aunt and uncle do not see you as a miscreant. And it matters not what our parents and officials thought of you back in The Hollow. All Thomasin, Samuel, Rose, and I ever saw you as was a friend. Even John thought of you as a hero." My words draw a long-buried emotional response from Henry. "Trust me when I say that you are not thy father. And I know it is strange to see such regard for your family name, but you deserve all the recognition that you receive. You are the most wonderful person I have ever known. You need not prove it with excessive chores or by trying to earn your place on this farm. It matters not what thy name represents in Warren Hollow because in this land it is that of greatness."

Henry nods, appreciative of my words and likely overwhelmed at the conversation that has unfolded on this unsuspecting morning. We lie together on the mattress and converse no further. My talks with Thomasin made it clear that we all hide struggles, and it is liberating to address the things that create distance between us. While I still feel guilt for keeping this secret from Henry and the others, I believe that this conversation was the first of many instances that will strengthen our bond and allow us to heal.

In the next few moments, I find comfort in our silent embrace. My breathing calms and I attempt to slow my intense heartbeat. All the plans I had before supper vanish from my mind, and I decide to lie here with Henry for the time being.

Commotion within our home startles me. I look around the room, realizing that I must have fallen asleep next to Henry. As usual, Henry allowed me to sleep while he stealthily departed our chamber. The smell of fish and vegetables fills the air, indicating that our meal is likely ready. Slowly I rise from the bed, fastening my makeshift hand and exiting the room while I wipe the sadness from my eyes. Henry and I's conversation took much effort, and I wish not for the others to notice any signs of sadness. Surely I will inform Thomasin and Samuel when the moment presents itself, though I do not wish for that to be tonight. Dinner smells delightful as I traverse the hallways and make my way down the stairs. Nicholas and the others seem gathered in conversation as I approach and do not acknowledge my presence with their usual exaggeration.

"Once we finish, I need each of you to help me decorate our farm," Nicholas exclaims while eating quickly.

"And what do we decorate for, Nicholas?" I ask as I enter the room, shaking my tiredness and becoming attentive.

"I shall explain, but first, I'd say it is time to feast!"

Thomasin offers me a smile as we all make our way to the table, hungry and confused by such a circumstance. Henry also acknowledges my presence, putting his arm around me as we take our seats. He seems to be feeling better by this hour and in good spirits after our discussion. It already feels as though the barrier between us has been destroyed.

Supper is generally a celebration in itself, but this evening appears to be overly special. Amelia prepared fish, vegetables, cider, mincemeat pies, and pudding that shall last for days. We fill our plates and revel in such a wonderful feast.

"Now, how was your trip to the village this morning?" Nicholas asks.

"It was mostly well, aside from the chilling weather," I begin, "and those sisters bothering us again. I think they followed us, for reasons of which we are uncertain. But we learned of their childhood and their grandmother, Clara, from Simon the merchant."

"Aye, those girls are likely curious about your journey. Their grandmother is a caring woman, although she lacks the awareness she once held. Was Simon lost to the ale?" Nicholas asks with a smirk.

"I'm afraid so," Thomasin adds, "just as old Phillip and seemingly everyone else in Bedfordshire."

"As expected," Nicholas replies with a laugh as we begin to devour our meal. Nights like this do not seem real in comparison to the nights of hunger and sadness back in The Hollow. Even before the witch trials, Mother and Father struggled to bring more than stale bread to the table.

"All of this absurd drunken behavior is likely to flourish in the coming weeks. And do any of you know why?" Amelia asks, eagerly waiting to explain. We look at each other and shake our heads in confusion.

"Christmastime!" Nicholas shouts while leaping from his chair.

Perhaps Rose mentioned such an event in one of her writings because it sounds familiar, although none of us are fully certain of what this 'Christmastime' entails.

"Yule? Midwinter? Christmas?" Nicholas spouts as we smile in confusion.

"This was likely forbidden back in their homeland, Nicholas. I apologize for his eagerness," Amelia whispers while leaning in our direction. "Nicholas, would you please explain?"

"Certainly!" Nicholas shouts with enough enthusiasm to spread his excitement. "There has been much commotion over the years surrounding this holiday. For a time, it was forbidden across the land. Then it was not, then it was once more. But as you can tell, we do as we please here in Bedfordshire. There is no harm in a good celebration and Christmas is the grandest time of year to celebrate!"

"And what is it that we are celebrating?" Samuel questions Nicholas.

"A time of joy, many days of good will, and faith. We shall decorate our homes, drink through the nights, and celebrate just as you all have done for All Hallows Eve. Although, Bedfordshire is much more involved with Christmastime, for this is our largest observance of the year. Though it is still a time of controversy so many other villages across the colony do not feel the same. Would you all like to help us decorate after supper?"

"Of course!" Henry answers with joy. The others are excited for this occurrence, and I cannot deny the feeling of exhilaration as well. Especially given the controversial views of this holiday, which is partly why we favored All Hallows Eve.

Christmastime is a festival that Warren Hollow must have forbidden, as we knew not of such an occurrence until today. Winter was nothing more than a dark time in The Hollow, often full of worry, hunger, and desperation for spring to arrive. But my friends and I live for any celebrations, so we are eager to get involved.

We finish our feast in haste so that we can begin to decorate. Nicholas and Amelia continue explaining the traditions and magic surrounding this time of year. Henry and Samuel make jest of Nicholas's excitement for the allowance of public drunkenness and gambling in the village. I am relieved to see that Henry is well after our discussion. He continues offering subtle glances and smiles throughout the night, perhaps in a way to verify that I am also fine. I grant him the same smile in return, wishing to ease his worry and allow him to properly enjoy himself.

Samuel and Henry assist with moving furniture for decorations and bringing in bundles of wood for the fire that will burn in constant through the winter. While drinking and gambling seems joyful, Thomasin and I assist Amelia and share her fondness for the less chaotic activities.

"I shall teach you how to make a wreath. 'Tis a simple and beautiful decoration for our door," Amelia explains as she gives us materials. We stare in awe as Amelia provides evergreens, branches, flowers, berries, and other natural materials preserved from the land. "Follow my motions and you will see that it is rather effortless."

"It be no issue for me to handle this," Thomasin tells me quietly, worried that I will be unable to build the wreath with one functioning hand. Her concern is appreciated, although I wish not for special treatment or sympathy.

"We shall do it together," I announce cheerfully. Thomasin smiles as we begin to follow Amelia's movements in building the wreath.

"Do keep a close eye on Henry and Samuel in the coming weeks, and I must do the same for Nicholas. This time of year brings joy, but also chaos. Most drink too much and engage in wassailing!" Amelia exclaims.

"What does that entail?" I ask Amelia with a laugh at such an odd phrase.

"Further excuses for the men to become drunken fools! The wealthy fall victim to ridiculous performances and entertainment from the most outgoing individuals. They sing and act like animals in exchange for payment, or oftentimes, something to drink! 'Tis harmless if conducted in good will, but we have seen this turn to harassment and conflict. We will undoubtedly get some excitement at our door."

Thomasin and I laugh at the foolishness of such a celebration. It is hard to believe that these actions can be taken with little consequence or question of faith. The slightest of odd behaviors would have someone facing conviction in The Hollow and I am constantly amazed at the difference in Bedfordshire's law. Yet, I feel eagerness to join in the coming festivities. Surely this will be a winter to remember.

"And now, you must do it like this," Amelia instructs as she continues to build the wreath. Thomasin and I mimic her every move. While I am unable to assist with the complex motions, I simply hold the materials for Thomasin and contribute when possible.

"When does the official day of Christmas occur?" Thomasin asks.

"We still have some time," Amelia starts, "although Nicholas and I choose to decorate early. Perhaps too early but we love this time of year. Bedfordshire acknowledges Christmas for twelve days, with a grand feast on both the first and final day. You will notice other members of Bedfordshire beginning to decorate in the coming weeks, so the village will look magical. This signals the start for those who engage in mumming, which I believe is far worse than the reveling!" We look to Amelia and laugh as she shows irritation for the odd behaviors that are to come. "'Tis all but the same, but these maniacs often visit in disguise, or cause commotion in the tavern. The same few members of the village end up jailed for taking the festivities to the point of danger."

I listen in disbelief at the complexities of such a celebration that was unknown to us before supper. Drinking, visiting friends, gambling, feasting, and honoring a sacred time of year for twelve days is truly a wonderful occurrence. The Hollow did not recognize anything outside of faith with positivity. A few pumpkins on a porch and a fire were the extent of acceptable behavior before Thomas arrived. But here, it's as though celebrations are the most important happenings of the year.

Henry and Samuel run around the house in cheers, placing decorations and sharing the excitement. I recognize the foliage near the hearth and on the tables to be that of mistletoe, holly, evergreens, and other vegetation from Rose's teachings and writings. While visually appealing, Rose taught me the significance of these plants in my younger years. This atmosphere takes me back to a memory in her home when I was but a child.

"And this mistletoe shall protect your home, ward off disaster, and bring joy."

As I remind myself on most days, John would have loved every moment of this. Perhaps he never understood the significance of All Hallows Eve at his age; rather, I think he enjoyed the forest and saw that I was excited, so he was excited. Nonetheless we created many memories together that I shall cherish for a lifetime. 'Tis challenging to fully engulf myself in happiness as the thought of his death and moving forward often stops me.

Amelia ends my despair with praise for our progress. We are nearly finished so Thomasin holds our wreath next to Amelia's with pride and shows the others. They compliment our work and take the wreaths to place on the outside of the doors.

Most of our home is now decorated and we all slowly walk around to admire each other's progress. Nicholas adds more logs to the burning hearth while Amelia gathers cups of cider. Night creeps through the windows as we sit near the fire in merriment, watching the first snowfall that steadily builds alongside a wicked chill. Flames dance on the walls and illuminate the decorations as each of us drink beyond our limits and continue feasting on tonight's supper.

  This coming celebration is quite unexpected, but an opportunity that fills us with rejoice. I use the evening hours to document our discoveries in Rose's journal, which is an act that I have committed to since we departed Warren Hollow. I sit quietly in the presence of the others, taking in the festive scents and sights around us with an eagerness for all that Christmastime entails.

VII

Lord of Misrule

Snowfall covers the ground across all of Bedfordshire. Frost coats the windows of our farm, and the smell of smoke is constant from the everlasting fire. Cabinets are filled with rations, and the farm is officially prepared for the vicious winter ahead. Each day entails joy and merriment rather than chores and duties. Christmastime draws near so Bedfordshire prepares to acknowledge the festivities that Nicholas and Amelia enacted in their home over the past few weeks. I cannot pass judgment on their fondness of this celebration, for we did but the same with All Hallows Eve back in The Hollow.

It's as though the preparation is a holiday in itself. As soon as the first leaf fell from the tree each year, Thomasin and I rallied our friends and devised plans to outdo the previous year's activities. We contemplated how to craft decorations or what to wear or which foods we should eat. And now, preparing for Christmastime in Bedfordshire is a refreshing and similarly festive experience. Although I do struggle with bouts of sadness and guilt in the midst of happiness. John is not by my side to craft his own decorations or to frolic in the snow. Ezekiel is no longer leading our group with plans of how to sneak around the restrictions. And I hold a deep longing to share this holiday with

Rose, as she enjoyed these events more than any of us. But since the moment we said our goodbyes to that life of old, I use every day to honor and remember those who sacrificed everything for our freedom.

My struggles have unfortunately reemerged in recent days. I sense that the others worry for me, though I wish not to be a burden on this farm. Things were going well in the weeks after All Hallows Eve, but this newfound level of joy has evoked a guilt that turns all happiness to distress. Nights are full of sleepless agony, and the days turn to a never-ending feeling of anxiety. Today is certainly one of those days because I realize that John and Rose will be absent through all of the celebrations, and there be nobody else that I would like to share my first Christmas with than my dear brother.

Each of us spent the morning crafting decorations for the younger children of Bedfordshire, which has helped to raise my spirits and shake my sadness. We prepared quilts, scarves, and a few other items that the less fortunate will find beneficial. While these moments can evoke horrific memories, I do find pleasure in giving to others, just as Nicholas and Amelia have done for us. All of Bedfordshire shares this fondness and respect for Nicholas and Amelia well beyond their farming contributions. The simple fact is that behind all the wealth and power, they are good people.

Everyone has been called to the meetinghouse this morning to formally address the festivities ahead. Once the service concludes, Nicholas and Amelia will spend the day distributing wreaths, children's dolls, and much of our excess food. Thomasin is stricken with another bout of illness, so Amelia elected to assist her in getting ready while Henry, Samuel,

Nicholas, and I leave for the service. Winter certainly brings sickness to all families and our conditions from last winter are still affecting me to this day.

Nicholas and Samuel make their way to the door, so I prepare my scarf and the heaviest of clothing to shield myself from the cold. I offer one last bout of assistance to Thomasin, who as always, refuses any help. This is a shared trait of stubbornness that neither of us will admit. 'Tis my hope that her illness shall pass so that we can all enjoy the next few weeks in the fullest of health.

"Henry," Nicholas shouts as he bids farewell, "we are off to the meetinghouse!"

Henry cleared a path around the home so that we do not have to traverse through the snow. He spends hours carving paths and ensuring that we can reach the barn or any other structures on the farm with ease.

"I am grateful for your efforts, Henry, but I believe that Emelie wishes not to find you frozen solid one of these mornings," Nicholas claims jokingly. I laugh, watching Henry as he pretends to be unbothered by the cold.

"It be no trouble, Uncle. Truly I do not mind," Henry replies.

Henry continues to assist around the farm beyond what anyone would expect. Perhaps he still feels a responsibility to earn our stay or to fill the role that his father tarnished. Nonetheless, Nicholas and Amelia are grateful for his contributions but constantly express that this time of year is for rest. Henry and Nicholas lead ahead of us, lost in conversation about work on the farm. Samuel and I have a moment alone together for the first time in recent memory.

"I hope that Thomasin's illness soon passes. How do you feel, Samuel?" I ask him.

"To my surprise, I feel quite well. Perhaps we shall be fortunate enough to avoid this sickness. I am happy that Thomasin is well enough to attend today's service, though she would likely come regardless!"

"True," I say with a laugh, "she is not one to admit when she is ailing. And how are you faring through this celebration? We have had little time to speak as of recent."

"Things have been terrific. I am grateful for all the time spent with Pastor Noah thus far. This has allowed me to strengthen my faith, but at my own will this time," Samuel replies.

Samuel is always pleasant to converse with. He stood by my side through the worst of moments back in The Hollow, so it brings me joy to see him adjusting so well. It was Samuel who first knew that my hand needed to be removed, and he was also the reason we remained undetected in Rose's home. Though underneath his genuine happiness, I sense that Samuel struggles with inner turmoil just like the rest of us. Perhaps we shall never fully know what occurred in those months after he sacrificed himself and stayed behind with Reverend Gregory. While I was often praised as our savior and a figure of power, it was all thanks to Samuel and his courageous sacrifice. And while I shall never question his reasoning or speak of it, I believe that he and I shared a similar plan, or desire perhaps, for death at the culmination of our actions back in The Hollow.

All of us are trying to fulfill a purpose in this life. Before the disruption I was nothing more than a child, bored with my mundane existence and longing for solitude in the forest. The closest friends I had are the few with me today, and not even Mother or Father understood my desires. Most children in The Hollow felt this way, which is what led to our bonfire excursions of sin. While Samuel has always been one of the most generous people I know, his devotion to faith is a result that was quite unexpected. It is another example of how such trauma has completely redirected our lives.

Is this not the result you desired? Freedom, a new home, a new life? Why do you question yourself or the paths of others?

"Did you ever think that your destiny was to be in the church?" I ask in a straightforward manner.

"It be fact that I lost my faith for quite some time back in Warren Hollow," Samuel begins with an honest tone. "Before everything happened, all of us were devout to the church. But the death of Reverend Nicholas brought evil to our home. Our parents changed, as did everything we knew about our way of life. Then after that night in the courthouse, perhaps I became involved with the church to protect everyone else. I felt that I needed to do so. And that is why I chose to leave The Hollow behind and come with you all. What good is serving in the church if it is for survival, or repentance for guilt? Although I learned much from Gregory, and most of it was a pleasant experience. Here in Bedfordshire, I have the chance to serve on passion and good will, rather than punishment."

I understand Samuel's words as though they are my own. We did not choose to endure such punishment, but we must find the good in our survival. Samuel was thrown into a path he never wanted but it allowed him to find his purpose and make the circumstance his own. Henry was an outcast in the eyes of most, but now in Bedfordshire, he is becoming one of the hardest working and well-respected farmers. Thomasin also has the opportunity to start anew without the playful notoriety that troubled her in the past. And my future is whatever I choose it to be. 'Tis difficult and shameful to accept at times but, this tragedy has reshaped our lives for the better. We lost our home, loved ones, and nearly everything we know; but through the tragedy, we are starting to find ourselves.

The raging weather puts an end to our meaningful conversation, as the snowfall has gradually gained momentum since our departure. We enter the village near Phillip's home, and I laugh to myself as he falls while clearing the snow from his porch. There be not a time in this plantation without someone making a drunken fool of themselves. While there is nothing but happiness in Bedfordshire, I believe that Christmastime will certainly bring the conflict that Amelia warns of. Some of these people act like wild animals that are waiting to break from their cages. Today's meeting to discuss the safety and plans for this time of year needs no further justification.

We walk side by side with other members of Bedfordshire, offering greetings and shielding each other from the cold. Our trek to service is much more pleasant here than the miserable silence and dread back in The Hollow. Nicholas and Henry rush to hold the doors open for everyone, asking us to save a seat for Thomasin and Amelia upon their arrival. I let out a long breath of relief as the warmth of the meetinghouse greets us. More than one fire burns in this building to fend off the treacherous weather outside. Quickly I remove my wool hat and scarf while searching through the pews for a seat.

We find an opening in the first few rows and get settled for service. Samuel greets Pastor Noah who sits one row ahead, and I take my seat while Nicholas and Henry approach. 'Tis likely that a member of the court will lead today's proceedings, as Pastor Noah exclusively handles church services. People continue to fill the meetinghouse, some already drunk and indulging in the Christmas merriment early. Nicholas explained that the purpose of today's meeting is to address Christmastime and the weeks of celebrations ahead with a mind for safety. Decorations shall fill the homes and paths of Bedfordshire in the coming days, which is something I am eager to witness above all other happenings.

    A tap on my shoulder pulls me from my thoughts and I turn to see Abigail and Rachel sitting in the row behind us. 'Tis the first time I have spoken to them in weeks, so I immediately feel awkward. Chrystopher also sits at their side, fully engaged in the interaction that is about to occur. While Samuel is near and the others make their way, I feel outnumbered and vulnerable without Thomasin.

    "Hey there," I say while exaggerating my smile.

    "It is nearly the greatest time of year, Emelie. We are so excited for Christmastime. Who do you think shall be the Lord of Misrule for this season?" Abigail replies.

    "What is the Lord of Misrule?" I ask curiously.

    "Well," Rachel begins, eager to clear my confusion, "they say we must be respectful and now refer to it as *'The Lord of Christmas'* instead. It is nothing more than a drunken fool elected to oversee the celebrations. Though Mr. and Mrs. Miller have done this many years in the past and brought respect to the position, but Simon the merchant or even old Phillip have guided us. Perhaps it shall be you this year!" Rachel exclaims.

I scoff at her idea, unable to hide the absurdity of granting me such a role. While it sounds interesting, this honor could not simply go to someone who only arrived but a few months ago. Though who's to say this could not be a possibility for any of us in the future?

"That does sound exciting but seems likely that the role will go to someone of higher regard," I reply.

"But Emelie," Abigail begins, "you be the most important person here today. You can do whatever you desire, you need not hide such power around us any longer."

She cannot possibly believe that I am still a witch. We discussed such foolishness many times, but they hold me to this high regard with certainty. And the worst part is that they are not afraid. Rather, they are still eager to befriend someone they believe to be wicked.

My next few words must come with caution, as I do not aim to make a fool of myself in front of all these people. Instead, I smile while formulating insults in my mind rather than speaking them aloud.

"How could you be the Lord of Misrule?" You would need to speak prayers and read scripture. You mustn't do this, Emelie, it will cause you great harm!" Chrystopher pleads with genuine concern as he leans forward. His imagination at such a young age is adored, though still outlandish.

"Some say that Griffin murdered his wife because she was a witch!" Rachel adds.

"No, you fool," Abigail interjects, "Griffin the butcher was the one bewitched! For it is simple history!"

I let out a sigh, understanding that these three individuals shall never comprehend that I am not a witch. Chrystopher does not bother me, as he is younger than Abigail and Rachel and I have always had a mind for children. Perhaps it is the innocence of my brother that shaped this tolerance. Though it is absurd for these sisters to believe that a real witch sits before them. This fascination is quite troubling and validates the reason Thomasin and I have avoided them since that morning near the port.

"Aye, prayer would burn me from the inside, and this very place would cause me agony if I was a witch. But I am no witch! I have spoken scripture at every service, so I cannot be a witch!" I express forcefully while keeping my voice low, but also clearly displaying frustration. My gaze bounces between Abigail and Rachel for a few moments, both of whom are oblivious to my growing anger. "I am no witch," I repeat again in a serious but calm tone. The sisters nod and look at each other with a playful grin to emphasize their doubt while I turn around to end our conversation.

I attempt to regain my composure so that conflict is avoided. Thomasin is usually the one who loses control, but she is not present and I feel as though I am surrounded. Although I do not want Nicholas or Amelia to see me lash out, especially while they know I am already unwell. A conflict could remove me from this meetinghouse or even Bedfordshire. While this was but a harmless encounter for the most part, my heart is pounding and my hand is shaking once again.

Instantly I feel sorrow for losing my temper, although Abigail and Rachel need to understand that this is nothing more than a dangerous fantasy. I can only imagine what stories they tell the others in Bedfordshire. This is attention I do not wish to attract. Reverend Thomas called us witches out of fear and disgust, and this never phased me. But it is quite uneasy that

Abigail and Rachel call us witches with honor and glorification. 'Tis my desire to never hear the word *'witch'* for the rest of my life or to have anyone accuse me as such. A wave of relief rushes over me as I spot Thomasin and Amelia making their way to our seats. Slowly they maneuver through the crowd and Thomasin sits directly at my side. It seems that the proceedings are moments away, so everyone halts their commotion.

"How do you feel?" I whisper to Thomasin, hoping she fails to notice my distress.

"Improved. Although I would feel even better without the sisters from hell behind us," Thomasin replies. I let out a laugh at her words, thankful to see that she is back to her normal self after a difficult morning.

"You missed all the excitement. I may have lost my temper for a few moments," I explain. Thomasin looks surprised, perhaps impressed at my words. "They asked foolish questions about me being unable to pray, because they still think us to be witches."

"They are idiots, Emelie. As I said before, 'tis best for us to distance ourselves from them and their curiosities," Thomasin replies, nearly loud enough for the sisters to hear. I agree with her words and no longer want to acknowledge the lunacy and obsession of Abigail and Rachel or their infant companion. Today is supposed to be full of joy so I shake this unpleasant interaction and draw my attention forward. All nerves begin to pass with Thomasin at my side.

"Hello everyone, 'tis great to see you all on this cold winter's morning." These words come from a man, Ambrose, who Nicholas explained as one of the head officials of Bedfordshire. Unlike Pastor Noah, he is younger in his age and is appointed to speak on matters beyond church service in the meetinghouse. He stands tall, appearing well kept and proper. Although I have not had the pleasure of meeting him myself, he does seem pleasant so far with his growing presence around the village. Much more so than any of the officials back in The Hollow.

"With the weather outside and the increase in drunken behavior, I would say that Christmastime is soon to be upon us!" Ambrose exclaims as the crowd erupts with cheers. "However, we must remember to be considerate of thy neighbor and do not pamper yourself beyond your means. The foundation of Christmastime is in faith and family so do not spoil the festivities with overindulgence in rum and violence. Poor actions will be met with severe punishment." The crowd nods in agreement with his words, including the people who will undoubtedly cause this mischief that this statement pertains to.

Ambrose carries on with regulations and warnings for what seems like an eternity before concluding the meeting with an eagerly awaited announcement. "And as we have done year after year, a Lord will be appointed to manage the revelries. We shall observe the twelve days of Christmastime, with celebrations starting on a glorious Christmas Day. And after consideration of all candidates, we honor Giles Harman as this year's Lord of Christmas."

The meetinghouse applauds Giles as he makes his way forward. He is close to Nicholas in age, though he is much smaller and is evidently not a farmer or fisherman. His appearance is clean, and he clearly dressed in anticipation of this opportunity. Nicholas mentioned him previously as Bedfordshire's most prominent tailor. I try my best to join in on the clapping and blend in, but it is difficult with one functioning hand. 'Tis my hope that attention is not drawn to my odd behavior. Although life is much more manageable with this makeshift hand, I still face bouts of insecurity and shame in moments like this.

"I thank you for all thy support," Giles begins, "this is a celebration that I love so deeply. After praying on this regard for many years, it be my honor to lead us through this year's twelve blessed days of Christmas." Giles' family rushes to embrace him at the front of the crowd, his wife and children thrilled for his opportunity to fulfill this role. It brings a tear to my eye to witness such a happy and supporting family. Mother and Father never shared the same love for celebration back in The Hollow, instead, it was met with scorn and loathing.

"I damn Christmastime and all who celebrate it!" A voice shouts from the back of the meetinghouse. Silence falls across the room as we direct our attention, watching as none other than Barnabas Wilfred stumbles his way through the aisle. He looks ragged and worn down. More so than he should at his age, which is likely close to that of Nicholas and Amelia but with the appearance of an elderly peasant. His clothes are covered in dirt and snow as if he spent the past few days outside.

"Leave this place at once, Barnabas, or you will certainly regret it," Ambrose demands.

Barnabas pays little mind to this warning as he is clearly drunk and working his way to the front of the room. He aggressively drinks from a cup that likely contains ale or rum. "I should be this so-called Lord that you praise!" He fends off the people who attempt to intervene, looking only to cause a scene and make a fool of himself. Now standing much closer to

Ambrose and Giles, Barnabas throws his cup with great force. Thankfully his aim is quite poor, and everyone is unharmed by the attack. Other officials and onlookers rush to detain Barnabas, forcing him back and out of the doors. The head of Bedfordshire's tavern, Solomon, must be restrained as he looks to launch his own attack at Barnabas. Nicholas mentioned the long history between Barnabas and Solomon, as the tavern is Barnabas's favorite place to spend his days. He often drinks himself into oblivion and causes chaos among travelers and guests.

"It should be me! I shall slaughter you, Giles!" Barnabas screams as the doors close.

"My apologies to you all," Ambrose expresses, "for this is not what Christmastime shall entail. He will be jailed, per usual, and do take his thoughtless words with little regard."

"He needs to be exiled, once and for all!" a voice shouts from the crowd, with cheers and agreement from others.

That exchange was quite unsettling to witness. Perhaps this is normal behavior in Bedfordshire, with threats such as murder being dismissed as nothing more than drunken ramblings. And that is likely all it shall be, but I will not take these words lightly. I have seen firsthand how chaos can unfold in the safest of places.

This commotion signals the conclusion of the meeting, and everyone is eager to shift their focus back to decorations and preparing for Christmastime. Nicholas and Amelia rise from their seats, gathering the decorations we constructed and wishing to congratulate Giles. When Nicholas is not the Lord of Christmas himself, which is said to be quite often by Rachel, he still makes contributions and gets quite involved with the festivities. This is apparent by the many gifts that we helped him craft for those without the wealth and means to properly celebrate.

Henry gives me a quick embrace, informing me that he shall assist with clearing a walking path outside. Samuel also departs to talk with Pastor Noah and his other acquaintances in service.

"Hello girls, how fares thy grandmother on this day?" Nicholas asks Abigail and Rachel. Momentarily I forgot their presence behind us.

"She is well, sir, although she has fallen ill and could not join us," Abigail replies.

"Well, that is unfortunate. Do let us know if we can provide any assistance to you all." They smile at Nicholas, quickly glancing at Thomasin and I as we all rise from the seats and prepare to depart. "In fact," Nicholas begins as he turns back, "would you care to join us for supper tomorrow? We shall offer the first of many celebrations to come for you and your grandmother."

Thomasin and I nearly implode from Nicholas's words, as he has invited these lunatics into our home. Though I cannot be mad at Nicholas, for he knows not of the complexity and delusion that these girls share. He is only trying to aid the less fortunate with an innocent gathering. While I wish to beg Nicholas for reconsideration of his offer, I understand that it is not my place to dispute. This thought is shared by Thomasin who prepares to intervene, although I whisper that we mustn't. She understands my words but matches my sharp gaze of anger and irritation.

"That would be wonderful!" Abigail exclaims. Nicholas's invitation seems to bring them as much joy as the election did for Giles. They look at each other with smiles, unable to contain their excitement. Catching me completely off guard, Abigail leans forward and pulls me in until we are cheek to cheek. She holds onto me with a tight embrace for an uncomfortable duration as though we are the closest of friends. Her strength is intimidating, and I show my discomfort by backing away until she finally releases her grasp. Thomasin stands ready at my defense and Nicholas is oblivious to the entire situation. He bids us farewell before departing to assist with the coming celebrations.

"We will see you tomorrow!" Rachel claims as they rush off.

I turn and notice Chrystopher is still sitting in his seat, watching closely without any intervention. I feel sorrow for his absence in the conversation and nearly invite him as well until he draws his attention forward and departs upon noticing my gaze. I begin wiping at my cheek and signal to Thomasin that we should depart as well. She agrees, though not before once again acknowledging Abigail and her fondness for me. She speaks not a word, but her eyes and gestures are all that is needed. I brush off her claims, trying my hardest not to laugh once more and give Thomasin the satisfaction of being correct. Surely Abigail is aware of Henry and I's relationship and the repercussions of such behavior, though I sense that she does not care in the least for either circumstance. Nonetheless, this morning brought more than enough excitement, so I wish to return home.

Preparations for Christmastime are well in motion as we depart the meetinghouse. People are hanging wreaths and other decorations on their homes and nearby structures. Smells of cinnamon and other festive foods fill the air from open fires and roasts. Some gather in their yards to sing carols, and children slide down ice on the path while throwing balls of snow at each other. They attempt to construct figures and shapes out of the heavy snow and disappear head-first into larger piles. The weather is brutal and the snow falls intensely, but this is most fitting around Christmastime. Some of the wealthy members like Nicholas and Amelia hand out cups of ale and servings of pudding at makeshift merchant stands. While I wish to join in on the merriment, the uneasiness of tomorrow's visit looms in my mind.

VIII

Sojourn

An evening of dread is fast approaching. We are but moments away from the sisters' arrival and my wish is to hide in Henry and I's chamber. Perhaps I did not want to address their behaviors initially and felt that they were misunderstood. The people of Bedfordshire are nothing like those back in The Hollow, so I believed they were harmlessly interested in our past. I even see a reflection of myself in Abigail and Rachel, as they burn with the desires that I too shared for many years. A meaningless existence in The Hollow was not something I would settle for, and I always knew that there was more to life than farming and faith.

Over the past year my friends and I shared enough experiences for a lifetime. But 'tis not our long journey or family history that interests these sisters; rather, it is the witchcraft at its core. The conduit used to ruin our home, murder my brother and friends, and rip me from the very course of my life. It cannot be denied that their vision of witchcraft is hindered and there must be a distinction between Rose's teachings and this so-called black magic. This was my promise to Rose and the reason I often spend hours reading her scrolls or documenting my own knowledge. Perhaps I can use this visit today to teach the sisters and help them understand, in order to prevent a similar chaos in

Bedfordshire. There be enough writings on my shelf to teach even the most simple-minded individual. When witchcraft is mentioned, and I hold no doubt that it shall be rather quickly, I will use the opportunity to enlighten them.

Nicholas wishes to provide Abigail, Rachel, and Clara with his own rendition of Christmas Day. While all of Bedfordshire shall act in observance for twelve days, the people of less fortune inevitably face hardship. Surely young Chrystopher will spend many days alone, never receiving a warm meal or gifts while his father is off fishing and partaking in other drunken behaviors. This is likely the case for many commoners in this village, so I understand Nicholas's reasoning and know quite well what it is like to be on the opposite side of fortune.

Nicholas and Amelia worked tirelessly to prepare goose, mincemeat pies, peaches and pudding for dessert, and also plenty of wine and rum. The first day of Christmas is nearly upon us but it's as though Christmastime began weeks ago. Scents of lavender and rosemary fill the halls as I make my way to Henry and I's chamber. While all the activities and foods are delightful, it is the simple smells and sights that truly engulf me day after day. It was the same when I escaped to the forest on an autumn day in The Hollow or when we would gather at Rose's home for a bonfire. For it would be impossible to fully express the way I become one with the sensations in these moments.

Snow falls heavily outside and winter's chill creeps through the windows. I hear Samuel tending to Thomasin as I pass their chamber, and once again this illness has kept her bedridden for most of the day.

"I am growing quite fond of Christmastime," I tell Henry while entering our space. "Perhaps even more so than All Hallows Eve."

"Maybe you should wait until these twelve days of Christmas come to an end before making such a bold statement," Henry replies.

"It is truly magical, and a shame that this was kept from us our entire lives back home. If Warren Hollow was more like Bedfordshire, then everything would have been fine."

"It be a different place," Henry begins, "with different struggles and different people. These fishing plantations care little for restrictions and are not ruled by faith. The Hollow was crumbling around us. Even without the witch trials, it would have survived two, maybe three more winters at best before collapsing. And faith gave our parents meaning. Our conditions were so horrid that it was surely God's punishment for our wickedness and untamed behavior."

"I am sorry, Henry, for all the years that your father took from you in this place because of his foolishness," I say sympathetically.

Henry smiles as he sits next to me on the bed. "If everything did not happen the way it did, then we would not have found each other. I would not have friends like Thomasin and Samuel, and you would not be by my side."

I appreciate the comfort I find in our early morning conversations or before nightfall. While Henry is busy helping around the farm or in the village, he still makes time to remain by my side to no end. To experience the magic of Christmastime in this wonderful house with my loved ones is cherished.

"Thank thee for always calming my nerves. This is a morning of worry. Abigail and Rachel shall soon be here, and their antics are difficult to handle. Maybe I can help them understand that I am nothing more than a commoner, like Simon or Phillip," I explain.

"You mustn't forget that you were also our leader and savior not so long ago. 'Tis easy for anyone to recognize the power and spirit within you, even when you do not recognize it yourself. This was proven back in The Hollow. So, it is no surprise that this is recognized here by people who see your arrival as a severance of their dreary existence. And we shall all be by your side, so if they act foolishly then they can leave our home immediately," Henry assures.

His words bring a smile to my face and it is clear that he still holds me to such a high regard. These situations tend to pull me between this new life and the one I left behind. Months of answering to the others and giving them hope, even at times when I had no hope myself has certainly molded who I am. Or as the others say, perhaps this tragedy allowed my true self to shine through the barrier that I hide behind.

Over the next few moments, I gather all the writings from the shelf. I spread them across the bed and wish to prepare a clear explanation for the sisters. Some of the writings are journals like the one I left for the others in The Hollow. Others include recipes, notes of experiments, healing remedies and instructions, and some contain writings on the darker side of witchcraft. Rose was exploring the idiocy that some people believed, such as preparing witch cakes or sacrifices for a ritual. She wrote of symbols and dark forces that entice women to sign The Book of the Beast. 'Tis common that I recite a lengthy prayer after reading some of these wicked scrolls. The line between reality and delusion blurs at times and calls to those with burning desires. Some of the contents were a shock at first glance, but as Rose concluded through all her research, these behaviors hold no significance. In her own words, *"It be important to immerse thyself in the bad of the world, dealing with it firsthand and understanding what is out there, in order to recognize the good."*

I finish organizing the writings and depart to join the others downstairs while Henry does the same to check the path outside. The food is nearly finished so Abigail and Rachel will arrive at any moment. Perhaps they will not act out of turn with their grandmother in attendance. 'Tis strange to worry for the actions of people who are my age, as this would be expected from a child in infancy. Nicholas and Amelia prepare the table for our grand feast and Samuel adds logs to the fire while Thomasin rests nearby. Her prolonged illness causes much disruption to her enjoyment of Christmastime and has started to concern me. Henry makes his way from the outside, covered in snow and joined by Abigail and Rachel. The very sight of these girls brings tension to the room, or perhaps it is my own paranoia. Nicholas and Amelia rush to greet them, explaining all the foods that we shall enjoy and the events of the evening.

"And where is thy grandmother?" Nicholas asks.

"She struggles with illness on this day. It is tearing through all of Bedfordshire at the moment. But she wishes a blessed Christmastime to all of you," Rachel explains with a perplexing tone.

"What a shame," Amelia states sympathetically, "then you must be sure to take her as much supper as thy can carry once you leave."

The girls begin to look around the home in awe. Abigail and Rachel share the same level of surprise that I held upon our arrival months ago. They offer a greeting to me and Thomasin without any strange behavior. One by one we sit at the table; Abigail makes certain to claim the chair next to me. I await a snide remark from Thomasin, but this illness has stolen her humor for the time being. It appears that her only focus is enduring the meal without losing consciousness or getting nauseous.

Eventually I notice that Abigail changed something about her appearance. I look at Rachel, who also shares this alteration to her look. Both now wear ribbons in their hair; Abigail's is a scarlet shade and Rachel's is as white as the snow. They took measures to dress formally for this dinner, as I would have done the same when visiting the most prestigious homestead in the village. While they are strange, their beauty admittedly leaves me stunned, perhaps envious, in these instances.

"Do you like it?" Abigail asks, noticing my gaze before I can look away. She turns her head so that I can see the ribbon as it flows side to side.

"Yes," I begin with uncertainty of what to say, "it is lovely."

Abigail smiles from ear to ear and moves excitedly in her seat. The sisters look at each other and rejoice as though this was the grandest approval they ever received. Abigail leans towards me and reaches beneath the table to squeeze my hand in her usual excessive compassion, but I fail to react before she grabs hold of my makeshift hand. Her smile fades as she looks down and quickly pulls away. She looks back up with confusion and sympathy, along with what seems like immediate regret. It's as though she is about to cry out of embarrassment or sorrow for my situation.

"It is quite alright. A tale for another time perhaps," I whisper to Abigail as she nods, and we both face forward. Surely she noticed the steel boulder attached to my arm in place of a hand prior to this moment, though I often wear gloves or keep it concealed so it is likely that she may not have. Perhaps this could dissuade her from such affection in the future, which is my hope so that I do not need to eventually address it myself. The realization that they will surely ask how I lost my hand causes further dread and uneasiness.

We start our meal and everyone is cheerful, aside from Thomasin. She is in no mood to deal with any foolish behavior should it arise. Although difficult, I understand that I must show apprehension and ignore any idiotic questions. These sisters are full of surprises, as the next statement from their mouths or their actions are always a mystery. Aside from their enthusiasm and Abigail's overbearing fondness, things have been relatively peaceful thus far. They dine with proper manners and do not bicker with each other or look to engage in mischief. For a moment I relax and enjoy the meal as well. Nicholas and Amelia spoil us with wonderful feasts so I am always sure to show appreciation.

"Is everyone eager for the arrival of the first day of Christmas?" Amelia asks aloud.

"Of course," Samuel begins, "we have many plans within the church. Pastor Noah will let me assist with a service before the celebration's end!"

"How wonderful, Samuel. And what about you, Henry? You must spend some time enjoying this time of year, outside of the barn that is!" Amelia remarks in a teasing manner as we all laugh.

"Aye, perhaps I may take a few days rest to enjoy the merriment," Henry replies. He still feels this need to prove his worthiness, perhaps to himself.

"Does Bedfordshire have an apothecary? Or has there ever been an apothecary in this plantation?" Thomasin asks. Although acting without ill-intent, she continues to press for this to be my future. I was unsure of how anyone would react to such a role, though we shall find out at this very table.

"There was, many years ago. But he had little involvement in the healing or non-traditional practices of which you likely speak. He was much more present in bringing goods to Bedfordshire and even managing the currency. This was long before our physician, Timothy, took such a role. For what do you ask?" Nicholas questions.

Thomasin looks at me and smiles. I notice that Abigail and Rachel are also staring directly at me. They appear as though this answer could shift the course of their lives.

"I think that Emelie would make a fine apothecary. Given what we have endured and all she has learned from our apothecary, Rose, back in Warren Hollow. If you need an expert on healing, witchcraft, or anything beyond the words of faith, then Emelie is your destination. With respect to common practices and beliefs," Thomasin shares with a smile. Her explanation was honest and did not shy away from this role's separation from faith and reason.

"I must agree," Henry interjects enthusiastically, "you study those writings and hold knowledge that could be quite useful here."

"Writings?" Abigail asks curiously, nearly inches from my face.

For a moment I wish to disappear, frightened by the reaction that Nicholas and Amelia may have. Since our arrival, I diverted nearly all attention aside from these sisters, and it has been relatively peaceful. To take on such a role would make me an outlier in this community. Although, I must remind myself that Rose was not executed for her practices. Apothecaries are much more traditional in other places and this previous apothecary in Bedfordshire likely faced no judgment or scrutiny. I took an oath to educate those around me about Rose and her life, and to help others understand something sinful and bizarre.

"That is a great idea," Amelia interrupts, showing no contention. "People are always looking for a healer. And holding such knowledge would be useful in this village. I think that is a fine path for you, Emelie."

"Would you be so kind to show us these writings you speak of?" Rachel chimes in, struggling to conceal her desire for information.

"Perhaps after supper I can retrieve some of those writings to help you best understand the means behind our conviction. I planned to surprise you and do so anyway," I reply.

The sisters look at each other with excitement. While such a response was expected, my hope is to enlighten them and ease their obsession with the dark forces. As we spend more time together, it is evident that their interest is within the darkest side of witchcraft, rather than components of nature and healing. They obsess over the rituals and fantasy of magical powers, so it is my goal to banish these foolish thoughts from their mind. If I find success in educating Abigail and Rachel, then there may be a possibility to fulfill this role and educate countless others in Bedfordshire.

The conversation begins to shift once more as we devour the meal before us. Our portions are never-ending, and I struggle to finish my pudding after overconsumption of goose and pie. Nicholas continues sharing tales of Christmastime and further explains the history and how it came to be such a glorious holiday in Bedfordshire. Abigail and Rachel contribute memories of Christmastime in the days of old, receiving gifts from their neighbors and frolicking in the snow. Their stories never consist of positive memories involving their mother and father. It seems that their parents were not happy individuals before their deaths, though I feel no desire to ask of their past.

The others are still baffled at the fact that Christmas was never observed in Warren Hollow, but they understand the difference in lifestyle in comparison to a struggling village where faith and law are intertwined. We do mention that days like All Hallows Eve were usually not an issue until all facets of life shifted when the slightest of issues arose.

Samuel discusses his involvement and progression within the church, and we are pleased to see him doing so well. He has found peace in his life, which is something I hope will unravel for me in the near future. I cannot deny that life in Bedfordshire exceeds all expectations and the freedom is unimaginable. While my hatred for Mother and Father shall meet no end, I desired a different ending to our relationship. Before the witch hunts and persecution, my home was loving and happy place. As we discussed many times since our departure, the hope is that Reverend Gregory has restored order and some level of happiness to our birthplace.

The candles across the table are nearly extinguished and all of us have reached our limits of consumption. We are gathered as family and friends, discussing pleasant memories and making new ones at this very moment. Cheer fills our halls and the merriment carries through all of Bedfordshire. Nicholas is certainly lost to the alcohol and perhaps even I have consumed beyond my means. But it is all in jest and there is no harm in enjoying such an occurrence. It brings me joy to know that twelve more days of celebration are approaching. Amelia begins to clear the table and conclude today's gathering while we laugh at Nicholas who struggles in his intoxication.

"We have this under control, go enjoy the rest of your evening!" Amelia instructs the rest of us while playfully slapping Nicholas. She wants no further assistance, so we leave the kitchen and make our way to the warmth of the fire. Samuel helps Thomasin to her chair and Henry rushes to clear the snow from the walking paths around the farm.

"Can we see those writings now, Emelie?" Abigail asks at the first opportunity to do so. I forgot about this agreement I made and begin regretting my decision. Although I recognize that this is a chance to educate them. 'Tis my hope that their obsession with witchcraft, or me specifically, shall end after tonight.

"Very well," I begin, "I shall retrieve some of the writings and bring them down."

I enjoy one last moment of warmth by the fire before departing to the chill of the upstairs. It is a bit unnerving to show anyone what I hold so sacred. Henry, Thomasin, Samuel, and even Nicholas and Amelia have viewed some of these writings, but nobody else has yet to do so. Our chamber door is shut so I push it open and endure the wave of cold air that greets my arrival. The window is cracked slightly open, so I rush to pull it shut and preserve the heat. Floorboards sound beneath me as I make my way to the bookshelf. One by one I pull the scrolls and journals from the shelf, placing them across the bed to determine which I would like to present. Suddenly the sound of the chamber door prompts me to turn around and discover that Abigail and Rachel stand peering into the room.

"We are sorry to disturb you, Emelie, we only wish to assist you," Abigail says. They push the door fully open and make their way into Henry and I's chamber. Momentarily they scan the room before noticing the writings on the bed. With no hesitation they rush over, eager to get their hands on all that I promised to show them.

"Perhaps you could talk to us in here," Rachel suggests, "as we feel improper to ask such questions in the presence of others."

I let out a subtle sigh, reluctant to be alone with either of them. Once again, they followed me when it was undesired, and I immediately sense a shift in their behavior. It's as though the manners and respect at dinner were merely an act, concealing their true intentions and curiosities while around others. Nicholas and Amelia are unaware of these behaviors, but I see directly through this veil they present. "Very well," I reply, eager to end this situation as quickly as possible.

The girls take their position over by the window as I stand near the bed while preparing my explanation.

"This is my collection of writings, experiments, and research that I brought with me from Warren Hollow. Our apothecary, Rose, documented all the work that she conducted over the years. She aided the ill and spent a lifetime understanding nature and developing remedies. Even officials of high regard would visit her with family members who had fallen ill."

I continue my explanation while the sisters pay close attention to every word. "Rose taught me many things in my life, like how to read or how to disperse an ache in the stomach. And then, witchcraft began to tear through neighboring communities. People were frightened, unsure of what it was exactly, all while accusations and murder were unfolding. And due to Rose's status as a magical healer, it was believed that she worked for the Devil. So she was hung by the neck, which was soon to be a fate for each of us. After months in prison, we were finally given the choice to prove our innocence. The few of us here today chose to leave our home and start a new life," I explain.

John's death, the helpless nights in prison, Thomas's ruthlessness and eventual murder, or how I lost my hand are all occurrences I wish not to share with these sisters. None of those details are of importance in proving that witchcraft is not something to desire.

"And so you see," I begin, "I am no witch. Thomasin is no witch, nor Henry or Samuel. And I made a promise that I would spread this truth, bringing justice to Rose and all our torture. Many good people lost their lives, and it must be understood that Rose was a healer, but nothing more."

The girls stand in complete silence, taking in my words and not engaging in their usual playfulness. Perhaps I was successful in teaching them the truth. "And what are these other writings?" Rachel asks as she points to the bed.

"This one," I say as I grab one of the scrolls, "is a collection of recipes and instructions for healing all sorts of illness. Rose describes the combinations of ingredients that can bring someone back to full health. And this," I pronounce while presenting the next journal with the black covering, "holds all the knowledge that Rose uncovered with witchcraft. She tried to understand this plague and was to present her findings to the court. This is quite the collection of sinful and dark behavior, and I find it best not read unless absolutely necessary."

Oftentimes I shy away from this particular collection. Rose tried for years to understand the motivation behind serving the Devil and such willingness to engage in dark magic. From sacrifices to conjuring of spirits, this writing is the darkest side of witchcraft that must be handled with caution. I continue presenting each of the writings while explaining what they entail.

Eventually, I reach the last binding. "This last piece is my own work. I actively use this to document our struggles, all that we endured through imprisonment and life after. My hope is to someday use this to help everyone understand that Rose was innocent and executed on the basis of falsity and fear. Over the past year I've contributed my own findings on healing, witchcraft, and anything that Rose would have continued to pursue."

This journal is one that I hold much protection over. Nobody else, not even Thomasin, has seen the contents hidden within. I documented the truth between Rose and Thomas, which only Henry knows. Vivid details of John are also included, along with all that I can remember from my childhood with Mother and Father.

"Thank you for sharing, Emelie!" Rachel exclaims. The sisters take a few moments to stare at the large collection of writings on the bed that I presented. More than enough insight was shared in this room, so I wish to end our conversation and place the writings back on the shelf. I pull each of them into my arms as Abigail steps forward.

"Could we look at some of those writings before you put them away? Perhaps the one with the black cover?" Abigail asks.

"I am sorry, Abigail, surely we can have further discussion in the future. But these are quite personal and best kept in my hands," I claim. Clearly this is not the answer she had hoped for, but I shared enough information to satisfy her. I move towards the shelf while struggling to carry all the writings.

Abigail rushes to stand before me, making one final attempt to change my mind. "Please, Emelie," she pleads.

"Abigail," I mutter with noticeable frustration, "please step out of my way."

"Emelie, I only wish to observe one writing, just for a few moments," Abigail begs.

"No!" I yell without further explanation. Abigail refuses to move, and I feel all the writings slipping from my incapacitated grip. Forcefully I push past her, wishing to quickly reach the shelf.

Catching me completely off guard, Abigail latches onto the stack of writings in my grasp. We struggle back and forth as she desperately tries to break anything free from my hands. "Please, let us see just one!" Abigail yells.

"Let go of me!" I demand. Our struggle continues as Rachel offers no assistance with her sister. We move around the room, bound in a fight for control. Abigail becomes aggressive, which is unnerving and unexpected. She revealed many sides of her personality since we first met, though this anger is unlike anything I have seen. I fail to notice that my provisional hand is coming loose as we grapple for control. With one final pull, Abigail breaks the components that fasten the hand to my arm, sending the writings all around the room as my makeshift hand crashes to the floor. Abigail stands in complete shock, staring at my arm and instantly regretting her decision.

"Emelie," she mumbles in desperation, "do forgive me."

My emotions shift from embarrassment to fury as tears form in my eyes. Abigail stands stuttering before me, and without any thought, I finally lose myself to anger. Forcefully I strike Abigail across the face. The blow is devastating and Abigail stumbles back with blood instantly dripping from her nose. All the commotion turns to silence as the three of us stand completely still. Rachel gathers the loose pages and writings from the ground behind me while I never break my gaze from Abigail.

"Get out," I demand, quietly and emotionally.

Neither Abigail nor Rachel dispute my command. Rachel finishes organizing the writings into a pile as Abigail makes her way to the door. Quickly the sisters disperse from the chamber, and I now stand alone with my rage. I start to cry, embarrassed by losing my hand and the foolishness of thinking I could spread this knowledge to them. Pathetically I begin to meddle with the hand in hopes of reattaching it to my arm. All the commotion alerts Henry who rushes through the door in a panic.

"Emelie, what happened? The sisters left in such haste!" Henry yells as he observes my condition and the aftermath of our conflict. He gathers the writings and places them back on the shelf.

"I only tried to do what is right, Henry, but I fear that nobody shall understand our truth." The night was going so well, and I cannot blame anyone for what happened. Those girls are unhinged and perhaps it is my own ignorance that led to this.

"Nicholas and I shall repair this first thing in the morning. It will be good as new and you need not worry," Henry assures as he pulls me into his arms on our bed. Overcome by emotion, I lean into Henry as I peer out of the window and watch the falling snow. My surroundings fade and I am taken back to those long nights in the prison of questioning my will to survive while looking outward for answers.

IX

Solivagant

The Christmastime festivities in Bedfordshire are accompanied by a vicious cycle of winter weather. Today is the coldest in recent memory, far beyond any nights in the prison. If such a chill was present back in Warren Hollow, we all would have lost our lives on that very first night. Those conditions led to the eventual loss of my hand and stole the lives of others, but the weather in Bedfordshire is unmatched as we are a day removed from Christmastime.

    A great reception awaits on tomorrow's first day of Christmas, although today brings all but happiness. Last night's confrontation affected me more than I care to admit. At first I felt anger and admittedly have yet to shake it, but I also feel sorrow. There is a burning pain within me for Abigail and Rachel because they can take little blame for such an outcome. I understand the loss of a mother and father in some ways, but I had friends to help me endure. These girls were left in the care of a senile grandmother, with little capability to guide them through life. In this existence of hardship and monotony, our arrival was an answer to their prayers. We provided them a purpose, or an escape rather, and it matters not if this is of faith or benevolence. Yesterday was a mistake on my part because I should not have leaned any further into their desires. While I wish I could pass the blame, it is impossible for me not to hold myself accountable.

"You cannot do this, Emelie," Thomasin affirms with dispute. "After what they have done, it is wise to leave this be!"

"I wish I could, Thomasin," I reply, "but I must make this right."

My plans draw anger from her, and reasonably so. Nicholas and Amelia are unaware of the issues that unfolded after last night's supper, and they wish for the sisters and their grandmother to have a meal for today. They left in such haste after our encounter, so Nicholas is arranging for the leftovers to be delivered. He planned to do so himself, but after much contemplation, I elected to travel to their home and deliver the meal. Henry, Samuel, and especially Thomasin are opposed to the idea. Each of them suggests that there is nothing left to be done. Our efforts to create a tolerable friendship failed, and after yesterday, distance is perhaps the only solution. 'Tis likely that nothing positive will come from further efforts. There are plenty of other children and friendly individuals that we encountered in Bedfordshire, and we could build much healthier friendships. But I simply cannot shake the urge to make one final attempt. Not to be friends, but to at least put this fantasy to rest and resolve yesterday's conflict.

Thomasin's illness grows more prevalent each day, which is starting to spread fear across the farm. I understand her desire to protect me from these sisters and she is unable to do so in her current state. Things would have ended much worse if she was also in the chamber yesterday.

"I shall return in haste, and there be no need to worry. This meal will be delivered to their grandmother, and I will be home before the sun goes down," I explain as I prepare to brave the weather outside.

"You do not need to do this, Emelie. 'Tis not your responsibility to help them. And none of this is your fault, you cannot fix these sisters. The only one that you must fix is yourself!" Thomasin shouts with anger. She recognizes the harshness of her explanation and immediately shows regret.

Her words stun me and pierce through my impenetrable barrier. We had our share of squabbles in our younger years, but Thomasin never spoke to me in such a manner. My reaction causes the anger to subside, and she apologizes for her choice of words. I cannot blame her for such a statement. This claim is valid and surely it is frustrating to watch as I help these sisters while failing to acknowledge my own struggles or safety. Thomasin is always by my side when I awaken from nightmares or when the sisters become too aggressive. So surely she feels helpless while I run rampant with my foolishness as she is bedridden. Though her words are true, no matter how much they sting at this moment.

"I will soon return," I reply, giving Thomasin an embrace and preparing to depart.

I will not hold her words against her, for she only wishes to protect me. Everyone on this farm tries to protect me, especially from myself. But I made a promise to Rose and my brother that I would help people understand. That was my only intention in showing Abigail and Rachel those writings. In turn, I validated and fueled their desires beyond what even they expected. It is unclear what I will say on my visit, but I do feel guilt for striking Abigail. Perhaps I shall issue a simple apology and leave them with this meal.

Without further hesitation I push through the doors and out to the cold. I hold a large plate of yesterday's supper that I must shield from the vicious weather. Henry is off in the barn with Nicholas, and the light of a lantern indicates whatever nonsense keeps them occupied. Samuel remains at home with Amelia as they tend to Thomasin, and I depart to reach Abigail and Rachel.

This moment reflects last winter in Warren Hollow. It feels as though I am in chains, held captive by Reverend Thomas as we struggle through the storm. I keep my eyes to the ground and my feet moving forward while recalling his threats and demands. He took me to my home as a means of torture on that day, and in some ways, this feels but the same. But there is no crazed Reverend forcing me to do this; it is at my own will. Even I am uncertain of my persistence, given all that has happened. My safety is of little concern as I place myself in these dangerous situations.

And to what end? How far will you allow this guilt to guide you?

My thoughts return to torture me once more. I often dream of the horrors that I faced back home, reliving my brother's death or the executions. But this is no dream, and I have willingly condemned myself to whatever shall meet my arrival. Just as Henry refuses to listen to his aunt and uncle, no amount of contributions are ever enough. Or Samuel, who has fully engulfed himself in the church. We all have a purpose that we want to fulfill as a means of justification or guilt. 'Tis all but the same and I see that now. These girls may present just as much lunacy as Reverend Thomas. Yet, I managed to guide all our friends through months of hardship. We faced starvation, death, loss of faith, and somehow survived. They claim that I gave them hope and our survival was of my doing. This was something I refused to believe, but if they swear it to be true, then perhaps I can find that power once more to save these sisters from themselves.

For a moment I begin laughing to myself. After all that happened and all that we have gone through, once again I find myself struggling in the snow. Even with Christmastime upon us and a warm home waiting, I brave the blistering winds by choice. It is of my own free will to endure such conditions in an attempt to help others.

Perhaps I was lost in thought longer than anticipated because I already wandered through the outskirts of Bedfordshire. There is not another soul in view as I walk the icy path. Doors are closed and smoke indicates the constant fires in many hearths. 'Tis my wish to quickly return home as well, back to the warmth and to my own family.

Suddenly I realize that I am not alone in this blizzard, as an oncoming individual moves into view. Perhaps it is old Phillip, inebriated and searching for his home in the snow. Or maybe it is Griffin Osmund, the murderous legend of Bedfordshire. Nonetheless, I continue my stroll past a few houses and structures while moving closer to this mysterious figure. This person is engaged in a shouting match with the homeowner, and I soon recognize their voice. It is Barnabas Wilfred, engaged in a quarrel with our Christmas Lord, Giles.

"I demand to speak with the Lord of Misrule!" Barnabas shouts, clearly inebriated. He stands outside of Giles's home, shouting demands and making a fool of himself.

"Leave this place at once, Barnabas! You bring fear to my children, hath thou gone mad?" Giles replies.

There be no officials or anyone to interfere and restrain Barnabas. My thoughts urge me to keep moving rather than placing myself in further danger.

What assistance can you offer to Giles? Will you restrain Barnabas yourself, with a loose hand and carrying leftover supper?

Ignoring my thoughts, I divert from the path and approach Barnabas with serious intent. Giles has since retreated into his home while trying to keep his children away from the window. Barnabas does not notice me through the heavy winds until I stand within arm's reach.

"This does not concern you, witch!" He yells, slurring his words. For the first time since back in The Hollow I am referred to as a witch in an insulting manner. Not in the way that Abigail, Rachel, or Chrystopher use this word, nor the respectful manner of Pastor Noah. It's as though Reverend Thomas stands before me, spewing insults and justifying his cruelty at my expense. In an act that would make Thomasin proud, I do not show restraint in my response.

"The last person who damned me a witch lost his life!" I shout, full of confidence and anger.

"I do not fear you," Barnabas begins, "or whatever magic you shall use against me. Now, be gone!"

"To what end do you wish to harass Giles? Do you really think they would make a drunk like you the leader of Christmas merriment?" I ask. While this is no business of mine, I cannot watch while this man terrorizes our new home. Such a disruptive figure in The Hollow would have been exiled, perhaps killed even, but this place follows a law that Barnabas narrowly walks. A night in the prison is but a charity that he welcomes.

My words bring a pause to Barnabas, and he begins to process the statements I made. Why he wishes to hold this position of regard is puzzling, perhaps even to him.

"I'll prove my worth!" He demands through drunken ramblings.

While I do not know much of Barnabas, it is said that he was once held to high regard in Bedfordshire. A fire many years ago took his small farm and his wife. Since then, he became the village nuisance, causing chaos and wallowing in his sorrows. I notice the anger growing inside him and he lunges in my direction. A simple shift of my weight and a step to the side leaves him plummeting to the ground.

"And how will anyone respect you with disruptions in service, harassment of an innocent man, or spending day and night lost to ale? Stop such behavior, and perhaps you can reclaim thy reputation," I explain to Barnabas, standing over him as he lays in the snow.

He gives no reply to my words, although every remark is heard. I have given enough energy to this man, especially in a situation where my interference was not asked for. Looking to the home, I notice that Giles and his family watch from the window. As I begin to leave, I offer a quick wave and a smile. They show appreciation for my actions and offer the same in return.

Taking a glance back, Barnabas returned to his feet and stopped his harassment near the home. He mumbles to himself of how he will kill me and Giles as he disappears into the blizzard. Perhaps he shall stumble back to the tavern or get lost in the forest. 'Tis my hope that my presence brought some good to the Harman household. Giles can now return to planning festivities without any fear or conflict. My tolerance for such nonsense has grown quite thin and it is difficult for me to ignore. Before All Hallows Eve back in The Hollow, I watched as a mother scolded her child without reason, and then I offered compliance when Mother and Father welcomed John's death. Perhaps my recent behavior spawns from guilt or an attempt to erase my inaction in the past. Eventually my involvement in these situations will have consequences. But my thoughts remain true, and death is not a fear of mine. Each day removed from the prison is a blessing that I shall use to bring good to others.

    With no further interruptions I locate Abigail and Rachel's home. The snow continues to fall around me, and the heavy winds nearly knock me to the ground. As I approach, I recognize that their home is in worse shape than the surrounding structures. It reminds me of my home back in The Hollow; still put together but struggling not to collapse on itself at any given moment. With the absence of a father in this home, the condition is understandable. I knock at the door, hoping for someone to quickly answer and let me inside. After a few moments I hear the undoing of locks and feel anxious to confront these sisters once more. However, 'tis neither Abigail nor Rachel who answers, rather, it is their grandmother, Clara.

    "Yes?" She asks, smiling with obvious signs of confusion. At a glance I recount Nicholas's words of her current condition. Clara is struggling to identify me and seems frail in her elderly age.

    "Hello there, I am Emelie. Abigail and Rachel had supper with my family yesterday and I come with leftovers," I explain.

    "Well, that is very kind of you, Elizabeth. Please, do come inside," Clara insists as she holds the door open. Rather than correcting her I offer a smile of gratitude. She seems harmless in her condition, and I see no reason to be anything but kind. As I walk inside, I notice that the home is mostly standard. It appears mundane like most homes in Bedfordshire while I make my way to their table. Clara passes by to sit in a chair near the hearth. Her joyous behavior continues while she stares with clouded eyes at the logs as if a fire is burning.

"Are Abigail and Rachel home?" I ask curiously. To my surprise, the sisters have not rushed to greet my arrival.

"Oh, those girls listen to me not, Elizabeth. They are your daughters so perhaps they shall listen to you. The Lord knows that they care little for my words," Clara explains with a laugh, rocking in her chair.

I now realize that she thinks of me as her late daughter, Elizabeth, the mother of Abigail and Rachel. Sorrow overcomes me at this life that Abigail and Rachel must endure. 'Tis no wonder they seek an escape from this life by any means necessary.

Carefully I arrange the food on the table, relieved that some of the feast has kept its warmth through the snow. Before I take my leave, I do wish to find the sisters and speak with them. The staircase sits just past the kitchen area, so I begin my ascent to the upstairs. Each step makes the wood creak as though it shall break beneath me. Upon reaching the top, I notice the door to one of the two rooms is open. Carefully I make my way inside, not wanting to scare the sisters or go where I am not welcome. This room is undoubtedly that of Abigail and Rachel, as they each have their own bed and a small area for themselves. Nothing appears out of the ordinary aside from an open chest full of hair bows and other apparel. This must be Abigail's, as the scarlet red shading spans across all the accessories inside. There are no sinful writings or altars devoted to witchcraft or black magic. Instead, it appears to be completely normal.

A commotion outside draws me to the window and I notice the sisters emerging from a cellar. Chrystopher is with them as well, but he seems to be leaving in haste as they push down and lock the doors. They send him on his way as fast as possible. He falls face-first in the snow on his exit while they continue to shout and I cannot help but laugh at such clumsiness. Abigail mentions my name, and they point to their home. I suspect they heard me from below and rushed to finish their activity with Chrystopher.

Cautiously I make my way from their room, not wanting them to notice my exploration. I race down the stairs and over to the table just as they make their way inside. In an act of desperation, I pretend to finish organizing the feast before noticing Abigail or Rachel.

"Emelie?" Rachel asks curiously.

I turn with a smile, ready to greet their arrival and give an explanation.

"Hello there," I say, looking back and forth at both of them, "it seems that you have forgotten the rest of the food on your way out yesterday."

Abigail is hesitant at first, her face swollen and bruised from our encounter. But I cannot blame her indecision, for I feel the same. "You brought us food?" she asks. They look over the table and then back to me.

"Yes, Nicholas wishes for everyone to have an early Christmas supper. And he wanted you to be well fed before tomorrow's festivities," I explain.

Rachel keeps her distance, but Abigail pushes forward and steps before me.

"I am sorry, Emelie. I should not have acted so impolitely yesterday. It was wrong of me to do so, and I hope you can forgive me. We care little for witchcraft, and only thought of it as a means to impress you," Abigail pleads with an honest tone. She takes a few glances to my hand as she speaks.

"There be no need, Abigail. I am sorry for losing myself to anger and striking you. Perhaps it was my own doing that caused this quarrel between us. I only wanted you both to understand what witchcraft truly entails. It is an evil force, one that I do not want confused with all the good that apothecary practices can bring. But I know how it can be enticing and was once in the same state of mind as you both. So, I would like to put this situation behind us and speak no more of witchcraft or the wickedness out there," I say sympathetically but sternly enough to emphasize my demands. Abigail's claim of caring not for witchcraft is surprising, though I do wish it to be valid.

"So, you do not hate us?" Rachel asks.

"Of course not, Rachel. I do not wish to hate anyone in Bedfordshire. Even Barnabas, who I had the most unfortunate encounter with on my journey over."

"Barnabas," Abigail begins, "did he cause you harm?"

I notice as her hand makes a fist and begins to shake. She clearly does not take kindly to anyone causing her friends distress.

"Well, only one of us struck the ground with their face," I reply with a laugh. Abigail relaxes at my humor.

"We thank thee and would also like to carry on as friends. Perhaps someday we can become the closest of friends, without false obsession over witchcraft to do so," Abigail proclaims.

I offer her a smile, joyful that this gesture cleared all feelings of malice between us. While I plan to keep a distance from these sisters, I felt the need to apologize and make things right. Though my actions were antagonized and likely a rational response, I cannot fight the sympathy I feel for Abigail and Rachel. Things may improve between us moving forward and the witchcraft nonsense has been put to rest. This was my final plea for friendship and peace, and I know that Rose and John would be proud.

The next few moments carry on in joy and merriment. Abigail and Rachel prepare to devour the feast, and I bring Clara a portion to her chair. Although confused in her current state, she thanks me for visiting and recites a Christmas blessing. The sisters spend a few moments discussing tomorrow's events before I depart. They explain that everyone gathers in the meetinghouse for the first day of Christmas and how the food and decorations are magnificent. Though this visit has gone rather well and I would not mind staying longer, I understand that there is much to do for tomorrow and wish to assist Nicholas and Amelia. With a final farewell, I depart back into the blistering cold.

Just as today's journey began, I am alone with nothing more than the soothing sound of snowfall hitting the ground. But I find peace in these moments of solace. This gives me the opportunity to reminisce on my brother and the past life that seems to be but a fading memory.

"Hello, Emelie," a voice calls, catching me by surprise. This greeting comes from Chrystopher as he rounds the side of Abigail and Rachel's home. Rather than stopping, he offers me a nod and continues on his way. His hands are full of quilts and he struggles to drag a chair through the snow. This interaction catches me off guard as we nearly collide and I only have time to reply with a smile. Out of curiosity I slow my pace to a halt, listening as Chrystopher makes his way around the back of the home. He begins to unlock the cellar, tossing his materials down the few stairs and pulling the doors closed behind him while scanning the area. Uneasiness begins to wash over me at such a strange interaction.

I turn to follow Chrystopher but realize that both sisters stare at me through the open front door. They show no emotion and never break their gaze while whispering to each other. We are trapped in a standstill that seemingly has no end until Abigail makes her way from the door.

"Please do not tell anyone, Emelie," Abigail urges. "Chrystopher stays in our cellar when his father is away. They will make him sleep in the meetinghouse if this is discovered. But we keep him warm and spend our time down there as well. He would much rather be with us for a few nights. It is only for one, maybe two days at most!"

"I shall not say a word, Abigail. Let us know if you need any further means of warmth down there or if Chrystopher wants any assistance moving his supplies. Henry or Samuel will gladly come your way to help. Why does Chrystopher not sleep inside of your home?" I ask.

"Our grandmother does not always act well with visitors. She attacked him in his sleep not long ago and claimed he was an intruder. Officials scolded us and Chrystopher was punished by his father for not staying at home. So, we find it easier this way. And we have made the cellar our own space for amusement."

"I see. The farm always has more than enough space if he would like to spend a night in our company. Surely Nicholas would not mind," I tell her.

Abigail smiles and nods back to Rachel who disappears through the doorway. "You are truly a wonderful friend, Emelie. We are so fortunate to have met you." She approaches for the embrace that I feared was imminent during my visit. I reach out to initiate this friendly gesture now that we have made progress, though I am still hesitant with any physical contact. Rather than stretching her arms out and pulling me in tightly, she grabs both of my shoulders and places a kiss on my lips. It happens so fast, and I am completely taken aback. My only reaction is to get away, so I push her chest to create space between us.

Rather than lashing out or turning this situation into another conflict, I use all my strength to remain composed and address her actions with reason. Abigail stares back at me, unsure of what to expect but not backing away or raising her defenses.

"I, and everyone back at the farm are most delighted to have met you and Rachel, and to call both of you our friends. But Abigail, friends are all that we shall be," I tell her sympathetically. "For Henry and I are courting, and this could have great consequences if anyone saw." Surely Abigail understands my explanation, though I still felt the need to offer total clarity. She does not give a reply, though I can see the hurt in her expression. Tears begin to form in her eyes no matter how hard she attempts to hide her emotions. Abigail nods and quickly turns back to go inside. Her odd behaviors finally make sense. Thomasin was valid in her assumption, and Abigail acted on her true desires. She no longer sees witchcraft as a viable way for us to bond and failed to control herself. While Bedfordshire follows loose regulations, this is an unspeakable engagement with great consequence in any community.

"Abigail!" I call out to gain her attention before she is out of sight. "Shall we see you both tomorrow to celebrate the first day of Christmas? We may need thy assistance when the drunken antics begin."

She turns back and smiles at my words. It seems that she is relieved to know that our friendship was not ruined by her actions. "We will see you there! Many Christmas days of celebration await!" Abigail enters her home, and I am finally on my way back to the farm.

Surely Thomasin, Samuel, and Henry will not believe the unraveling of events that has occurred. Perhaps this shall be enough for Thomasin to find humor through her illness, and she will boast for days of how she was right. She tried to warn me on numerous occasions, but I paid no mind to Abigail's deeper intentions and assumed her desires to only be that of witchcraft. Though I gave her my honest thoughts so perhaps this will be the end of their pestering. Her actions were not appropriate, but I understand that neither Abigail nor Rachel are of sound mind. And while I wish to admit it not, something about Abigail has intimidated me from our very first encounter. Perhaps it is her overwhelming personality or the fact that they tower over me in height, but I always feel the need to act with caution in their presence. Maybe I am simply paranoid, or jealous of the way they carry themselves so freely.

Nonetheless I quiet my thoughts and hasten my speed to leave the area. I laugh to myself at the recounting I must tell upon my arrival. Surely this will be more frightening than any fireside tale.

"It went quite well today. The sisters apologized and I did as well for my assault. I am happy to share that it is resolved, and we can all be friends moving forward. They will even leave us alone with the witchcraft nonsense, for that was but a ploy. So Henry, I must warn you that Abigail wishes to take thy place. And while it pains me to say it, you were right, Thomasin. Abigail kissed me right in front of thy home. Did I forget to mention that they have a child sleeping in their cellar?"

The recollection of events leaves me in disbelief, though I am satisfied to have some form of resolution as we officially enter the holiday. I feel proud of my determination and can sense some of the guilt and worry dispersing. There is much to be done so I make my way back to the farm with anticipation that nothing but joyful bliss awaits.

X

The First Day of Christmas

The first day of Christmas has officially commenced. This was obvious from our awakening by a few ecstatic members of Bedfordshire who chose to surprise us with caroling. It is a beautiful winter day; the temperature has risen and the snow falls moderately. Thomasin's illness has subsided for the time being, and aside from the strange ending to yesterday's encounter, I greet the day with high spirits and positivity.

Nicholas and Amelia snuck from their chamber in the early hours of the morning to prepare us a wonderful breakfast. One by one we make our way downstairs to watch the revelers outside and applaud their performance as they sing and dance like fools. While this behavior is still odd to me, it seems to be nothing more than harmless jest, so I welcome all the Christmastime traditions. A fire burns in the hearth and the table is lined with porridge, biscuits, bread, and other delicious foods that I do not recognize. We start the day around the table, showing appreciation to each other and excitement for all that Christmastime has to offer. Even Henry elected to join us instead of clearing the snow from the path or tending to the animals. I cannot deny my feelings of gratitude and love for the family that surrounds me. To find peace and the ability to celebrate such a glorious time of year is a blessing.

Nicholas rises from the table and rushes around the corner as we ponder on whatever surprise he shall enact. He comes back into the room carrying a large box and drops it on the table. "It would not be Christmas day without the giving of gifts," Nicholas claims. We leap from our chairs and eagerly gaze at the box before us. Nicholas reaches in and begins handing each of us items that they have prepared.

Samuel stares in awe at the bundle of religious scrolls and a large bible he is given. It seems to be made of high-quality materials and crafted with fine detail. Henry is handed an entire outfit of clothing, from a wool hat to a jacket and boots. Surely an appropriate gift for the winter months and something that will help him fight the cold on his long days outside. Amelia makes her way to the box, pulling the next gift and handing it to Thomasin. They give her a silk scarf, one that makes all of us gasp in awe. Something so luxurious is worn by few members of Bedfordshire. An accessory this elegant would have been a dream back in Warren Hollow. Thomasin recognizes the significance of such a gift and begins to repeatedly offer her gratitude.

And now it seems that I am the last one waiting. Nicholas jokes that the box is empty until Amelia reaches in while I stand eagerly at her side. I cannot believe my eyes as she hands me a beautiful journal, bound in leather and accompanied by a quill pen and ink. The pages are empty and clean of any dirt or damage. Rather than continuing to write on loose pages or at the end of Rose's work, I can now start documenting everything in an organized binding of my own. This is a gift that I shall cherish forever. Once more, each of us offers thanks to Nicholas and Amelia as we finish our breakfast feast and begin preparations for the day. 'Tis hard to believe that the next twelve days will hold nothing but celebration.

We spend time utilizing our gifts throughout the rest of the morning. It is difficult to determine what I should write about or where to formally begin. Perhaps I should start with the knowledge of Rose and Thomas's relationship. If there is a chance to make anyone understand the events that occurred in Warren Hollow, then surely this must be the focal point.

The next few hours passed by as I sat writing among the decorations and Christmastime scents from the kitchen. I described Rose, the arrival of Thomas in anticipation of Reverend Nicholas's death, the secret relationship that formed and the child to be, and our questioning in the church prior to All Hallows Eve. This seemed like a fitting end for the time being. Recollecting such memories is not a pleasant situation so I decided to halt my progress and prepare like the others as they rush around me.

Everyone dresses themselves and anticipates the celebration in the village. This is my signal to also get ready, so I make my way to Henry and I's chamber to hide the journal out of sight. The details enclosed in this binding are not to be seen by anyone other than Henry, as he is the only one that knows the truth of our conviction. I feel shameful for hiding such a secret from Samuel and Thomasin for this duration. Perhaps I owe it to Thomasin and Samuel as my own gift of Christmas to enlighten them of the truth. Whether the perfect moment arises or not, I will speak of everything before the last day of Christmas.

The time for celebration is near so we depart from the farm. Each of us carries offerings of decorations, food, ale, and anything that we can bring to the village. Groups of officials, children, and those already intoxicated pass us on our walk. We stroll by carolers and families who bid us merry Christmas. Everyone is in high spirits, and the festivities surround us as we traverse further into the village. Children play in the snow and parents sing and cheer around fires. Thomasin receives compliments for her beautiful scarf and many members of Bedfordshire revel in Nicholas and Amelia's presence. But they do not seem to mind the attention because they receive nothing but respect and honor from all who approach. 'Tis strange for the rest of us to be held to such a regard, as we were nothing more than servants and untamed children in our past life. So I find gratitude in the attention, even from Abigail and Rachel who we have yet to see on our way to the meetinghouse.

Bells ring through the village and signal the start of the festivities. Pastor Noah stands just outside of the meetinghouse with Ambrose and welcomes us in from the cold. Inside is just as cheerful and festive as the rest of Bedfordshire. Families are in high spirits and decorations fill the meetinghouse from the floor to the gallery. The pews are so full that we must disperse and sit apart for today's service. Luckily I remain close to Thomasin as we find seats.

"Can you believe the magnitude of this celebration?" Thomasin asks.

"It is a bit odd, but truly wonderful. I cannot imagine such merriment back in The Hollow," I reply.

"Of course not. Even before Thomas and his nonsense, we usually honored All Hallows Eve in secrecy. To see hundreds of people celebrating is astounding," she expresses.

"It truly is."

"You know," Thomasin says as she grabs my hand, "we deserve every moment of this happiness. Things are going quite well for us in this place. I think we have done well for some witches who nearly met death last winter. And now you have found thyself a close friend in Abigail. Awfully close I must say," she claims in a teasing manner.

I roll my eyes and shake my head in disagreement. "Henry and thee find amusement in what happened yesterday, but I fear that I shall never be the same! If Rachel fancies you then I will encourage her to pursue all desires as she sees fit!"

We laugh at my unforgettable encounter, though I sense this to be a lighthearted moment to talk with Thomasin about Rose.

"There is something you must know," I begin as my laughter fades.

Is it finally time to tell Thomasin the truth?

"Back at Rose's home, I found something before we departed," I start, struggle to continue. Thomasin pays close attention to my words, fully unaware of the truth that I am soon to reveal. "I made quite the discovery. Rose was–"

My words get interrupted by cheers and shouts for Pastor Noah and Ambrose as they make their way to the pulpit. Thomasin turns her attention forward and whispers, "Do tell me after the commotion."

It feels as though my heart may beat out of my chest at this moment, but I shift my attention forward like everyone else. While this time was not the most appropriate to tell her the truth, perhaps it would have been easier to speak it without being alone or in the middle of a crisis. I try to calm my nerves and tell myself that another opportunity shall soon arise. Now is the time for celebration so there is no reason to ruin such a day.

"Hello everyone, and merry Christmas to all," Ambrose begins. "The first of twelve yuletide days has arrived. During this time, we shall see celebration, giving, good will, and honor for this sacred holiday. As for what this year's Christmastime shall entail, please welcome your Lord of Christmas," Ambrose announces as he steps down and begins to cheer for Giles.

Giles rises with his family and makes his way to the front of the crowd. He is visibly ecstatic to hold this regard and always seems to be the happiest member of Bedfordshire. Per usual, he presents himself with another finely crafted coat. The cheers die down as Giles prepares to speak.

"It is an honor to guide us through this magical time of year. We will give credence to faith, spend time with family, and some of us shall drink more than we can handle." His words draw laughs from the crowd, and cheers from those who raise their cups to validate such claims. "And by Epiphany, we shall remove our decorations and return to labor. But we will look back and say that these twelve days were the best in Bedfordshire's history!"

Everybody cheers once more and shows excitement for the days of celebration that await. Giles seems to recognize me as he steps down from the pulpit, taking an extended look and offering a smile. Pastor Noah then assumes his position and aims to give a quick service. His conclusion shall let loose a crowd of avid chaos, as the meetinghouse feels ready to explode. We listen to his words, showing respect to faith but eager to celebrate.

Minutes pass as Noah gives a wonderful sermon, but he recognizes the urgency as his conclusion draws near. Like all services here in Bedfordshire, he ends with an extended prayer. We bow our heads and repeat his words under our breath. "And now," Pastor Noah yells, "do not sit here while the festivities await! A merry Christmas to you all!"

He steps down and the meetinghouse shifts into a wonderful chaos. People are not fighting or causing any harm; it is a chaotic eruption of song, frolic, and everyone forcing their way outside. Thomasin and I slowly make our way down the aisle, greeting others and smiling at all the merriment that surrounds us.

"I believe your name is Emelie?" a voice asks from behind. I turn and recognize it to be Giles, our Christmas Lord.

"Yes sir, it is nice to meet you on this first day of Christmas," I reply.

He smiles, drawing himself closer as we continue fighting through the crowd. "I wanted to offer thanks for your handling of that troublemaker, Barnabas. It was not an intervention asked of you, so you have my gratitude."

"I know all too well how it feels to be harassed and tormented by someone so vile. I simply could not watch as he made a fool of himself and scared thy children," I explain.

"Perhaps your encounter with Barnabas has brought some sense to him, because he has yet to cause mischief or be seen by anyone on this day. I thank you once again, Emelie, and

I will see that any Christmas requests you or your family have shall be fulfilled!"

"I thank thee, and best of luck in containing the madness for twelve days!" I shout as we go in separate directions.

"Your encounter with Barnabas?" Thomasin asks.

I laugh at her words, wishing not to make any more of a fuss over yesterday's situation.

"He was being a drunken fool outside of Gile's home so I could not simply walk by," I tell her.

"And you were unharmed?"

"Yes, 'tis Barnabas who met the ground with his face before stumbling off."

Thomasin shakes her head and lets out a laugh. "Someday your heart shall lead you to the grave. First the sisters and now the village disgrace, do you aim to gather your tools and hunt for this Griffin Osmund next?" She asks playfully as we exit the meetinghouse.

I understand the concern in her words. Back in The Hollow I cared little for the misfortunes of our home and the miscreants who inhabited it. But after all that we have gone through, I feel an obligation to ensure the happiness of everyone. And perhaps I act without a concern for safety because I welcome the danger if it makes a difference. The suffering that we endured is something I hope nobody here shall ever experience, and my survival must come with a purpose.

You cannot save everyone.

My thoughts remind me of the rationality that I ignore. Some people cannot be changed, and some situations will be unpleasant, even on days like today. This is something I have little control of. But if the opportunity arises to make a difference, then I will continue to do so. Even if I willingly place my own well-being to the side.

A gust of wind hits us as we finally make our way through the meetinghouse doors. We spot Henry and Samuel who found their place at a nearby fire. A few other people our age gather in this area, and I notice Abigail and Rachel standing nearby as well. They are engaged in mischief with Chrystopher, sneaking him rum and laughing as he spits it out in disgust.

"I suspect that we shall see little of my aunt and uncle in the coming days," Henry tells us while scanning the area with a smile. "Did you ever imagine that we would take part in such an event? Look at the sights around us!"

"Never. Our All Hallows Eve celebrations were but a few of us gathered around a fire. I think that a gathering of this scale would have benefitted Warren Hollow," I tell Henry.

"I only hope that Reverend Gregory restored that place, but this is a different life here in Bedfordshire. And without faith guiding our every move, there is little commotion like our parents feared. The only issue is excessive drinking," Henry replies.

It is true that this distinction between law and faith helps to maintain order. But this is a town built on fishing, with little care for religious supremacy. These people pray, go to service, and still live a life devoted to God. But the reach of faith is not into the laws and structure of village operation.

"And here we are," Thomasin begins, "gathered around a fire once more, talking of the past and its horrors."

"We do spend much of our time doing so," Samuel notes as we laugh at the fact. It is difficult not to make comparisons to Warren Hollow, and I find myself doing so nearly every day.

A woman passes by with a cart of what appears to be cider. Each of us shows gratitude and takes a cup, except for Thomasin.

"Art thou not thirsty?" I ask. "You do not wish to be out of your skull within the hour?"

"I do not," she replies, offering no explanation or jest with her words. It seems that she has no interest in further discussing her decision. Perhaps she is fearful that her illness could worsen, or she wishes to remain vigilant, so this is likely a wise choice.

Our moment is disrupted by a ball of snow that crashes into the back of my head as I take a sip of my cider. Henry and Samuel look behind me and laugh, so I turn to notice that Abigail initiated an attack. Abigail, Rachel, and Chrystopher subtly laugh and looking around the area as though they are innocent. Before I can react, Thomasin reaches down to the snow and creates a ball herself. She throws it forcefully and lands a direct hit on Rachel's face. We stand in silence while onlookers gather, staring at each other and curious how this shall unfold. Thomasin reaches down again to forge another projectile without any hesitation. The sisters do the same and now it is my turn to get involved. It is a bit of a struggle to craft a ball of snow with one hand, but I do so and quickly toss it at Abigail.

We all smile and laugh at such foolish behavior; even Thomasin seems to be enjoying herself. Those nearby soon notice the recreation and start to get involved. Our playful banter turns into a large-scale battle outside of the meetinghouse.

Children, adults, and even some of the officials join in on the festivities. Balls of snow fly and strike me with force, though I simply return fire and try my hardest to hide behind others and land shots of my own. Some begin building mounds of snow for cover and hide behind merchant carts or their friends. Henry spots Nicholas and Giles as they leave the meetinghouse and lands a clean hit on his uncle. Nicholas rushes to get involved and smashes a handful of snow on Henry's head.

  Everyone is laughing and cheering at the ongoing battle. Members sing, dance, and frolic in the winter weather with their loved ones. At this moment I officially accept my adoration for Christmastime and all that it entails. I met acknowledgement of All Hallows Eve and other holidays with apprehension, although I believe that no progress will be made without vulnerability. These coming days could grant Samuel, Thomasin, Henry, and I release from the darkness of our past. 'Tis impossible for any distress to overcome the love that surrounds us. The decorations, happiness, snowfall, food, gifts, and yuletide spirit are magical. This is our first of many Christmas celebrations in Bedfordshire and these coming days shall forever change my life.

XI

And So It Begins, Once More

We emerge from our chambers with an ache in our heads and a pain in our stomachs. Overindulgence of cider and pie proved to be quite unwise. Perhaps I shall refuse to drink ale or feast upon pudding for the rest of Christmastime.

The day starts with a peaceful silence through our home. Each of us recuperates from the intensity of our first Christmas celebration by sitting around the hearth and sipping tea. Amelia prepared a light breakfast, and the mere smell of bread makes me want to heave.

Festivities lasted deep into the night, and we did not arrive back to the farm until well after dark. Hours passed while we paraded around the village singing carols and drinking beyond our limits. Although we feel debilitated, yesterday was a wonderful experience. Nicholas explained that the days are often balanced with celebrations and rest, so I am thankful that we have no presence needed in the village this morning. Today is to be a time of relaxation and recovery for most. Henry tends to the animals and plows the snow with Nicholas, Samuel reads from his bible and constructs sermons, Amelia prepares light meals while decluttering the kitchen, Thomasin will spend most of the day sleeping off her looming sickness, and I will write in my journal until my hand refuses to cooperate.

The snowfall gradually worsened throughout the morning, and the temperature dropped once again. 'Tis my hope that the weather clears before tomorrow's events. Nicholas mentioned that the next festivity shall be a meal in the meetinghouse tomorrow evening and will be much less chaotic than yesterday. This does sound pleasant, as it will take a few days before I am ready to partake in another wild night. It is said that the first day of Christmas is only matched by Epiphany, which is one final gathering to indulge before decorations come down and farming plans proceed for the spring.

Thomasin rises abruptly from her chair and rushes to vomit in the kitchen. Amelia runs to her aid, and I follow close behind. She assures Amelia and I that she is well, only regretful of her choices yesterday. Though I recall her declining the cider and fail to remember her indulging in a single cup of wine, rum, or beer. Her sickness has been ongoing, so perhaps it is time to call upon a physician in the village.

"Amelia, do you know of any physicians in Bedfordshire?" I ask.

"I am fine, 'tis no need to worry," Thomasin interrupts before Amelia can answer.

"Thomasin, someone should look at you and help solve this illness," I recommend assertively.

"That may be a good idea," Samuel agrees as he joins us in the kitchen. "You have been ill for some time, so seeking treatment is wise."

"I only need sleep. Not any treatment," Thomasin replies in a serious tone.

She is not one to accept help or admit when she is unwell. But this has gone on for days and each of us recognizes the need for intervention. And just as Thomasin says to me, her stubbornness shall take her to the grave.

"How about you go and rest through the morning. And if you awaken with the same sickness, then someone can take a look at you," I barter.

Thomasin begins to vomit once more. Rather than disputing, she nods her head in agreement and makes her way to the hearth to get some rest. I sit by her side, watching in sorrow as she struggles with this strange ailment that troubles her. Thoughts of her contracting the plague or another vicious illness on our journey to Bedfordshire begin to cause me distress. Carefully I pull the journal back into my lap to remain occupied by further documenting our struggles. The journey continues as I write of our criticism in the church and the revolt that followed.

'Tis hard to blame us for wanting to escape on All Hallows Eve after such animalistic observation.

Then came our celebration, which I articulately describe in great detail. The weather, decorations, masks, and all other aspects that made for a wonderful celebration while it lasted. Even the unfortunate conviction that followed. I write and write as the hours pass, documenting our injuries, Rose's death, and the dreaded months in the prison.

A knock at the door pulls me from my thoughts. Thomasin awakens and we curiously look at the door and ponder who visits. Nicholas, Henry, and Samuel are nowhere in sight, so Amelia advises us to carry on while she discovers who has come by on this day of rest. She unlocks the door, revealing it to be Pastor Noah, Ambrose, and a few other officials that I do not recognize.

"Hello to you all," Amelia begins, "we were not expecting company. What brings you to the farm?" She invites them inside while Thomasin and I fix our posture in their presence.

"We apologize for such an unexpected visit, but I am afraid we come bearing unfortunate news. Is Nicholas around?" Ambrose asks. Samuel also hears the commotion and joins us from the upstairs, surprised to see these visitors in our home.

"I shall find him at once. Do make yourselves comfortable," Amelia requests as she dresses herself to brave the cold and venture to the barn. Quickly she makes her way through the door, and we are left with this sudden crowd around us.

"Is everything alright?" I ask curiously. Their stature indicates that something is awry.

"We meant not to interrupt. How do you fare after the first day of Christmas?" Pastor Noah asks with a smile.

"Thankful that today is meant for relaxation," I reply with a nervous laugh. "But Thomasin has struggled with illness for quite some time, and we think it would be wise for a physician to observe her."

"That can certainly be arranged," Ambrose ensures.

Amelia pushes through the door with Henry and Nicholas close behind. They enter and shake the snow from their clothes while rushing straight to the fire.

"What a festive surprise to see you all so soon!" Nicholas announces playfully as he greets the visitors.

"As we told your wife, Nicholas, we come with unfortunate news," Ambrose expresses in a serious tone.

Each of us offers our full attention as we eagerly await their announcement. "Last night," Ambrose begins, "there was a death in Bedfordshire. 'Twas Simon, down at the port. He was found in the early hours this morning, floating just off the dock in the near-frozen water."

Shock and sorrow fills the room. This is quite an unexpected misfortune to have occurred during the festivities. Christmas is to be a time of merriment and joy, but death has come on the first of twelve days. A similar fate could have happened to any of us, as we were lost to ale for many hours.

"Simon is intoxicated more times than not, but he knows better than anyone how to conduct himself in such a condition. I've seen him man a fishing vessel with rum in both hands, so such an accident is quite odd," Nicholas claims.

"Indeed, Nicholas, 'tis very odd. We have reason to believe that this was no accident. It be murder," Ambrose states.

Each of us rises to our feet at this revelation. We look to each other and then our visitors for answers.

"Barnabas was not at his home this morning. An active search is already in motion," one of the officials adds.

"I saw him taunting Giles but a few days ago. He spoke of how he would kill him," I share without any hesitation.

Ambrose listens to my words with full attention. The officials are caught off guard by my intervention, but they show me respect and listen attentively.

"Barnabas is certainly at the center of our search. And I assure you all that Giles is safe with his family at their home. But, may I ask of your past?" he replies while looking directly at me.

Suddenly the suppressed emotions return just as quickly as they departed. I fight the trembling that starts in my hand. Do they think we held involvement in this tragedy? To what end do they make a connection to us?

Please Lord, I beg of thee. It cannot be. Do not let Ambrose say what I suspect he is about to say.

"Yes," Thomasin answers, fixing her posture and saving me from my anxiety. My concern is noticed so Ambrose and the others signal for us to take a seat. They sit as well, easing my mind for the time being. I know not what they shall ask, but the respect granted is appreciated.

"Back in your homeland, you dealt with the likes of witchcraft?" He questions.

And so it begins, once more.

"I'm afraid so. Accused of it even, and sentenced to death by a Reverend gone mad. Why do you ask?" Thomasin demands.

"Well, we seek to better understand this plague. It may have spread to our village. We fear that what happened to Simon is not of normality. But such information mustn't leave this farm."

Thomasin and I look at each other, prepared to be accused and ready to fight if convicted.

"Not you of course," Ambrose states, realizing our panic. "Unless Simon had reason to bite off his own tongue and tie a rope around his neck, we believe that he was made to suffer greatly. Perhaps Barnabas was enacting some sacrifice? We do not fully understand how it works, but does this sound familiar to you?"

"Our friend, Ezekiel. He met a similar, near identical fate at the hands of Reverend Thomas. Many lashed out during questioning, and as punishment, his tongue was removed before his hanging," I add to the conversation.

"I see," Ambrose mutters as he takes in my words and rubs his head. "This does seem similar. Was this typical behavior for someone considered to be '*bewitched*'?"

"We know little of true witchcraft. I stand by the belief that there were no witches in Warren Hollow. Ezekiel's death was a showing of power by The Reverend and even the most evil witch could not match the brutality of Thomas," I explain.

They do not fully understand the extent of our past or witchcraft. In fairness, we wished to speak not of The Hollow unless asked, but I understand the confusion surrounding such a horrific death. It brings me peace to know that the church and court came hand in hand seeking guidance rather than placing us in prison. Thankfully they hold enough sense to see us as incapable of something so awful. Though if Barnabas is proven innocent, this conversation could unravel differently. But just as I have done with documenting our experiences or informing the sisters, my goal is to make everyone understand the truth of our story and what they believe to be witchcraft.

"If you would like," I begin, "I could examine Simon's body."

Everyone in the room is stunned at my words, even Nicholas and Amelia. Nicholas grows impatient and starts calling for an end to our questioning. He only wishes to protect us, but my involvement could do so as well. This is an opportunity to get on the better side of this tragedy. Although witchcraft is unlikely to be the motivation for Simon's death, taking time to observe his corpse and gain confirmation will grant us esteem and contain mass chaos.

"I shall look at his body, only to verify that witchcraft is not intertwined. But if Barnabas is to blame, then surely he has a reason for doing so and will act again. Whether it be witchcraft or another motivation, it would be wise to protect Giles until Barnabas is found. I can help you solve this before it spreads," I tell Ambrose adamantly.

"Then I shall do but the same," Thomasin declares as she rises from her chair, fighting visible signs of distress. She will not adhere to any pleas for rest.

"We will also join you," Henry announces as he and Samuel come forward. Pastor Noah nods to Samuel, recognizing his courage and willingness. Nicholas is still worried, wanting to shield us from such a sight. Perhaps they fail to comprehend the horrors of which we endured before arriving in Bedfordshire. Henry eases his uncle's worry, and we all look to our visitors for approval.

"Very well. If you are willing to do so, then we best be on our way. Your involvement is appreciated and could very well uncover why this happened." Ambrose takes a step forward and lowers his voice with honesty. "Admittedly, we are not certain of what we are dealing with. I must warn you that what awaits is not a pleasant sight."

'Tis quite a strange situation; from being accused of witchcraft to assisting officials determine if it be a possible motivation for murder. Barnabas's absence certainly indicates that he could be involved. But what motivation led him to harm

Simon rather than Giles or Pastor Noah? Could a drunken fool truly enact such a vicious crime? While it is certainly reasonable to place the blame on Barnabas, I speak not of the fear that he could be innocent, or yet to be discovered as another victim. If so, there is a much darker situation unraveling in Bedfordshire.

XII

A Watery Grave

This day of rest has taken an unfortunate turn. Rather than spending time relaxing by the hearth and writing in my journal, I traverse the bitter cold to examine a corpse. But this time Henry, Samuel, and Thomasin are by my side, so I do not brave these conditions alone.

Amelia ensured that a warm supper would await our return as we departed from the farm. Ambrose and Pastor Noah lead a small group in front of us as we follow them to the port. The snowfall reached a gentle steadiness at this hour, though the temperature is wicked. Our group is silent as we walk along the path to the village. Yesterday we traveled this path in merriment, joking and eager to celebrate the first day of Christmas. But as I told myself from the moment we arrived, happiness can turn to malevolence in an instant. Thomasin stays close to me as Samuel talks with Pastor Noah and Henry discusses the situation with Ambrose up ahead.

"What do you think we shall find?" Thomasin asks.

I shake my head, unsure and nervous at the sight that awaits. "This is truly a sight I wish not to see. But they are desperate, and they came to us for help. This is a good thing, Thomasin," I explain quietly.

"Yes," Thomasin begins, "I was but seconds away from attacking if we were accused."

"And I as well. But they approached rationally and listened to our words. If this was back home, we would already have ropes around our necks. Surely they do not see us capable of such a crime here. My hope is that we can observe poor Simon's body and confirm that it be nothing more than an act of brutality," I tell her.

"But," Thomasin continues with hesitation, "what are we to do if this is not Barnabas? If he is found drunk on the other side of the village and cleared of accusation? Or if this is clearly an act of witchcraft?"

"We best hope that Barnabas is to blame, and with simpler motivations," I reply, directing my gaze ahead and hastening my pace.

This is a valid concern, but I mustn't spread fear to Thomasin or the others. While Barnabas is an awful man and we have openly seen him threaten to take the lives of many, I ponder on his capabilities regarding such an evil act. Though for the sake of our safety and reputation, 'tis my hope that this is nothing more than a blatant murder with clear explanation.

We fight through the snowfall until the port comes into view. The sun has yet to illuminate through the clouds and snow, so our view is hindered. I begin to feel uneasy with each step, as what we are about to witness will surely be unsettling. I recall Ezekiel's murder, and it is a visual that will never leave my mind. All the friends and family that died over those long months burden me as well, even Reverend Thomas who I butchered myself. Memories of their lifeless bodies haunt me every night.

"His corpse is over here. I must say, it is not pleasant," Ambrose warns. He points us to the edge of the dock as we move forward. The dock sways beneath us in the wind and the wooden planks creak with every step. Ambrose leads the way while Pastor Noah takes Samuel beside the dock to reach the water. Henry notices my uneasiness, so he squeezes my hand for reassurance. A subtle trail of blood comes into view beneath us, leading to where the obvious struggle began. The wood is chipped and splattered with blood that shines through the layers of snow and ice. Nearby a section of the railing is broken, which is likely where Simon was thrown over. I run my hand along the wood, noticing a piece of rope that was tightly wound around the wooden rail. Ambrose points over the broken wood, indicating that Simon is just beneath.

Briefly I close my eyes and take a deep breath of the sea's air, preparing for the unpleasant sight that awaits. I move forward until I peer through the broken railing. The water is nearly frozen over, but Simon's body is no longer floating freely. He was removed and lies motionless on the land with people around him.

"One thing is for certain; Simon was murdered. He was attacked here," I verify while pointing to the trail of blood, "and eventually made his way to this railing. Perhaps he collapsed or even fought back for a few moments. Either way, he probably lost his tongue here in submission as the rope was fastened around his neck. But neither the wooden rail nor the rope was strong enough. Both failed immediately and sent him crashing through the ice to drown."

My explanation relayed the obvious, but our guidance is the reason we are here. Henry nods at my words, believing that my recollection is reasonable and accurate. Simon made a good distance before succumbing to his attack because the blood trail extends across the dock. The attacker may have been unprepared for such a struggle in Simon's drunken state.

"Are you certain that his tongue was removed? Perhaps he bit through it as the rope tightened?" I question Ambrose.

"I am positive that it was removed by force. Given the blood around us, and the precision in which it was cut. This was done with intention and accuracy. Would you like to take a closer look?" Ambrose asks.

We nod, so he leads us off the dock and down to the others. "Given the struggle that occurred, I would be surprised if the attacker left unharmed. Barnabas, or whoever did this, is likely to have injuries of their own," I explain.

"That is a fair revelation, and we will certainly consider this assumption," Ambrose replies, showing appreciation for my input. And just as I speak these words, I notice the wrapping of cloth around Ambrose's wrist. He becomes wise to my gaze and lets out a subtle laugh while raising his arm. "The consequences of tending to the fire after far too much ale."

I smile at his words and quickly shift my focus so that Ambrose does not think that I am accusing him of any wrongdoing. Although the drunken mishaps of Christmastime will certainly bring some bruises and injuries, signs indicate that Simon fought until the end and could have inflicted damage of his own. Whoever did this may surely stand out or even visit the physician. As we approach the body, Samuel and Pastor Noah are leading a subtle prayer. Everyone makes way for Ambrose who kneels over to adjust the body. Gently he turns Simon's head and pulls his mouth open. His tongue was severed beyond any doubt.

"Whoever did this acted with skill," Henry adds. "This cut was cleaner than some I have seen through a lifetime of farming and butchering. The tool was much sharper than the average knife."

It is obvious that Simon suffered a horrific death. He has stab wounds on both sides of his body and Ambrose turns him over to reveal a large wound on his back. This was likely the initial blow, leading me to believe that the attacker acted with stealth and aimed to catch him off guard. But this was not enough to incapacitate him so a few more slashes were given. We continue analyzing the body and surrounding area until none of us wish to be in this situation any longer. Ambrose regroups and guides us back to the path.

"I thank each of you for helping us today. We have a search underway for Barnabas, and we will send word once he is located. After what you have seen, do you believe that witchcraft is of concern?" Ambrose asks.

I look at him with a bit of uncertainty. "It is difficult to truly say. Our experiences and knowledge from the apothecary back in Warren Hollow do not include suffering as a typical component. The so-called sacrifices are conducted with animals or with a bit of blood. I did not see any symbols or indications of dark magic near his body, so it is unclear. The attacker wanted Simon to suffer beyond any doubt, and we only saw such brutality from our Reverend who had gone mad. This is but a reenactment of his behavior. True witchcraft, if you will, was used to bring about healing back in Warren Hollow, not murder," I explain.

Ambrose takes in each of my words as he always does, paying close attention and allowing for a full explanation. "I see," he begins. "If curiosity is to arise in Bedfordshire, would thy be willing to further inform us of what witchcraft entails? Some may share this fear, and it would be wise to keep the chaos contained. We can only do so through knowledge, and clearly there be no experts here."

"Certainly. I have been writing of our experiences and all that we know, and would be happy to share if necessary," I reply.

Ambrose nods in appreciation before bidding farewell and making his way back to the body. The four of us look at each other before making the journey back home. It was a traumatic occurrence to witness but I am thankful for Ambrose and everyone who sought our wisdom on this matter. While Bedfordshire has had its fair share of tragedy in the past, this murder surely caught everyone by surprise. It is likely that Ambrose will return for further information on witchcraft so I must continue documenting our experiences in the new journal and keep Rose's writing ready for display.

"Do you think this was Barnabas?" Samuel asks aloud.

"I have my doubts, as I'm sure the rest of you do as well," Henry answers. "The blade was sharp, and it took someone with strength and hatred to inflict such damage on poor Simon."

"And what are we to do if it is not Barnabas? Surely this was not a random act of violence. We must act with caution until Barnabas is found," Thomasin adds.

"Perhaps they will find him before the day's end. His reasons will be known and that shall be the end of it. There are still many days of Christmas ahead and this is a time for celebration," I reply, wishing to ease the fear.

"It be our luck to join this community on the cusp of Griffin's return. He hath come to finish the work of the Devil and wreak havoc on us," Thomasin adds as we all laugh.

"It could have been that old drunk, Phillip. Perhaps they got into a quarrel over who drank the last of the rum at yesterday's feast," I interject.

"With such brutality it seems as though Reverend Thomas walks among us," Henry claims, bringing an end to the laughter. I cannot shake the thought of Ezekiel on his knees, unable to speak as blood pours from his mouth. Reverend Thomas was the only man I've ever thought capable of such atrocities, so it is hard to ignore these vivid memories when today mirrors the past.

"If this happened back in The Hollow, we would already be locked in a prison cell. We must comply and help in any way we can," I announce.

"And I will say it again," Thomasin starts with a smile as she nudges my arm, "Bedfordshire needs an apothecary. If today is any indication, they already look to you for guidance. You can help these people, and we all believe you should do so."

I offer a smile as each of them stares at me. For a moment I feel proud of the knowledge that I hold and the respect that was shown to us today. This was precisely how Rose was utilized in Warren Hollow initially, answering the call to illness or any strange occurrences.

"For now, I will focus on writing in my journal. And we shall see what comes of it," I reply.

Not once do I deny the role they force upon me. Each of them offers support and wishes to see me do well in Bedfordshire so I am not entirely opposed to the idea. From informing confused sisters to regarded members of the court, I have done well in drawing the truth from the misconceptions so far. There is still much for me to learn so I must spend the next few days writing of our experiences and searching through Rose's writings. Surely they will call on us for assistance if Barnabas is not found, or if he kills again.

"Why do you think this has happened? If it is not Barnabas, then who could do this to someone in this peaceful village?" I quietly ask Henry as we walk side by side.

"All shall be revealed, likely before the end of Christmastime. But please, Emelie, do not put yourself in danger for this," Henry pleads.

He knows me all too well.

We arrive back at the farm, and I can smell the supper that awaits. Henry retreats to the barn in his usual fashion to tend to the animals and clear the path before feasting. The rest of us are eager to get inside and feel the fire's warmth. Nicholas and Amelia are joyous at our return and exaggerate their happiness for supper. Perhaps they believe we are affected by such horrific sights and attempt to provide comfort. Though while it was unpleasant, nothing shall compare to what we witnessed back in The Hollow.

One by one we readjust to the warmth and prepare ourselves for the evening. Henry makes his way inside and joins us at the table. Tension feels a bit high at the moment, as today's events certainly caught all of us by surprise. And for the first time, Nicholas and Amelia received a glimpse into our past and the struggles that each of us conceal.

"So," Nicholas starts nervously, "did you provide clarity to the situation?"

"Yes, Uncle," Henry replies, "Simon did meet quite the tragic end. All signs point to Barnabas as the culprit. Yet his whereabouts are unknown, along with any possible motivation."

"It is truly unfortunate, especially amid Christmastime! And what of the witchcraft nonsense they spoke of? Was this idea proven as false?" Nicholas asks.

"For now, although nothing is to be confirmed until Barnabas is locked in the prison. Such a brutal attack needs an explanation," I add.

"They will find him, drunk in an alley or asleep in the forest; and for his sake he best not be found wandering our farm!" Nicholas shouts. Amelia tries to calm Nicholas as his anger swells. "Simon worked that port for years, and Bedfordshire lost its best fisherman. This will affect all of us, well into the spring!"

Nicholas's words present a valid issue. Perhaps Simon's importance in Bedfordshire was a motivation for his murder. This action may not have been the result of a drunken rage or a personal quarrel. Bedfordshire will undoubtedly suffer without Simon, and this could be a reason for his death. If that be true, then members like Pastor Noah, Ambrose, Giles, or even Nicholas could be in danger. Although it is far too soon to make such an assumption or to ponder on why someone would aim to weaken the village. All we can do now is wait in agony until Barnabas is found.

"So, what is in store for the third day of Christmas?" I ask Nicholas, silencing my thoughts and shifting the focus of our supper conversation.

"Yes," Nicholas begins, calming himself and wiping his face with a cloth, "Giles decided that we shall dine in the meetinghouse tomorrow. It will be an evening spent with friends and family. We usually sing songs, feast, and drink for those who are ready for more merriment. Then an evening service from Pastor Noah will follow. 'Tis set to be a wonderful night, one of the finer days of Christmastime I must say."

The tension starts to disperse, and Nicholas regains his composure. Perhaps a lovely evening in the meetinghouse will help to ease everyone's fears. Surely Barnabas will be found by then, so tomorrow will be a brighter day. My wish is to revel in the Christmas spirit and continue indulging in the festivities. Although, it would be unwise to ignore what happened today. Like everyone at this table and across all of Bedfordshire, I will remain on high alert and keep my guard high. We cannot predict what awaits in the days ahead until Barnabas, or whoever did this, is found.

XIII

Recidivism

Commotion interrupts my sleep in the early hours of the morning. Like most days, I try to block the noise by holding a pillow over my head. Nicholas and Amelia could alert all of New England as they prepare breakfast while caroling, holding obnoxiously loud conversations, dropping plates and bowls, and all else that makes it sound as though our home shall collapse. With gratitude and a bit of annoyance, I sigh as I lie wide awake. A pounding continues beneath, although the source is difficult to determine. Suddenly I suspect that this is not a typical joyous morning. I slide the pillow from my face with hopes to eavesdrop on what is unfolding in our home. Anxiety overcomes me at the realization that the room is entrapped in total darkness, so it is not yet morning. We are in the midst of the night, and the smell of breakfast is absent.

    Carefully I sit up in bed and notice that Henry is not by my side. He is not even in the room, so I rise to my feet and make my way to the window. My heart begins to race and my body resorts to its usual trembling that accompanies distress. Snow falls heavily outside, and I notice the illumination of a lantern. A visit at this hour cannot be pleasant. I open our chamber door and spot Thomasin doing the same down the hall.

"Thomasin, what is the hour?" I ask, practically still asleep.

"I am not sure, but something is happening," she replies.

We make our way down the stairs, listening carefully as Nicholas is engaged in conversation at the door. The wind blows past us on the stairs and sends a chill through my shaking body.

"I do not understand, Phillip. Please come inside and explain thyself," Nicholas whispers. Rather than intoxicated and full of jest, Phillip appears serious and fearful in his visit.

"I cannot, Nicholas. All of Bedfordshire has been summoned to the meetinghouse at once! The only reason I am here is because I was appointed without choice. It is not safe, so I must go!" Phillip yells as he begins fighting his way through the snow. He is panicked and none of us have the slightest indication of what is happening. Nicholas shuts the door and stands in silence for a few moments.

"Uncle, why does Phillip visit at such an hour?" Henry asks.

Nicholas turns around, surprised to see his entire family standing directly behind him. He changes his expression and tries to hide the panic with merriment.

"It seems that our third day of Christmas is to begin earlier than expected," Nicholas explains. And for the first time, I am caught by surprise as he loses his joy. Although he cannot be blamed. Yesterday's events and now whatever awaits would hinder the Christmastime cheer for anyone.

"We should go right away," Nicholas states while handing us our coats and coverings.

"Surely we must take a moment to prepare ourselves. Perhaps we should gather some leftovers and breakfast for the others," Amelia adds with enthusiasm, attempting to hide her concern.

"Phillip's words were heard by all; there is no time to prepare!"

Within moments I went from a deep sleep to traversing the snow through the night. Our only light is that of Nicholas's lantern as he leads the way. Henry holds me tightly as we push through the darkness to reach the village. Perhaps they have found Barnabas, or they aim to raise our spirits with a Christmas surprise.

It would be foolish to believe that whatever awaits is festive.

"I am sorry," I say out loud. My words are not directly aimed at anyone or provided with any further explanation. It is impossible to shake the feeling of responsibility for all the hardship that has befallen Bedfordshire since our arrival. Simon lost his life, whispers of witchcraft are starting to hold weight, and these first few Christmas days are surely ruined.

Nicholas and Amelia work tirelessly to spread the merriment and provide us with a wonderful first Christmas. These unfortunate circumstances as of late are beginning to affect them and I feel solely responsible.

"There be no need for sorrow, Emelie," Nicholas begins. "You are looked upon with respect and honor for your assistance, and whatever awaits is not thy doing. There are still plenty of Christmas days ahead and Bedfordshire will prevail."

His words are reassuring. Bedfordshire certainly has a history of tragedy, but our arrival caused an undeniable disturbance. Each of us makes notable contributions to the farm and the village, although I am certain that there are whispers out of sight and this misfortune is not a coincidence.

    We rush through the snowfall as the village comes into view. Other people line the paths and appear just as confused as the rest of us. Neighbors attempt to find their friends and officials guide everyone in the direction of the meetinghouse. Something must be terribly wrong.

    Smoke fills the air as we venture further, rendering our view obstructed with every step. People crowd around and soon we are all stopped in the center of the village. I wave my arms in front of my face to clear the smoke, realizing we left in such haste that I did not fasten my makeshift hand to my arm. This causes embarrassment so I drop my arm out of sight.

    Screams of terror surround us as we try to make sense of the commotion. A small shed is engulfed in flames nearby. Some people try throwing snow to calm the flames, but Nicholas urges each of us to keep moving. I notice other small structures are also burning as we push forward.

    The village has erupted into total chaos. Structures are crumbling and people are fighting to reach the meetinghouse in a panic. Though what draws my attention are strange symbols painted on many of the homes. I stop dead in my tracks and stare as we pass Abigail and Rachel's home. Their grandmother, Clara, is trying to rub off a marking painted on their door. Abigail and Rachel pull at their grandmother, but she refuses to advance without cleaning the mess. Nicholas notices their distress and urges each of us to move forward.

    Amelia puts her arms around Thomasin and I while Samuel and Henry push through the crowd. We are at too great a distance to hear what is said but Nicholas strays to help the sisters and their grandmother. He grabs her hand and guides them through the crowd behind us. Curiosity overcomes me so I break free and maneuver back to Abigail and Rachel's home until I stand just outside of their door. The marking is a red cross, although it is upside down. This is present on many of the homes and structures around us. Each is nearly an identical, inverted cross painted in the darkest shade of red. Reverend Nicholas referred to this as The Cross of Saint Peter back in The Hollow, though Rose wrote of this symbol in an entirely different context. With both sides of my knowledge, surely its usage is quite obvious in this instance.

 This situation is becoming too much to bear. I lose control and start to cry from the overwhelming chaos surrounding me. People are shouting, structures are on fire, and it seems that all of Bedfordshire has fallen into total distress. The involvement of witchcraft is all but confirmed as I stare at these symbols of sacrilege. Rather than taking the lead and composing the others with bravery, I cower like a frightened child. Tears fall as I cover my ears and my entire body shakes. My emotions are uncontrollable, and I am thrust back into the memories of Warren Hollow. Visions of Rose, Ezekiel, and John's death race through my mind. Thomas's shouting pierces my ears alongside the blood curdling screams of Thomasin as he attacks her in the cell. A sting in my arm rehashes the memory of Henry severing my hand. Slowly I sink to the ground, muttering the same words repeatedly to myself. "Make it stop, make it stop, make it stop."

 Suddenly I feel a forceful embrace from behind. Someone rushed to my aid and holds me tightly. They pull my arms away, allowing me to hear once more. "It is me," Thomasin expresses calmly as she peers into my eyes. "We are alright, Emelie. 'Tis time to keep moving to the meetinghouse. You mustn't look at that any longer."

Thomasin helps me to regain my composure. For a few moments I lost all control. I felt like a frightened child and retreated into traumatic memories. I hold onto her tightly as she pulls me to my feet. My breathing slows and I try to stop my hand from shaking. Abigail pushes through to join Thomasin at my side, helping to calm me and keep us moving. She assists in guiding my steps and uses her coat to start wiping me down.

"Oh," I say with a laugh through the tears, "of course I chose to incapacitate myself in a pool of paint." Abigail wipes my hand and arms furiously, as I am now a shade of red in the night.

"Emelie, I do not think that is paint," Thomasin replies shakily.

Stains of red cover my clothes and skin. Abigail tries to clean me but there be no use. I raise my hand and soon realize that it is not paint at all. A quick smell verifies that I am covered in blood. My breathing starts to escalate but I try my hardest to stay calm. Without any words I remove my coat and throw it to the ground.

We finally reach the meetinghouse, and I have grown numb to the pandemonium. Pastor Noah ushers people inside and helps to calm everyone. We regroup and Nicholas gets Clara and the sisters seated. Thomasin thanks Abigail for her assistance and guides me to a seat in the middle of the room. She never leaves my side, recognizing that I am still in a daze from the mayhem. Amelia, Nicholas, Henry, and Samuel soon join us, and we all take a minute to breathe. They try to wipe the blood from my skin but I offer no reaction. Many familiar faces crowd around us until the meetinghouse is filled from front to back.

Most shout for explanations and cough from the smoke, some even covered in blood just like me. Ambrose rushes to the pulpit and waves his arms to take control. Slowly everyone stops their panic and awaits his words.

"We find ourselves in a bit of chaos," Ambrose begins. "As you all know, Simon lost his life on our first night of Christmas. But moments ago, someone lit fires and slaughtered much of our livestock. We suspect the Devilish symbols to be inked in blood."

The crowd erupts with shouts of fear. I am surprised that Ambrose was wise to the deeper meaning behind these taunting symbols. Perhaps he held more knowledge on witchcraft than he cared to express yesterday. Nicholas leans to Henry and asks if he checked the barn. Both are now worried for our own animals as Ambrose continues.

"Why this happened is unknown. Truly there must be a purpose, and we will uncover it. But this is not all that happened tonight," Ambrose explains.

"Where is Barnabas? He killed Simon!"

"No, it be Griffin! Back to terrorize us again!"

"We are all bewitched!"

Accusations and assumptions fly around the room while Pastor Noah and Ambrose struggle to maintain order.

"Please, everyone! Although unpleasant, I must share the worst of all. 'Tis why you are here. There has been another death," Ambrose shouts.

The room falls silent as everyone looks for their friends and family. Even Nicholas is taken aback. I scan the nearby faces while Ambrose tries to explain what is unraveling. Clearly it was not Phillip because he woke us in the night. I saw the sisters leaving their home with their grandmother and they sit before us. Solomon was standing guard at his tavern with a rifle. Many court officials, clergy members, children, and even young Chrystopher sit amongst us.

Who could it be? Simon was a man of power in Bedfordshire. Was someone similar targeted as well? Perhaps you were accurate in assuming that this butcher has a higher objective in mind.

Nicholas is undoubtedly the grandest farmer and one of the wealthiest members of Bedfordshire. Pastor Noah stands at the front of the room along with Ambrose and the other elected officials. And then suddenly I realize who is missing from the crowd.

"Our Lord of Christmas, Giles, is dead. He left to gather wood for an overnight fire but never returned. And there he was, rope around his neck and hanging from a tree behind his home. The fires and other misfortunes started before we could even get him down," Ambrose states.

People cry out in fear over this information. Nicholas is distressed and I struggle to believe it myself. Giles was a kind man who wanted to give Bedfordshire a perfect Christmas. He was grateful that I stopped Barnabas outside of his home, and I was eager to grow closer with him during these twelve days. This is the second person who died after we shared an encounter. The possibility of Gile's blood staining my clothes and skin makes me ill.

"His wife and children are locked safely in the prison. Anyone else who wishes to join them shall follow me after we disperse. There will be no celebrations on this day, or the next. We suspect that the snowfall will also be drastic in the coming days, so it is best to remain at home unless told otherwise. Alert officials immediately if you know or see anything suspicious!" Ambrose instructs, signaling that the meeting is over. Although inappropriate, I cannot help but find amusement in the fact that the prison is where the victims shall go for safety. They are now trying to keep the wickedness on the outside.

"All of you stay here until I return, and then we shall get back home together," Nicholas demands as he rises from his seat. He makes his way to an official, pointing at Clara and likely asking for them to escort her and the sisters home. Clara is blind to the commotion, smiling and sitting as though we attend a traditional service. Three of the officials follow Nicholas's request. Abigail comes over and embraces me tightly before departing. Surely the situation is dire if I am finding comfort in her arms and Thomasin welcomed her earlier assistance. Though she is not making her usual advances or seeking anything other than safety at this moment.

"Both of you be careful," I tell Abigail as she maintains her grasp. "And I thank thee for helping us back there."

Abigail nods and walks back to her grandmother so they can all depart. She speaks to Nicholas and points to Chrystopher, likely explaining that Chrystopher should go with them so he is not left alone in his home. Nicholas sends officials to gather Chrystopher with the sisters. He makes his way around the meetinghouse, answering questions and providing guidance for those in a panic. His behavior reminds me of my own when I became the leader.

Ambrose grabs Nicholas's arm and stops him in his tracks. He whispers something in his ear that shakes Nicholas to his core. Nicholas nods at his words and eventually comes back to us so we can also depart. He grabs hold of Amelia's hand, as does Samuel to Thomasin, and Henry to me.

"We must stay together and remain at home for the time being. I instructed officials to hold post outside of our farm, along with Clara's home and a few others. We have nothing to fear, although I do not wish to take any chances," Nicholas explains. His actions are wise and reasonable.

"First Simon, and now Giles. Perhaps there is a bigger meaning to this madness. The greatest fisherman is murdered, and now the Lord of Christmas. Whoever is doing this may very well be trying to corrupt Bedfordshire," I say to finally share my thoughts.

"Do be careful, Uncle," Henry begins, "if Emelie's words are true, then you would certainly be of interest to the murderer."

"Let them try to corrupt our farm. I will send Barnabas or whoever this be straight to Hell!" Nicholas shouts in anger.

"Calm yourself, Nicholas," Amelia begs.

Nicholas slows his breathing and tries to remain unaffected by the state of our village. We make our way outside in a line, each of us aware of our surroundings and ready for an attack from all sides. Smoke continues to fill the air, although most of the fires are extinguished. People try to clean the vandalism from their doors, and the sun slowly begins to peak over the trees. Rather than leaving the meetinghouse with joy, everyone exits with cries and panicked whispers.

It causes deep sadness to know that Giles was taken from his wife and children. He brought happiness to Bedfordshire and was eager to lead us through this holiday. And now, we shall celebrate by being locked in our homes while a murderer runs rampant in the village. With each passing moment my faith in Barnabas being the culprit fades.

"Of what did Ambrose speak to you back there in the meetinghouse?" I ask Nicholas. Although Nicholas likely wishes not to discuss this any further, I feel that it is necessary for all of us to have the truth.

"He told me," Nicholas struggles to find the correct words. "Giles was murdered horrifically. His wounds were similar to Simon's, although this time the rope was intact. And like the markings painted on many of the homes, there was a word drawn in blood near his body."

"What did it say, Uncle?" Henry questions.

"Witch. In the snow beneath his hanging corpse," Nicholas mutters with no further explanation as he walks ahead of our group.

All doubt can officially be put to rest, it is verified that someone welcomed this plague to our new home. Two respected members of Bedfordshire were brutally slain at the start of Christmastime with this motivation. And it is puzzling for Barnabas, a drunken fool, to still be missing. Perhaps I underestimate his wickedness, and he is behind the misfortune around us. Or perhaps he is another victim, soon to be discovered nearby without a tongue. Witchcraft is being used to conceal the deeper intentions of whoever is behind this, just as we have seen before. We told Ambrose that the first crime was not gruesome enough or fully indicating of witchcraft, though this murder clears all uncertainty.

"Reverend Thomas thought us to be witches, but he was merely an idiot driven by power. I truly do not know what to make of this here. Do you think this be a true case of witchcraft?

Is there such a thing?" Samuel asks as we walk the path to the farm.

"I was thinking the same," Thomasin interjects in agreement. "What say you, Emelie?"

"I do not know. The witchcraft accusations back in The Hollow were based on lies. But something is different here. Maybe there truly is a witch, or someone bewitched amongst us. It does sound foolish, but I am no more certain than anyone in the meetinghouse," I explain.

"We mustn't rule anything out. Maybe it is Barnabas, or something much worse. Perhaps we were wrong about witchcraft being entirely nonsense," Henry adds.

Each of us offers our insight and bafflement at the situation. We have not a clue as to why this is happening, or if witchcraft actually holds truth. Perhaps it was naive of us to assume without absolute certainty that people cannot make covenant with The Devil and wield such sorcery.

Could it be real? You considered witchcraft to be misunderstood and false, but now you think otherwise? Was Rose a practicing witch?

It is likely fantasy, but we cannot ignore any possible motivations. There could very well be an active coven in Bedfordshire behind the chaos. And while most members of this village seem pleasant, we truly do not know anyone beyond introductions. Perhaps the court is corrupted, or some members are not as honest as they seem. Our exposure to witchcraft was limited to accusations and brutality from a Reverend gone mad. We know little of what occurred in those neighboring communities or deep in the forests that the village members feared. While Thomas was an unstable man, perhaps he did hold some valid knowledge on witchcraft after all. Rose would know better than anyone what is happening here so I will search through her writings over the next few days of confinement at the farm.

I care not to admit that there is humor in the fact that we are searching for truth in witchcraft. From the chaos to the murders, it is odd to watch a similar unraveling of events on the opposing side of our own experiences.

Officials follow close behind until we walk through the door of our home. Nicholas instructs each of them to stand guard at all points of entry. And now we must simply wait under lockdown. Maybe they will find Barnabas and he will confess to motivations of witchcraft and corruption, or maybe Barnabas is already dead like I suspect. An approaching blizzard shall complicate the madness even further. Each day of Christmas has brought unimaginable misfortune and there are still many days ahead.

XIV

Lull

Any signs of chaos are absent as we wait patiently for news from the meetinghouse. Each of us slept late into the next morning and started the day without the commotion of any visitors. In fact, nothing out of the ordinary unraveled since our return to the farm. We spent the entire third day of Christmas resting, trapped from the snowfall and comforting each other in the safety of our home. Officials scoured the trails and checked in on us routinely, so it feels safe within our confinement. Nicholas and Amelia grow more reserved with each passing day, and it is obvious that Nicholas struggles to maintain his joyous composure. Last night's supper was not a massive feast and Thomasin's illness worsened. We didn't celebrate Christmastime or gather as a family outside of meals. The day passed with minimal interactions or conversations, but it was not out of anger or resentment. Each of us feels uneasy and frightened by what is happening to our village. And just as quickly as the day began, we found ourselves locked in our chambers through a quiet night of minimal rest.

The fourth day of Christmas has commenced, and an unsettling stillness is upon us. I wait nervously for a messenger to come at any moment and inform us of further dread or Barnabas's capture.

In truth I am quite shaken from all that has happened, perhaps even embarrassed at my inability to keep my composure that night. The sounds and sights became too much to bear, and I cowered amid the commotion. My actions leave me ashamed. Though I wish to admit it not, I was simply terrified; frozen in fear and taken back to The Hollow. Today I want to remain occupied by writing in my journal and tending to Thomasin, who struggles once again with her condition. Samuel stays by her side in their chamber and Nicholas requested that an official calls forth a physician. This was a long overdue evaluation, as her health continues to decline and her illness has no end. We watched as disease led to the death of many elderly and infant members of The Hollow over the years, so it is quite worrisome. Thomasin knows of my willingness to help but often prefers that each of us gives her space.

The snow falls heavily outside, and I grow tired of sitting by the fire and writing in my journal. Rather than reliving memories of torture, I'd much rather prefer making new memories on this fourth day of Christmas. Though it is selfish to complain of boredom when innocent people are being slaughtered in the village.

Henry invited me to assist him with his afternoon duties in the barn, and I was ecstatic at the opportunity. Although the temperature is chilling, I gladly accepted such an offer, and it seems that the time has come. He verifies that I have the warmest of clothing as we make our way outside. Subtly I smirk at his overbearing protection. I noticed Henry giving me quick glances this morning and I pretended not to notice. Henry seems nervous in my presence and is likely concerned after all that has happened.

We greet the officials and head towards the barn. Snow continues to fall as clouds of darkness loom overhead. I stand back as Henry pulls the barn doors open. A gust of wind forces snow into the barn and Henry rushes to pull the doors closed behind us and light his oil lamp. The inside of the barn is quite dark with the doors closed and much colder than the temperature outside.

"Are you certain you wish to handle these animals?" Henry asks with a laugh.

I smile at his words, scoffing at his doubt for my contributions. "I grew up in nature, Henry. There be not a day that I returned from the forest without dirt and insects all over me. Tending to farm animals is no bother and I am grateful that they were spared that night."

"Very well, wouldst thou like to assist with the cows or the chickens?" Henry replies.

"The cows are mine!" I shout. He laughs at my enthusiasm. It brings me joy to be surrounded by the many cows, chickens, pigs, goats, and sheep in our massive barn. Each animal serves a purpose on our farm and Nicholas ensures great care for them. While the family wealth and reputation stem from the endless crops and vegetable gardens, the animals are merely used as companions that provide us with further resources. We produce our own milk, eggs, meat, and supplies like wool directly on the farm. Having such resources would have been impossible through the long winter months back in The Hollow. It is with gratitude that I no longer drift off to sleep with pains of hunger and I constantly remind myself of the luxuries that bless us in our new home.

I locate my favorite cow and sit on the nearby stool. After a quick greeting and a brushing, I begin the milking. Henry gathers fresh eggs laid by the chickens and places them in a bucket for cleaning and meal preparation. He then starts the shearing among the sheep, which is a fascinating process to observe.

"Do you feel alright, Emelie?" Henry asks.

"Illness has yet to overcome me, and I am still alive. So I am well. 'Tis my hope that this physician can bring Thomasin back to better health. I worry for her these days," I reply.

"I am certain they will make her well. But aside from illness, we should discuss these atrocities around us."

"Well," I begin with an exhale as I move to another cow and grab a fresh bucket, "it brings me great sorrow to watch Bedfordshire endure this. I shall not soon forget the fires or the blood dripping from the homes. That was frightening and took me back to The Hollow. I cannot shake such thoughts, they drive me mad most days."

"It is truly unfortunate, and I was quite worried for you." Henry stops his shearing and stares at me with a sympathetic gaze. "I am always here for you, Emelie. You need not go through all this alone." It is not like Henry to express such emotion so I can sense his awkwardness. But he puts his comfort aside to provide reassurance.

I nod at his words and look away out of shame and desperation. His desire to console me is appreciated, though I often panic and distance my emotions from the outside world. But I do not understand this separation that I create, so it angers me. Constant comparisons to The Hollow and reminders everywhere I look are taking me down a dark path.

Henry senses my desire to move forward in the discussion. I wish to tell him the truth of how I feel, but instead I sit in silence while I scream on the inside.

"I am relieved that we are not to blame. They act with reason here and right now we must focus on staying safe. Once Barnabas is found he will spend the rest of his days in prison. And our Christmas celebrations will resume. 'Tis what Giles would request," Henry explains with exaggerated optimism.

"I hope so, Henry. We must stay close to Nicholas. For if my assumptions are true, he is undoubtedly a target."

"My uncle, or anyone for that fact, will not leave the farm until we are cleared to do so. I think it is a wise choice for us to remain in confinement."

I finish filling my pale and take a moment to pat each of the cows as I pass by. Henry continues his shearing while I pull the loose wool from the sheep's skin. Life on the farm is delightful for all of us. The village is but a few minutes away and we are surrounded by wildlife and nature. My desire to experience a life among the forest is fulfilled. Tending to these animals is something I enjoy because I had little experience doing so back in The Hollow. Perhaps I carry a sympathy for the animals, just as I do for the children in my life. These delicate creatures judge us not and I find peace in their company. And when my desire is solitude, I can spend endless hours traversing the fields of crops or the nearby forest with the massive trees. It is a simple life and one I do not take for granted.

Each of us worries in constant of Barnabas's whereabouts, if another murder is happening at this very moment, or if we shall safely reach the twelfth day of Christmas. But at this very moment I find peace alongside Henry and these wonderful animals. As Christmastime continues, I spend significant time reminiscing on our past life in The Hollow. Guilt often overcomes me in these brief bouts of happiness; a remorse that I cannot shake to this day. An utmost fear of mine is losing all memories of my brother, and it haunts me when I cannot recollect John's voice or appearance with fine accuracy. This realization leads me to tears on most days and the long nights are filled with viciously documenting memories before they are lost in time.

Henry rushes to comfort me when I leap from the bed during the night, eyes full of tears and shaking as I eagerly write in my journal. He understands my pain and remains by my side in the moments when I become a recluse. And with each passing day it seems as though the guilt and penitence only continue to grow within me. But I believe that resolution in Bedfordshire will bring resolution within myself. I put faith in the idea that Christmas was going to be a time of healing and progress.

I do my best to conceal such agony from the others, though Henry is wise to my emotions. The others also approach me with caution since our return to the farm. 'Tis my hope that they understand I do not wish to act so wretchedly, and I would never intentionally push them away. Dealing with such atrocities in our new home before properly confronting our struggles in the past has created deep complications.

"Perhaps I should go and check on Thomasin. Thank you, Henry, for this wonderful afternoon," I profess genuinely. This much needed retreat has strengthened my spirits, and I am forever grateful to Henry and his never-ending efforts.

Henry smiles at my words, appreciating my company and assistance with his farm chores. "I love thee, Emelie," He replies.

We embrace for a few moments as I provide equal words of affection. Each day on this farm strengthens the bond between us, even through all my struggles.

    I exit the barn and rush through the brutal conditions to assist elsewhere. One of the officials recognizes my haste and opens the door so I can quickly make my way inside. The comforting warmth of the hearth and the smell of supper's preparation leaves me in a state of delight upon my arrival. Nicholas and Amelia move silently in the kitchen, so I make my way towards them with hopes of brightening their moods.

    "Supper smells delicious, as always," I say aloud. "What shall we be feasting upon?"

    "Today is also much less of a feast. We need to make our rations last until the Christmas celebrations return," Nicholas discusses with a bit of gloom. "Although, do prepare yourself for turkey, cider, corn, cranberry, and a surprise pie if there be an appetite for dessert!"

    "That sounds lovely, Nicholas. And I promise thee, this is still a feast!" I reply enthusiastically.

    "The pie is also full of cranberries," Amelia whispers with a laugh. Nicholas hears her remarks and tosses a bit of cranberry her way. The tension begins to lighten, and things seem joyous for the moment.

    I cannot imagine the fear, stress, and anger that grows within Nicholas. Although he has his moments of doubt, Nicholas puts forth an effort each day to honor Christmastime and remain positive.

    "Do you have any updates on the whereabouts of that physician?" I ask, eager for Thomasin's evaluation.

"They ensured his arrival before supper. 'Tis difficult to say when exactly, but he should be here any moment. Tongue in mouth and head still attached, God willing," Nicholas replies.

It seems that our crude sense of humor is beginning to wear off on Nicholas, as his statement draws a laugh from me and a gentle nod of shame from Amelia. I offer a smile and leave them to continue preparing our feast. Henry raised my spirits so I feel the need to do so for the others.

The fire begins to dim in the hearth while I carefully adjust the wood and add the final log to the pile. This is unsuccessful and the flames fade away, so perhaps I shall ask Samuel to help me retrieve more wood. Silence fills the rest of the home, which indicates that Thomasin achieved rest in her weakened state. This morning was perhaps the worst of all, so I am thankful that she will soon be evaluated.

And just as the thought enters my mind, a knock at the door indicates that this physician has arrived. My attempts to light the fire yielded poor results so I leave the hearth and rush upstairs to alert Samuel while Nicholas answers the door.

"The physician is here," I whisper through the cracked door to Samuel who sits with Thomasin as she sleeps. Carefully he rises from the bed, trying not to disturb her during his exit. He thanks me as we make our way down the stairs.

"Samuel, this is Bedfordshire's best physician, Timothy. He will banish this illness from Thomasin by the day's end!" Nicholas claims.

Timothy laughs at such a formal introduction, taking a moment to shake Samuel and I's hands. He is an older man, likely close in age to Pastor Noah. I recognize him from service in the meetinghouse, although we have not had the chance to properly meet until now. The large spectacles on his face stood out to me prior, as these accessories were only worn by a few officials back in The Hollow. Many of the elderly members in Bedfordshire own these because they are said to assist with vision.

"Hello Samuel, and you must be Emelie," Timothy begins with a smile. "I shall give Thomasin a proper evaluation, but please tell me of the troubles that plague her. And precisely for how long."

"She has fallen quite ill as of late," Samuel begins, "seemingly worse by the day. It started not long after All Hallows Eve and leaves her fighting nausea through the day. That is if she does not start the morning by vomiting in the privy."

"I see," Timothy replies while listening to Samuel's words. He opens his case of tools and devices that will be used during the evaluation. "There can be many causes for this illness that she faces. A new home with unfamiliar surroundings is often the culprit. I do not suspect this to be a case of the plague or disease, because the rest of you are unharmed. She may be sensitive to the crops, or even the animals. Perhaps a summer asthma still lingers or a poor reaction to the inclusion of fish in her diet."

"Fish, or nearly any of these foods were not common back in our home village," I add.

Timothy nods, and I believe any of his ideas could be a rational cause of her illness. Bedfordshire offers an entirely different way of life in comparison to Warren Hollow. From the food to the climate, I am surprised that Thomasin is the only one who constantly faces difficulty from these changes.

"Would you be so kind as to lead the way?" Timothy asks Samuel. Nicholas returns to the kitchen while Samuel guides Timothy upstairs.

"Timothy said that we are to have a remembrance for Giles and Simon tomorrow at the meetinghouse. Perhaps we can prepare some candles, and assist where we are needed," Nicholas speaks quietly to Amelia. I listen in secrecy from the hallway, just out of sight.

"They think it wise to leave our homes while Barnabas is on the loose?" Amelia asks with concern.

"If we stay together then nothing shall arise. I will instruct the officials to escort us to and from the meetinghouse," Nicholas replies.

"I fear that the others in the village are beginning to talk, Nicholas. Thoughts of witchcraft and bad omens are starting to surround this farm," Amelia whispers so that nobody else hears.

"We will not tolerate such foolishness. Each of them has made a fine member of themselves, and I will see to it that our names are not confused with the true evil out there!" Nicholas begins to raise his voice out of anger.

Rather than another feast, Bedfordshire will hold a vigil for those who have lost their lives. Amelia does have valid reasons to fear for our safety with such a bold decision to depart our homes. Surely Barnabas, or whoever killed the others, will be waiting for another opportunity to act. Perhaps that is the goal of this event, as the officials will wait in the shadows for Barnabas to reveal himself. They will have eyes on all of those in attendance so this may very well be a trap. For our safety, I hope that this is the case.

The people in the village are starting to ponder on ideas of witchcraft. We expressed our wicked past in front of everyone, and life was calm in Bedfordshire before our arrival. Surely these ideas will be linked to our presence soon enough, and I feel shame that Nicholas's reputation could be impacted because of us.

Samuel makes his way down the stairs and interrupts the conversation in the kitchen. To conceal my eavesdropping, I rush to the hearth and call Samuel to my aid.

"This fire will not cooperate!" I yell, pretending to be frustrated. "Would thy help me gather more wood?"

"Sure, yes!" He replies, visibly nervous and worried for Thomasin. I hope to take a few minutes with Samuel and free his mind of this trouble, just as Henry has for me. I throw him his coat and make my way to the door. The cold stings my skin as we exit, which reminds me that many months of winter are still on the horizon. Samuel pulls the door closed behind us and our journey to the woodpile shall be brief.

"Timothy is said to be the best physician in all of Bedfordshire. He will have Thomasin in high spirits upon his departure," I tell Samuel reassuringly.

"I feel great sorrow for her," Samuel begins. "She does not deserve this lasting illness."

"Thomasin will get through this," I tell Samuel while placing my hand on his shoulder, "and soon we will all be celebrating Christmastime once more. We have not been informed, but I overheard Nicholas and Amelia talking. Timothy brought news of a remembrance service to be held in the village tomorrow. They will honor Simon and Giles, and hopefully restore the merriment back to our homes."

"Thank thee for this information. I must prepare a few words for the ones we have lost. But we must act with caution tomorrow," Samuel advises as we approach the wood pile.

He pulls some logs into his arms and grunts as I stack a few more nearly past his chin. Samuel begins to struggle, and we both laugh at the amount of wood he must carry back to the hearth.

"I am afraid that you must carry all this wood alone," I tell Samuel, waving my makeshift hand in a pathetic and exaggerated manner. We continue our playful banter as we traverse back through the snow.

Samuel carries enough wood to last us well through the night while I carry a single log with pride for my contributions. Although it is obvious that gathering wood was a ploy to have a moment with Samuel, it seems that he is rejuvenated from this moment of peace. He aids Thomasin tirelessly through her illness, so I try to provide relief when possible. Our private conversations are always enjoyable, all the way back to our time in Rose's home or the basement of the courthouse. We understand each other and share a connection that is absent with anyone else in our home. He knows my guilt and grief better than Henry or Thomasin, perhaps because of his own suffering that he tries to conceal. While Samuel remains positive and has made progress, I still see the darkness within him.

"Wait," I tell Samuel before we enter the home, "there is something I must tell thee." Suddenly I am regretful of my words, wishing not to ruin this moment of peace. Though I understand it would be selfish not to tell Samuel of my secret, for he deserves to hear these words.

"I'm afraid that our conviction in The Hollow held more secrecy than any of us knew. Thomas had deeper motivations for our torture," I explain.

Samuel places the logs on the ground and stares at me, unsure if I am telling a fable or speaking in truth. Perhaps he is just as surprised as I am for choosing to do this right now.

"When we were leaving Rose's home, I found one of her writings that I failed to notice before. It was a journal, just like the one I spend night and day writing in. That journal held many secrets that she wished to expose," I explain.

"Of what secrets do you speak?" Samuel asks, now realizing that I am not acting in jest.

I take a deep breath and prepare to enlighten Samuel. This seems even harder than when I told Henry, though this secret must be shared. "I do not know how, but Rose and Thomas grew fond of each other upon his arrival. They met in secrecy, and eventually, she carried a child. Thomas was fearful of such a sinful truth, so he used witchcraft to keep his secret. He killed Rose before her pregnancy was evident. Our actions in the forest soon followed so he needed to continue the fantasy that led to our torture. But he knew we were innocent all along."

Samuel takes in my words, reliving all the horrific memories and understanding that we were never guilty of anything more than sneaking from our home. "He knew we were innocent," he mutters to himself. "Thank you for telling me this, Emelie."

"It is with sorrow that I did not do so sooner. The thought of losing any of you to that place brought me great fear and I did not want you to return. Although it was wrong of me to hide the truth and prevent any of you from making your own decision. I am sorry, Samuel," I remark with shame.

We stand in silence for a few painful moments. Samuel is lost in thought while I look for any escape from our current situation. "I," he begins, "I feel as though I should be mad, or even sad. But I feel nothing. In fact, I understand why you have chosen to do this. Back in the courthouse when Ezekiel attacked Thomas, I was not sharing the fullest of truths either. It is true that Ezekiel eventually lost himself to anger and attacked Thomas, but it was much less of a fight than I explained. I wanted the final moments of our friends to be heroic; and instead, many pleaded for their lives as they were slain on their knees. Most by their own parents. But I wished to give us hope and create a positive memory of them."

These words take me by surprise but further reassure that I am not alone in my secrecy. We believed that a massive brawl ensued in the court, one where many of our friends died heroically for our freedom. This was not fully the case and perhaps there was no fight at all. Samuel carried this tragedy, just as I have done with my own knowledge. And in this very moment, I watch as Samuel achieves the relief that I so desperately search for.

"I understand, Samuel. I shall not speak a word of it. Before we left, I ensured that Gregory would receive that journal so everyone in the village would know the truth. I have yet to tell Thomasin, but Henry is aware of this. It is my only hope that someday you can forgive me, though I do not expect any of you to do so," I tell Samuel emotionally.

"There be nothing to forgive. God has already forgiven you, as do I," Samuel expresses with a smile. A wave of relief rushes over me, just like when I spoke these words to Henry. Perhaps Samuel is stunned by this truth and understandably so. His confession also takes me by surprise, but I understand the reasoning. He struggles with guilt and inner torment just like me, and it is my hope that he shall soon overcome this darkness.

We make our way inside with no further words of the past. Samuel organizes the logs atop the scalding ash, and a fire is raging within moments. He turns and offers an exaggerated bow while I reply with applause for his success. We take a moment to sit by the fire, warming ourselves and fighting the sting of the cold. Warren Hollow suffered through many cold winters but the weather here in Bedfordshire is unmatched. We have yet to begin the new year, and snowfall already layers the ground. The frigid temperature also makes it seem as though the dead of winter is upon us. I am eager to witness the blooming of flowers, and the return of farming come spring. Our arrival was close to All Hallows Eve, so we missed the beauty of summer.

Please let Thomasin return to good health and overcome this illness that troubles her. She hath done no wrong and suffers unjustly.

I find myself praying for the safety of my dear friend while dozing off near the hearth. It is true that I made peace with my faith and even enjoy service in the meetinghouse, though I cannot deny my past of shifting beliefs and doubts. This troubles me alongside the rest of my guilt, but I pray and remain devoted to my religion. Samuel helped greatly in strengthening my faith and even listens to my doubts and prays with me upon my request. He already forgives my apprehension and does not hate me like I feared. But when I get lost within my own thoughts, there is nothing that can tame my misery. Prayer is overcome by Thomas's shouts as they fill my ears and swirl around me.

"Speak of thy deception at once!"

"Stop!" I cry out, drawing the attention of Samuel and startling myself back to reality. It was not my intention to speak aloud in my restful state but today has brought an abundance of doubt, fear, and shame. Sometimes my thoughts become unbearable, and while the peacefulness of today has been enjoyable in comparison to the tragedy of the last few days, it certainly does not help my worries from thriving in the stillness.

Sure enough the chamber door opens above us, and Samuel rises to prepare for Timothy's findings. We listen as he makes his way through the hall and eventually down the stairs. Nicholas and Amelia emerge from the kitchen, and I also rise with hopes of positive news. Timothy finishes his descent and seems to be in good spirits. He offers us a smile and fastens his case of tools in his hands.

"I conducted my evaluation," Timothy begins, "and there be no need to worry."

Each of us offers a massive sigh of relief and I feel a great deal of fear dispersing.

"Although I will not share the details, at Ms. Thomasin's request, she does not face disease or a plague of any kind. This new lifestyle presents many changes to her health. It is quite common for young travelers to face such maladies. This could have certainly happened to you as well," Timothy claims while looking directly at me. "Nonetheless, I gave her remedies for the discomfort, and instructions for recovery were properly discussed."

"We thank thee greatly, Timothy," Nicholas answers with appreciation. Timothy offers a farewell to each of us while Nicholas guides him to the door. Within moments, Timothy is positioned in the center of the officials as they depart. Nicholas shouts outside to Henry that supper is ready. Samuel makes his way to the stairs, but I stop him in his tracks.

"Go and enjoy the feast, I shall sit with her," I tell Samuel. He is apprehensive for a moment but appreciates my request and complies. Quickly he puts together a serving for Thomasin, making sure to get the largest piece of turkey and more than enough cranberry. Samuel gives me the plate, and I thank him before departing to the stairs.

"I shall return for dessert," I announce as I leave the room. Sounds of Henry and Nicholas laughing while telling stories brings a smile to my face. Carefully I climb the stairs and make my way through the hall, trying my hardest not to drop the heaping pile of food. Thomasin is asleep as I enter so I position the plate on the edge of the mattress and warily sit at her side. She is weakened from this illness but seems peaceful for the time being. Realizing that she is not stricken with disease nearly brings me to tears, as I care deeply for Thomasin and our bond is unmatched. We are truly sisters and without her I would have never made it out of that prison.

Minutes pass while I reminisce on the memories of our childhood; the two of us taking John to the forest or spending time together with Rose. The room grows darker as the sun falls from the sky, and the evening draws near. Thomasin senses my presence while awakening and looks at me with surprise.

"That physician says I will live to see tomorrow," she mutters jokingly.

"What a shame," I reply, matching her energy and pretending to desire a different result. We smile at each other as she rises in the bed.

"I brought you supper, if you have any hunger."

"So long as it is not another night of cranberry! If so, I feel that my sickness may take me!" she exclaims.

I laugh while presenting the plate of food and pointing to the mound of cranberry that awaits. We both nearly leap from our skin and I drop the plate into Thomasin's lap as Nicholas aggressively pushes the door open. But it is not just Nicholas; Amelia, Henry, and Samuel follow close behind him. It seems that they brought the dessert to us.

"There is no need to have dessert around a table when we can do so in bed!" Nicholas shares enthusiastically. One by one they surround us, gathering near the bed and filling the room with positivity. Some of the pie spills onto the floor and the quilt but we laugh and feel nothing but happiness. The realization that Thomasin will recover brings life back into the farm and Christmas merriment is back in full effect for the time being. What lies ahead is unclear and Bedfordshire's current situation on this fourth day of Christmas is not ideal. But I wish for this moment to never end. Yesterday's monotony and today's experiences with Henry and Samuel were an instance of healing that we all desperately needed. The brief moments spent with everyone on this farm remind me that through love, each of us will triumph this darkness.

XV

Memento Mori

A cloud of uneasiness hangs overhead through every moment of this false comfort. Christmas memories were created and Thomasin was finally evaluated yesterday, but isolation during merriment does not serve any of us well. Such stillness causes my thoughts to run rampant and slowly tear me apart. Needing an escort to leave the farm, traveling only in groups, and guards at every entrance is not a proper way to celebrate Christmastime. Today's memorial is meant to restore order and show the people of Bedfordshire that we will overcome this hell. It is my hope that the gathering proceeds without issue, as another murder or indication of witchcraft will send Bedfordshire into total disarray.

    Nothing out of the ordinary occurred during our isolation, which further leads me to believe that this butcher is an intelligent member of the village. If it were Barnabas, or God forbid Griffin Osmund, they would not comply with the ordinance. Though an attack yesterday would have been far too obvious. Instead, this murderer is abiding by restrictions and waiting to strike. And what better time than the first official gathering in days? Perhaps I am wrong, and Barnabas waits in the shadows with motives of witchcraft and sorcery. Only time shall tell. Henry will keep eyes on his uncle, Samuel will stay close to

Pastor Noah, and I will watch for any disturbances around Ambrose or other officials of the court. We carefully formulated this plan and shall not allow anything to happen to those around us.

'Tis a shame to experience our first Christmas under these circumstances, but we are familiar with sacred holidays bringing the worst of behavior. We are fortunate to face no accusations for the time being, though this may change if another murder takes place.

Everyone seems to be in high spirits on this fifth day of Christmas. Thomasin awakened with a positive attitude and now holds the knowledge to control her illness. Henry and Nicholas spent the early hours tending to the animals and clearing the snow for today's adventure, while Samuel and I assisted Amelia with reinforcing decorations and clearing the kitchen of its mess. I found a few hours to write in my journal and nearly finished our tale in The Hollow. Soon my words will stand alongside Rose's wonderful writings and scrolls, and I am eager to express our story to everyone in Bedfordshire once Christmastime passes.

Yet, secrets remain between us because I have yet to inform Thomasin of the truth. Henry and Samuel took my words relatively well, but I am uncertain how she shall react. Henry met my explanation with a glimpse into his childhood and Samuel used the opportunity to let go of his own secrecy. When the perfect moment arises, I will tell Thomasin everything about Rose and Thomas.

Our journey into the village had a positive momentum with eagerness to honor those who passed. While we are still escorted by guards and on high alert, Christmas cheer is resurfacing through the calamity. There were no homes engulfed in flames or animals slaughtered in their pens, but tension is still high through the village as we pass other members with similar concerns.

A crowd of armed officials stood guard at the entrance of the meetinghouse upon our arrival. There will surely be an immediate defense if anyone tries to launch another attack today. Nicholas spent time visiting Giles's family and offering his condolences. Those who lost their homes or suffered at the hands of the murderer elected to move to the meetinghouse's shelter area until matters are resolved. It is with sadness to look at Giles's wife and children, as I understand what it is like to suffer such a loss. Their first days of Christmas included losing Giles and moving between the meetinghouse and the prison for safety.

And here we are, awaiting a service from Pastor Noah in the meetinghouse. Samuel generously offered to speak on behalf of the victims. I give Abigail and Rachel a greeting as they find their usual spot in front of us. They assist their grandmother in getting comfortable with hopes that she shall not cause a scene. Their story is also one of tragedy that brings me sorrow. Abigail and Rachel lost their parents and were left in the hands of someone who requires more care than they do. Chrystopher is their only true friend who also comes from a broken home. The desire for a better life burns within each of them. Though I have made peace with the sisters and our relationship improved greatly since my visit to their home. Perhaps after this chaos ends Nicholas can arrange for proper care of Chrystopher and better assistance for the sisters and their grandmother.

"Good evening to you all," Ambrose begins as the crowd draws silent, "we thank thee for joining us on this day. Christmastime is nearly halfway over so it is our goal to restore the festivities in Bedfordshire. Unfortunately, Barnabas has yet to be jailed."

This revelation draws anger from the crowd and shouting follows. It is puzzling how a drunken man like Barnabas remains hidden from the entire village. They searched his home and the forest tirelessly, yet there are no leads on his location. Perhaps he is already dead and shall never be found. There must be a reason for this disappearance, and I suspect all will be revealed before the twelfth day of Christmas.

"If anyone knows where he is, then please come forward and express it. There has been no further crime committed since our previous meeting. Perhaps our Christmas celebrations can proceed, but with undeniable caution. Tonight is to be a time of remembrance and honor for those who have met their end unjustly," Ambrose explains.

He takes a step down from the pulpit and signals for Pastor Noah to begin his service. Samuel takes position by his side and makes each of us proud of how far he has come. It's as though I can see into the future, watching as Samuel one day leads Bedfordshire's congregation. After our conversation, I believe that Samuel found his purpose. He seems happier, no longer allowing the guilt of the past to torment him. My only hope is to find this same peace, but I cannot deny my worsening state with each passing day.

Upon leaving The Hollow I had not a care in the world. All of us were eager to move forward and remained occupied with months of travel and interaction. Though when we found our home in Bedfordshire, all the weight began to push me into the ground. Positive memories of my brother fade to his lifeless body before me; a sight that will never leave.

While I would kill Thomas again in an instant, enacting a murder has certainly taken its toll. Those months in the prison and losing my entire way of life changed me. Most nights I hear Thomas's screams and feel the pain of losing my hand. Often, I get lost in my thoughts while writing and find myself back in those dreadful moments. Memories of Rose and Ezekiel hanging from the tree are ingrained in my mind and always waiting in the darkness when I close my eyes. These past few days tested my strength, but I believe progress was made. Henry and Samuel now hold the truth, and I will inform Thomasin as soon as possible.

Pastor Noah begins his service with a dedication to Simon and Giles. He talks of who they were and the contributions they made to Bedfordshire. Though usually a drunken mess, Simon was a wonderful fisherman and an essential component in Bedfordshire's many years of prosperity. Giles was a kind man, a loving father and devoted husband. He cared deeply for the festivities and was honored to be our Christmas Lord. This community was unprepared for the atrocities we face, but a sudden massacre could not have been predicted. Losing one or two more members of regard like Nicholas, Ambrose, or Noah would leave Bedfordshire in shambles. Each of us bows our heads and follows along with prayer when guided, though we keep our sights set for indications of an attack. Surely the guards are waiting for the slightest of notions as well, and none of us will feel safe until this nightmare is resolved.

A sudden commotion in the row before us steals my attention. It seems that Clara is becoming perplexed and shouts at the sisters while they do their best to restrain her. Her illness takes her further into confusion with each passing day and it is with difficulty to witness. Others also begin to take notice until Clara causes a total disruption of the service. Officials rush to calm her and ease her worry, but no efforts prevail. Clara calls for her daughter and scolds the sisters for misbehaving. Abigail and Rachel have done no wrong and it seems that the officials are now ushering Clara out of the meetinghouse. Nicholas calls for an armed escort because this could be the perfect opportunity for another murder. Soon they depart and I cannot help but worry for their safety. They are one of the only families in Bedfordshire outside of the meetinghouse, so I desperately pray for them.

Ambrose helps Pastor Noah to regain order as he concludes his service. Final words are given alongside reassurance for Christmas celebrations, though it may be difficult for everyone to recapture the joy after what occurred thus far. I cannot pretend everything is normal until Barnabas is found and the crimes come to an end. Talks of witchcraft spread and we will eventually be on the forefront of the accusations if nothing changes. But people are hesitant to involve us due to our connection with Nicholas and Amelia.

I understand their concerns, and it makes perfect sense for a wave of tragedy to follow unknown travelers who bring a past riddled with witchcraft and mystery. Perhaps I would accuse one of us if I was not in the very situation they question. Each of us has done well to assimilate into Bedfordshire so accusations are not greatly focused on us yet. This may soon change if Barnabas is found innocent or becomes the next victim.

Rather than rising from the seats and engaging with friends and neighbors, everybody remains silent. We all sit hesitantly, not wanting to leave the safety of the meetinghouse. Ambrose senses the tension and suggests a Christmas gathering at this very moment.

"Stay as long as you would like, everyone is welcome to remain here for the time being. Gather by a fire or indulge in the feast that we shall put together. And when you wish to return home, we shall line the path and ensure a safe departure," Ambrose ensures. His words are appreciated and help to ease the fear. Nicholas instructs each of us to remain close and to not leave the meetinghouse until we are all together. He and Amelia begin making their rounds, greeting neighbors and facing unwanted praise in this time of tragedy. Samuel remains with Pastor Noah, shooting us glances and verifying that his elderly friend remains unharmed. Henry signals that he shall follow his aunt and uncle so Thomasin and I are left to watch over each other. Ambrose is protected by a gathering of guards, so it is unlikely for him to be attacked at the moment.

"Perhaps we should stay here through the rest of Christmastime," I express jokingly. It is hard to deny the feelings of safety and care within these walls.

"We cannot live in fear, and the murderer is likely in here with us," Thomasin replies with unsettling honesty. Slowly we make our way through the crowd, avoiding attention and ready to indulge in a feast that none of us expected.

"If it is not Barnabas then who could it be?" I ask Thomasin.

"I am unsure of what to believe. His disappearance must have a connection to the crime, whether he is already dead, or the cause."

"A similar thought runs through my mind. I have not seen him since our encounter outside of Giles's home. He shouted that Giles would suffer and now he is dead. It seemed to be nothing more than drunken ramblings, but we shall know for sure any day now."

Our conversation continues as we choose the various desserts and drinks that have been presented. It was unexpected for this to be anything more than a vigil, but Ambrose was wise to turn this to our next celebration. The stress begins to lighten as the meetinghouse fills with laughter and cheers. Most people stack their plates with ham and take large cups of cider, though I take a plate full of Christmas pudding. My actions provide humor to Thomasin, and she laughs at my eagerness to devour what has become one of my favorite desserts. We turn our attention to the doors as officials push through, guiding Abigail and Rachel back into the meetinghouse. They look around for a few moments, surprised at the celebration and relieved that everyone dismissed the earlier disruption.

"Over here!" I call to them.

The sisters spot us by the large table and rush to find seats. Normally I limit their company, but I wish to calm their worries and spread some of the cheer.

"Hello to you both, did thy grandmother make it home safely?" I ask.

"Yes, they helped to get our grandmother home and guided our return. We do not wish to be near when she acts in such ways. 'Tis not an easy situation," Abigail replies.

"What caused her confusion?" Thomasin questions.

"It takes nothing these days. She gets frightened if she sits near the hearth for too long or sometimes gets lost behind our home. All this chaos worsens her, and she does not even understand that there have been murders," Rachel explains with a bit of sadness.

"That is truly unfortunate. We will help in any way that we can. Nicholas cares for your grandmother, and he cares for the two of you as well. As do all of us," I express reassuringly.

"Thank thee," Abigail replies, seemingly ready to end the discussion of their burden.

It feels strange to share such a normal conversation with the sisters. This has been the case since I visited their home after our conflict. Abigail may finally accept that we are to be just friends, but they seem to have matured in recent days. We sit together as the minutes pass, watching the celebration grow around us and eating until we cannot handle another bite. Chrystopher also makes his way over and the sisters amuse themselves with their playful torture. We laugh and take some time to appreciate the joy and festivities. Though I never drink any alcohol and shall remain fully prepared for whatever may arise. I notice that Thomasin is also on high alert. She scans the room to locate Samuel every few moments and keeps an eye on our surroundings. Rather than fully enjoying the merriment, I try to place myself in the mindset of the murderer.

How would you react to this sudden Christmas celebration? Would you be involved, hiding among the crowd and waiting to stealthily launch an attack from the inside? Or are you outside of the meetinghouse, waiting for any drunken attendees to wander home in the darkness? Where are you, and who are you?

Nobody seems to be acting out of the ordinary. The sisters returned unharmed and there are no signs of calamity. Clara sits guarded at home with officials just outside of the door. Everyone else is in the meetinghouse, from Ambrose and Timothy to old Phillip. I gaze through the crowd and find no indications of anything but drinking and Christmas cheer. But I know too well that this is far from over. If a mass attack was to be enacted, then it would have happened by now. This butcher is waiting and has other plans in mind. Only time shall tell.

Nicholas and Amelia traverse to our table and are relieved to see us enjoying ourselves. Henry and Samuel are close behind, indicating that our time in the meetinghouse draws to an end. This celebration will likely last through the night, but we are all tired and eager to feel the warmth of our home. The sisters also appear ready to leave so Nicholas suggests that they join our group as we all depart. We pass through the meetinghouse and the midst of the celebration. None of the tragedy is being ignored, but in the spirit of Christmas and Giles's wishes, happiness is momentarily restored. Tomorrow is uncertain and we do not yet have resolution, but tonight is a break from reality.

Henry and Samuel push us into the center of our escort with Amelia for the most protection as we reach the outside. Guards stand on all sides of our group, especially protecting Nicholas. Though frigid temperatures appear to be the only concern on our trek back home. We make our way down the path as the commotion in the meetinghouse begins to fade.

Our journey is met with the darkness of the path. A whistling of the wind and echoed footsteps on the frozen ground are all that surrounds us. Although we move in a group of nearly ten people, most armed and prepared, an uneasy feeling overcomes me. The homes are all dark and the rest of the village is entirely empty. Few lanterns light our way so the moonlight above is the primary guide. It feels as though something horrific shall occur at any moment. Nobody dares to speak a word, not even Abigail and Rachel. Perhaps this year's Christmastime gave them the adventure they always desired, and their childish behaviors are at rest. Abigail was true to her word in not mentioning witchcraft since our discussion, so perhaps she spoke the truth in only showing interest to grow our friendship.

"Elizabeth!" A voice shouts in the distance. At first we hear nothing else, but with each step a faint cry in the distance grows. Our group immediately stops, and the guards raise their weapons.

"Elizabeth, let me in!" The voice shouts again, more distinct as we are fully alert.

"I," Abigail begins, "I think that be our grandmother!"

Quickly the sisters push through the group and rush to their home. Each of us immediately follows while urging them to slow down. The voice continues to call out as we move closer. Soon we all stand in front of the sisters' home, desperately searching the area for their grandmother. A pounding around the back of the house indicates that something is happening. Nicholas runs alongside the officials while we are urged to remain in place.

"You can come around, slowly," Nicholas shouts.

Abigail and Rachel lead the way behind their home, and a crowd surrounds their grandmother. She stands in the snow without any shoes or coverings, pounding on the cellar door. The sisters rush to her aid with tears in their eyes, disturbed by what they see.

"Grandmother, what are you doing out here?" Rachel asks.

"I must get inside, Elizabeth, for your daughters disobeyed me once again!" Clara shouts, confused but nearly laughing as though it is a jest. "They locked this cellar, but I must stop the pounding beneath the floor. For that is how I can sleep once more."

She continues struggling with the door until Nicholas pulls her away. Clara is confused, thinking that she speaks to her daughter and is engaged in a playful trick with her granddaughters.

"It is us, Grandmother, Abigail and Rachel. You are just confused. We play no games, and it is not safe out here," Abigail explains.

It appears that Clara is trying to understand these words but still attempts to undo the locks on the cellar door. She seems unbothered by the frigid temperature and it is clear that she will need additional care moving forward.

"Let us all go inside now," Rachel says as she puts her arm around Clara. Carefully she guides her around the house and back inside.

"I am sorry for her actions, she knows not what is happening. She has fallen down the cellar stairs more than once in the night, crying of a pounding beneath our home. So we keep it locked. Usually she does not wander, and we even put her to bed before returning to the meetinghouse," Abigail explains to our group, nearly embarrassed.

"It be true," one of the officials interjects, "I helped them lay her to bed myself."

Abigail takes a quick look at each of us and forces a smile before joining her sister and grandmother inside. The same official immediately takes his position at the door, likely guarding them through the night and ensuring Clara will not wander outside again. Nicholas scolds him for allowing her to venture outside in the first place, and takes a moment to confirm that there be not a sound coming from the cellar.

"She likely heard Chrystopher down there in recent nights. He was to be staying with the sisters for the first few days of Christmas, though I saw him in the meetinghouse, so their cellar is empty," I quietly remind Henry, Samuel, and Thomasin.

"Perhaps we should be on our way," Nicholas instructs. Our group regathers and we slowly begin advancing from the sisters' home. "Something must be done for Clara. These girls do not deserve to handle such a burden on their own. We must find a solution in the morning," he whispers quietly to the officials at his side. I cannot help but agree with Nicholas's words. While her actions are involuntary, Clara is putting herself in danger. If we did not come to her aid, then she could have injured herself or faced the murderer. Elderly people with similar struggles were present back in The Hollow, but Clara's state is much more severe than anything we have experienced.

The edge of the village is within sight, so our journey home reaches its conclusion. As we progress through the night, the temperature continues to drop rapidly. It is safe to say that we are all nearly frozen and eager to light the hearth before escaping to our chamber for the night. Now that we are into the early hours of Bedfordshire's sixth day of Christmas, I do hold gratitude for today's vigil. The remembrance service was delightful, and the following reception helped to restore positivity in this dark time. Though the events with Clara were unsettling and I wish for Abigail and Rachel to receive assistance.

"Finally," Thomasin rejoices shakily as the farm is now in view.

"Perhaps I should check the animals and ensure that all is well," Henry adds as we walk the path.

"It can wait until morning, Henry. Surely they are all fast asleep," Nicholas replies.

"I do not mind, Uncle. We can rest further into the morning if things are handled now. If this storm is to worsen then we may be trapped inside well into the afternoon," Henry tells Nicholas.

"Do be careful," I urge Henry. Two officials join Henry by his side as he departs from the group. The thought of anyone separating at this point frightens me.

"It seems that the wind has blown the doors open again, Uncle," Henry shouts as he walks to the barn. Nicholas shakes his head in frustration as we continue moving closer to our home. Our group takes a few steps forward before Nicholas stops dead in his tracks.

"No," Nicholas mutters aloud to himself. I look up and a wave of fear flows through my body, nearly bringing me to my knees. There is blood across the front of our home, covering the windows and staining the wood of the porch. A trail of blood drips down the steps and through the snow before us. And sure enough, a massive, inverted cross is painted on the door. Broken bottles of wine and rum lay scattered across the stairs. The officials raise their weapons and shout for all of us to come together.

"There is more," Nicholas says as he approaches the door. There is something else painted beneath the cross.

"You mustn't go any further," Amelia urges.

Nicholas ignores her pleas and instructions from guards while approaching the door. We notice that the door is not fully closed as it shutters back and forth from the wind. Some of the windows are broken as well.

"Your ... time ... has ... come," Nicholas repeats as he struggles to read the inscription on the door. He begins walking backwards down the stairs in a state of shock, glass breaking beneath him. It is clear that this nightmare is far from over and death awaits us all.

"Wait!" Henry shouts in the distance. We turn and notice that he is sprinting from the barn with the other officials. He is covered in blood and indicates that the harassment extends beyond vandalism.

"Do not go inside! We must leave at once!" Henry shouts as he approaches, nearly out of breath and shaken to his core.

"Tell us, Henry, what did you find?" Samuel asks in a panic.

"It is the animals. All of them are dead! The entire barn slaughtered," Henry shouts through tears.

Immediately I lose control of my emotions and join the others in tearful despair. I loved each of those animals, as did the rest of us. We would take time to groom them and even talk to them as though they could respond. Thoughts of Henry and I's magical morning in the barn rush through my mind and my body fills with anger.

"We, we must go. Back to the meetinghouse right now," Nicholas instructs, fighting through his words and visibly disturbed. And soon we are off, sprinting through the snow and struggling to follow the path that our footsteps carved moments ago.

"My farm," Nicholas repeats to himself. We continue to run faster than ever before. And sure enough, I am trapped in another memory of the past as thoughts of Warren Hollow fill my mind. I feel the chains around my waist and the blood pouring from my head. My hand is once again stinging from the cold, although I look down and remember that I no longer have a right hand.

Eventually we hit the edge of the village, but our pace never slows. Smoke fills my lungs from the many hearths that are in use, and the meetinghouse quickly comes into view. Guards outside of nearby homes recognize our actions. We pass Abigail and Rachel's home, the official still in position near their door. Nicholas shouts something incomprehensible to the numerous guards lining the path and homes as we pass. Soon the festive commotion fills our ears as we reach the entrance to the meetinghouse. I slow my pace so that Nicholas can force his way past as we approach. He turns to verify that we are all present and pushes through the meetinghouse doors. One by one we fill in behind him, eager to put a barrier between us and the farm. Each of us struggles to catch our breath and Thomasin collapses with exhaustion on the floor. All eyes fall upon us until the meetinghouse goes silent.

These days of peace are over, and it seems to be our families turn to face off with this assassin. Yet there mustn't be any confusion, for I awaited this very moment with a vengeance.

Whoever is behind these crimes is likely staring back at us right now. Boldly I meet the gaze of every onlooker, challenging whichever fool believes that they shall provoke our family and live to tell the tale.

XVI

Hysteria

Hours pass as I drive myself mad with delirium. We share accusations amongst ourselves well into the day and fail to make sense of the situation. Seemingly every member of Bedfordshire was present at last night's celebration. I recall every face in the meetinghouse, and my list of suspects draws thin. At first I did not believe Barnabas to be capable of such atrocities, but nearly everyone else is accounted for. Finding bottles outside of our home was also further pushing the belief of Barnabas as the culprit. The outlandish idea of Griffin Osmund returning to continue his slaughter in Bedfordshire is also pulling closer to reality. We must expect the unexpected and assume nobody is innocent for the time being.

Thoughts of a higher purpose fill my mind, with motivations like Reverend Thomas. Perhaps an official or respected member of the village aims to take control and must clear his path of any contention. But this feels personal, much more so than a jealous official or the drunken ramblings from Barnabas. The way in which Simon, Giles, and these poor animals were executed surely holds a deeper meaning. Markings on the homes and all the destruction must mean something. If this was an official, surely they would not want to destroy the civilization in which they intend to lead. Unless it is all a ploy;

someone can rush to save our home from the witches that they falsely create. Surely whoever stops this madness will be a hero, and just like Reverend Thomas, they could be utilizing neighboring misfortunes to their advantage.

    Ambrose also gained further insight into our past and may have entrusted this knowledge with the murderer, or Ambrose could be the murder himself. Giles's death was far worse than Simon's, so perhaps Ambrose aimed to remove any doubt and learned from our uncertainty. I keep his so-called burn from the hearth in the back of my mind. Then there are the sisters, though it seems that their fascination has come to pass since I respectfully declined Abigail's advances. Abigail and Rachel spoke not a word of witchcraft since admitting it was a means to grow closer with us. Solomon also seems to be unhinged, and there are plenty of members who could conceal their identify through false drunkenness. As we repeated to each other for hours, it could honestly be anyone.

    Our return to the meetinghouse was met with chaos and hysteria. Nicholas explained our findings to everyone, and panic immediately ensued. Families rushed to find their loved ones and departed to search their own homes for similar destruction. Ambrose attempted to maintain control, but the meetinghouse was in disarray. A crowd of guards surrounded us since the moment we arrived, as Nicholas is now the target of a coming attack.

    Officials walk the paths through the blizzard and patrol all surrounding areas. The farm is being thoroughly searched and restored at the moment, so we are likely locked down in the meetinghouse for the time being. It is now clear that this murderer waits for the perfect opportunity and will not act in such a guarded area. They may target Nicholas, but an unsuspecting victim who leaves their home could very well be next. Talks of a manhunt are underway and a mob is forming to conduct a search for Barnabas.

"We cannot wait as Barnabas slaughters everyone around us. It would be wise to gather our weapons and search the forest until we find him ourselves! If it was of my power, we would have exiled Barnabas years ago!" Solomon shouts.

It seems that Solomon, Bedfordshire's primary taverner, has taken the lead in guiding this charge. Ambrose tries to deter this behavior while more people share this belief with each passing minute. This group departs from the meetinghouse to begin their search, armed and ready to implement justice.

"What am I to do?" Ambrose asks Nicholas. He appears defeated and lost control of the home he is expected to protect.

"Let them go. Just ensure that they bring him in alive," Nicholas advises.

He still firmly believes that Barnabas is to blame. While this is one of the few viable options remaining, I hold doubts until this is confirmed. Barnabas caused chaos and engaged in many conflicts over the years, but he is nothing more than a drunk. His only concern was to make a fool of himself and bring misery to those around him. It also makes little sense to think that Barnabas could suddenly have motivations of witchcraft and the skill to act with stealth and precision. Each of the murders left little evidence behind, if any, so why would he become reckless at the farm?

We watch silently as Nicholas takes charge and guides everyone through the panic. It was quite evident from the moment we arrived that he is of great importance in this village.

Amid chaos it seems as though Nicholas holds more regard than any official. Though it is hard to blame Ambrose or Pastor Noah, as they have not faced anything like this under their rule. Nicholas is a powerful individual, and I feel awful for the tragedy that he and Amelia now face. Each of us is fearful, yet we remain prepared and ready to act on a moment's notice. These unfortunate occurrences blur the passing of time, though we are approaching the afternoon on Bedfordshire's sixth day of Christmas.

"Are all of you well?" Nicholas asks as he returns to us.

"Yes, Uncle. Just as we were when you asked moments ago," Henry replies.

"And how are you, Nicholas?" I reply. He looks at me for a few moments, providing nothing more than a gentle nod.

"We will get through this," Nicholas claims before walking away. I do sense a bit of apprehension, even potential anger, towards us. Maybe Nicholas is frightened and struggling with ideas of how to keep us safe. Or maybe he blames all of this on our arrival. For now, I elect to stay out of his way. While I wish to raise the idea of Barnabas potentially being innocent, any involvement will draw more attention towards us. This situation grows shockingly similar to The Hollow by the day, which is potentially why I am so bothered. The idea of Barnabas being murdered before proven guilty is unsettling. But Nicholas also wishes for Barnabas to be captured alive so surely they will abide by his request.

"How are you faring, Aunt Amelia?" Henry asks.

She smiles at his words, trying her best to remain composed. Her positivity has yet to falter, though I sense it is a challenge for her to maintain the joyous demeanor.

"As well as expected. Our poor animals did not deserve such cruelty," Amelia replies while nervously fidgeting with her quilt. The destruction of the farm troubles each of us deeply. Not knowing who did this or with what motivation is perhaps the most frightening realization. While I know that it would be nearly impossible for anyone in the meetinghouse yesterday to be guilty, I refuse to blindly place any blame on Barnabas. My worst fear is that he will be found and executed, but the crimes continue after his death.

"You are shaking again," Thomasin whispers to me. I failed to realize that the racing of my mind is causing my body to panic. She grabs my hand and pulls herself closer.

"I am starting to dislike this Christmastime celebration. There be too much murder and mystery," Thomasin explains. Her playful conversation gives me comfort and helps to ease my mind. While I wish to join her in jest, I feel that she is deserving of complete honesty.

"It must be quite obvious, but I have been a mess as of recent," I begin emotionally. "All of the death and chaos is too much to bear. I simply cannot control myself and I fear that it shall lead me to madness."

For the first time I openly acknowledge my struggles to someone other than myself. They are all undoubtedly aware of the issues I face so it does not seem justified to deny such pain. If I ignore my current state any longer, I fear that it shall eat me alive. At this moment I am finally addressing the simple fact that I need assistance with my healing.

"I understand, Emelie. Only the four of us truly know what we had to go through. And this too shall pass, for they act in haste so this will get resolved. Everything shall return to normal by the end of Christmastime," Thomasin claims reassuringly.

That is if we are all still alive. We may not even live to see the seventh day.

"I apologize. I mean not to be so distant and bothersome. What frightens me the most is my newfound inability to act in moments of distress."

"There be no need to apologize."

We sit passing the time with no further words, watching as officials come and go. I can tell that Thomasin appreciates my honesty, more so with myself than the words I speak to her. A blizzard rages outside and further hinders the search for Barnabas and the efficiency of the guards. Most officials take breaks to find warmth from the cold until Ambrose shouts for them to remain guarding the doors outside. Samuel helps Pastor Noah lead a small service for the other members of Bedfordshire who join us in the meetinghouse. Giles's family is still present, along with some elderly members and those with small children. The rest joined the search while everyone else barricades their homes.

"Nicholas," an official calls out as he approaches. Each of us also gives our full attention to this conversation. Samuel rejoins our group and each of us rises from our seats. "We thoroughly searched your farm. Aside from the broken windows and vandalism, your home remains unharmed." Each of us lets out a massive sigh of relief. "Though true to your findings, all your animals have been slaughtered. Some members offered to provide their cows and chickens in the coming days."

"That is quite generous. I thank thee for this information," Nicholas replies. The official leads his small group back to the outside as quickly as he came. We all stand in silence and stare at each other.

"This was intentional," I begin as all the eyes fall upon me. "All of it. If they wished to harm us, then surely they would have waited until we arrived back home. There is a reason behind it, or else we would likely be dead."

"I think you are right. They could have lit the farm ablaze when we went to sleep, or attacked us on the path," Samuel adds in agreement.

"But why?" Nicholas asks. It does not appear that any of us can provide an answer. We did not come to Bedfordshire with enemies, and any connection to our old lives is separated by a great distance. Nicholas and Amelia are also treated as royalty so nobody would dare to consider them an adversary.

"They weakened the port and hindered all order surrounding Christmas. Complications with farming would make matters drastically worse. It is hard to deny a pattern," I explain.

Nicholas listens to my words attentively while going through all possibilities in his mind. Perhaps Ambrose or Pastor Noah could fall victim to this butcher in the near future as well. Or the death that would cause the most panic of all would be Solomon. Without his ability to bring alcohol and visitation to Bedfordshire, many members would surely lose their minds. And if this was a personal attack by Barnabas then Solomon would have been the first to meet his end. It is unclear why I am so keen on Barnabas's innocence, but I cannot shake this belief until it is proven inaccurate. Our unjust conviction in The Hollow could be the deeper reasoning.

"I am sure that they will find Barnabas. Once they bring him in, we will get a confession," Nicholas replies.

"And what if Barnabas is proven innocent beyond any doubt?" Henry questions.

"Then it is but the same. We shall be ready to face any danger that is brought before us. Each of you will be safe, for I guarantee it. Nobody will tear apart our village, our farm, or our family!" Nicholas shouts as he departs.

It seems that Nicholas is growing impatient with the tragedy surrounding us. Maybe he is scared; surely anyone in his position would be. This murderer is still unknown after days of searching and ongoing attacks. Christmastime is meant to be a break for members like Nicholas or Ambrose. Rather than coming to the village for celebrations and merriment, we are locked in our homes and watch helplessly as friends and family are slaughtered. We will be under supervision at all times until resolution is achieved.

The fires destroyed barns, sheds, and even some people's homes beyond repair in recent days. Watching as an established community begins to crumble is unsettling. But even through all the tragedy, Bedfordshire remains strong and determined. Officials protect us for hours on end and provide comfort to anyone in the meetinghouse. Even yesterday's celebration was a fine attempt at restoring the cheer of Christmastime. Samuel, Henry, Thomasin, and I try to pass the time by solving this madness ourselves. This revelation of the murderer targeting the leaders of Bedfordshire seems to hold truth, so I am thankful that Nicholas listened to our ideas.

"Ambrose, Barnabas, Solomon, or even old Phillip could be to blame," Henry explains as we gather subtly in the corner.

"We mustn't forget Abigail and Rachel, or even their grandmother," Samuel adds.

Thomasin laughs at the idea of Clara being a murderer. "For all we know it could be Pastor Noah, or that physician, Timothy."

"Surely the others ponder on such accusations with us in mind. With our past and the coincidence of our arrival, we must act with caution," I quietly remind the others while scanning our surroundings.

As we ponder on potential murderers a commotion near the doors steals our attention. Everyone in the meetinghouse rises and listens to the shouting and uproar that is swelling.

"Stay behind me," Nicholas instructs as he rushes towards us. Within moments the doors fly open as a crowd forces their way through. Solomon leads his mob and urges everyone to move out of the way. A gathering of guards also enter alongside many other members of Bedfordshire. And to our surprise, it seems that these members captured Barnabas. He appears beaten and dirty, fighting the crowd that restrains him against his will. They drag him across the meetinghouse while pushing through pews and anything in their path.

"It is Barnabas! Go and gather everyone who is not present in this meetinghouse with haste," Nicholas instructs a few of the officials who guard us. They rush through the doors and into the blizzard. Confused faces fill the meetinghouse and stare in horror at the sight of Barnabas.

"Release me or I shall kill you all!" Barnabas shouts.

"You will cause no more harm to Bedfordshire, murderer!" Solomon replies as they beat Barnabas into submission. Henry senses my desire to get involved so both he and Thomasin urge me to remain in place.

"Take him away!" Nicholas shouts as he approaches the group. They obey his words and usher Barnabas into one of the private rooms. And just as it was moments ago, the meetinghouse grows quiet and still. The four of us are unsure what will happen next. This mob located Barnabas rather quickly, which is strange after so many days of officials conducting searches.

Unless there be someone in power who was intentionally misleading the search. Why was it so easy for a few vagrant members under Solomon to locate Barnabas when an entire group of officials under Ambrose could not? This capture brings more questions than answers.

I watch the door as Phillip, Timothy, Pastor Noah, and seemingly everyone else in Bedfordshire makes their way inside. Abigail and Rachel come through guiding their grandmother, appearing confused and afraid like everyone else. They quickly spot us and rush to our side.

"I wish not to be here. Why are we here?" Clara asks in a panic. It seems that it was a struggle to remove her from her home, and the sisters fight to keep her calm. She pulls towards the door, but Abigail has a firm grip on her arm.

"Is it true that they found Barnabas?" Abigail asks.

"Aye! Solomon gathered a small group of men who went to search for him. They were gone no more than a few minutes before they returned. We know not of how, but they brought Barnabas back!" I explain.

"That is great news!" Abigail exclaims with a smile.

"Perhaps, though I am uncertain of Barnabas's guilt. If I am correct, then this could be the beginning of something much worse," I say quietly to the sisters.

Abigail releases her grandmother and remains still, staring into my eyes and appearing fearful. I look at Rachel who stands in a similar stature. She gazes at her sister then back to me. They seem hesitant or confused by my words as if I confessed to involvement. Immediately I regret sharing my thoughts aloud.

"I see," Abigail replies, breaking from her fear to chase after Clara who aims for the doors. She takes a few glances over her shoulder in my direction.

"So you think someone else is causing this chaos?" Rachel asks timidly.

"It be just a desperate thought. Although Barnabas is detained, so it is best to hear from him first before pondering any further," I claim. It would be wise to keep our reasoning brief with anyone outside of our family. My words seem to have frightened the sisters, or perhaps they are now frightened of me. I only wished to keep them safe, but I sense that they took my words as a warning.

We await patiently for any further developments. It is hard to decipher the shouting and commotion unraveling behind the closed doors. Abigail and Rachel maintain their distance while I try not to look in their direction. My words did not seem wicked as I spoke them, but Thomasin urges me to pay it no mind.

"This could be the end," Samuel whispers, "perhaps Barnabas will confess, and Bedfordshire will recover."

"Do you think that to be true?" Henry questions.

"I would like to believe it. But it would be wise to remain on high alert at the moment," Samuel replies.

His words are wise and replicate my thoughts. Rather than relief at the sight of Barnabas, his presence made me feel even more unsettled.

How did they find him so quickly? Where has he been all this time? Surely this would be too easy.

"Grandmother, please!" Abigail shouts as she tries to calm Clara and force her to sit. She is experiencing another frantic episode and wishes to leave the meetinghouse. The struggle is interrupted as Ambrose appears from the private chamber. Many in attendance begin to shout for answers, asking of Barnabas and calling for his death.

"Silence all!" Ambrose shouts. Everyone calms down and eagerly awaits an explanation.

"It is true that Barnabas sits in this room behind me. Solomon found him in the tavern, covered in blood and disoriented. He tells a tale of confusion and deceit, so how he arrived at the tavern is unclear," Ambrose explains.

"Did he confess?"

"Why did he do this?"

"Is he bewitched?"

Shouts from the crowd continue as this explanation only causes more hysteria. The fact that Barnabas was suddenly in the tavern is odd and perhaps there is truth to this tale that he speaks. If Barnabas enacted his crimes with stealth and precision, then why would he return to the tavern amid a massive investigation for his whereabouts? It would not be strange if he was found hiding in the forest or a barn rather than in plain sight.

"Something is not right," I whisper to Thomasin. She does not reply, but I sense that she shares a similar notion.

"We will present Barnabas to you once he has calmed. For now, he is restrained so that he can harm no one else. Bedfordshire is safe!" Ambrose claims. I show apprehension at such a guarantee. It seems as though someone carefully constructed his capture, escaping into the night while Barnabas is executed on falsity.

The rest of the officials exit the room, shouting insults and threats to Barnabas as they close the door. Nicholas also emerges from the chamber, appearing emotionless and unsatisfied with this resolution. He walks past Ambrose and makes his way to our area. Amelia pleads with Nicholas for information, but he leaves her questions unanswered as he passes.

"It is not Barnabas," Nicholas mutters.

We look at Nicholas who sits on the pew, shaking his head and showing disappointment.

"Are you certain, Uncle?" Henry asks.

Nicholas nods, providing no further explanation to validate the belief that we all share. This means that the murderer is still among us, ready to act and catch everyone by surprise. We observe the crowd with growing panic.

"It could be any of them," Thomasin whispers.

"I know. We must stay close and watch for any signs of disorder," I quietly reply.

We listen as the crowd shouts to Ambrose and swells with anger. They believe that Barnabas is to blame and wish to punish him with violence. Even Nicholas was blind to any doubts, only now realizing that Barnabas is innocent after standing face to face with him. This exact reasoning is unknown, but Nicholas would not make such a claim unless he believed it to be true.

"Let us face him right now!"

"He must answer for his crimes!"

The crowd grows impatient and begins storming the chamber. They pound on the door and fight with the guards who urge their peace. The four of us maneuver to the back of the meetinghouse, wishing to avoid all the conflict that is unfolding. Other officials surrounding the exits make their way inside to calm the mob, leaving us completely vulnerable to the outside. Nicholas also rushes to restore order near the pulpit. Defenses falter and attempts to break down the chamber door are nearly successful.

"If they get through then Barnabas is as good as dead!" Samuel shouts.

"There is nothing we can do to stop this," Thomasin replies.

We feel helpless but understand that involvement may place the target on us. These people are dangerous after losing loved ones and spending Christmastime in fear. But we know the feeling of facing such a force while innocent.

"Grandmother, you cannot leave now!" Abigail yells, drawing our attention to the nearby doors. Clara is nearly halfway through the door while Abigail fails to restrain her. There are no longer guards to stop her from leaving and the sisters are unable to control her. She does not understand what is happening, and it seems that the commotion frightened her. Both Abigail and

Rachel shout for any officials to provide assistance. Their requests are met with little response as the focus is still on the chamber door that is nearly broken down. The sisters desperately look in our direction for guidance.

"Emelie, please help me block the door so my grandmother does not leave!" Abigail yells. I begin to thoughtlessly move towards the door before I am restrained.

"Stop," Thomasin commands as she tightly pulls my arm. I look at her with confusion, then quickly understand that this could be some form of deception. Abigail may wait for me to get close and plunge a knife into my chest before anyone could reach us. While such an occurrence is quite unlikely, we wish not to take any chances. The meetinghouse doors are now wide open.

To provide some form of assistance, I begin calling for any officials around us. Clara pushes through to the outside and the sisters rush to alert the crowd. Anxiously I look all around the meetinghouse, hoping to find someone who can stop her. All pleas are ignored while any officials assist in restraining the crowd. Suddenly I cannot believe my eyes while gazing from the window. Through the formation of frost and ice, I spot Barnabas sprinting through the night. I quietly alert the others and soon Henry, Samuel, and Thomasin also watch as Barnabas struggles to make his escape. He has ropes and chains around him, but moves hastily into the forest.

"Do not say a word," I begin, "this could be our chance to prove his innocence before they find him again."

We watch as he struggles through the snow until disappearing into the darkness of the forest. The mob bursts through his chamber door just as he falls out of sight.

"Where is he?" Solomon yells.

Ambrose pushes through the crowd and is stunned upon entering the private room. Everyone forces their way inside, shouting for Barnabas and tearing the area apart. It is unclear why I hold so much faith in his innocence or compare his situations to ours. While Barnabas may not be a maniacal murder, he is still far from innocent in anyone's eyes. He ruined nights in the tavern, corrupted service and festivities, and instilled fear in all of Bedfordshire. Perhaps if the circumstances were not dire then I would have little care. But we are wise to the fact that his death shall bring false security and further mayhem.

"He hath gone through the window!"

"How did he escape?"

"Quiet!" Ambrose shouts to regain order. And soon all commotion comes to a halt. The mob slows their movements until the meetinghouse falls silent. A faint noise in the distance captures everyone's attention.

"Do you hear that?" Nicholas asks Ambrose.

Suddenly our attention is drawn back to the front of the meetinghouse. Something unpleasant is unraveling on the other side of the doors. Nicholas raises his hand to stop the others as he cautiously moves forward. A blood-curdling scream makes all of us nearly jump from our skin.

"Grandmother!" Abigail yells as she emerges from the crowd and runs to the doors. Nicholas grabs her into his arms and prevents her from leaving. She struggles to break free while a crowd of officials and Solomon's mob lead the way outside. They pause for a moment in horror before raising their weapons and shouting instructions to the inside.

"It is Barnabas! He hath killed again!"

Rachel helps her sister break free and they traverse to the front of the crowd. Soon their screams ring through the meetinghouse and it is apparent that their grandmother has fallen victim. We move forward until I barely have a view of the outside. I spot Clara, lifeless and covered in blood in the snow.

"No," I whisper to myself. All sound begins to fade and my heartbeat races. While I am disturbed by the fact that another murder has been committed, I refused to help Abigail and Rachel, so I feel responsible. The sisters pleaded for my assistance, and I did nothing.

"Listen," Thomasin shouts while placing both hands on my face, "if you had followed Clara outside, then it would be you no longer breathing. It took but one moment of chaos for this to happen."

My panic intensifies as I shake my head and struggle for breath. "I could have saved her. They asked for my help, and I refused," I reply emotionally.

"Trust me, Emelie, stopping you was a wise decision. That would be you out there in the snow. Blame me if you must, but your life would have ended."

Her words are true, and I am grateful for her anticipation of the danger. Though I cannot help but to envision a better outcome if I had found a way to assist them.

"Find Barnabas and execute him at once!" Solomon yells to his group. They disperse in all directions, armed and ready for another hunt.

"It was not Barnabas!" I yell, unable to contain my doubts any longer.

Soon all eyes fall upon me, and I feel the tension building.

"What say you?" an angry individual calls out while approaching.

"I saw Barnabas run into the night behind the meetinghouse before we heard the screams. It would be impossible for him to have done such a thing," I explain.

Henry and the others are worried and fear that I shall face repercussions. But just as Solomon proved tonight, the time to be silent is over if we wish to end this.

"Whoever is to blame wants you to believe that it is Barnabas. And perhaps I would believe it as well if I did not witness his escape to the forest," I shout.

"The child speaks of fantasy!"

"Barnabas must be killed!"

"Emelie bewitched him!"

The final shout of witchcraft catches my attention. I stand frozen in place at the realization that it is Abigail who claims Barnabas is bewitched. Through her tears and emotions, Abigail comes forward and speaks irrationally.

"They brought witchcraft to our home and bewitched Barnabas to do the Devil's bidding!" Abigail yells while pointing to me, Samuel, Henry, and Thomasin. Nicholas pushes forward and attempts to shield us from the swelling anger.

"Why do you say this, Abigail? I shared the misfortunes of our past with you. So how could you claim us as capable of such cruelty? I am sorry that I did not help thy grandmother, but this is not the way to proceed!"

Rachel joins her sister in passing the accusation to us. I am taken by surprise at this revelation and cannot understand why Abigail and Rachel, of all people, would accuse us of the very thing they hold to such regard. Upon thinking that I was a witch, these sisters practically worshipped the ground beneath me. And now they aim to join the others and put our lives in danger. Perhaps they are in shock, desperate for answers and angry at my lack of assistance. Or perhaps Abigail waited patiently for the opportunity to seek revenge after I rejected her affection. I scold myself for revealing my doubts to the sisters moments ago.

"We know you are more than capable of such cruelty. You fled your home after butchering the Pastor when he discovered your evil ways. And now," Rachel continues while turning to face the crowd, "Emelie and Thomasin have come to our home to corrupt Christmastime and spread their wickedness!"

Her words draw a gasp from the crowd and even I am completely stunned. How the sisters hold this information is unknown, as I have made certain to conceal these details of how our escape actually happened. Only Nicholas and Amelia are wise to the truth, so I am left in bewilderment. My ability to formulate a response has diminished and shouts of witchcraft surround us. Everyone now believes us to be evil and causing the madness. Our presence was approached with rationality until this very moment. But out of anger for my lack of assistance, the sisters turned this into a witch hunt.

"Come with me," a voice calls from inside the meetinghouse. We turn to see Pastor Noah signaling for us to join him. Ambrose and Nicholas push us back through the doors. Quickly we rush inside while Henry and Samuel keep distance between us and the crowd. "You must all go to the prison. 'Tis the safest place until we can settle this nonsense. It is foolish to believe any of you are to blame," Noah explains.

"We thank you, Pastor Noah. I swear that we hold no involvement in this mess," Samuel replies.

"I believe you, Son. Ambrose, get them there safely," Noah instructs.

The prison is but a few steps beyond the meetinghouse and stands miniscule in comparison to the magnitude of that in Warren Hollow. Bedfordshire has little crime so perhaps it has only ever been inhabited by Barnabas. It is honestly an extension of the meetinghouse, rather than its own structure.

"We will stay here and try to calm these accusations," Henry explains to Ambrose. "It is Emelie and Thomasin that they fear, not us."

"No!" I yell at Henry's request. I fear for their safety if Henry and Samuel do not join us in the cells.

"These people are angry, but they will bring no harm to any of you. I will not allow it," Ambrose claims. "I agree that it is best if the two of you retreat to the cells until we can restore order. And once Barnabas is located, all these accusations will stop."

"But you must believe me that Barnabas is innocent. We watched as he ran to the forest moments before Clara was murdered," I plead.

Ambrose nods, never officially agreeing but showing no signs of doubt. The mob shouts from the outside while trying their best to enter the meetinghouse. I give Henry a tight and reluctant embrace, as does Thomasin to Samuel.

"I convinced an entire village of our innocence, so surely I can do it again," Samuel claims with a smile.

I give my deepest faith to Samuel. Henry will also protect us from the outside and Nicholas will silence all negativity surrounding our family. They will listen to him, even during the chaos.

"We must go," Ambrose demands.

I take a final look at Henry, Samuel, Nicholas, and Amelia before departing.

I beg of thee, keep my family safe from all that may come.

With a desperate prayer, I prepare for our imminent return to confinement.

XVII

Tranquility

The cell feels familiar whilst the door locks behind us. It's as though I am home, reliving the vivid memory that has haunted me each night since our departure. 'Tis a strange feeling to be back in confinement because I never truly escaped the prison of my mind. Dusk brings sleepless nights and echoes of the bitter cold, screams, death, and paralyzing fear until dawn. No matter how far we span from Warren Hollow, its wicked grasp may never be broken. This was not the outcome that any of us could have anticipated.

"Emelie, you must devise an escape! Just as you have before," Thomasin pleads.

I turn, meeting her gaze and offering a despairing reply. "I'm afraid it would be impossible. We shall be trapped until our execution."

Through all the chaos and misfortune surrounding us we cannot help but make a mockery of our current situation. Thomasin jokingly pulls at the cell bars while I pretend to scream for help. We came a long way, but all paths led back to imprisonment. And while this time we are not exposed to torture or cruelty, 'tis all but the same.

"It is strange to think that we are now in a cell for our own protection," I admit.

"Certainly," Thomasin replies as she begins to make herself comfortable, "though I find it hard to believe that anyone back there would have harmed us. They are fearful, and this precaution shall keep us separated from the madness on the outside."

I agree with her words but struggle to move past the actions of Abigail and Rachel.

"I do not understand why those sisters accused us of witchcraft. We were good to them, through all their mischief and awkwardness. Perhaps they seek revenge for my lack of assistance, or Abigail still holds my rejection against me," I tell Thomasin in a defeated manner.

"How did they know of our history with Reverend Thomas? Did you speak of it with them, even by accident in conversation?" Thomasin asks.

"Never," I reply sternly. "Only Nicholas and Amelia know the truth. And I trust Nicholas would have kept this secret for our safety. I acted with caution when the scrolls and writings were presented as well."

Perhaps word spread across the colony. But just as I trust Nicholas to keep our secrets, I have faith that none of our friends back in Warren Hollow, or Reverend Gregory, would speak the truth we aimed to bury. Pondering in prison has become a joyous pastime of mine, though I wish not to travel the line of sanity once again in a cell. We shall be locked away for a day, two at most, and hopefully things will die down while we are confined. Though I am doubtful of such resolution and fear that the worst is yet to come. This murderer has grown ruthless and could have easily killed me instead of Clara.

"Do you remember," Thomasin begins as she pulls me from my thoughts, "all those nights back in The Hollow? Struggling to survive, not knowing if we would see the sun rise through our window."

"Aye. No amount of happiness in Bedfordshire will allow me to forget. Or perhaps it is I who prevents resolution and fear the loss of those pleasant memories as I exile the wicked ones. Most nights I awaken in a panic, shouting and pleading until Henry pulls me to reality. Sometimes I rush through our chamber door and believe that the guards forgot to lock us in."

Thomasin understands my struggle. "We all still face misery from the past. Even Samuel and Henry, though they occupy themselves with chores and desperately search for a purpose. But deep down they struggle just like you and me. We all suffered through those nights in the prison, the torture, starvation, and bitter cold. It is not easy to move forward but I would like to," she admits.

"And how do you handle those days? The ones where you wake from a nightmare or when it seems that something awful shall come at any moment? It's as though I never made it out of The Hollow. The weight has become too much to bear, and I fear that these Christmastime misfortunes may take me to the grave," I also admit with vulnerability.

"Perhaps I conceal my emotions well. And I understand that our family is by our side. Nicholas and Amelia may be confused by this darkness, but they will stand by us until this comes to an end," Thomasin explains.

Reassurance that none of us are alone in this despair brings me a moment of validation. I am wise to my fondness for struggling in solitude and how I distance everyone from the torture that tears me apart from the inside. It feels as though I deserve a bitter ending in death and misery. But this is not what Rose or John would wish for. They died so that we could achieve happiness and freedom, although I have yet to truly break free.

"I am afraid," I whisper tearfully to Thomasin, "that I shall forget John. His little face begins to fade in my mind, and I fear that I will lose all my brother. So I cannot move on."

"You mustn't torture yourself, Emelie. John shall be a part of you forever and you will never lose those memories. From his birth to his death, you gave him a life worth living. Perhaps you can write all your fondest memories with John in one of your journals. For I have many stories of our childhood that could be contributed as well. Though our time in The Hollow ended poorly, we had years of happiness. Like the many bonfires with Rose or the mischief in the schoolhouse," Thomasin explains with a smile.

Her gesture is appreciated and allows me to finally address the reason behind my troubles. Surely murdering Thomas and the hardships of the prison bring me misery, although I fear that finding resolution will also be acceptance of my brother's absence. But it is not fair to condense John merely to the moment of his death.

Thomasin is right; our lives in The Hollow were much more than the darkness brought on by Reverend Thomas. Her ideas are valid, and I wish to rush home and begin writing the tales of our childhood, like taking John to the forest, Ezekiel causing mischief in service, or when I first crossed paths with Rose. This is what I should be documenting instead of our torture.

"Thank thee. Without you I would not be here today," I admit.

She smiles as we sit together in this cell. Thomasin begins to laugh at our current situation once more and I cannot fight the urge to do so either. Our lives are an insanity that holds no comparison to the wildest of tales.

"And to think they found All Hallows Eve wicked back home," Thomasin claims playfully.

"It brings me sadness to watch this wonderful village struggle through such a joyful time. These twelve days would have been wonderful without the murder, chaos, witchcraft, and whatever else unravels on the outside," I reply.

"Perhaps next year's celebration shall be less chaotic, although we must reach the end of this year's Christmastime first. Can you even recall the day?"

"I believe it is the early hours of the seventh day. 'Tis a shame that this time of merriment is spent in a prison. But so long as we are behind these bars then the murderer cannot reach us. Unless it is you that be the butcher of Bedfordshire!"

"Wait, that would all make sense," Thomasin begins while fixing her posture, "with the others now accusing us, the murderer could act in a similar state of mind. As long as we are in prison everyone else may be safe. Ambrose supported placing us here, so maybe this is his way to hide if he is the murderer. He has taken quite an interest in our past. It could even be Pastor Noah or any of those people in this village. The list is endless. I was quite certain that it was Abigail and Rachel until last night. Whoever it shall be is quite intelligent, drawing the focus to the back of the meetinghouse and then striking in the front."

"That is all true, no action was taken during our days of peace either. Then once everyone is together, it happens again. Maybe they will lose control and strike while we are locked in this prison. Then everyone will see that it is not you, me, or Barnabas," I explain.

"There is nothing else we can do. So long as we are safe, that is all that matters for now. But we have endless time to make assumptions and solve the riddle in this cell. Perhaps our best option is to get some rest," Thomasin suggests.

I nod, agreeing that we have gone far too long without sleep as I begin to adjust our makeshift bed on the floor. No words are needed as we go through the same motions of preparing to rest. Though Ambrose provided us quilts for comfort, food, and resources so we will not lose our lives to the cold or starvation.

Once again, we find ourselves bound together on the floor of a prison cell, yet I cannot help but to find comfort in our situation. This is familiar and nearly brings me to a euphoric state. 'Tis odd that I am more relaxed on this cold floor than in the comfort of Henry and I's chamber. Rather than struggling to quiet the chaos in my mind, everything goes silent. Neither panic nor guilt torment me and within moments I begin drifting off peacefully.

Thomasin's sudden movements awaken me in a state of confusion. My instincts take over and I jump to my feet, panicked that today is the day that Reverend Thomas shall execute us.

"My apologies, Emelie. For I tried my hardest not to disturb you," Thomasin says, sitting in the corner and facing the wall. After a few moments I gather myself, realizing that I am no longer a prisoner in Warren Hollow. I let out a long exhale and struggle to calm my shaking body. Nervously I pace back and forth in an attempt to dismiss the fear.

You are not in Warren Hollow.

"I meant not to scare you, but I feel a bout of sickness coming,' Thomasin explains as she leans forward. Quickly I join her on the floor as my panic subsides. I sit by Thomasin and place my arm around her for comfort as she begins to vomit. It seems that her sickness has returned, or never fully left.

"If we are to be stuck in this cell together then I may contract this illness that plagues you. But I want it not," I state in a playful manner.

Making light of the situation is also a desperate attempt for me to hide the struggle I faced moments ago. Thomasin continues to vomit, unable to acknowledge my words or reply. As we sit together in silence, a wave of nerves overcomes my body at the realization that this is the perfect moment for honesty. A situation in which Thomasin and I are finally alone so that I can disclose the truth. My mind is still racing, and Thomasin is likely not in the mood to hear of my deceit, though I prepare to speak the truth in full before this anxiety causes hesitation.

"While we sit here in this cell, I fear there is something you must know. Back in Warren Hollow—"

"Actually, Emelie," Thomasin interrupts my words and catches me by surprise, "there is something I must share. You likely have suspicions and deserve to know the cause of my illness. I suspected such an occurrence long before that physician, Timothy, conducted his evaluation."

"What plagues thee?" I ask, trying to subtly calm myself from the explanation I was about to deliver.

Thomasin adjusts her posture and slides closer, removing the various quilts between us and her coat. Taking a deep breath, she pulls my hand into hers and gently guides it to her stomach. At first I am confused, and then Thomasin smiles as my jaw nearly drops to the floor.

"You are with child?" I ask in nothing more than a pathetic whisper.

"Aye," she replies tearfully and joyously, "and will be unable to hide it much longer. I wish to keep such a secret until these Christmastime horrors are over. For I want there to be no worry of my situation."

This circumstance was completely unexpected. I never thought of her condition to be that of bearing a child. Sensitivities from our travels and acclimating to this land led all of us to believe that a common sickness was to blame.

"Does Samuel know?" I ask.

"He does not. You are the first, but I will tell him and everyone else once this has all come to pass. It was my plan to share on the final day of Christmas, and I still want to do so," Thomasin replies.

"I shall not say a word. Truly I cannot believe this, Thomasin! Perhaps it be one of those Christmastime miracles that Nicholas speaks of," I revel, pulling her in for a joyous embrace.

"The physician gave me methods of temporary relief, but I will soon require regular visits into the village for proper care. And come summer, I shall bring forth a child into this world."

Her demeanor shows signs of happiness but also fear, and reasonably so. Bedfordshire will be a fine place to raise a child, as we have a wonderful home and a caring family. Though we are not far removed from childhood ourselves so I would share a similar concern in her position.

We sit joyfully in conversation for what feels like hours. Discussing our own childhoods and how she will never treat her child as her mother hath done to her. Predicting it to be a boy or girl and whose features it will share. The sun dims on this seventh day of Christmas as we continue our conversation into the late hours of the night. And while I do not tell Thomasin, I fear for her safety until this massacre is resolved. I plan on getting her home and devising an immediate plan of action. If there is no resolution when we leave this prison, then we must stand aside and wait no longer. But as we all understand, this cell is unfortunately the safest place for both of us on this night. Slowly I sink back into the comfort of the hard prison floor. I adjust the quilts and all our supplies to ensure Thomasin's comfort. Our conversation slowly fades until we both try to rest once more.

Through all the chaos and hardship surrounding this crumbling village, I cannot help but find joy in Thomasin's pregnancy. She shall be a wonderful mother, as I expressed many times through our conversation. And Samuel shall be a wonderful father.

We are all unsure of what the future holds in Bedfordshire. For now we are living in the moment, finding our place and putting little thought into the years ahead because we still struggle with what is behind us. Perhaps we shall remain on the farm, or each depart and find our own homes nearby. Henry may desire a farm of his own and Thomasin could want the same for Samuel and their child. And perhaps I will pursue the idea of offering apothecary services to Bedfordshire, or I will assist Henry if he is to stay with Nicholas and Amelia. Regardless of our ambitions, there will not be a future for any of us if this situation continues. I worry for the safety of Henry and the others on the outside, as most people assume Barnabas to be the culprit. They likely hunt him in the forest while the murderer walks through Bedfordshire without a care. We made it clear to Ambrose and the others that we will not spend much time in this prison because we are useful on the outside.

"Emelie, art thou still awake?" Thomasin asks.

"Aye," I whisper.

"What was it that you wanted to tell me earlier? Something about back in The Hollow?" Thomasin replies, bringing the thought back into my mind that escaped the moment she spoke of her pregnancy.

"Perhaps we should get some rest, there will be plenty of time to discuss tomorrow," I reply nervously, now unprepared to speak the truth.

"Emelie, I know there is something you have been wanting to tell me for quite some time. I can sense it when we are together. You were never good at keeping secrets."

I let out a long exhale and prepare to give Thomasin the truth. She lays behind me and we both face the wall. Perhaps it will be easier to discuss without looking directly at her, so I never adjust my position.

"Back in The Hollow, I be afraid that there was more to our imprisonment than witchcraft. In fact, witchcraft was never the issue. Thomas and Rose shared a secret." I take a moment before continuing, but Thomasin never interrupts. "They concealed clandestine interaction, and eventually, Rose carried Thomas's child. But she became wise to his viciousness and planned to expose their truth. Thomas knew this would ruin his reputation, so he used witchcraft to condemn her. And eventually he needed to follow through when we were caught in the forest." I take a deep breath and give another moment for Thomasin to ask questions, but she never speaks a word. "Our torture and accusations held no truth, and it was all to keep Thomas's secrets buried. He knew there be not a witch in Warren Hollow."

We lay in silence, aside from the rigorous beating of my heart. My eyes shift up and down the dark wall, desperate for an escape or any reaction from Thomasin. Instead, she remains silent, never yelling out or asking any questions. Of all outcomes, this was not the reaction I expected.

"Say something," I command through a panicked whisper. Thomasin has yet to respond, although I feel her tighten her embrace from behind and pull me closer.

"I know, Emelie. I have known for quite some time."

Her words leave me stunned.

"You knew this? Did Samuel or Henry tell you?"

"They did not," Thomasin replies as she slightly rises from the ground. "I watched you leave that journal with Robert at our departure. His reaction told me that there was more to our situation. But I chose to ignore it and wondered from time to time on our journey what you discovered. Then eventually I read through some of the writings you brought with us not long after our arrival. I suspected my pregnancy and thought Rose might have some remedies for my struggles, but instead found this truth."

"You were aware this entire time?" I ask aloud once more, feeling tremendous guilt for my secrecy.

"Why did you keep this from me, Emelie?" Thomasin whispers.

"I acted out of fear. At first I was frightened but wanted to tell each of you. After all that we endured, I told myself that this truth would send you back home. Or worse, that it would lead you to believe that our torture was for nothing, and that Rose or John's death were for nothing. It became difficult to share through the summer and nearly impossible upon our arrival to Bedfordshire. But such justification was a lie, to you and to myself," I admit, turning to face Thomasin tearfully. "Honestly, I was selfish. I did not want this revelation to make you, Henry, or Samuel leave my side. I could not go back there. For that place took too much from me." Pathetically I glance down to my makeshift hand. "And I could not, or would not, allow myself to survive on my own. The three of you are all that I have left and the fear of losing my friends made me act selfishly. Especially you, I could not move forward without you in my life. So, I hid these details and never imagined how deeply it would haunt me. Truly, I am sorry."

It would be foolish to think that Thomasin, Henry, or Samuel would not resent me for my selfishness. I told myself it was the best option for our safety and kept this secret out of my own cowardice. And while Thomasin's reaction is uncertain, I feel a massive wave of relief. No longer will this secret cause me intolerable guilt. Though I may lose my closest friend, she deserved to know the truth and act on her own will. To realize her knowledge from the very beginning brings me shame. For keeping such a truth from my dearest friends, I feel that I have matched Reverend Thomas in his cruelty.

"There is nothing to forgive, Emelie. You saved us," Thomasin states, pulling me closer. "After losing your brother and your faith, you spent months ensuring our survival and getting us to this wonderful place. You stopped Thomas and saved my life. Because of you, we are all free and order is likely restored back home. Giving Robert that journal certainly made a difference, for Gregory would have guaranteed it. And you even lost a hand. To this day, I am uncertain of how you survived after Thomas's attack in the prison. I thought you were dead on the floor. Seeing you in such a state frightened me and still leaves me unwell. It was as if you rose from the dead to keep us going. That is when my faith was restored, and it was all because of you. We found a home and soon I will have a child. You need not carry this guilt any longer."

Thomasin embraces me as I cry in her arms. Her gratitude is something I would have never expected, and I feel the chains of Warren Hollow beginning to break. The truth has been revealed and no longer do I need to carry such guilt and fear. Everyone is still here and none of them resent me for my actions. Henry and Samuel even used my confession as an opportunity to do the same. I shall never see the inside of Warren Hollow again.

No further words are exchanged as we lay together in our cell. It feels as though John and Rose are watching over me at this moment of happiness, relief, and rebirth. I shall let go of our torture and live the life we fought so desperately for.

Although not ideal, our current situation restored some level of balance to my life. A strange comfort has taken me since our arrival to this cell, and it seems as though I needed such conditions to reach a breakthrough. No more secrets are concealed, and yet, all my friends are still by my side. Although shame for keeping the truth from Henry, Samuel, and Thomasin when there was no need is something I will force upon myself for quite some time.

And just as we begin drifting off to sleep once more, a noise down the hall causes both Thomasin and I to rise from the ground. A lantern illuminates the walls, so we rush to the bars of the cell.

"Who is there?" I shout.

"I apologize for the interruption at this hour," a man replies, "but we got him!"

The voice is that of Edward, a guard I recognize from the meetinghouse. He often patrols the outside during service and was one of our many escorts back to the farm. Edward has come to Nicholas's aid in recent days, and we are grateful for his efforts. We gasp as Edward moves into sight, dragging none other than Barnabas down the hall. They move past our cell and continue down the hall until Edward reaches their destination. Barnabas is placed a few cells down the hall and across from us.

"Do not pay him any mind. And he knows better than to even raise his gaze in thy direction. This fool speaks of nonsense and he hath gone mad. Ambrose gave me the order to release you both from this cell and take you home," Edward explains as he passes by.

"We would rather stay here, just through the night. 'Tis late and we wish not to make the journey back home at this hour," I reply. Thomasin nods to my words, recognizing a critical opportunity that has fallen in place. This may be our only chance to talk with Barnabas and discover the deeper truth to what is happening. Edward throws Barnabas into the cell and checks the lock multiple times before returning.

"If you are certain, then I shall inform Ambrose of your request. Do let me know when you wish to leave. I will be standing guard at Barnabas's cell through the night," Edward says with a nod as he makes his way back down the hall.

I peer through the bars to Barnabas's cell before returning to our mattress. We must take any opportunity to speak with him, though it will be difficult with Edward standing guard. The proper time will not arise through the night, so the only option is to once again try and rest. Carefully we lay back down, pretending that plans are not already in motion.

"Edward will eventually leave, and that is when we must speak with Barnabas. We need to know how he escaped the meetinghouse or where he has been," I whisper to Thomasin.

'Tis a shame that three innocent members of Bedfordshire sit in prison while the true murderer roams free. They likely sleep soundly in their home, plotting another attack without any suspicions surrounding them. Time is drawing thin if we wish to prevent another assault. But this reign shall soon come to an end, and we have been granted an incredible advantage. We will not leave this prison until we have answers. By sundown tomorrow, we may single handedly bring this nightmare to an end.

XVIII

Face to Face with Evil

Sunlight shines through the barred window and warms my skin. 'Tis a strange feeling to rest so soundly in a prison cell. We are comfortable and anticipating a day of progress. A morning that brought sunshine was often a determining factor in life and death back in The Hollow's prison. We lost many friends on those days where the sky was gray and the sun failed to rise.

Thomasin and I revive from our slumber of interruptions. I remain hopeful that Barnabas will cooperate, as we may be the only ones capable of saving his miserable existence. Though it is difficult to look past the progress made within our own cell. Thomasin entrusted me with the secret of her pregnancy, and I finally revealed the truth of our conviction. While still regretting my actions, I am glad that I found the courage to speak the truth to her. There are no more secrets or struggles that we must face alone. With all that is going on, it is critical to remain honest.

"Of what do you believe this eighth Christmas day shall bring?" Thomasin asks sarcastically. "I suspect a day of murder, accusation, witchcraft, and worst of all, more cranberry pie."

"That is likely," I reply while rising to stretch. "But we have a chance to solve this, Thomasin. Surely Barnabas can provide some useful information."

"Aye. While I enjoyed a night of reliving our capture, I am ready to depart from this place as soon as possible. If Edward does not leave then we must find a way to make him do so," Thomasin explains.

I peek through the cell and see Edward still standing guard down the hall.

"Edward, can we please speak with you?" I call out.

Thomasin is correct that there is no more time to waste. If we can speak with Barnabas and leave this cell, then we have an entire day ahead of us to make progress. Edward gathers himself after a night standing guard and moves in our direction.

"A good morning to you both, and apologies for the interruption in the night," Edward calls out as he approaches. "Art thou ready to leave this place?"

"Actually, I wanted to ask a few questions if you do not mind," I reply.

"Of course not, child. What troubles you?"

"Well," I begin, acting helpless to show no signs of our plan, "we are frightened to return to the outside. What happened out there yesterday? Do they still wish to harm us?"

"We want not to die!" Thomasin adds to emphasize our fear.

"There be no need to worry. Yesterday brought no excitement and families remained in their homes until Barnabas was found in the forest. Everyone understands that you both played no role in these murders. None of the attention is in your direction anymore. The terror has come to an end so we shall get you back to the farm, which is currently under restoration as we speak. Ambrose will personally take you there," Edward explains.

I exaggerate signs of relief. "If that is true, then could you send for him now?"

"Certainly. I believe there are two guards just beyond this hallway, so if you are ready then I can instruct them to bring Ambrose straight to thy cell."

"Thank thee, Edward," Thomasin adds.

Edward smiles and makes his way back to Barnabas. We will use the opportunity to question him when Edward leaves. Though our time will be short so we must be concise and hope for cooperation.

"What will we ask him, Emelie?" Thomasin whispers.

"We must know who freed him from the meetinghouse and where he has been these past few days. Then how he ended up in the tavern," I explain quietly.

Surely Barnabas's words could help us to make sense of this situation. We know he is not the murderer so we can potentially solve this and inform everyone else. We watch as Edward checks the lock and returns to us.

"I will soon return," Edward ensures as he passes. Quickly he makes his way down the hall and out of sight, indicating that we have little time to question Barnabas.

"Barnabas!" I yell. "We must speak with you!"

"If you wish to make it out of this prison alive, then surely you will answer us!" Thomasin adds.

A few moments of silence pass until we hear movement from Barnabas's cell. Our words have likely caught his attention so now we eagerly await his reply.

"I do not know you, and I do not wish to. Leave me to spend my last living moments in peace!" Barnabas replies angrily.

"We know you are innocent!" I shout back, matching his intensity. My words bring about further silence from his cell, but it seems that our conversation has drawn to a close as the prison doors open once again. Edward wasted no time with his absence.

"My apologies, but the others are nowhere to be found. They are likely assisting with your farm or somewhere nearby. We can wait for their return, or I can quickly go find them if you would like," Edward explains.

"Yes, please do find them and send for Ambrose. We wish not to remain in this cell any longer," I plead.

"Very well, are you certain that you feel safe with a brief absence?"

"That man has spoken not a word to us, and we really wish to leave this place," I reply in a pathetic tone.

Edward falls for my act once more. He checks the lock to our cell before doing the same to Barnabas's cell. "I shall be gone no more than a few minutes at most!" Edward shouts as he moves hastily.

The doors close behind him and our conversation shall continue. I offer Thomasin a subtle smile to acknowledge our skill in manipulation and dramatics. It does not feel pleasant to lie and pretend with Edward, though it must be done for the greater good. We earned ourselves a few moments alone with

Barnabas and surely this opportunity will not be possible after we exit the prison.

"Barnabas, we do not have much time. So if you will, please answer what we ask of you," I call out.

He is waiting for my words, as our claim of his innocence caught his attention. "And why do you think of me as innocent?" Barnabas asks, curious and less aggressive.

"While you are a vile member in this community, we know you are nothing more than a sorry drunk. This chaos is far too calculated for someone of your standards," I shout, holding back no insults.

"I remember thee. From outside of Giles's home, or I think that was you," Barnabas replies with poor memory. "Did he send you to make a mockery of me in my final moments?"

"Giles is dead, as I am sure you heard. But we cannot waste any more time. We need to know of your whereabouts. Why were you hiding for all those days?"

Barnabas offers a laugh at my remarks, perhaps amused at Giles's death or my questioning.

"I moved from one prison to the next. After that morning, I spent the day at the tavern with an ache in my head thanks to you. And once I made it home that night, I was attacked. Attacked in my own home! When I awakened, I could not see. I was chained at the wrists and ankles, unable to move with a cloth on my face."

"Who did this to you?"

"Do you think I would be in this prison if I knew? I would have told those pathetic guards, though they are probably behind this. They all wish for me to die, but I think it was

Solomon. He followed me from the tavern and took me captive in my own home," Barnabas claims.

Given what we already know, this explanation would make little sense. Many members of Bedfordshire dislike Barnabas and wish death upon him. Solomon likely holds the utmost hatred for Barnabas, constantly dealing with his drunken behavior and tossing him from the tavern. But after gathering a mob to find Barnabas, Solomon would not assist with his escape from the meetinghouse. He was also in view from the moment they returned that night.

"So, you were held captive?" I continue questioning.

"Aye! With little food and not the slightest of rum, or even beer. It drove me mad. The attacker never spoke to me, even when I begged for a meal. Each time they returned, the door slammed so viciously that it ached my pounding head. Eventually I heard commotion on the outside, but I was bound and had a cloth nearly shoved down my throat so I could not call for help."

"And how did you escape such hell?" Thomasin asks.

Barnabas laughs. "Escape? There was no need! He went behind me and started to choke me with a rope. He pulled hard enough that I felt my throat crushing and my head nearly falling off. I thought that was the end of my time in this god-forsaken life of misery. But then I awakened just behind the tavern. So I rose from the ground and broke a window to get inside, caring only for a drink after days of torture. I thought it a proper way to repay Solomon after he tortured me. He can torture me, but I shall never stay away!"

This explanation is quite strange. Barnabas was allegedly held captive for days in a place that nobody thought to search.

And then he is suddenly freed outside of the tavern, right in the middle of the village without anyone noticing. Before he was located, any of our potential suspects were all in eyesight. Every last one of them was with us in the meetinghouse. Even those wicked sisters were near the entrance when Barnabas made his escape.

"And in the meetinghouse, how did you escape once again?" Thomasin asks, remembering a critical component of our questioning.

"My chains were loose, and the window was smashed forcefully from the outside. I saw it happen with my own eyes, so I pulled free and climbed right out. They were to execute me moments later, just as they will now before the day's end. There be no reason to fight it," Barnabas remarks, moving away from the bars and maneuvering back to his bed.

It seems that Barnabas feels defeated from the torture and is submitting to whatever fate awaits him. He cares little for our questioning or intentions and finds bliss in this confinement as well. There are no onlookers to harass him and nothing to interrupt his rest. Everyone on the outside despised Barnabas long before these Christmastime misfortunes so this is but a regular day in his eyes. But if I learned anything from The Hollow, it is that past status and regard certainly influence conviction during these troubling times. And with Barnabas being the most hated man in Bedfordshire, he practically asked to be the prime suspect. While he is innocent in this aspect, his reputation has been earned and cannot be disputed. But part of me wishes to find redemption for Barnabas and save his life.

If he is put to death, then the outcome will be further chaos. The murderer will likely strike again, or worse, they may use this opportunity to end their massacre. Everyone would simply return to the festivities, never uncovering who was actually behind this madness. Then the murderer would wait until the spring or autumn to articulately devise a plan, killing Nicholas or Ambrose when least expected.

"No, I won't allow it," I pronounce aloud, nearly a whisper meant only to myself. Thomasin turns and shares my disdain, not knowing my true worries but likely formulating her own.

"I don't think Barnabas will be of any more use to us. But Emelie, we uncovered critical information. We must find his cage; a shed, a hunter's cabin, an attic, or another makeshift prison. Truly somebody in this village knows more of this and we can act immediately once we return to the farm," Thomasin replies.

While we did not receive enough information to make our own accusations, Barnabas was still helpful in his reluctance. Someone is on the verge of getting away with pure wickedness and Barnabas shall die to keep the secrets buried. Or we could also be drastically incorrect. Barnabas's arrest could be another piece of this malevolent puzzle that the murderer is using to prevail. Everyone will return to Christmas festivities with Barnabas in prison and this will lead to the next attack. The meetinghouse could be locked and set ablaze, the food could be poisoned, or the murderer could infiltrate our homes while we rest.

Another lesson I learned from our friend, Reverend Thomas, is to always remain one step ahead. If this murder is close to us, like Ambrose or Timothy, then they know of our deeper thoughts. Ambrose could have placed us in prison to plan his next move, using Barnabas as a scapegoat and even letting us die if needed. While Ambrose is a trustworthy and kind man, I do not put such actions past any of these individuals.

My contemplation is interrupted by Edward as he makes his return. He enters the hallway and hastens his speed back to our cell.

"My apologies," he begins, nearly out of breath, "it seems that the others were called elsewhere. I had to cross through the village and request Ambrose myself. He is finishing up at your farm but will join us shortly. Your uncle said that he would also accompany you back home."

"Thank thee, Edward, you have been very kind," Thomasin says.

Edward smiles and makes his way to Barnabas's cell. He stares inside without speaking a word, which indicates that Barnabas has likely fallen asleep after our encounter. Carefully Edward checks the lock and repositions himself to stand guard.

"Though it was with amusement to reminisce, I hope to never see the inside of a prison for the rest of my days," Thomasin expresses.

"Agreed," I assert with a laugh, "though I found that our time was well spent."

"Aye," she replies as she puts her arm around me, "we face even more confusion with this butcher and now each of us are admitted liars. Can we even trust each other?"

"Just as I told Reverend Thomas, 'tis you behind all this madness. Do you plan to kill me and keep this secret of yours?"

"If need be," she claims while trying to wrap her hands around my throat. We laugh and wrestle with each other for a few moments until a commotion in the hallway catches our attention. It seems that Ambrose arrived with our escort, so we gather our belongings and prepare to leave the cell. I bend over to fold our many quilts and retrieve my coat.

"Who goes there?" Edward calls out.

His words bring halt to my actions. Thomasin and I look at each other, slowly turning to see what is happening.

"Art thou lost? This area is restricted," Edward states, more aggressively in his tone.

"Emelie?" Thomasin whispers. I signal to silence her words as we cautiously make our way to the bars of the cell.

"Do not take another step!" Edward yells. He clearly does not like the sight of who approaches and begins struggling with his musket. Edward was unprepared for any disruption in the prison and we begin to panic.

"Stay away from the bars, children!" Edward yells. We ignore his words, peering down the hall to see who is approaching. I am taken aback as I gaze through the bars. Someone is rushing down the hall towards Edward.

"Would you shut thy mouth! I intend to get some rest before meeting my death!" Barnabas yells, unaware of what is unraveling.

This individual passes by our cell and I am stunned by their appearance. They wear a hooded outfit; solid black to conceal all features. I have never seen anything like it in my life. It resembles a cassock, but black from hood to boots. I notice a large blade in their hand behind their back as they pass by.

"Edward, he is armed!" I yell.

Nervously Edward fidgets with his musket but is unable to successfully load it in time. The hooded individual rushes forward and stuns Edward by pushing the musket into his face. They struggle for a few moments, but Edward was unprepared and unable to properly defend himself. Barnabas shouts in confusion from the cell while Thomasin and I watch in horror. I try forcing our cell open, but this lock is impenetrable without the key. The assailant swings the knife, and Edward blocks the strike with his musket, gaining an advantage by landing a devastating blow. Edward knocks the assailant face-first to the ground. He mounts the attacker in an attempt to subdue them. It appears that Edward has prevailed, until he fails to recognize the attacker reaching for their blade.

"The knife, Edward!" Thomasin shouts to warn him.

The attacker reaches the handle of the blade and builds a firm grip while Edward tries to restrain him. Edward attempts to block the coming attack, but the blade strikes his hand and cuts straight through the skin. He falls on his side and tries to slow the bleeding from his wound. Slowly the attacker rises to his feet, struggling through the damage and wishing to finish this assault. Before anyone can react, the blade is plunged directly into Edwards stomach. Edward shouts in agony as the attacker removes the blade, striking him again, and again, and again. I fight the urge to cover my ears and escape from the brutal sound of this murder. Briefly I look away to Thomasin as we both prepare for battle. The murderer stands before us on the other side of our cell, and perhaps our time has come.

Edward lies motionless on the floor of the prison, bleeding profusely and drawing minimal breath. The attacker searches Edward's coat to retrieve the cell keys and pulls the knife from his body.

"Emelie," Thomasin whispers, "now would be the time to find another shard of ice."

I scan our cell but there are absolutely no objects that could be used in our defense. We are helpless against this attacker, but we will fight until the end. Edward could have easily won this battle if he was prepared. This is not a towering demon or the irrational belief of Griffin Osmund. There be no sorcery or witchcraft involved. Rather, this murder is of normal stature and would likely be of little danger if unarmed. The fact that the monster terrorizing Bedfordshire is a normal individual draws more fear than I care to admit.

It seems that we are not the attacker's primary concern at the moment. Barnabas stares from the cell in complete shock. He is unsure if this is to be his savior or his bringer of death.

"What do you want with me? Is that you, Solomon?" Barnabas asks. "It be you that kept me in that place and then freed me from the meetinghouse. And now you have come to free me again?"

The attacker offers no reply but raises the key to the lock of the cell. We all watch anxiously as he turns the key until the lock releases.

"Do not trust him, Barnabas!" I yell nervously.

Barnabas is not thinking rationally. This person kept him caged like an animal while enacting a murderous rampage in Barnabas's name. They did not come to this prison just to murder a guard. The cell slowly opens until there is no protection between Barnabas and this attacker. Thomasin and I are frozen in place, watching as Barnabas begins to trust this hooded figure. And it is true that Barnabas is a large man who could easily overpower the attacker if he chose to do so. But all hope of Barnabas's redemption is fleeting as he steps forward from the cell. He stares at the shrouded face of the attacker before advancing down the hall. Each step pulls further on my anxiety and Barnabas is now a few steps removed from our cell. This attacker follows closely behind, matching Barnabas's steps as they maneuver through the hall.

"Please, Barnabas. You can end this now. Save us all," I whisper as he comes into range. He turns his head slightly at my words but offers no reaction. This could be Barnabas's opportunity to save Bedfordshire and put an end to this murderer's reign.

Rather than stopping, he slowly continues his steps forward. Barnabas is almost out of sight, so the attacker passes directly by our cell. This person is even more benign in intimidation than my initial observation revealed. They give no attention to our presence. After all that we endured in Warren Hollow, a faceless shadow is nothing more than a child before me. While their murders are gruesome and methodical, I sense all of this to be for a dramatic spectacle.

Suddenly Barnabas stops in his tracks. He is no longer moving forward and comes to a complete standstill.

"Of what will come of me once we leave this place?" Barnabas asks nervously. He never turns, but adjusts his gaze so that he is nearly peering back over his shoulder to his guide. There is no reply from the other side, his question is met with complete silence.

"I will not go back to that place!" Barnabas yells.

After weighing the outcomes of this situation, perhaps my words clouded Barnabas's mind. In a heroic manner, Barnabas uses all his strength to turn and swing at the attacker. He can be the hero who saves us and finally earns respect within the community. Though acting with good intentions, Barnabas's change of heart is to no avail. His offensive was slow and uncalculated, and I fear that even old Phillip would have sensed the building offensive. The murderer ducks under Barnabas's arm as he swings, stabbing the knife directly into his rib cage. Barnabas falls to the ground with the knife stuck deep in his side. He grunts and struggles in pain while the attacker towers over him.

Slowly the assassin kneels down, staring into Barnabas's eyes as he rips the blade from his body. With one final gasp, Barnabas succumbs to his injuries while the murderer wipes the blood from the blade on his clothing as a final sign of disrespect.

Thomasin tightens her grip on my arm at the realization that it is now just us and the hooded assassin. This is also recognized on the other side as they turn to face us for the first time. Rather than cowering in fear, I stand my ground and offer no emotion. One step at a time they make their way to our cell, sliding the blade across the bars and taunting us from the outside to induce fear. And as history repeats itself, I stand face to face with evil, once again. I stare back intently, showing no signs of fear. In fact, I simply feel nothing.

"So, it be you that terrorizes Bedfordshire?" I ask, already knowing the answer. No response is expected so I continue my gaze into the darkness behind their hood. I recognize that the attacker is taller than I am, but slender in their build. Surely this is not farmhand or a blacksmith. While these details shall serve me well, this is the stature that many men in Bedfordshire share, so it is not a groundbreaking revelation. Although it could help to narrow our search if we survive this encounter. To Thomasin's surprise, and admittedly my own, I offer a subtle laugh in the face of this attacker.

"You are pathetic," I claim boldly. The attacker is caught off guard, losing their composure and becoming enraged. They slam the knife into the bars to cause panic, but still, I am unshaken. I do notice, however, that the blade is strikingly similar to Reverend Thomas's. It could be mistaken for the same blade that came with us on our travels if it was not tucked away in my chamber on the farm.

Is that you, Reverend Thomas? Risen from the grave so I can send you back?

Though the blade surprises me, I still do not back down. The attacker raises their hand with the key and shoves it into the lock of our cell. We brace for an attack, but they do not proceed. As I suspected, this is another act of intimidation. Barnabas was but a loose end that needed to be severed, and drawing fear from Thomasin and I is a bonus. But the intimidation is failing and this is recognized. Once again their hand grips the key, preparing to turn the lock and open our cell.

"If you come into this cell, you will die," I declare sternly. Thomasin matches my intensity, and we both stand ready for battle. Perhaps this attacker does not like their odds, or they aim to strike in another instance. Edward inflicted noticeable damage so they could also be in immense pain. We stand trapped in a face-off until the murderer backs away from the cell, key still in lock, and abruptly escapes down the hall.

We hear Ambrose and our escort coming through the other side as the assailant rounds the corner. Immediately they notice that something transpired and begin rushing to our aid. Footsteps echo through the prison in our direction. I turn to Thomasin who appears ready to faint. She lowers her guard, holding her stomach and struggling to catch her breath. Thomasin stares back at me and I am unable to determine if she is impressed, frightened, or believes that I have truly gone mad.

"How did you do that, Emelie?" She asks.

It was likely unwise to taunt this butcher, though I simply felt no fear. We imagined a wicked beast roaming the outskirts of the village, mutilating people and cutting out their tongues. For a moment we event contemplated the existence of real witches or the legend of Griffin Osmund. But this hooded being is but a minor Christmastime nuisance; a coward, nothing more than a pathetic harlot who finds thrill in torment.

"Well," I turn to Thomasin and stare directly into her eyes, "I faced the Devil before, and I won."

XIX

Homecoming

Though the world may very well be collapsing around us, Thomasin and I find temporary relief in returning to the farm. Our previous exit from a prison was followed by months of hiding in the forest and the eventual journey that led us here. But not this time. We are not going anywhere and shall defend our home to the best of our ability. The description of this masked assailant has spread through Bedfordshire overnight like a plague. Officials, merchants, and even children are fully aware of this hooded attacker. Many bring forth their own so-called sightings and encounters, though I believe it to be pure paranoia. And while I swore upon honesty, Thomasin agrees that some details of our encounter are best kept unspoken. We told most of the truth, but failed to mention the damage inflicted by Edward. It be likely that this assassin is facing injury after their nearly failed attack. This knowledge gives us an advantage and will allow us to potentially determine the attacker. Our names have also been cleared so all eyes fell from us as quickly as they came.

  I think of all the wonderful Christmastime celebrations that were destroyed by this butcher. Those first few days were wonderful, as we grew closer with Nicholas and Amelia and prepared for endless days of merriment. Today is the ninth day of Christmas and we would likely be traveling to the meetinghouse for yet another magical celebration. The food, decorations, and pleasantries fill my mind of what could have been. Instead, Bedfordshire was turned into a battleground. Respected and vital members of the community were viciously executed, along with raging fires, vandalism, slaughtering of animals, accusations, and total hysteria. A mob formed to convict an innocent man while the true murderer roamed free and continued their reign of terror. Barnabas is dead, and the village is in shambles.

Our current situation resembles the time in Warren Hollow before we faced imprisonment. Families are accusing each other of being the murderer and everyone is instructed to remain at home while constant patrols fill the paths and outskirts of the village. Whispers of dark magic and witchcraft are spreading because this assassin is believed to be wielding divine power. But we saw the genuine truth before our eyes and know this to be highly inaccurate. The killer is nothing more than a normal individual, perhaps even a respected member in the community. All efforts by officials to resolve this issue failed, so I doubt that an identity will be uncovered today. And we are certain that the mayhem is far from over after the display in the prison.

Thomasin and I informed Henry and Samuel of our findings, though we do not wish to trouble Nicholas and Amelia with more outlandish claims. Nicholas is struggling much more so than he already was prior to our temporary conviction. He has gone days without rest and works tirelessly alongside Ambrose and the others to find resolution. Perhaps he is also afraid, as it was quite evident that the target is still set on Nicholas. Clara and

Edward were merely caught in the midst of a bigger affair. So as a precaution, many village officials assisted in barricading the farm upon our return. All accessible windows and doors remain guarded at all hours of the day. Amelia attempts to spread joy through the home, though I sense her own faltering faith. It brings me immense sadness to see such a loving family and community struggle through this travesty. They had a happy life on this farm, and I find guilt in knowing that our arrival could have triggered these events.

 My suspicions of our ties to this grow stronger with each passing moment. It was all but confirmed after our encounter in the prison. Maybe this killer wishes to torment us as a means to weaken Nicholas. Or maybe all that happened is directly because of our presence. I cannot shake the resemblance of the blade that took both Edward and Nicholas's life. It crossed my mind that this hooded figure could be the ghost of Reverend Thomas. Given the methods of murder, incredible stealth, and weapon of choice, this idea is no less valid than the other accusations shared. Locating the knife was admittedly my first instinct when we arrived back at the farm.

 And to heighten the intensity, the four of us have been unsuccessful in our efforts. I am certain that the knife was hidden away with my journals and writings upon our arrival. Henry recalls using it without my knowledge while assisting Nicholas in the barn shortly after All Hallows Eve. While this could be the truth, I believe he may have hidden the blade after one of my nightly terrors. And now that some time has passed, he likely forgets its whereabouts. Samuel and Thomasin claim they have not seen a glimpse of the blade since back at Rose's home. And while I may be paranoid, I hold firmly that the weapon was nearly identical to that of Reverend Thomas. This knife's appearance is burned into my mind after what it was used for. Surely a weapon of such virtuosity could have made those precise cuts and easily severed the tongues from the victims if it removed my hand with ease.

"Do you suspect someone wandered into our chamber and lifted the blade from its hiding place?" Henry asks. While this does sound ridiculous, I know better than to view anything with certainty. This killer came and vandalized the farm so we cannot assume that they did not take further action.

"Unless we locate that god-forsaken blade, we will not know for certain. When the opportunity arises, you must go and search the barn," I instruct.

Doing so will be easier said than done. At a glance, a small militia guards our doors from the outside. We are prisoners in our home, though it does bring some sense of security. It may very well take sorcery to infiltrate the fortress that has become of our farm.

That is until one of the guards reveals themselves as the murderer and slaughters us all.

Between our extensive questioning from Ambrose and smothering of food and treats from Amelia, the four of us tirelessly scour every bit of this home to find the blade. Our next move is unknown if the blade is found. But if it is not found, our suspicions of ties to this matter are confirmed. Of all the weapons of choice to enact a massacre, there must be a connection to the singular weapon that came with us from The Hollow.

I sit near the hearth to take a moment's rest and ponder on where else we can search, and more importantly, who would have stolen this weapon. Nicholas owns countless muskets, tomahawks, and much deadlier farm tools than a singular knife. Truly I wish for it to be found or the hooded killer to be found for that matter, so that all of this can be put to rest. Though we will likely not be that fortunate and instincts tell me that our outlandish suspicions are true. While I care not to admit, I find myself to be fully invested in this mystery with high spirits. Uncovering the identity of the butcher and putting an end to the chaos has eliminated much of my personal torture and grief. This is now my purpose and devising a way to save Bedfordshire brings me rejuvenation. Slowly I am pulling that brave and confident leader back to the surface, and I cannot deny my love for such a feeling.

Who would have known about this knife and why do they wield it? Did someone follow you from The Hollow? Why would any of this be about you? Why, why, why?

As I lose myself in thought, Nicholas enters the room before I can solve the mystery. He appears hesitant but still the caring and thoughtful individual that welcomed us all those months ago.

"How are the two of you handling things?" Nicholas asks.

"We are pleased to be back home," Thomasin replies.

Nicholas forces a smile at her words, likely feeling guilt or responsibility for what we endured in the prison. "I deeply apologize for what the two of you seen. Perhaps if we were but a moment sooner Edward and Barnabas would still be alive."

"This killer would have found another way to carry out their plan. They wait for the right moment and strike when victims are vulnerable. If it was not in the prison then surely it would have been when Edward left for patrol or while Barnabas was escorted for his trial," I express. And while it is unfortunate, this is an undeniable truth. This murderer acts precisely and with the skill of a seasoned assassin. They blend into the crowd and murder swiftly at the perfect moments because nobody knows who they are.

"Have you spoken to the sisters after Clara's death?" I ask curiously.

"Aye. They spend their days in the meetinghouse. Surely we will find some arrangement for them after this all comes to an end," Nicholas explains.

"I see," I begin as I rise, anxiously fidgeting with the logs in the hearth. Once again, the sisters were accounted for and even Ambrose was on the other side of the village. "It be a shame that Clara was caught in the crossfire. She did not deserve such a fate."

Nicholas nods his head in agreement. While Clara was often a burden and those sisters are strange, Nicholas cares for all the less fortunate members of Bedfordshire. I fear that Clara's death took a toll on Nicholas.

"Why those sisters shouted such accusations is a mystery. They nearly got us killed," Thomasin adds.

"They were frightened. Their grandmother was just murdered, and they were in a panic. The four of you are good friends to Abigail and Rachel, so it be confusion," Nicholas explains.

Though most people would place little attention on their outburst, it does not sit well with any of us. Nicholas claims fear and desperation for their words but I do not believe this as accurate. Abigail and Rachel were fascinated by our past, nearly obsessing over the outlandish ideas of witchcraft and black magic. And Abigail could not resist the urge to act on deeper feelings for me. Somehow, I will confront the sisters about their display in the meetinghouse and apologize for my lack of assistance. If they were not standing before us while Clara was murdered and Barnabas escaped, I would undoubtedly make my own accusation towards them. But with most of the misfortune that unraveled since the beginning of Christmastime, Abigail and Rachel have been in eyesight. Which is also the case for Ambrose, Solomon, or anyone who could remotely connect to the crimes. I fear that focusing on the sisters or Ambrose as our primary suspects could be a waste of valuable time. If we are to uncover the truth, then it will require a revitalized approach.

"Samuel and I scoured the cellar and shall search the barn at our first opportunity," Henry announces while entering the room, unaware of his uncle's presence.

"And what is it that you be searching for, Henry?" Nicholas asks.

Nervously we all remain silent, not wanting to alert Nicholas of our secret plan in motion. I shoot an assertive gaze at Henry, though I cannot blame him for alerting Nicholas. Thomasin and I forced Henry and Samuel to search our home for hours on end.

"Nobody is supposed to leave through those doors. What is it you believe to be in the barn?" Nicholas attempts to maintain his composure but we sense his growing impatience. Amelia is also drawn to the conversation, so I stand anxiously with eyes locked on the dying fire in the hearth.

"Henry, I asked thee to explain yourself," Nicholas demands while taking steps forward.

"Uncle, there is no need for anger. Please, calm yourself and I will explain," Henry replies desperately. Nicholas now stands face to face with Henry, and it feels as though chaos could erupt at any moment. For the first time we are seeing another side of Nicholas. The cheerful and loving man seems to have vanished from this guilty, aggravated, and fearful being before us.

"It was my blade!" I shout, shifting the attention from Henry.

"My father gave me a special blade when I was but a child learning to hunt. This is the only thing I have left to remind me of life back home. And now, I fear that it is missing," I explain while trying my hardest to force tears. The atmosphere begins to lighten as Nicholas calms himself. "All I wanted was to find that blade. It reminds me of my brother, John. Though he was far too young to wield it himself, I was to give it to him as a gift. Perhaps I left it in the barn or lost it on our journey. I miss my brother, and I miss my home!" I shout with dramatic emotion. Nicholas backs away from Henry and rushes to comfort me.

"I am sorry for losing my temper. I am sorry to all of you. But if your blade is somewhere on this farm, we will not rest until it is found," Nicholas states genuinely. He then looks to Henry and nearly begins to cry himself. Samuel and Amelia come closer until Nicholas signals for everyone to join us. Henry also moves forward and soon we are all gathered in a tight embrace.

"These are troubling times in Bedfordshire," Nicholas begins tearfully. "We lost control and people are dying unjustly. Christmastime is nearly over and there is no order. But we shall get through this together, with prayer and determination. I only ask that none of you leave the farm for the time being. It is not safe, and we must remain wary."

"Of course, Uncle," Henry replies.

It seems that Nicholas has been concealing his true emotions. He understands the dangers of leaving the farm and his outburst is justifiable. Now is not the time for secrets or to sneak from our heavy protection. But nothing shall get resolved if we remain in place, waiting fearfully for the killer to strike again while progress is stalled. The people of Bedfordshire can search, but they will never uncover the true identity of the assassin. It is likely that the murderer is also helping with the search, potentially covering their tracks and emphasizing false leads.

With these warnings and fears spreading through the walls of our home, my goals remain unchanged. I feel guilty for lying to Nicholas about our true suspicions of the knife, but keeping him calm will allow us to continue formulating our plans.

Amelia announces that supper is nearly finished, so we disperse to prepare for the lovely meal that awaits. Even though we are all fearful and struggling through this misfortune, Nicholas and Amelia continue making an effort to provide large meals and deliver faltering Christmas merriment.

"Thank thee," Henry whispers as we make our way through our chamber door.

"I am sorry that we troubled thy uncle. He is a good man who cares for our safety," I reply.

"Perhaps he is right, Emelie. We are putting ourselves at risk by leaving the farm," Henry replies.

I understand his concerns but fear that nothing will get resolved if we do not act on this ourselves. After what we experienced in the prison, it would be unwise to think that this killer will not come for us next. They infiltrated one of the most guarded places in all of Bedfordshire so they could easily make their way onto the farm if they chose to do so.

"We must find the knife, then we can disregard these suspicions," I explain.

Quickly I take another look through all our belongings to ensure that the weapon is not in our chamber. And like the many searches we conducted, the knife is still missing. Nicholas will also search for this blade so if it is in the barn or anywhere on the outskirts of the farm, then surely it will be located. The only thing we can do now is enjoy the feast that awaits.

"And once we are done, Henry, please remind me to search through some of Rose's writings. She must have ideas on how to best approach this situation," I say as we exit our chamber. While Rose is no longer with us, her lifetime of knowledge guided our very existence since our first encounter all those years ago. 'Tis a burning desire to hold one final conversation with her. Rose's wisdom brought stability to any situation, and though she lost her life before watching us mature, I hold no doubt that she would be proud of us to the fullest extent. Although, I would also receive a scolding for my determination.

"When will you learn, Little Emelie? Risking your safety once again to fight a cause that will consume you. You hardly know these people in this new land, so why do you make such an effort to save people like Barnabas or those sisters? But I know you, and you know better than

anyone that I would do the same. 'Tis blatant lies to say I wouldn't. I understand that you will not stop, even with the risk of losing your life."

Truly I miss those long conversations with Rose while we would tend to her garden or make jest around a bonfire. If I was agitated or complaining of Mother and Father, Rose would take me to her garden until all was well in my mind. We spent hours together as I complained of issues that held little significance.

Samuel and Thomasin disrupt my thoughts as they join us for supper. I wish to escape through the window and search the barn myself, yet I understand the importance of sharing a meal and temporarily putting my plans to rest. These moments have become sacred and cherished while our future is uncertain. It seems that the moment when Nicholas and Amelia gave us those gifts was a lifetime ago. All the happiness seems so distant through the tragedy. Regardless, everyone is trying to recapture some form of happiness so I must do the same. We walk to the table and stare in amazement at the glorious feast that awaits. Nicholas and Amelia made an effort to celebrate our homecoming and momentarily bring Christmas back to the light.

Guards are rushing in to take their own portions that Nicholas and Amelia prepared for them. One by one they retrieve rations and return to hold their posts on the outside. Even while supplies are limited and spirits are faltering, Nicholas remains dedicated to caring for those around him. He looks out for everyone and constantly validates his positive reputation. We begin to fill our plates with servings of meats, vegetables, and even a pie that Amelia found the time to bake. We pour cups of cider and fall into conversations of humor and joy.

"I must say," Nicholas begins, "this is truly the most eventful Christmas of my lifetime!" Though the reasoning is not favorable, nobody can help but to laugh at such an accurate statement. "And what do each of you make of our Christmastime customs here in Bedfordshire?"

"Well," Thomasin begins dramatically while pretending to get lost in thought, "the decorations are lovely. And all this food has been even better. The strange people who come to sing us songs and put on an agonizing performance also brought amusement. Though I think we could all do without the murder, fires, and time spent locked in prison."

Nicholas nods, playfully accepting her words as though they are totally normal.

"You mustn't forget the frigid temperatures outside," Samuel adds.

"I see. Perhaps next year I shall reclaim my position as Lord of Misrule, as you kids call it. And I will ensure that we do away with the murder, fire, and prison time for next year. Ah yes, and I will see that we can keep the sun in the sky and the snow from falling," Nicholas exclaims.

"You are all bad influences on my uncle, that is for certain!" Henry adds. We carry on with laughter and forget the troubles that await us on the outside. For the first time in days, we feel like a proper family once more. Smiles fill the room, and the festivities are back in effect, even if it is for a few moments. There is simply nowhere else I would rather be than with these people I love dearly.

"So, what do each of you plan for yourselves come spring?" Amelia asks.

Subtly I shoot a look to Thomasin who will be more than occupied in the coming months. In a few short days she will send shockwaves through our home with a glorious announcement.

"I will be assisting Pastor Noah even further with service," Samuel begins enthusiastically. "He believes that I will soon be ready to lead if need be. And by the time the spring greets us, I will certainly be a regular deacon!"

"How splendid! And what about the rest of you?" Amelia questions.

"Henry and I shall have this farm up and running like never before. Our greatest season awaits now that I have a helping hand!" Nicholas declares.

"Perhaps only time shall tell," I begin, "although the apothecary idea continues to swirl in my mind."

The others are excited to hear me acknowledge this desired profession that they practically beg of me. They believe this to be a fine path forward and I see little reason to dispute such an idea. While I would need to work with Timothy and strengthen my knowledge of traditional healing and medicines, I am well equipped on the side of the odd and unknown. Thomasin never shares her ideas, as her future is one of uncertainty. She is likely fearful of Samuel's status in the church or how Nicholas and Amelia shall react to such news. But I see no reason to worry about acceptance. With the regard that Nicholas holds and his efforts through this tragedy, it is unlikely that any of us would face scrutiny moving forward.

"And what about you, Aunt Amelia?" Henry replies with a question of his own.

She smiles at his interest. "Well, I suspect that I will be right here on the farm. As fishing season resumes, I shall be roasting and boiling until none of us can fathom another bite of fish. And I will take the occasional trip into the village to stay familiar with current happenings."

It is a wonderful feeling to ponder on future normalcy. As Nicholas mentioned, we will prevail through these trying times together. And while each of us has moments of weakness, the bond within these walls is unbreakable.

"How could I have forgotten?" Nicholas asks himself, attracting our attention. "Some of our friends outside found a collection of tools, knives, and other items out in the barn. Perhaps you could go and check at first light tomorrow and see if this blade of yours is included. Just be sure to have some of the officials guide you, they will be posted just beyond the door. And if it is still missing then I will see that the blacksmith recreates your dagger to the finest detail."

"Thank thee, I shall do so first thing in the morning," I reply with appreciation.

We continue gossiping and celebrating at the table until the candles dim and the last of the daylight vanishes. The snowfall rages outside and we eventually make our way to the hearth. Nicholas carries on with endless tales of Christmas while we match his enthusiasm with our own stories of All Hallows Eve. Our conversation carries through the flickering flames of the fire until each of us struggles to stay awake. Samuel and Thomasin assist with setting the fire for the night before heading to their chamber. As Henry and I prepare to depart, Nicholas pulls his nephew aside to offer a sincere apology for his earlier behavior.

"Deep down, Nicholas is a troubled man," Amelia whispers to me. "This village has exhausted him over the years. But since all of you arrived and brought Henry back home, it's as if he is a new man. We are so glad you came."

Her words are far too kind for the trouble that we brought upon them and this entire community.

"It is I that needs to offer gratitude. You accepted us and expected nothing in return. Even knowing our past and the awful things we did to survive. There shall never be a way to properly thank you and repay all that you have given us," I state thoughtfully.

Amelia shakes her head in disagreement at my words. Neither her nor Nicholas ever expected anything in return. They welcomed us as we were struggling to survive; never criticizing our past or the events that brought us to their door. Instead, they provided love and kindness. Though we have a dangerous path forward, I believe that it is owed to Nicholas, Amelia, and all of Bedfordshire to somehow end this travesty. We are on the cusp of greatness in this new life and will not allow this assassin to take anything away.

Our conversations diminish and it is finally time to rest. We thank Nicholas and Amelia once again for the wonderful evening and make our way to our chamber.

"I know it is quite late, but you wanted me to remind you about searching through those writings. Perhaps it would be best to do so in the morning," Henry mumbles, struggling to stay awake as we climb the stairs.

"Thank thee, and I believe you are right. I will pull a few from the shelf so that I can start promptly tomorrow. But it is time for rest," I reply.

We pass through the hall, hoping not to awaken Samuel and Thomasin who are likely fast asleep. Henry carefully opens our chamber door and pulls it shut behind us. The moonlight shines through our room and a chill in the air makes me shiver. Carefully I make my way to the bookshelf, trying not to make the floorboards creek from my steps. It has been quite some time since I utilized any bindings or journals other than the magnificent one that Nicholas and Amelia gifted me back on the first day of Christmas.

Where should I start?

I stare at the writings on the shelf, unsure of which binding could prove as the most useful. "Of course," I whisper to myself while reaching for the journal with the black cover. This holds the darkest and most outrageous ideas surrounding witchcraft and magic, so surely our current situation may share similarities with its contents. And while I may collapse from my exhaustion, I cannot help myself but to open to the final pages and glance at Rose's findings. The beauty of her writing always amazes me, and it brings me comfort to see the words as they come from her hand.

"Where is it?" I ask myself with confusion. Upon flipping to the end of the binding, Rose's plans of exposing Thomas are nowhere to be found.

"Is everything alright, Emelie?" Henry asks while struggling to stay awake.

"Sorry, it seems that I mistook this for another writing," I express while presenting the journal. But as I raise my hand to show Henry, the moonlight shines across the cover and confirms that this is in fact the one I was looking for. In a state of perplexity, I rub my eyes and quickly pass through the binding until realizing that nearly half the pages are missing.

"Something is wrong," I disclose while my panic swells. I flip from cover to cover, and the words are simply not there. Hastily I rush to the window so that I have light to confirm my suspicions, and I notice that the pages have been torn out. Henry rises from the bed and joins me as I rush back to the shelf.

"No," I mutter with the last bit of breath before it escapes. Now fully alert and scanning desperately, I realize that something else is missing from the shelf. And it is not just a simple binding of medicines and remedies. The original journal that I was using to document everything from Warren Hollow is gone. Details of John, the bonfire on All Hallows Eve, my parents, and our escape were written in that scroll.

"How did I not notice?" I ask myself. "It is not here!"

"What is missing, Emelie?" Henry asks desperately.

"My journal that contains everything! All that happened to us was written in that binding, and now it is missing!"

"And this is not it?" Henry asks while pulling another writing from the shelf. He holds the journal that Nicholas and Amelia gifted me. Suddenly a wave of terror nearly drops me to my knees. I have not touched any of the other writings since I received that new journal. It was so beautiful, and I instantly wanted to rewrite our story from the very beginning. No longer was I going to vandalize Rose's bindings with my own scribbles. Days passed as I wrote for hours on end in that new journal, never giving a second thought to anything else that sat on the shelf. And now the only other documentation of our past is gone, along with critical pages of Rose's findings on the darkest side of witchcraft.

"When thy aunt and uncle gave me this journal," I say while taking it from Henry, "I stopped writing in the other ones. This gave me a clear way to document our past, so it did not seem necessary to continue vandalizing what belonged to Rose."

"Well, I am sure that it is around here somewhere. Perhaps you left it near the hearth or it fell behind a shelf. Do you remember when you last used it before they gifted you the new one?"

Think, think, think!

Thoughts race through my mind of its potential whereabouts. I spent so much time filling the pages of the new journal that I merely forgot of the old one's existence. Desperately I force my eyes shut while recounting my steps.

When was the last time you physically held the journal in your hand? Surely you were writing in it until the moment you received the new one from Nicholas and Amelia.

My eyes shoot open as I recall the exact moment I last saw the journal. My body is paralyzed with fear and my hand shakes uncontrollably at this revelation. The deception that occurred in this very room leaves me dumbfounded and admittedly impressed. Recounting a certain sequence of events shows just how naive I was from the beginning.

"I remember," I whisper while turning to Henry as he desperately awaits an answer. "Abigail and Rachel stole my journal."

XX

The Plan

We gather around the shelf in Henry and I's chamber while trying not to alert Nicholas or Amelia. I recount the sequence of events over and over in the exact place that it occurred. Henry, Samuel, and Thomasin listen carefully to my words and assist with the reenactment.

"And you did not see Abigail or Rachel with the journal in hand?" Samuel asks.

"I'm afraid not. When my hand broke loose during the struggle over here," I explain while moving into position and pointing, "and the writings spilled across the room all the way to there, my focus never left Abigail. Rachel scurried behind me precisely where you stand," I point to Thomasin, "while gathering the scrolls and bindings. With the sudden chaos I paid her no mind and thought it only to be a kind gesture. Surely this is when she stole the journal and any other pages that be missing!"

"How did it take so long for you to notice its absence?" Thomasin questions.

"Henry rushed to our chamber once the sisters fled. He was the one who gathered all the writings and placed them back on the shelf because I was trying to fix my makeshift hand. I paid no mind to the mess. And then I received the journal from

Amelia and Nicholas shortly after, which is where I conducted all my writing since."

"And you also believe this is when they stole the dagger?" Samuel replies to my explanation.

I nod, finding this to be quite likely. "I searched with Nicholas earlier today and none of the items in the barn were the missing dagger. Rachel could have easily taken that as well while Abigail distracted me. Perhaps she spotted it under our bed while gathering the writings. Or they might have returned to our chamber when they vandalized the farm if they are behind all of this. And Henry," I say as I turn in his direction, "if you believe that you did not misplace the knife then it is foolish to think otherwise."

Henry confirms that he did not hide the weapon as a means to bring me peace of mind. And it was not in the barn, so I have no other option than to assume Abigail and Rachel stole the writings and the dagger.

"We should tell my uncle everything. He can pass our thoughts to Ambrose. We have strong evidence against them," Henry claims.

"If we are to accuse Abigail and Rachel of causing all this mayhem then we must be certain. They are strange, and we have reason to believe that they stole my writings and the knife, but we need proof," I explain while compiling my thoughts. "Nearly all the murders happened while they were accounted for. When Barnabas was freed and Clara fled through the doors, Abigail and Rachel were in eyesight. And on the night the farm was vandalized, they had a guarded escort. It would be unwise to alert anyone of our findings for the time being, as Ambrose could also be to blame. Until we know for certain, it could honestly be anyone and we mustn't place ourselves in danger."

Our situation is one of immense difficulty. Everything indicates that Abigail and Rachel could be behind this tragedy around us. Though even with this belief I hold much restraint in openly accusing them of such wickedness. We were falsely accused and imprisoned back in The Hollow, never having the chance to defend ourselves or prove our innocence. And if we are wrong, Abigail and Rachel would suffer in the prison without reason. Or if it be Ambrose, he would know of our every move and use it to his advantage, or simply murder us as well. Many members of Bedfordshire visited our home recently, from revelers to the physician, so the list of suspects is endless.

"Must I even ask if you have a plan?" Thomasin remarks. She suspects that I devised a strategy through the night, so she rolls her eyes at my gaze of ambition. "And if I am to guess, this plan is one of danger and serious risk?"

"Precisely," I reply with a smile. Though all of us understand that this is not a matter of jest. They are well aware that I shall place myself in danger to reach a solution and will not tolerate any dispute. "I noticed a schedule in which the guards outside take their breaks. Just after supper, there is a brief instance where only one guard stands in front of our home and one in the back. The others are likely off patrolling through Bedfordshire so this is when I will escape."

"And there it is," Thomasin says while shaking her head at my words. Henry and Samuel immediately disagree while Thomasin smirks at her anticipated danger of my plan.

"You would risk your life and leave this farm?" Henry asks.

"I must, Henry. This could be our only opportunity to end this. If I sneak to Abigail and Rachel's home, perhaps I will find all that we need to make our accusation. It is already the tenth day of Christmas, so time is drawing short if they plan to act again. I fear that Nicholas or any of us are not safe until this is resolved. There is a reason we are still alive after the encounter in the prison."

"I will not let you leave alone. If this is how we are to proceed, then I am joining you," Henry replies with a serious tone.

I stare at him for a few moments without a response. His desire to protect me is rational, so perhaps it is wise for him to join me. "Very well, we shall go together. But I need the two of you," I command while turning to Thomasin and Samuel, "to remain here and distract Nicholas. After supper I shall fake a sickness, and we will exit from our chamber window. But they mustn't know of our absence."

Samuel and Thomasin nod, understanding their role and the importance of our stealth. If Nicholas suspects we are leaving, he will place guards at our chamber doors and at every window. We must act with caution and quickly run from the farm once we break free. Then we will avoid patrols and any attention on the way into the village. And if we find evidence of Abigail and Rachel being the hooded demon of Bedfordshire, then all will be resolved.

"For now, we must draw no suspicion. I shall take some time to write in my journal as normal and the rest of you should carry on as though it be a normal day," I advise while ending the reenactment.

"I am off to assist Nicholas with the morning chores, so I will be out in the barn," Henry explains while departing.

Thomasin follows behind Henry as they descend the stairs. Samuel stays however, potentially wishing to ask more of the plan. He peeks his head out from the door, waiting until Thomasin and Henry are out of sight before pulling it closed. We now stand alone as I prepare to answer whatever further questions he may have.

"Can I ask thee something?" Samuel starts, appearing a bit nervous.

"Of course, Samuel. I understand this plan is not the most efficient or safest, but we can make it work," I reply.

He shakes his head, more so at himself than my answer.

"Actually," he begins, "it is not about this plan at all."

I take a step closer and show interest in whatever he may ask. "Then what is it, Samuel? What troubles thee?"

Samuel takes a deep breath, appearing reluctant to further his questioning "Is," he struggles to finish, "is Thomasin with child?"

I stand frozen, mouth hanging open and unsure of how to proceed. "Is ... she with child?" I repeat back, unable to provide anything other than his own words. Rather than staring blankly at Samuel I attempt to mutter some sort of explanation. "Well, she—"

"You do not need to tell me, it was an unfair question to ask so abruptly," Samuel replies. "She has all but confirmed it these past few weeks with her sickness and other sudden changes. I apologize, Emelie, and know not why I ask when the answer is quite obvious."

The tension in the room begins to lighten at Samuel's confession. He spent significant time caring for Thomasin recently so surely it all but revealed itself. It seems that none of us are well versed in keeping our secrets from each other.

"She wished to tell you," I say while placing my hand on his shoulder. "But with all this madness, she did not want to cause any commotion. But once Christmastime has come to pass, surely she will tell you herself."

He nods at my words, sympathizing with her reasoning. "I am to be a father," he whispers to himself, accepting the reality of his suspicions. I offer a smile and watch as he displays the same signs of happiness and fear that Thomasin showed in the prison.

"Aye, a wonderful one at that," I reply. He smiles as I pull him in for a comforting embrace. "But for Thomasin, we must remain focused. We can end this tonight and ensure a future of safety."

"Of course," he replies, pulling away and preparing to leave the chamber. "Let us finish this." Samuel turns back just before passing through the door. "Thank thee. For all that you have done and continue to do for us every day. I see your pain and believe you are the only one who can truly see mine. Perhaps you and I will someday free ourselves from this hold of the past. Please, Emelie, do act with the utmost caution tonight."

I stand alone in the room, staring at the bookshelf and taking a moment of silence in an attempt to control my emotions. While usually brief, conversations with Samuel always strike deeply. It cannot be said enough that Samuel and I share a unique bond. He carries heavy guilt from The Hollow and prevents himself from fully accepting our torture or moving forward. This is something I understand, and I shall pray that this child brings him a new beginning. Samuel is establishing himself as a respected member in Bedfordshire, so a bright future is within reach. The idea of a regarded church member raising a child will likely be overlooked due to our status and connection to Nicholas. We noticed from the very beginning that this place ignores nearly all the bounds and constraints of life elsewhere. Religion is quite prevalent, but has no ties to law or celebrations like All Hallows Eve or Christmastime.

We are so close to the end, and I want nothing more than to restore normality to our lives. Once we find proof in the sisters' home, this nightmare will come to pass. Though my thoughts never shift from the absolute certainty needed to make our accusation. And if the sisters are responsible for our suffering, then this is more mercy than they have shown to any of the victims in Bedfordshire.

What if you are to find nothing? Perhaps Henry will remember that he hid the dagger, and the journal will also reveal itself? If not the sisters, then who?

Anxiety grows as the day progresses. This is a feeling that will worsen until I reach the sisters' home and search every room and cabinet in sight. We sit at the table for supper, eating the leftovers of yesterday's feast and pretending that it be a normal day as the sun dims in the sky. Nicholas and Amelia do not suspect our plans so things may go rather smoothly. I fake laughs and engage in conversation while feeling disgusted that deception has become my expertise. But I tell myself that it is for the greater good. Lying to Nicholas and Amelia does not bring me joy, but just like Thomasin in the moments after The Reverend's death, I believe that they shall forgive me. I plan on making it clear that I act for no attention or regard. In truth, I would prefer that we are given no credit if Henry and I find evidence. My desire for the future carried over from The Hollow; to remain unseen and live a simple life. Samuel and Thomasin will start a family of their own, progressing in the church and finding peace. Henry may start his own farm or take over for his uncle one day, and I will be by his side with my own apothecary services.

As we continue eating our meal, I look around the table in bliss. The anxiety fades through the love and happiness that flourished between us. Nicholas and Amelia provide more than we could ever ask for. Because of them, the ragged survivors of witch trials in faraway lands have a future. And the time to secure that future is now.

Supper concludes and I fail to recall any of the current happenings around me. It all unraveled in a blur. My focus is narrow and set only on making our escape into the village. Throughout the evening, I watched the snowfall gradually build outside so our likeliness of being seen is low. Guards will remain at their posts until the weather subsides, and our supper carried late into the evening. Departing to our chamber for the night will be of less suspicion than anticipated. Henry, Samuel, Thomasin, and I offer glances at each other while Nicholas and Amelia are oblivious. We are eager to act and wish to wait no longer.

"It seems that I caught Thomasin's illness, or the cranberry pie is not sitting well," I claim aloud. "I think it best that I get some rest for the night. Do you need any help preparing for nightfall?" I ask Nicholas and Amelia.

"Not at all," Amelia replies with concern as she comes closer. She holds me and gently brushes my hair to comfort me. "Go and get some rest, we are just about done here. And do let us know if you need anything through the night."

"Thank thee, perhaps I just need some rest," I reply, preparing to leave the room.

"I shall be right behind you, Emelie," Henry adds.

I give him a smile and make my way around the table. As I pass by, Thomasin grabs my arm and gently pulls me down, stopping me right in my tracks. "Be careful," she whispers so only I can hear. I give her a nod and carry out my departure from the room.

Hastily I make my way through our home, climbing the stairs and maneuvering through the hall to our chamber. I open the window now to minimize all sounds during our escape. This is a technique that I mastered in my earlier years, though it shall be much easier on this farm. Mother and Father were closer in our small home back in The Hollow. The wood creaked beneath all movement and echoed through our entire home. But on this farm, I could smash the window or break down the front door and it would likely go unnoticed. Rather than lying in our bed for the time being, I dress myself for the vicious weather outside. Coats, scarves, and a glove are added so that I can face the cold with no issues. A chill sneaks through the open window and indicates a frigid night ahead.

And now I must try to get a few moments of rest. Our escape is in full effect so we must wait patiently. Henry eventually joins me in our chamber and shivers from the cold that creeps through the window. He also takes a moment to dress for the weather before joining me on the bed. We pass the time by sharing thoughts of our future in Bedfordshire and reminiscing on our past in The Hollow. It is quite evident that Henry does not miss his father back home and honestly does not have much he would like to remember from those earlier days. He was frowned upon by most for the mistakes of his father. Surely he finds much more peace on this farm with his true family. In honesty, I find my own peace in knowing that none of us have the slightest regret in leaving The Hollow.

The night begins to drag while we listen to Samuel and Thomasin finish their nightly routines and make their way past our door. Shortly after, Nicholas and Amelia also prepare to rest for the night. All light vanishes from the farm, so our escape is moments away.

"Emelie, I think now is our chance," Henry whispers. "I shall look to make sure."

Henry slowly makes his way from the bed, walking to the chamber door and stealthily pulling it open. He peers out into the hall and looks side to side before returning. "Let us be gone."

At Henry's command I rise from the bed with eagerness. We make our way to the window, looking down to our long descent. The climb is much steeper in comparison to my escapes back in The Hollow. Wind blows in my face and snow falls steadily, hindering my vision as I slide to the outside. My grip will also be in question as I only have one functioning hand. But there is no turning back at this point, so I maneuver to the outside and begin my descent.

"Hold on tightly, John."

It feels strange to squeeze through a window and climb down the side of our home without John on my back. His presence has been felt as of recent, and I pretend that he is with me once more as I begin my climb. Perhaps he is my guardian angel, watching from above as I go through the motions of my childhood. As I slide down and place each step, I envision John whispering in my ear with his excited mannerisms. I found the village that the two of us could only dream of; John drew his final breaths with a smile at thoughts of such a place.

And here I am, engaged in yet another escape. We'd climb from our home often back then, rushing into the forest to meet Rose and all the others. And while the purpose of this escape is not for a night of debauchery, 'tis all but the same. Once again, I stand in the snow while breaking rules and placing myself at risk.

A night on the outside always takes me back to those vivid childhood memories. While it is something I can now enact with free will, the desire for solitude in nature still burns within me from time to time. When I touch the falling snow or the wind stings in a prison cell, I truly feel alive. Nature was a place for me to escape from reality and find my truest self. Perhaps it would serve me well to recapture that passion of exploration in the forest once this is resolved.

We stealthily make our way from the farm as I am lost in thought. True to our suspicions, the guards are not out in full scale tonight. Our timing could not be more perfect as we make our way towards the village. The moon fails to shine through the snowfall and clouds in the sky, so we move in darkness. Henry stays right at my side while monitoring our surroundings. Now would truly be the time for the murderer to strike, but they would never predict our adventure.

Aside from our conversation with Barnabas, this is perhaps our final chance to gain an unsuspected advantage. I fear that if our plan fails, someone else shall die and Bedfordshire will fully spiral into hysteria. After the events in the prison, any of us could be next. Barnabas was but a loose end, quickly severed before he could uncover an identity. Time is running out if this murderer aims to wreak more havoc in line with Christmastime. Tomorrow is the eleventh day of Christmas, and I believe that the worst is drawing near.

"Are you doing alright?" Henry asks.

"Yes, we are nearly there," I reply. Even if I felt pain or the weather was worse, there be nothing that could stop our actions. I would crawl to the sisters' home if needed, but things are going well so far. We passed no one near the farm and the village is dark as we approach. Carefully we follow the path but stray off as we get closer to structures. Our destination is just beyond the edge of the village, so we are moments away as Phillip's home comes into view. Surely the guards will be making their rounds at any moment, and we are too close to be caught now. Being spotted would not help our innocence either, that is if we are not shot in a panic.

"They will suspect us if we are seen," I shout through the icy conditions.

"Aye, perhaps we should move quickly then," Henry replies.

Our speed increases as we march through the worsening snowfall and heavy winds. It is difficult to determine where we are, but I know that we must be close. I venture through terrible conditions more than ever desired, so I hope that tonight will be the last time for such an adventure. The four of us shared enough excitement for a lifetime and I am ready to find peace. While the journey to Bedfordshire brought wonderful experiences, I have not felt rested since before the chaos of the witch trials. Holding status from our connection to Nicholas bothers me not, but returning to a life of monotony would not be as terrible as we thought back in The Hollow.

"We've made it undetected," Henry proclaims with relief.

"Indeed," I reply, standing outside of the sisters' home. This was a day full of worry and disconnect. Perhaps I placed too much faith in obtaining happiness once this is over. I assumed that all the anxiety, guilt, and trauma from the past could vanish by securing our future. It may not be that easy, but I believe solving this will be a fine start. These feelings trouble me, although I wish to heal and acknowledge the need to do so. A prosperous future is what Rose and John died for. Rose would scold me and Samuel for the pain we purposely impose upon ourselves.

The cellar door shutters from the vicious winds as we circle the home. I stare at the cellar, thinking back to all the suspicious activity surrounding its secrecy. Rachel, Abigail, and Chrystopher ensured that it was locked each time I was near, and Clara had a strange fascination with whatever lies beneath. From Chrystopher's supposed occupancy to Clara's claims of constant noise, I feel foolish for ignoring the mystery of such a place.

"Perhaps we should check inside the home first. But we must search the cellar before we depart," I demand, eyes fixated on the cellar. The lock is still in place, so we will need to break it open in order to get inside. We continue circling until we return to the front of the home. Henry moves a few steps ahead of me to verify that the path is clear. We sneak our way up to the front door and it is also locked. Twisting the handle and pushing with force is an unsuccessful attempt to get inside.

"I can get us in there, but it would mean breaking the door. Do you think that be wise?" Henry asks.

Our list of crimes is endless on this night. Does one more offense hold any significance?

"We have no other choice. This is our only chance, Henry. If there is nothing inside, then we will leave and return home. But if we find what is needed then surely we will be forgiven."

Henry nods at my words, understanding that breaking into a home is a minimal crime in comparison to what is unraveling around us. "Very well," he says while preparing to break the door.

With a deep breath, Henry bends his knees and turns until his shoulder is facing the door. His body tenses as he lunges forward and slams his weight into the wood. The first attempt is unsuccessful, but the locks are audibly loosening. If the snow wasn't falling and the winds weren't so wicked, surely all the neighbors would hear this commotion. Henry braces to once again throw himself forward. This attempt is also unsuccessful, but it sounds like the locks are on the cusp of breaking.

"Once more, Henry. Surely that shall do it," I cheer, impressed by his strength and praising his efforts. Rather than using the force of his shoulder, he elects to face the door directly. The door swings open from a forceful kick as the locks fly from the hinges. We scan for a few moments to verify that nobody heard us. Our surroundings seem clear, so we prepare to enter the darkness of the home. With no time to waste, the only thing left to do is cross this threshold and uncover the truth.

XXI

Trapped

The atmosphere of this empty home is tense and daunting. No signs of life exist, as the sisters have not returned since Clara's murder. An awful stench was released when the door opened, so we maneuver through the home with caution. Rather than locating a dead animal or another victim, the putrid smell comes from food on their table. As we move closer, I realize that the meal I brought many days ago is still on the table, rotting and covered in insects. I look away and cover my nose out of fear that I shall vomit from such a sight. The sound of the insects devouring the food fills my ears and echoes through the home.

"Excellent, I am starving," Henry says jokingly. "Though I think you deserve the first bite."

I shoot him a wicked glare through watery eyes while holding my nose and trying to regain my composure. Henry searches through the room until he locates an oil lamp. We now have a light to guide our search through the cold and empty rooms. It seems that the meal I provided was untouched after that day. Allowing the food to spoil and ignoring the mess for days on end is unsettling behavior. Our search continues as Henry leads from the kitchen into the area with the hearth, which appears free from ash or embers. Clara's rocking chair sits vacant near the window. Sadness overcomes me at the recollection of her brutal end. Though often confused and troublesome for the sisters, Clara was kind and did not deserve such a horrific death. If the goal is to corrupt Bedfordshire and eliminate its grandest members, then I do not understand the motivation behind her murder.

The home does not seem out of the ordinary as we continue our exploration. I expected to stumble into the lair of a beast, and yet, nothing beyond the food is of concern for the time being. Still, I remain vigilant and cannot shake the feeling of uneasiness. Nothing peculiar reveals itself in this area so Henry suggests we move to the upstairs. After a brief search around the hearth and through some chests and shelves, this floor appears to be clear. While it is strangely empty and mundane, we cannot prove their guilt from this otherwise normal living space. Surely the chamber upstairs is where Abigail and Rachel would keep the stolen journal and writings. Each step creaks beneath us as we make our way to the sisters' room. Our only light is the oil lamp in Henry's hand, and I watch as shadows move across the walls from the flame.

As we reach the top, panic ensues at the thought of leaving empty-handed. If we do not locate the journal, then we are truly at a loss with our accusations. It would be impossible to determine the killer's identity without so much as an indication of where to begin. These sisters and Ambrose certainly raise the most suspicion, but until we have any solid evidence, we are simply running in circles with blind assumptions. And we will not find another opportunity to escape from the farm.

Before I let doubt fully creep into my mind, I tell myself that we still have the rest of the home and the cellar to search.

Discovering that the sisters are not to blame would be joyous, but then we are simply at the mercy of this assassin. Although, a lack of evidence would still not proclaim total innocence for Abigail and Rachel in my eyes. Though if I lack proof and continue my pursuit on intuition, I am no better than Reverend Thomas and our parents back in The Hollow. Time would also be wasted trying to prove their guilt if the assassin is in fact someone else. The thought of me misplacing the journal also looms overhead and I constantly question my own sanity.

"Through here," I tell Henry while entering the sisters' chamber. I rummage through a bed and any accessible areas.

He places the lamp on a shelf and immediately begins searching as well. Henry tears apart the other bed, removing quilts and lifting the mattress to check everywhere. "Nothing," he shares defeatedly.

My heart begins to race and I feel the nerves growing with each passing moment. We both react to the sudden slamming of the cellar door. Clara's words of a constant pounding fill my mind, but I was truly unprepared for such an aggressive occurrence. It sounds as though the lock has broken and the cellar is open. I listen to the banging of the door as it swings freely in the wind. But for now, I must refocus on the bedroom.

"There must be something!" I shout in a panic. I search their shelves and find no traces of the journal or other writings. Their chest of accessories enters my mind, so I drop to the floor and find it under one of the beds. "This has to be it," I tell Henry in a panic.

He helps to slide the chest across the floor as I aggressively pull at the lock. The lid releases and the chest swings open, revealing the same accessories that I noticed prior; useless hair bows, a scarf, and a ragged sweater. My frustration is evident as I aggressively push the chest away. We searched the home and failed to locate any writings or the dagger.

"What are we to do?" I ask emotionally.

"We've done all that we can, Emelie. Surely the cellar is open so we can search it on our way out, but there is nothing here that we can use against them. You said it yourself that it would be unwise to accuse the sisters if we did not find anything. Let us search the final room on this floor before departing. Then we shall devise another plan tomorrow," Henry explains optimistically.

Dread overcomes me as I reorganize the room before venturing into the hall. There is one last room to search, though I suspect it will be empty as well. It will be difficult to remain positive moving forward. After conquering Reverend Thomas with near-impossible odds, it feels quite defeating to fail this time. Perhaps I placed too much faith in this plan, thinking I could solve this so easily and gain the upper hand. But after all that we have gone through, none of us shall willingly submit. Our resources are limited and time draws thin, but we will regroup at the farm and determine how to move forward.

"This room is also empty," Henry claims as we scan the final area. Similar to the rest of the home, this space is plain and unalarming. A small bed sits in the corner, likely where Clara used to sleep. The rest of the room is situated with minimal items beyond a chair and a shelf. Henry makes an effort to look under the bed and search through the shelf, but it is to no avail. Their cellar is likely to be the same, containing nothing more than tools or vegetables.

"We should return to the farm," I say defeatedly. Henry fixes the quilt on the bed before we exit the room. My mind is racing with thoughts of who could be the murderer. Unless Abigail and Rachel are master assassins and hid the evidence elsewhere, further proclaiming their guilt is a waste of time. It seems that the likes of Ambrose, Timothy, or even Solomon could be next on our list of potential murderers. Perhaps Nicholas and Amelia hath gone mad and terrorize the village. They have been wonderful and gracious to us since the moment we arrived, but we have only known them for a few months at most. I could never mention such a thought to Henry, though I will keep it in the back of my mind as our desperation swells.

"The cellar is likely small, so we can search it with haste and make our way back to the farm," Henry explains.

"I thank thee for all of your help," I begin as we start to descend the stairs, "perhaps now we should shift our focus from the sisters onto other–"

"Wait," Henry interrupts while grabbing my arm. His actions take me by surprise as I nearly lose my balance on the stairs.

"What is it?" I ask with confusion.

"Listen," Henry whispers while turning his head to hear down the stairs. I also hear a faint sound that seems to be voices below us. Footsteps follow until we realize that someone is entering the home. Henry extinguishes the flame of the lamp while we cautiously retrace our steps to the upstairs. As we round the corner into the sisters' room, we hear the commotion of two people entering below us.

"This front door is also broken, just like the cellar!" a voice yells.

"What say you?" another replies.

"Someone could be in here. We must check each room to be certain!"

Henry and I look at each other then desperately scan the room for a place to hide. I pull the door until it is barely open and follow Henry who made his way to one of the beds. "It's our only option," he declares while pointing to the other bed. I drop down and crawl beneath, trying not to make any sounds on the fragile floorboards beneath us. Henry pushes the chest from underneath his bed and struggles to take its place. This could truly be the end if we are discovered. Explaining our innocence would be impossible, even to Nicholas and Amelia. Shuffling below indicates that the men are conducting their search.

"It smells awful in here, Ambrose," one of the men shouts.

I look across the room to Henry who I faintly see through the darkness. We now understand that Ambrose is one of the men beneath us, likely joined by one of his guards.

"Never mind that, we must search for the girl," Ambrose replies. "Please make thyself known, Abigail! It is unwise to run off during these troubling times!"

"She puts us all at risk with such foolish actions. Those sisters are an abomination," the other man proclaims.

"Do not speak ill of them! They lost their grandmother and are frightened like the rest of us. Perhaps you would like to speak instead on how she escaped so easily under your watch!" Ambrose orders, with noticeable anger.

Though the details are unclear, it seems that something happened at the meetinghouse. Perhaps there was some sort of disagreement or conflict, and Abigail fled into the night. The men continue searching below us and calling out for Abigail as we listen from beneath the beds.

"Solomon had no right to confront those grieving children!" Ambrose shouts to the other man. "He frightened them, and he will find himself with a rope at his neck if anything is to happen to her!"

A commotion with Solomon caused Abigail to flee. This is why Ambrose visited their home, only to discover that it has been broken into. Though as long as we remain hidden, he will suspect it to solely be Abigail. And just like all the other circumstances surrounding Abigail and Rachel, it is a strange coincidence. While it seems extremely unlikely, the mere thought of Abigail and Rachel knowing of our presence in their home brings me uneasiness. And even if this was all coincidental, Abigail could panic and rush to the farm since she is not here. Nicholas will question our innocence if Abigail is present and we are not. Ambrose will likely make his way to the farm as well if Abigail is not soon found.

"Henry," I whisper in a panic, "we must get back to the farm. They will search there as well."

"We cannot go anywhere at the moment," Henry replies. Until Ambrose and his guard exit the home, we are unfortunately at their mercy. It is my only hope that they conduct their search and move on. And once the opportunity arises, we will rush back to the farm.

We cease our conversation at the sound of footsteps climbing the stairs. I slide further under the bed, praying that we remain hidden. Light shines through the hall and the bedroom door is pushed open. The floor creaks under heavy footsteps and I hold my breath while trying not to make a sound.

"Search quickly and get back down here!" Ambrose shouts from below. The man mutters something under his breath while shining his lantern through the room. After a few moments he leaves our space and makes his way into Clara's chamber. I let out a sigh of relief as he descends the stairs.

"It is empty, Ambrose. She is long gone," the man claims.

"She could still be close by. I need you to wait here in case she comes back. God forbid her sister escapes as well. It is not safe for them to be running through the night! I will send word once she is found. Until then, do not leave this home," Ambrose instructs while preparing to depart.

"You wish for me to wait here? Alone?" The man asks timidly.

Ambrose is audibly displeased with his companion, as he shouts incomprehensible insults while making his exit. Henry and I stare at each other, accepting that we are now trapped while Abigail could be wreaking havoc or Ambrose makes his way to the farm. Our primary suspects are both wandering through Bedfordshire alone at night so surely their safety is at great risk. And if the morning comes and brings their deaths, perhaps we are helpless and it would be time to flee this village. Regardless, remaining in this room through the night is surely not going to serve us well. Finding a way to escape is necessary.

Escaping is what you do best, so do it now!

While I wish to rush from under the bed and down the stairs, I understand that this would not be wise. The guard that Ambrose stationed here is clearly afraid and likely drunk, so he may shoot us on sight. Each of the windows on this floor are too small to squeeze through, so our options are limited.

If Abigail was not already here prior to our arrival, then she would recognize our search and confirm that she did not break down the door. This cannot happen while we are still inside, or anywhere but the farm for that matter. But it seems that we cannot go anywhere at the moment. We shall capitalize on any chance to escape, but that opportunity has yet to arise. I listen as the guard paces below us, checking the windows and watching the open door.

"I do not see a reasonable way out of here, Henry. We must wait. But when the moment arises, we will get back to the farm," I whisper.

"Aye. There is nothing we can do until then," Henry says in agreement.

We wait under the beds for what seems like hours. The room has become frigid and the floor is terribly uncomfortable. Every so often I will crawl out from under the bed, believing that the guard left his post until we hear his footsteps return or a progressively worsening cough. We are likely nearing sunrise, so our time is drawing thin.

"We cannot wait any longer, for it has been hours. 'Tis nearly morning, and they will see that we are gone. It would be a miracle if they do not already know," I whisper to Henry.

"Have you heard any footsteps recently?" He asks.

"I have not. Perhaps he returned to the meetinghouse. We should go and check."

Slowly I crawl from underneath the bed, rising to my feet and trying not to make a sound. I look out the window and notice that the sun is just starting to break through the darkness. The cellar is still open and swinging in the wind. But another sound in the distance catches my attention.

"Are the bells ringing?" Henry asks in confusion. I put my ear to the window and listen as the bells of the meetinghouse begin sounding off in the distance.

"Something is wrong," I tell Henry while watching from the window. There be no service or gathering at the meetinghouse that would warrant the toll of the bells this early. "We need to move."

While I worried for the safety of the others on the farm, it seems likely that Ambrose or Abigail did not make it through the night. We creep down the stairs and the guard is nowhere in sight. The door is wide open from our forced entry and screams in the distance start to echo. Tears fill my eyes at the thought of whatever misfortune awaits. Rachel would be devastated if her sister succumbed to the assassin, and Bedfordshire will collapse without Ambrose's leadership if it be him instead.

"Henry, I do not like this," I say nervously. We move to the outside and I shield my eyes from the brightness of the snow. This morning is absolutely freezing. The wind blows aggressively and almost knocks me to the ground. Carefully we round the house, and I am caught by surprise at the sight of an official. He sits in the snow near the cellar in visible distress. "What happened to you?"

Henry rushes to aid the man as he rises to his feet. He cannot stand on his own and seems to be suffering. Vomit and blood surrounds him in the snow.

"I ... fear it be ... poison," the man mutters. He coughs aggressively while Henry supports his steps. I recognize his voice to be that of the man who accompanied Ambrose and guarded the sisters' home through the night.

"We must get to the meetinghouse!" Henry shouts.

"No, we should return to the farm and check on the others. Wait here for just a moment," I demand in dispute. I run to the front of the home and see members of Bedfordshire flooding the surrounding area. People are rushing in all directions and devolving into chaos.

"Wait!" I yell to a stranger passing by. I grab her arm to slow her down, trying to make sense of who is dead and how poison is involved. "What happened? Was it Ambrose or Abigail who fell victim? Was it both of them?"

"In the meetinghouse," she begins, "it is horrible!"

"What is?" I ask with concern. It seems that my assumptions were incorrect, and neither the farm nor those wandering the night were targeted.

"We are poisoned! It must be arsenic!" the woman shouts while breaking away and continuing her panic.

I run back around the home to Henry and the official. "Those in the meetinghouse were poisoned, it has nothing to do with Abigail or Ambrose. A woman indicated that it be pure madness!"

The sound of the bells is deafening alongside the screams and panic around us. People force vomit on the path in a desperate attempt to rid themselves of poison. Guards continue rushing by as we make our way forward on the path to the meetinghouse. Henry hands the guard off to another passing group of officials who are better equipped to assist. I scan viciously through the crowd for any signs of Ambrose, Nicholas, or even Abigail. Things are moving quickly, and it is all a blur. My body begins to shake as my breathing intensifies.

You are in control. Do not allow this to happen. Breathe.

Rather than falling to the ground and facing defeat from my own emotions, I remain strong and contain the overwhelming urge to cower. Now is not the time to lose control. Henry holds my hand tightly to provide reassurance as we continue on the path.

"Have you spotted the others?" I ask Henry. "Surely someone alerted Nicholas by now."

"I have not yet seen my uncle. But we will find them when we arrive," Henry ensures.

The meetinghouse finally comes into view as we fight through the crowd. My internal conflict causes more distress than everything around me, but I am proud of myself for remaining composed. If we did not gain the knowledge of a poisoning, it could be said that the monster from a children's tale is loose in the meetinghouse. Not even the fires or the numerous deaths caused this level of chaos.

"There!" Henry shouts while pointing. I direct my gaze and locate Ambrose standing just outside of the meetinghouse. It is relieving to see him unharmed after wandering through the night. He shouts and tries to regain order as the crowd around him runs rampant.

"Ambrose! What happened here?" I call out as we approach.

"Henry, Emelie," he begins out of breath, "it is madness on the inside. I cannot contain it."

"Is it true that someone used poison?" Henry asks.

"Yes," Ambrose confirms, "though it shall not be fatal. Some became ill and chaos erupted before I could uncover the cause. But a concoction was found in the servings of wine and cider."

"And what exactly did you find?" I interject.

"We are not certain. It appeared to be jimsonweed, or perhaps lily of the valley. Someone placed this herbage in the drinks. It had to be someone inside the meetinghouse last night because we allowed no entrants after sundown." Ambrose continues his explanation with signs of guilt and regret. "We tried to calm the nerves with some minor festivities and merriment for those with nowhere else to go. But some unfortunate events led to a brief quarrel in the late hours of the night. Solomon acted out of sorts and caused quite the commotion."

Ambrose's mention of Solomon draws my attention. As the owner of the tavern, he holds access to all the wine, beer, cider, and other drinks provided in the meetinghouse. Perhaps Abigail saw something, and Solomon panicked.

"So, nobody is dead? Those who drank the poison shall live?" I ask.

"They will fall ill and vomit profusely through the day, but it is quite unlikely that this foliage could take a life in such a minimal amount. It is but a sick jest. This shall soon pass," Ambrose claims.

"We must warn my uncle," Henry says while turning to face me.

"Nicholas is already inside. Did you not follow his escort from the farm?" Ambrose replies with confusion.

Henry looks to me before thanking Ambrose and rushing to the doors of the meetinghouse. Any further conversation with Ambrose would likely not go in our favor.

"Wait," I urge while grabbing Henry, "he will not be pleased to see us in this place."

"It is too late, Emelie. He must be aware of our absence by now. I need to ensure that he is safe," Henry replies while pulling away and pushing to the inside.

'Tis nearly impossible for our escape to still be a secret. We were gone for the entire night, Abigail went missing, Solomon could be the assassin, and the next attack is unraveling. If only I could stand on a chair or climb the pulpit and make those around us understand that they shall live. My words would be ignored, so only time will reveal the survival of this heinous act.

I become doubtful of this current situation and begin to ponder. After all that happened, surely the assassin would carry out a successful poisoning. They murder with precision and act with nearly untraceable maneuvers. Perhaps this was a distraction to conceal a deeper incentive or as a means to taunt those who search for an identity. Nowhere is off limits and your life can be taken in the safest of places. This realization causes me to worry for our farm and the many guards and barricades. Is our home truly impenetrable?

"Uncle!" Henry shouts while rushing to Nicholas. At the center of the chaos, Nicholas turns and is surprised to see us.

"I apologize if my quick departure awakened you. But you should not have left the farm. It is but madness in this village," Nicholas explains.

I find relief in the fact that Nicholas is still unaware of our escape. It sounds as though he left the farm quietly, not wanting to alert the rest of us.

"I am sorry, Uncle, but we worried for your safety. We knew not what was happening," Henry replies, sharing the same notion that our escape remains a secret.

"I appreciate your concern, but I am well. Things are dire in Bedfordshire this morning. Abigail went missing last night and someone poisoned the refreshments. It was unwise to travel through the night without an escort. Please go and wait for me. I will regather our guards to take you back to—"

"Wait," I interject nervously, stopping Nicholas's words. "All the guards came with you before the sunrise?"

Nicholas hesitates before providing a response, now sharing the same concern that grows within me. "Well, yes. The farm was quiet as could be. We rushed into the village where all the chaos was happening."

My breathing intensifies as I stare back and forth between Henry and Nicholas. "This was but a ruse. All of this is a distraction," I say as tears fill my eyes. "The homes are unguarded, and the focus is on a mirage in the meetinghouse. We must get back to the farm!"

I turn and begin forcing my way to the outside. Nicholas and Henry shout for me to wait but there is simply no time. The entire village has fallen into this finely crafted distraction while the true malevolence unravels elsewhere. It is my hope that I am incorrect, but this series of events is too flawless for any coincidence. The farm remained heavily guarded for days, and with a simple distraction, it was left vulnerable in an instant. Thomasin, Samuel, and Amelia would be unprepared for whatever may come if Nicholas departed in secrecy. They are likely fast asleep without any care.

The cold air stings my face and fills my lungs as I break through to the outside. It appears that Ambrose is slowly regaining order in the surrounding area, as the screams and chaos are dying down. People comfort each other and start to handle their sickness with reason. Surely it was not a pleasant experience for anyone who ingested this poison. Watching people unexpectedly faint and vomit profusely would draw fear from anyone.

While the commotion slowly fades around the meetinghouse, my own emotions begin to spiral. The sun is rising on the eleventh day of Christmas, but I fear that this shall be the darkest day of all. And as I typically do in my most desperate of circumstances, I whisper a prayer as I rush out of the village.

I beg thee, allow my instincts to be wrong. They are completely unprepared and have no protection at the farm. Henry and I never thought that our escape would end in mass confusion. Let Samuel, Thomasin, and Amelia remain unharmed. Please!

Wicked thoughts fill my mind of what awaits. Perhaps the farm is engulfed in flames, or the murderer might attack me from behind as I run through the forest alone. Sounds of the village fade until all I hear is the beating of my heart and my heavy breath. Henry and Nicholas were unsuccessful in matching my pace, but I refuse to waste time by waiting or even turning my head to verify their position. While my safety is at great risk, all that matters is reaching the farm.

My suspicions were valid and there are no guards in these outskirts. Nobody passes by or is seemingly anywhere other than the meetinghouse. All patrols ceased on account of the disruption. It is unclear how long the farm sat unguarded, though Nicholas mentioned leaving quite early. I cannot blame him for choosing to leave in secrecy, for he only had our safety in mind.

Our farm finally comes into view over the vast crop fields. I stray from the path and race directly through what shall be a flourishing field of corn come spring. Even though the terrain is rough and the snow nearly reaches my knees, I never slow my pace. Dead corn stalks and stems beneath the snow hinder my steps, sending me face-first into the ground. Rather than brushing the snow from my hair or giving any acknowledgement to the pain, I simply rise to my feet and continue racing forward.

I reach the edge of the field with blurry vision and struggling breath. My heart races to the point of discomfort so I grip at my chest in agony beneath the thick layers of clothing. Nervously I raise my eyes and stare at our home. Everything slows as I glance back to see Henry approaching in the distance. He runs along the path and shouts for me to wait. And though I could knowingly be walking into a trap, I turn around and take a timid step forward.

One step at a time I move cautiously through the snow. The pain in my chest makes me want to collapse, but I need to keep moving. Our farm is silent, revealing no signs of whatever travesty awaits on the inside. Perhaps I am wrong, and our family is fast asleep. There are no screams, symbols painted in blood, broken windows, or smoke pouring outward as I approach. Nothing.

The illusion of safety fades as I reach the front door. "No, no, no," I repeat under my breath. The door is cracked open, so my fears are all but confirmed. Tears fill my eyes while I shake my head in denial. Nicholas would have made certain that any points of entry were secured before departing. And surely Amelia, Samuel, or Thomasin would have heard the door shuttering in the wind. My heart nearly beats out of my chest as I push the door fully open. I hold my breath and pass through, but it is no longer the entrance to a peaceful farmhouse that we call our home. Rather, it is the gates of Hell.

XXII

This Mortal Coil

A subtle wave of smoke from the hearth greets my arrival. Winter's chill fills our home because Nicholas likely forgot to place another log to burn before leaving. We always keep a fire going throughout the night so that the smoldering embers easily relight the hearth each morning. This holds no relevance as I desperately search for any form of distraction.

"Hello," I call out pathetically in nothing more than a whisper. I clear my throat and attempt to speak again. "Hello!"

Nothing. Only the sound of the door tapping from the wind. While I did not anticipate a response, I am merely biding my time at the thought of what my search shall reveal. Each step is torture, and this is undoubtedly the most frightening situation of my life. Not knowing what to expect is driving me mad. Reverend Thomas was predictable, sharing his plan of our execution and making his moves known for sport. But it was foolish to hold this assassin to that same degree of reckless honesty.

The entryway is unsuspecting as nothing appears out of the ordinary. Carefully I make my way to the area with the hearth. There does not appear to be any signs of disturbance here either.

Please, Thomasin, now would be a wonderful time for you to make your way down the stairs and scold me for waking you. "I'm sorry. There was a commotion at the meetinghouse, and I wanted to make sure you were alright. The day is just beginning so go rest for another few hours. I shall wake you when Amelia finishes breakfast and Nicholas returns."

Sunlight beams through the open door and windows, guiding me as I continue searching. My steps lead me to a trace of snow on the floor. I bend down, confirming my sight and recognizing the outline of a recent footprint. It is still wet to the touch, so someone walked through here moments prior. Slowly I rise from the ground and move forward until discovering another footprint. One by one these lead to the kitchen. As I reach the corner, I tighten my fist and prepare to face the hooded assassin. With a brief hesitation, I hold my breath and leap out with aggression.

"Amelia?" I mutter, standing in shock at the horrific sight before me. The floor, cabinets, and even the ceiling above me are riddled with blood. I try calling out to her once again, but I am unable to speak. She lies still, facedown and brutalized. My eyes never leave her body, and I must force each breath. It feels as though I am floating as I move towards her. My self-awareness is gone as I slip on the profuse amount of blood beneath me. All I can do is crawl to her side and slowly reach out to turn her over.

"Amelia?" I whisper once more. As I turn her corpse, I notice a large slash across her neck. I let out a shriek as she suddenly awakens and coughs intensely. Eyes barely open and face void of all color, she reaches up and grabs tightly onto my arm. Amelia is fighting to live and she is terrified.

"Emelie! What happened?" Henry shouts, bolting his way through the front door.

"In here! Hurry!" I yell. Within seconds Henry appears in the kitchen and is taken aback by the gruesome sight.

"Aunt Amelia!" He calls out.

"Henry, she is still alive! You must help me," I demand through tears.

He pulls a large cloth from the shelf as he makes his way over. Quickly he kneels down, signaling for me to move back so he can tend to Amelia. Henry pushes the cloth onto her neck to slow the bleeding while whispering to her. "You are going to be alright, Aunt Amelia. Nicholas was only a few steps behind me. Please hold on."

Amelia is fighting for her life, and it is but a miracle that she is still alive. I watch in horror while Henry struggles to save his aunt. My entire body is covered in blood, from my legs to my makeshift hand. With porridge and cider spilled nearby, it seems that Amelia was attacked while preparing us breakfast. She likely thought it to be a quiet morning and failed to notice the lack of guards.

"What do you need me to do, Henry?" I ask pathetically.

"We need to stop the bleeding. I may have it under control for the moment, so long as Nicholas and his reinforcements are close. I am not sure that she will survive this," Henry replies. "And what of Thomasin or Samuel?"

His words hit me with a thunderous force. "I do not know. I was only in here for a few moments before I saw Amelia," I explain. Carefully I rise to my feet and make my way to the bottom of the stairs.

"Thomasin, Samuel!" I shout at the top of my lungs, praying for an answer. "We need you to come down here and help us!" A few moments of silence pass as I burst into tears. "Please, come down here!" I shout, unable to control my emotions. "Thomasin!"

"This is not good, Emelie," Henry replies, sharing my concern. He attempts to stay strong, though I see him faltering.

"I need to find them. I need to make sure they are well," I explain tearfully while approaching the stairs.

"I do not think you will find anything pleasant up there," Henry claims, now failing to contain his tears. "Perhaps you should stay right here and wait for my uncle. He will come, and this will all be fixed."

It feels as though I watch from afar, relinquishing all control of my body as I begin my ascent. "I am going to wake them," I tell Henry.

He continues applying pressure to Amelia's wound and reassuring her. At this moment I am in a daze, spreading blood everywhere and reaching for the railing to maintain my balance. The stairs seemingly extend before me and the top falls out of sight. A snowy outline of footprints is visible on each step before me, and appear to be going up and down the stairs. Though my only concern is not to fall backwards into unconsciousness. My heartbeat continues to cause me pain, and my breath draws short.

Suddenly I find myself humming one of the carols that members of Bedfordshire would sing during the festivities. This is not something I have done before, but it brings me comfort. No longer am I in control of these peculiar actions. The thought of finding Thomasin in the same state as Amelia caused a complete disconnect. Perhaps this is an attempted shield for my own emotions, as my true self is certainly absent. I float up one stair at a time, humming and rubbing my chest.

As I reach the final step, it feels like hours have passed. While I wish not to admit it, this situation has finally broken me. My failure to identify the assassin brought tragedy to our home. Perhaps I missed too many opportunities to act and did not recognize obvious indications. A mob formed to accuse the wrong man, then we spent too much time in the prison and searching for a journal. The officials of the village were useless and even Ambrose failed us all. It would make complete sense that the struggles of the officials were intentional if Ambrose is behind this. But that matters not at this moment, and I must face the ultimate consequences of my own failures as I follow the killer's footsteps.

"Thomasin, Amelia prepared breakfast to greet the day," I call out as my words fade to a whisper. "Please reveal yourself so I need not come over there. I beg thee."

My legs are locked to the floor, unable to take another step and face the reality that awaits. It is my wish to move and gather myself, but my body does not comply. Though Amelia was still alive so acting in haste could allow for a similar outcome if Samuel and Thomasin were attacked.

What is wrong with thee? Compose thyself and move. You murdered your captor and freed a prison full of your friends. You can do this.

With a deep breath, I prepare to advance beyond the stairs. I am frightened, but this situation is of more importance than my inner struggles. If I truly wish to help the others then standing here like a coward is not the way to do so.

"I am here, Thomasin," I say aloud. The upstairs is wickedly cold, and I can see my breath with every exhale. Wind whistles through the hall and the wooden floor creeks beneath me. Henry and I's chamber door is shut, just how we left it before our departure. As I make my way down the hall, I notice that Samuel and Thomasin's chamber door is wide open. And it does not come as a surprise that the floor shows traces of blood. There is no more time to waste so I shakily walk through the doorway into their chamber.

 A pathetic attempt to grab ahold of the wall does me no good and I collapse to the ground. I scream at the top of my lungs, full of emotion and hyperventilating at the sight before me. "No!" I shout repeatedly. It is evident that we were far too late, and the assassin did not stop with Amelia.

 Sitting upright under the window, no longer displaying any signs of life, is Samuel. As I stagger towards him, it is with certainty that he is deceased. Samuel shows evident signs of struggle and multiple slashes across his body. His hands are covering a large wound on his stomach, which was likely the fatal blow. The furniture is out of sorts, so he clearly put up a fight. Thomasin is nowhere to be found, so my only hope is that she made an escape. While such a positive outcome is likely incorrect, I tell myself that Samuel's bravery allowed her to survive.

 "I am so very sorry. You did not deserve this," I whisper while gently sitting at his side. Another one of my dearest friends is gone. We understood each other and he was a wonderful friend since the days of our birth. John thought of him as a hero and I did as well; the true savior in our despair. Samuel carried a heavy burden from Warren Hollow and inflicted torture upon himself, just like me. He saw the damage I concealed and wished for us to find resolve together.

"Perhaps you and I can someday free ourselves from this hold of the past."

"I will, Samuel. For you, I shall try. But at the moment, it seems that this is our final goodbye," I express while slowly lowering him to the floor. "Thomasin needs me, and so does your child. I promise that I will fight for them until my dying breath. Goodbye, my dear friend."

Gently I lay the quilt from the mattress over his body. With staggering steps and a failure of balance, I make my way out of the chamber. I pass by the mirror and stop to stare at my reflection, rather than avoiding it as I have done each day since our arrival to this home. Moments pass as I stare dead into my own eyes as if I am face to face with a spirit from the past. The person staring back is a familiar face that I am ready to confront. Through a rugged appearance of dirt and blood, I see the person who beat Reverend Thomas all those months ago. My mentality shifts back into the state of revenge, survival, and determination that was long since buried. Whoever did this to us will pay dearly, by my own hand. Death could be the result for me and the face in the mirror, though I make peace with this and become one with the Emelie of old.

Commotion downstairs signals that Nicholas arrived with a swarm of guards and officials. Footsteps fill the home alongside shouting and panic. Rather than joining the others, I simply take a moment to myself and sit at the top of the stairs. I look down at my makeshift hand and watch as blood drips down the steel.

"Emelie!" Nicholas shouts as he appears at the bottom of the stairs. He has tears in his eyes and is in shambles as he makes his way forward. Henry stands not far behind.

"Samuel is dead," I reply calmly, interrupting Nicholas's advance. "And Thomasin is missing. I need to go find her. We must search the area right now."

Nicholas pulls me tightly into his arms. I hug him back to offer my own consolation. Though the only thing on my mind is finding Thomasin before she meets a similar fate, if she is not already deceased.

"We ... I ... need to find Thomasin," I mutter, trying not to confuse Nicholas with the fact that he be staring at two separate people inhabiting the same skin. The peaceful and naïve Emelie of Bedfordshire has called upon the vengeful, desperate, and animalistic Emelie of Warren Hollow. And together, they are out for blood.

"She will be found. But we must go. Amelia needs Timothy and his surgeons in the village. And they will take care of Samuel at our departure," Nicholas explains, pulling away and beginning his descent down the stairs. He stops for a moment to embrace Henry and tightly grabs his shoulder. Henry looks up to me and starts moving forward.

"Wait," I tell him as I rise. "You do not want to see it. I will be down in just a moment, for I need to retrieve some of the journals from our chamber."

Henry nods with confusion, but elects not to question my insanity while slowly making his way down the stairs. None of us will return to the farm for the time being, so I need to gather some of the writings and journals as a final attempt for clarity. While it seems like a desperate act, perhaps Rose's words can assist me in finding Thomasin. I push open the door and enter our chamber. The sun shines through the window, bringing a false impression of the beautiful day that awaits.

My bearings are out of sorts, so I lose my balance and slip into the wall. A journal slides off the shelf from the force of my collision. Thinking little of it, I bend down to retrieve whatever has fallen. Though suddenly I am taken aback. This is one of the collections that was missing. More importantly, it is the original journal that led to our escape and search of the sisters' home. Clear as day, I stare at the journal in a state of bewilderment.

How can this be? Did I overlook this journal in my desperate search? Was it here this whole time?

Doubt fills my mind as my breathing intensifies. We searched through every shelf and compartment on this farm and failed to locate this specific writing. And now, it found its way back to where it belongs. The thought of delusion also crosses my mind, and guilt overcomes me at the fact that our escape may have been useless and I am simply going mad.

Do I become someone else in my mind and take action without any awareness? Is it I who terrorizes this village and does these awful things?

Carefully I pull the journal from the ground and walk to the window so that the sunlight can shine on the cover. All the scratches and impurities are evident as I run my hand over the binding. I begin turning the pages, looking back to my early scribbles as they intertwine with Rose's words. Stories of my childhood, John, All Hallows Eve, and most importantly, the truth of our conviction. It is all here, and perhaps I am to blame for all that has happened. But as I reach the final pages, something falls from the scroll and floats to the ground. I watch as it drifts through the air, swaying peacefully and eventually landing with gentle ease. A thin cut of fabric lays before me. A bright red piece of fabric; scarlet shaded to be exact. One that could be used for accessories such as bows and ribbons.

XXIII

Watch Over Me, Part II

All doubt is officially put to rest. Our suspicions are confirmed, and Abigail held this journal in her possession. One miniscule mistake revealed her identity as I was moments from declaring a loss of sanity. And while I never saw her commit a crime with my own eyes, I have reason to believe that both her and Rachel are behind Bedfordshire's corruption. She came to this farm and used the opportunity to return the writings.

The room spins around me as I desperately revisit memories of these sisters. Our awkward introduction, following Thomasin and I to the port, their fascination with witchcraft, Abigail's deeper feelings for me, the distraction so they could steal the writings, accusing us in the meetinghouse, poisoning the provisions, and committing murder. Perhaps they did not expect Clara's death to cause a relocation to the meetinghouse. It became difficult for them to carry out their plans without free reign. They could no longer come and go as they pleased so a distraction was necessary in each instance. Clara's confusion was an opportunity to make an early entry or exit from each gathering. Abigail fled the meetinghouse and caused enough commotion for Rachel to stealthily poison the ale. They knew that this would leave the farm vulnerable.

But this sudden loss of freedom led to drastic measures of keeping their identity concealed. Barnabas was a loose end that needed to be severed. Stealing the writings and blade from my chamber was also something they viewed as a risk, so it was hastily returned to the shelf. Nearly all tracks were covered, aside from the ribbon that was forgotten in the binding. The attack on our home was conducted in haste, so they made a simple mistake. We were a step behind from the beginning, but this measly indicator was all that we needed.

Though if Abigail and Rachel are behind the chaos then I fail to understand their motivation. Thomasin and I were good to them and Nicholas was practically their guardian. Why they would want to weaken their home, ruin this time of merriment, and kill their grandmother is truly vexing. I suspect that their reasoning shall soon come to light, but I must proceed with the utmost caution. The blade is still missing and Thomasin has been taken, so their reign of terror is certainly unfinished.

An attempt to silence my thoughts does not calm my beating heart. This realization opened the gates of my emotions and a strange feeling washes over me. I have been in shambles since the moment I entered our home, and this discovery took the last of my poise. While I wish to run from the chamber and shout my accusations, a familiar feeling halts my movement, and I understand what is bound to occur. I drop the journal, and the room begins to spin as I fall into the door. My body sweats profusely and I shake uncontrollably. With the last of my strength, I reach for the window in a pathetic attempt for fresh air.

Air! The cold air will help! Must ... make ... it!

It seems to be a great distance away and getting to the window would be a feat of impossibility. I settle for the bed, which is nearly the same distance.

In one final act of desperation, I twist the doorknob and force the door open. The stairs are only a few steps away so I can call for help. My heart beats out of my chest and a sudden pain tightens my torso. I am scared to release my death grip on the doorknob because this is the only thing holding me upright.

They are waiting for you downstairs! Amelia needs assistance in the village.

I release my hold on the door and fail to take one full step before accepting my fate. Everything around me fades as my eyes close and I crash to the ground.

Air fills my lungs and I let out a gasping breath. I feel warmth on my skin and recognize that something is amiss. Rather than face down on the cold floor in our home, I am lying in a gentle plot of grass. My fingers run through the blades as the wind blows through my hair. It takes minimal effort to push myself to a seated position. Sounds of rushing water and birds chirping fill my ears. I shield my eyes to block the glaring sun above. This place is peaceful and inviting.

I have been here before.

As I rise to my feet, I recognize this to be a place of familiarity. It seems that I am back in the forest near Rose's home. But more importantly, this is where I awakened when Reverend Thomas nearly killed me in the prison. "John," I whisper, remembering his presence in this astral realm. My eyes shoot side to side, scanning the vegetation and animals that pass by. He is nowhere in sight, so I start to run as I search the area.

"John! I have returned and wish to find you!" I call out, my voice sounding strong and bold. The path ahead grows livelier with each step as I traverse deeper into the forest. My hand has returned as I push through the brush. I stretch each of my fingers and try not to make sense of the situation while desperately searching for my brother.

"There!" I shout, recognizing the space of our last meeting. John sat happily on a log nearby in my previous visit. A smile grows on my face at the idea of reuniting with my brother. We celebrated All Hallows Eve here, and this is where John waited for me. I often relive our previous conversation in this place and prayed for the opportunity to reunite.

All happiness begins to fade as I maneuver through the branches and into the clearing. Everything is the same, but John is nowhere to be found. The log sits absent, and John does not await my arrival. It seems that this space is empty, as I am the sole inhabitant of this dream. With one final glance, I leave the clearing and make my way back to the path. Thoughts of insanity and death fill my mind as I move forward. Perhaps the events in Bedfordshire were too much to bear and I retreated to the safest place I know. Or, I struck my head against the floor hard enough to end my existence. Either way I continue searching for whatever I am meant to find. This is a land of euphoria, much more so than the devastation and horrors in the other realm.

Suddenly I recognize a familiar line of lilacs, marigolds, and tulips. These flowers bloom beautifully in the sunshine and calm my sadness. As a child I always knew that I was close to Rose's home when flowers lined the path. Flowers would guide me to her if I ever lost my way, and I forgot how beautiful this homestead used to be prior to her conviction. I traced these steps hundreds of times with Mother and Father, John, and Thomasin, but mostly by myself.

"Rose!" I call out as her home comes into view. Rather than rundown and destroyed like we left it, her home is restored and thriving. The windows are no longer broken, and the cross is wiped from her door. Plants and vegetation around her fences bloom and decorations blow in the wind. Tears of happiness fill my eyes at such a site, and countless memories of my childhood come to the surface. Thomasin and I used to play for hours on end in Rose's home and the surrounding area, then this space turned into our bonfire gatherings as we matured. And much more recently, this was our shelter through the winter when we escaped from the prison. Just as I used to do as a child, I walk the path and climb the few stairs to her porch. With no hesitation I knock on the door. Nobody answers, so I knock once more while panic begins to swell.

"Can I help you, stranger?" A familiar voice calls from behind me.

Tears form and a smile grows wide on my face. There is no need to turn around in order to recognize the person who awaits. Slowly I take a step and look over my shoulder in awe as Rose stands nearby. She has returned to good health and her beauty shines as she smiles at me. Rose wears all black, from her hair accessories to her dress and boots, just like in all my memories. Her appearance was unlike anyone in The Hollow, and that fact remains true in this realm. Unable to control my emotions, I rush from the porch and meet her for a tight embrace. I hold tightly, never wanting to let go of my dear friend.

"What troubles thee?" She asks, pulling away and rubbing my face. I stare back into her mesmerizing blue eyes.

"Oh, how I missed you so!" I shout, trying to compose myself.

She smiles, never acknowledging my sadness or falling into a panic of her own. She is calm and peaceful, just as John was in this place.

"Come with me," Rose instructs while taking my hand and starting to walk, "let us tend to the flowers."

I smile at this notion because I loved to assist Rose with gardening as a child. "I have so much to tell you," I mutter.

She turns and smiles at my words as we walk, never loving her charm. The flowerbed near the stream comes into view as we move through the vegetation. "Wait," I say with enough force to stop our movement. "I must ask thee the same question I asked John. Have I passed?"

"Your curiosity has not escaped you, Emelie. This is an end of sorts, but you are still alive," Rose replies.

Though I am relieved, I still find confusion in this realm. "How, or why am I here? Last time I was slipping into death. Perhaps I was never close to death? Rather than a miracle, was all of this in my mind? Have I gone mad?"

"It is not I who brought you here, for we are both passengers in this place you envision near the edge of mortality," Rose explains with a smile.

I recount the moments before losing consciousness. A bitter pain struck my chest, and I lost control of my breathing. This was a pain I ignored for days among all the other struggles. Perhaps I panicked myself to death or am quite close as Rose alludes. But things are different this time and I do not wish to be here.

"I need to save Thomasin and inform the others! Samuel is gone; my dear friend was taken by those sisters! There was so much I needed to say to him, Rose," I shout in anguish as I sob. My sudden distress sends a shift through this place and my heartbeat echoes through the trees.

"Emelie, you will prevail, one way or another. You know exactly what it may cost you to save thy friends. But for now, would you assist me with pruning these flowers?"

I drop to my knees at her side. We begin shaping the flowers and removing the dead stems and branches. "Do you remember everything?" I ask.

"Of course," she begins with a smile, "I remember you and Thomasin running amok through these trees after teaching you both how to read. You would bicker and quarrel over who would take the first lesson." I laugh and reminisce on her words. "And as you got older, I remember you and your parents bringing little John to my home. We would treat him for hours and keep his health strong."

"No. I mean, do you remember things more recently?"

She pauses for a moment before resuming her gardening. "Well, as you children grew older, you would come less and less, no longer using my home as a place for sport." Her words bring me guilt, so I draw my attention to the ground as she turns to face me. "But then all of you came back. You were so mature and cared little for the bounds of Warren Hollow. We held those glorious fires in the night, breaking nearly every restriction your parents enacted," she recalls with a laugh. "I watched you all grow and saw it as the truest blessing. Were those not magical times?"

"They were the best times of my life," I reply with gratitude. "But Rose, I speak of thy death. All the torture you faced at the hands of Thomas. And I must ask, how did you come to fancy him?"

These words still do not hinder her positivity. She listens but appears to be free of any pain or worry, caring only to reminisce and tend to the flowers. "It matters not. We were not meant to be and could not be. Still, I played into his charm like a fool, never anticipating such ruthless aggression."

"I promise that everyone shall know the truth. I ensured it in Warren Hollow at my departure, and I live to tell your tale!" I tell her. And for the first time, her smile begins to fade. She stops her motions and turns to gaze directly upon me.

"No," she responds while shaking her head and pulling my hands into hers. "I'm afraid that my story has come to an end, Emelie. You need not carry this pain, this ... guilt and self-affliction for what happened." Her words continue as tears roll down my face. "You must live to tell your own tale. I know you are still trapped in the confines of Warren Hollow, but you must move forward."

"But John, and Ezekiel, and you. I cannot lose these memories, and I have done awful things. I struggle, Rose, every day. 'Tis true that I am withdrawn from myself and I do not know how to control these fears. My friends are dying and all I can do is cower amid the chaos. No longer can I lead, or even defend myself. I am afraid," I explain tearfully.

Rose pulls herself slightly closer as the world around us begins to ripple and fade. "You must listen carefully to my words, Emelie. There is a future for you, and one thing you must do to find it. Let go of the past," she holds me tighter. "Leave all this pain in Warren Hollow, but hold onto the pleasant memories. Lock those vicious writings away and retell every memory that you cherish instead. It is all a part of your story; a part of who you are. But it does not need to be all of you."

Her words rush over me like a crashing wave at the port. Perhaps this is all in my mind and Rose is merely the manifestation of a truth I refuse to accept. If I do not listen to those around me or my own words, then perhaps a rendition of Rose will allow for my cooperation.

When I visited this realm and found John, I never wanted to leave his side. But this time, my efforts are unfinished. I must save Thomasin and put an end to those wicked sisters.

"Well, it seems that we have done all we can for these flowers today," Rose says with enthusiasm, "I offer gratitude for thy assistance. Perhaps you should be on your way, Emelie."

"I agree," I remark while rising to my feet. "But Rose, there is something I must tell thee." She also rises, standing just before me and offering her full attention. That familiar smile stares back, reflecting all the wonderful memories from my childhood. The sun shines down and the vegetation flourishes around us. Perhaps it is all a figment induced by insanity or I lay on the floor bridging death, but I am grateful for this place. If this is deep within the confines of my mind, then I no longer need to worry about forgetting John or Rose. They will live on through my memories forever. Or if this is the heaven that awaits, then death is no fear of mine.

"I simply wanted to thank you. For pushing us to seek more in life and for being a wonderful friend. You made me what I am today, and I'm so sorry for what happened to you."

Rose stretches her arms out and signals for a final embrace. She wipes my tears as we hold each other tightly. I understand the chaos and danger that awaits when I awaken, so I take this final moment to appreciate the calmness and beauty. Whether in this astral realm or reality, I suspect this to be my final visit to Warren Hollow.

At this very moment I feel like the innocent child that once was. Long before John was born or I had any desires for a better life. Before Reverend Nicholas became ill and Thomas invaded our village. Before witchcraft destroyed everything we knew. Before Henry and I found love. Before all that I have become, was this very moment; Rose shaping my world with Thomasin at my side. And now, Thomasin is in danger so I must save her. I close my eyes and hold Rose tightly as the world around me becomes a blinding light.

A debilitating jolt flows through my body like a strike of lightning. I gasp for breath as though I am drowning and an unbearable pain shoots through my torso. With both hands I grab at my chest as my eyes begin to open.

"She is awake," an unfamiliar voice shouts. The room is blurred around me, and I succumb to a bout of delirium.

"What is happening?" I attempt to speak. Footsteps rush and a door slams close by.

"Emelie!" Someone shouts. Though still confused, I recognize this to be Henry's voice. My eyes adjust and I soon discover that I lie on a mattress in a dim room. Though I try to determine the current situation, my mind is void of all thoughts and recollection.

"What is this?" I ask.

Henry rushes to embrace me as my words trail off. "Oh, Emelie. I am so thankful that you are well. You gave us quite the scare back home!"

My chest pounds and it feels as though someone placed a boulder across me. "Henry?" I ask in a pained whisper.

"We are safe for the moment. There is no need to worry."

"Where are we?"

"We are in the meetinghouse," Henry explains with tears forming behind a subtle smile, "and Amelia shall live."

"Amelia, what happened to her? I am quite confused, Henry," I reply while rising to a seated position. Henry tries to assist my movements with visible worry. He likely wishes for me to relax but I disobey his command before it is given.

"You hold no memory of it?" he asks with kindness. I shake my head, feeling as though I remember something, but unsure of what exactly. "There was an attack. A vicious attack on the farm. We suspected such after an earlier diversion, but we were too late. Amelia was wounded, and I be afraid that—"

"Samuel!" I interrupt Henry's words. His brief explanation caused a flooding of memories in my mind. Though it is still hazy, I recall a commotion at the meetinghouse that left us in a panic. We were rushing through the snowfall, trying to get back to the farm because it was left unguarded. And then upon our arrival, we found Amelia in the kitchen. There was blood everywhere and Henry helped to save her life. The details are distant, but I recall finding Samuel. He was dead before our arrival.

"Wait! Where is Thomasin? Did we find her at the farm?" I ask with growing panic, my heartbeat bringing a deep pain to my chest as I struggle to remember.

"They are looking for her as we speak," Henry explains.

"We must go and find her. For she is pregnant, Henry!" I shout while rising from the mattress.

My words surprise Henry, and he slows his movements. Suddenly I regret sharing this secret, although the situation is dire and there is no time to waste. Surely Thomasin would not hold this announcement against me. "Why do we wait here? Who confines us to this place?"

"Nobody," he replies, leaving me bewildered. "We are here because we found you practically dead. I thought you had passed when I laid eyes on you."

What happened to me?

"Of what do you speak?" I ask Henry in nothing more than a whisper.

"You were on the floor and struggling to breathe. Things were dire for a few moments, but Nicholas and Ambrose helped to keep you stable until we made it to Timothy. He sees this as a severe bout of panic. No further treatment is needed so we brought you here to rest while his practice is occupied. But you could die if this is to happen again," Henry explains.

"And why was I in our chamber? Was I searching for Thomasin?" I ask with confusion.

"No. You were out of sorts and wished to retrieve a binding, a journal I believe."

"A journal?" I repeat. The faded memory of entering our chamber slowly returns. I recall my heart beating uncontrollably, struggling to compose myself, holding the wall, and eventually losing my balance. But I found something first.

Remember, remember, remember!

It was my new journal, or perhaps another writing that shared similarities to my journal. Though the binding that Nicholas and Amelia gifted me could not be mistaken if there be a room full of scrolls before me. I used the sunlight for some degree of confirmation. And it happened to be the original journal that was missing, so I became confused. Something was wrong. It was damaged or covered in blood. A dark shade of red fills my memory. Blood covered my journal like the rest of our home.

No; rather, I start to recollect that it was not blood at all.

I raise my eyes to Henry who notices my revelation. While it took a few pathetic moments to gather myself, I remember every detail of what I found. "Henry," I mutter with a shaky voice and a pain in my chest. "Abigail and Rachel are behind this."

XXIV

This Side of the Grave

Henry is surprised but never doubts my words. He knows that I would never make accusations unless I held absolute certainty. Though our day was full of death and despair, I ultimately found the evidence we needed.

"The sisters caused all of this madness?" Henry asks.

"Yes," I tell him sternly. "It was the journal. I entered the room and the missing journal fell from the shelf. Abigail made one small mistake. She was likely marking a page with ribbon and forgot to remove it. Her attack on the farm was a desperate attempt to once again cover her tracks, and she was so close to remaining unknown but knew we were on her trail. Perhaps they could justify stealing the journal out of curiosity if we realized sooner, but it be no coincidence that the journal appeared after the attack."

I watch as Henry unravels the situation in his mind. He slowly begins to connect all the events and make sense of the chaos.

"What do we do now?" Henry questions. "I should go to Nicholas, and I will tell Ambrose as well."

Henry rises and I quickly join him with a painful exhale. "Perhaps we should do this carefully. If Abigail or Rachel returned, then they could be waiting to attack. Who knows what they shall do if confronted."

They are not here, Emelie. Most of Bedfordshire is scattered, still suffering from sickness and hiding in their homes. Abigail never returned and Rachel supposedly went to find her."

"Well," I say while trying to formulate a plan, "is the sun still in the sky?"

"It is the early hours of the night. Perhaps a few hours passed supper time."

I was unconscious for longer than I thought. Though it is understandable as we did not get any rest on the previous night. We spent the whole day formulating a plan to escape and spent the night trapped in the sisters' chamber. And as the sun rose above us, our morning was filled with chaos and death. 'Tis no wonder that I nearly met my end in the midst of exhaustion and delirium. "And what of Amelia?" I ask.

"Timothy tends to her in his practice. My uncle is by her side, and they give positive news for the time being."

"We must go to her, but Thomasin is in danger. Tomorrow is the final day of Christmas and I wish not to find her corpse on display."

"Perhaps you should rest, Emelie. Though I know you all too well and understand that this would be foolish to request. But do promise that whatever this night brings, you will act with caution. I cannot bear to lose you," Henry urges while embracing me tightly.

"I swear it," I reply in nothing more than a whisper, doubting my words but wishing not to suffer any further loss. Thoughts of Samuel return and I fight tears from the horrific sight. I never anticipated seeing another one of my friends in such a manner after leaving Warren Hollow.

I pull away from Henry and take a few deep breaths. Pain radiates through my chest, but I will not succumb to fear. It nearly had me in the chamber, but Rose's wisdom gave me motivation to move forward. Perhaps it was all my own thoughts as insanity draws near. Regardless, Thomasin must be saved and I will do whatever is necessary to ensure that the sisters are brought to justice.

"There is a bit of commotion beyond these doors so we must remain composed," Henry advises. I nod at his words, prepared to face whatever awaits on the other side. Henry moves forward and begins opening the door. For a moment I close my eyes and formulate the best way to share my accusation. Doubt creeps in at the idea of making such a statement. This was the very action that tore apart our home, and now I will become the accuser.

You acted with reason and carefully uncovered the identity of this assassin beyond any doubt. So why do you still feel reluctant after the hell they bring down upon Bedfordshire?

A gust of wind blows through my hair as my eyes shoot open. Rather than chaos and despair, the meetinghouse appears to be calm. There are a few people in sight, most resting or fighting the aftermath of the poisoning.

"She is alive," a voice yells.

My presence is realized as I emerge from the private chamber. Henry stays by my side, holding my hand tightly and prepared to handle the attention together. We walk from the corner of the meetinghouse and slowly make our way through the pews. People stare as we pass, some rising and watching in disbelief. A crowd of guards swarms before us with visible concern.

"Are you alright?" An unfamiliar official asks. 'Tis likely that Nicholas gave firm instructions of our protection and care.

"I am well," I begin with a tired tone, "but I have some information I would like to share. Could you please call on Ambrose?" The guards look at each other and debate his exact whereabouts.

"He is with Nicholas and Timothy."

"No, he is in dispute with Solomon in the Tavern."

"I last saw him near the port!"

"Please," I say while slightly raising my voice. "Send anyone you can find. I know who is behind all of this and I must share it at once. My friend's life depends on it!"

They react as though I have spoken a miracle into existence. Fumbling over words and squabbling with each other nearly makes me laugh as they panic and rush to the door. Quickly they depart the meetinghouse and shout instructions on the outside.

It was unwise to think this would be a subtle accusation.

I look to Henry and offer a nod of confidence, ensuring that I am certain of the actions we are about to take. "Now we wait," I whisper anxiously.

More guards rush inside with other members of Bedfordshire. All eyes land upon me as they line the pews, but it bothers me not. I am taken back to those nights of power in the prison. My nerves slow and I fight the growing urge to smile. It may seem selfish given the circumstance, yet there be no denying that deep down I love this and always have. The power fuels me and makes me feel alive. I denied it in the past, but will do so no longer. I am not like other people, and Rose taught me that this is a wonderful thing.

The meetinghouse fills in a matter of moments. I decide to take a seat on the stairs of the pulpit, watching curious onlookers as they gather and spout rumors. While such attention fills me with insecurity and doubt, I do not mind from time to time. It will certainly take some adjusting to follow Rose's bold words, but this could be the first step in securing my future.

From the moment John was born, I cared for him more than I ever cared for myself. And upon his death, my sole purpose was to ensure everyone's escape from Warren Hollow. There has never been a single moment in my existence where I truly lived for myself. But tonight is of more importance than my own revelations, so my own progress can wait one more night. It would be unwise to assume that the next few hours shall be easy. We have no indication of Thomasin's safety, and I can only pray that she is still alive.

I apologize, Rose. Your kind words, or rather my inner voice of truth, must simply wait. Once Thomasin is safe and these sisters are exposed, I will bring my own safety to the light. But you, my brother, Warren Hollow, our torture, and the justice of your story are simply who I am. So what am I to be without this history? If I am fortunate enough to survive this night, then perhaps I shall find out.

Ambrose emerges through the door, and my composure begins to falter. This is now real, and I am likely about to pass a death sentence upon Abigail and Rachel. I cannot determine why this feels wrong, even with the proof and Thomasin's safety in the balance. From hiding in the prison for safety to passing my own accusations, our past has truly come full circle. These sisters did terrible things so why do I continue doubting myself?

Slowly Ambrose pushes through the crowd, making his way to the front and ignoring all pleas for his attention. His eyes remain locked on me and Henry with little emotion. The meetinghouse holds perhaps the largest crowd I have seen since the meeting to begin the festivities. Pastor Noah, Solomon, and nearly everyone in Bedfordshire is in attendance. Everyone except Abigail and Rachel.

Now standing feet away, I notice Ambrose's expression shift as he grows near. He tries his best to show sympathy but is unsure of how to proceed. This has been a horrific day in Bedfordshire, from the poisoning to the attack on the farm, and even Ambrose feels defeated. "Hello, Emelie," he begins. Ambrose is surprised to see me standing before him alongside Henry. "I understand that you two would like to make an accusation."

"Aye. That be correct. Though I fear it is more than an assumption or intuition. We know exactly who caused this hardship," I reply.

"I see," Ambrose begins while moving towards the room I recently awakened in. "Perhaps we should discuss this in private."

"There is no time for that. Thomasin's life could end if we do not act quickly. And I think it is only right that the people around us know as well."

"So, you wish to pass this accusation for all to hear?"

I offer a nod and remain at the bottom of the pulpit. He struggles for a few moments with doubt. Though he surely understands that further secrecy will drive Bedfordshire into mayhem, so he is conflicted. Solomon also pushed to the front of the meetinghouse with his mob, and they are ready for battle.

"Are you certain?" Ambrose asks one final time. He worries for our safety and for the chaos that a simple accusation can bring down upon someone. His concern is appreciated, although the time for private discussion is long past.

"Yes," I reply while ascending the pulpit. Henry joins me and Ambrose follows. The three of us stand above the fear and aggression of the countless onlookers. Ambrose signals for everyone to calm themselves and be seated. Some people abide by his command while most refuse to cooperate.

"Quiet yourselves and obey his command!" Solomon yells. He instructs his mob to line the pulpit, protecting us from any backlash and allowing this discussion to commence. I acknowledge his efforts and give him a subtle nod as I try to steady my breathing. It is with guilt that I suspected the involvement of Ambrose, Solomon, or any of these wonderful people.

"You can do this, Emelie," Henry whispers.

The meetinghouse falls completely silent. Nobody moves and all shouting ceases. "Now," Ambrose begins, "this has been a difficult time in Bedfordshire. Today was perhaps the worst in our history. While we are blessed to have lost not a soul from the poisoning in these walls at sunrise, I am afraid that the same cannot be said over at Nicholas's farm. Amelia is expected to live, but Samuel lost his life. He was becoming an integral member of this congregation, and we shall honor him in the days ahead. But Emelie and Nicholas's nephew stand before you today, willing to make a firm accusation." Ambrose turns to us as the crowd gasps. Solomon forcefully calms the voices until the meetinghouse is silent once again. "Emelie, we look to you with desperation. Please, inform us of your findings."

My gaze leaves Ambrose and I nervously scan the crowd. People stand wall to wall in the meetinghouse, ready to act on the first words that escape my mouth.

"I," I begin while my thoughts escape me. Henry squeezes my hand to offer support while I desperately search for the courage to continue. "I held suspicions in recent days. The manner of death among these individuals is no coincidence. Back in my home village, I had a friend named Rose. She was an apothecary who specialized in the dark arts and witchcraft. Much like the misfortune that happened here. Rose documented her findings across journals and scrolls for many years. Her writings were practically all that I kept from Warren Hollow. And not long ago, these journals were stolen. The chaos soon followed in a near-perfect rendition, and it seemed that the pages came to life in Bedfordshire. I know who is responsible," I claim, my words drawing emotion from the crowd.

"Who stole it!"

"This is the work of the devil!"

"Tell us, tell us!"

With a deep breath I continue. "Earlier today I discovered that the journal had been returned after the attack on the farm. We searched for days, but suddenly it was back on my shelf. I would have blamed my own stupidity but there was something left behind in the binding by mistake. It was a ribbon. A red ribbon to be exact. While I wish it not to be true, I believe that the twin sisters, Abigail and Rachel, are behind this wickedness."

My words hit the crowd with a heavy impact. People shout and search around the room, scanning for the sisters who are nowhere to be found.

"At ease, everyone!" Ambrose attempts to calm the crowd with failing efforts. "And this stolen journal leaves you certain that Abigail and Rachel are to blame?"

"I believe so. They visited us before the festivities began and distracted me in the chamber where the writings were held. I assume this is when they stole the writings, but in a desperate attempt to cover their tracks, they did not act with caution on the farm earlier today. If they stole the journal out of curiosity then so be it, but it cannot be a coincidence that the writing was returned at the time of the attack," I raise my voice over the crowd. My words fuel the chaos until the meetinghouse begins forming into a mob.

"We must find them!"

"Bring these wicked sisters forth at once!"

"They shall pay with their lives!"

"Just a moment!" Ambrose shouts to regain order. His forcefulness stops the madness. "Is there anything else you can use to connect these sisters to the attacks? Any deeper evidence? A weapon? A true sighting while in the act? Perhaps we need more proof before condemning them!" Ambrose tries to protect the sisters' innocence and reasonably so. He granted us the same level of reason when we were the accused.

What else led us to suspect the sisters? They will care little for odd behavior at supper or intuition.

"Yes, there is more!" I shout. "A finely crafted dagger is also missing, and we suspect they used this during the murders.

Abigail and Rachel will likely have it in their possession when they are found. But more importantly when we were in the prison, the attack was nearly compromised. Edward landed a significant strike during the scuffle. Surely this caused an injury or a scar."

"Of course! She speaks the truth!" Solomon announces while ascending the pulpit. His movements bring full cooperation to the crowd and some even take their seats. Solomon is a forceful figure, and I am relieved to have his sudden support and protection.

"I confronted Abigail about a wicked bruise on her eye. It was noticeable from across the meetinghouse. Perhaps I was drinking, and less than kind, but she fled before I could question her further. Surely that must be the cause!"

"How are we to be certain this is connected? Perhaps she fell or was caught in other mischief!" Ambrose explains conflictingly.

"No," Solomon replies in disagreement, "she was in pain and became hostile at the slightest mention. Why else would she run off into the night?" Ambrose attempts to formulate a response before Solomon continues. "I shall tell you why. She wished to cause a distraction while her sister poisoned the provisions! And now the both of them are missing, likely planning another attack at this very moment!"

Yes, continue connecting the pieces and unraveling their guilt before all of Bedfordshire. This draws closer to fact by the second rather than a foolish accusation from me and Henry.

Ambrose steps forward and pushes Solomon behind him. "I know Nicholas is a man of honor, and he would never act on impulse. And for the few months we have known his extended family, I know these two young adults to be but the same. Emelie, I place faith in your words, and we shall find these sisters at once."

Preparations to launch a so-called witch hunt are immediately underway. Some wave knives and tools in the air, ready to put an end to the chaos themselves.

"Ambrose," I yell while grabbing his arm, "The sisters must remain unharmed if they are found. They have Thomasin and we need to ensure her safety. For they could kill her out of desperation!" My panic begins to swell. While the efforts and support across Bedfordshire are appreciated, any irrational actions could place Thomasin in serious danger. And if the sisters are butchered, then we will never know their motivations.

"Child," Solomon says while drawing my attention, "after all that these sisters have done, death would be mercy for what awaits. Though mercy was not given to any of those who were murdered, including their own grandmother. I will see to it that they are returned alive." He shifts his attention to the mob and everyone in the meetinghouse. "These self-proclaimed witches must answer for their crimes! Do not harm them! If we wish to banish this wickedness from our village then we must bring them forward to understand! And it is suspected that they are holding a prisoner at the moment, so we must act with caution!"

His words draw no dispute from the crowd, which is a momentary relief. Even in the midst of rage, the most powerful men in Bedfordshire are still acting with reason. Barnabas was beaten and brutalized when discovered, but he was still alive. Some of our friends back in Warren Hollow were executed on All Hallows Eve at the bonfire, never having the opportunity to defend themselves or declare innocence.

Thomasin's safety worries me, especially with all of Bedfordshire now involved. And if Abigail and Rachel are as cunning as they have proven, then it is likely that they are somewhere nobody would expect to search. These people will rush to the outskirts and deep into the forest, while I believe that Abigail and Rachel are somewhere close.

"We will find these sisters tonight!" Solomon shouts while descending from the pulpit. "We must search the forests far and wide, and then through every path in this village; from the cemetery to the tavern!"

The mob swarms around Solomon as he rushes through the rows of vigilant members. It's as if they are ready to embark on a battle of tremendous size. Some shout of checking near the port and everyone is devising a plan for the hunt. Bedfordshire was disrupted and the Christmastime merriment has been destroyed, so these people wish to reclaim their home. But regardless of tonight's outcome, Bedfordshire shall never be the same.

The meetinghouse empties as people disperse in every direction. I notice that the sun has completely fallen from the sky, and our only guidance will be the moonlight. Solomon leads the charge forth while Henry and I stand with Ambrose, unsure of how to proceed. Pastor Noah is one of the few people remaining with us in the meetinghouse. He rises and makes his way forward to the pulpit.

"That was very brave of you, Emelie. Those sisters are strange, but I cannot believe that such wickedness burns within them," he ponders with sorrow.

"They will have a chance to speak on their innocence. Solomon will not harm them, and we will act accordingly if they confess to this heinous corruption," Ambrose interjects.

Pastor Noah turns and gently grabs my hand. He fails to recognize that he holds my makeshift hand but pays no mind and refuses to let it go.

"I deeply apologize for the loss of Young Samuel. He was a devout follower and wished to do tremendous things in this congregation."

His words pull on my emotions and I know that I will lose my composure if I attempt to speak. I gently nod to his words, trying my hardest not to falter. Henry shows gratitude to Noah and offers his own condolences, yet I can only worry for the night ahead. The time has come to end the madness around us. My thoughts race as I think of any indication to the sisters' whereabouts. They would not capture Thomasin if the plan was to escape from Bedfordshire. All instincts lead me to believe that their reign is unfinished, and they prepare for one final onslaught. Or perhaps Christmastime is only the beginning.

Where could they be? Abigail would not leave her sister in this village so surely they had a plan to reconvene after the poisoning. They must be nearby.

"Henry!" I yell while turning back to face him and Pastor Noah. My words interrupt their conversation and steal their full attention. "We never checked the cellar at the sisters' home. That is where we should start right away!"

We are immediately on our way into the night. Pastor Noah warns us to act with caution and explains that he will be waiting patiently should the sisters come and seek redemption.

He prays aloud and lights the candles around the pulpit. These actions bring me comfort as we exit the meetinghouse.

This momentary peace vanishes as we reach the outside. People are rushing through the village in a panic, using pine torches to light their search. Some check in the bushes and vegetation while others shout into cellars and tool sheds. They expect Abigail and Rachel to reveal themselves when clearly they shall never be found so easily. Solomon leads his mob beyond the village and into the darkness of the forest. I ask myself where I would hide in this situation. Surely it would be wise to find somewhere unsuspecting. A place too obvious to be searched. As we walk through the night, a potential location comes into mind; the sisters' home. Their home was searched thoroughly, and the guard was present through the night. Nobody would think to search there again and we know better than anyone what a fine hiding spot it was.

"Henry, we must search through their home again," I declare.

People push into us and rush as though a demon was let loose in Bedfordshire. A torch nearly burns me as a group of desperate members passes by. Henry is fortunate enough to receive a small oil lamp from a stranger as we move forward. The light is miniscule and appears to be nearly extinguished, though it is better than relying on the moon as it occasionally peers through the clouds and snowfall.

"You suspect that they returned to their home?" Henry asks. "We were there until morning and never saw them."

"I cannot say for certain, but the cellar must be searched either way. So perhaps there is no harm in searching again," I claim firmly.

Our pace increases as we maneuver through the night. I begin contemplating endless scenarios of how this all shall end.

How do you plan to confront them? What are you to do if Thomasin is already dead? Are you certain that Abigail and Rachel are to blame? Do you suspect that Thomasin could have been helping them this whole time?

As time passes, I begin doubting myself and pondering on irrational thoughts. My chest burns and I feel as weak as the night we escaped the prison. But we must remain one step ahead if there is any hope of succeeding. I anticipate a dramatic meeting, likely with a knife to Thomasin's throat and a deep explanation. Though perhaps it is selfish to assume that this entire calamity is because of us, or more specifically, me.

We start running as our destination comes into view. I breathe a sigh of relief to see that their home is left unharmed. It may be foolish to assume that they would retreat to a place so apparent, though something is telling me that this is correct. The sisters act with a high level of intelligence and outsmarted everyone in Bedfordshire. Their actions were nearly perfect, until they were not. Days of panic and unsuspected pursuit ruined their plans, which slowly accumulated into a trail of loose ends and evidence. And now, it is time to see if this trail continues in their cellar.

"Wait," I yell to Henry as he approaches the front door. "We must go straight to the cellar." He laughs at himself for so quickly forgetting this idea.

At a glance, the snow appears unbothered and there are no footprints nearby. This causes panic to know they may be elsewhere, yet I compose myself and reach the cellar door.

"The lock," Henry says while pointing, "it is gone."

For the first time since our arrival in Bedfordshire, this cellar is no longer under lock and key. Henry tenses as he signals for me to take a step back. He advances towards the door while making a fist with his other hand. The cellar effortlessly opens on both sides, and we stare down into a black hole. We look at each other but Henry wastes no time before taking a step down. I follow directly behind him, desperate to see what the sisters locked away. A breeze from underground sends chills through my body, as the cellar is even more frigid than the cold of the outside. Surely the explanation of Chrystopher occupying the cellar was a lie to conceal what actually awaits. I do not announce it to Henry, but I scold myself for overlooking such a blatant lie. Henry raises the oil lamp to illuminate our surroundings.

"I believe this cellar is empty," Henry claims defeatedly. The cellar is small, and we descend only a few steps before reaching the bottom. Henry must crouch in order to fit below the ceiling.

"Wait," I call out while pointing to the ground. Henry lowers the lamp and the light reveals footprints. They are faint and nothing more than an outline. I suspect that whoever came down here had done so a few hours ago. But this is a positive find and validates that someone was in fact down in this cellar. The light reveals a trail of footprints to a wooden shelf in the corner. We take a few steps and follow the markings until we can walk no further.

"Another lamp!" Henry shouts with excitement. He uses the last of his lamp to light the wick of this improved light source. The basement is bright and now much easier to search. There be nothing but boxes and canned goods, though I see a chair in the corner. I walk closer and let out a gasp as I notice chains and rope.

"Henry," I say to draw his attention. He walks over and also looks at the chair. "This is undoubtedly where Barnabas was held. Now it all makes sense. This place certainly fits his description of the dark prison. And perhaps the pounding that Clara heard was Barnabas fighting to escape! She was confused but trying to get into the cellar that night with a valid reason. If only she was successful, then all of this would have been revealed."

It makes me uneasy to know that Barnabas was held prisoner in this basement for days. The sisters are guilty beyond any doubt. I study the chains wrapped around the arms of the chair and the scratches on the floor from Barnabas's struggle for freedom.

"Emelie, you must see this!" Henry calls out. My eyes drift from the chair and back in his direction. He stands over an open crate. I look down and notice loose pages from torn bindings. The pages are dirty and battered, appearing to be covered in mud and damaged from the snow. I rush over to the oil lamp for light but already know that these are the contents of Rose's black book. It brings me anger to see her delicate research in such horrid condition.

"It be the missing pages, Henry. They brought these fantasies to life. All this nonsense on witchcraft and black magic was validated to them, and it is my fault!"

"You mustn't blame yourself, Emelie," Henry explains while providing me comfort. I wish to hear it not and understand that it is because of me that Abigail and Rachel learned these awful behaviors. It's as though I handed them a guide of how to manipulate those around them and cause chaos in this peaceful village.

"Samuel is dead because of me," I declare with guilt. "These sisters never would have known such methods of evil. And instead of letting the past die, I brought details of how to reach the same level of madness that unfolded in Warren Hollow!"

"You are wrong!" Henry answers while pulling me in front of him. "You acted with caution and aimed to tell the truth of our torture. From the moment we arrived, you wished to spread your knowledge and banish these awful thoughts from the world so that witchcraft would not plague anywhere else. 'Tis not a fault of yours that Abigail and Rachel refused to listen. And this is not an occurrence of witchcraft. Nor was our conviction back in The Hollow. This is but an attack from two evil sisters who fed their own wickedness, just like Reverend Thomas."

His words are reassuring, yet I continue to blame myself. I tried to educate them, though they were far more troubled than any of us could have imagined.

The next few moments are silent as I turn through all the pages that we found. The mix of Rose's dark knowledge and our stories of the past bring a subtle smile to my face. She was wise beyond her years and held a level of skill that I could only dream of achieving.

"Perhaps we should continue our search," Henry suggests. I exhale at his remark, subtly agreeing but never taking my eyes from the pages. My scan is nearly complete, as I wish to ensure that every page is accounted for. I discover an item left between the box and the wall while taking a final look before we depart. It appears damaged like the rest, but the material is unfamiliar. Slowly I unfold the damaged scroll, putting the torn pieces together and realizing that this is not a piece of Rose's work. Though difficult to decipher, it seems to be a map of Bedfordshire.

"Henry, please come here with the light," I request. He obeys as I spread the scroll open before me on the floor. We stand over the map and Henry holds the oil lamp close while I put the pieces back in their correct place.

"It is a map of Bedfordshire. I have seen this laid out in the tavern," Henry explains.

I also noticed similar maps in most primary structures in our village. "Look," I instruct while pointing. I turn the map around on the floor as I notice a marking near the edge. Slowly I crouch down and draw closer, recognizing that the fishing port is marked with ink. Henry draws my attention to another marking, which is precisely Giles's home.

"They marked the locations of the murders!" Henry shouts as we both make this revelation. We continue scanning as my finger traces the lines and validates his claims. The meetinghouse is also marked, likely due to Clara's murder or the poisoning. One by one we uncover markings at all the sites of misfortune, from the prison to the farm. Perhaps this was a tool used in their planning to achieve such stealth and precision. They memorized all the paths and studied these areas before attacking. I take a second glance at the farm, and it seems that there is a second marking that we nearly missed.

"Can you hold the light closer, Henry?" I ask while pulling my face closer to the edge of the map. "This seems odd to have two markings at the farm. 'Tis the only place in all of Bedfordshire with two markings."

"Perhaps it was accidental. Or to signify the death of both Samuel and Amelia?" Henry asks curiously.

"It be difficult to truly know. But the prison only has one marking for two deaths. If they are tracking murders, then this makes little sense. And we know that they act with perfection."

Henry drops down and uses his hand to smooth out the damaged map. His face is nearly touching the ground as he desperately scans.

"Emelie," He begins with a sudden rejuvenation, "if this is composed with fine accuracy, then I believe they marked our barn. Does that mean there shall be another attack on the farm?"

"Did Ambrose or any of the guards search the barn on their arrival?' I ask.

"Potentially, though I cannot say for certain. I was at Amelia's side and then tending to you until our departure," Henry explains.

The plan comes together with a clarity that makes perfect sense. Perhaps the sisters never left the farm. This would explain how Thomasin vanished so easily and why their basement appears undisturbed for quite some time.

"Henry, the sisters could still be there. Perhaps they used the barn to hide before making their next move, though with the commotion we failed to find any indications."

"We must inform the others at once!" Henry yells while making his way to the stairs.

"No," I reply, stopping him in his tracks. "A crowd could cause them to act irrationally and hurt Thomasin if they are still there. Solomon's encounter with Abigail all but confirms this. If we are correct in our assumption, then perhaps it is best that we confront them alone."

"I am not sure that is wise, Emelie. We know what they are capable of." Henry begins rummaging through the cellar for any weapons or tools.

"The others may detain Abigail and Rachel, but the slightest threat could cause them to kill Thomasin first. Her greatest chance of survival is in our hands, and our hands only. Let us go to the barn, and if our speculation is true, then we can end this before sunrise," I claim.

"Do you think they will cooperate?" Henry asks, handing me a small blade.

"Of course not. There is surely more to this sick plan that is unraveling," I reply with brutal honesty. It would be pure stupidity to suspect that this shall unravel with ease. Abigail and Rachel could have regrouped in the barn before departing, or still be there until making an escape at sunrise. But with Thomasin held captive, I believe they are waiting patiently for us to arrive.

We exit the cellar and our destination is set. I pay no mind to the pandemonium around us as people continue searching everywhere in sight. Though it is likely of no use, as Henry and I may have uncovered Abigail and Rachel's exact location. It is time to save our sister, save our home, and put an end to this madness.

XXV

Up in Flames

The chaos in the village is long behind us as we approach the farm. Henry and I established a plan on our brief journey out of the village. While we are still uncertain of what awaits, I convinced Henry to let me enter the barn alone. He will circle around in the shadows and enter through the back, catching Abigail and Rachel by surprise if needed. This plan is not one he agrees with, but I believe it is the best way to ensure Thomasin's survival. Neither of us know what to expect from these sisters, as they are unpredictable and dangerous. Perhaps we shall uncover their motivations behind all this malevolence alongside our rescue.

  I was told countless times by Thomasin and the others to avoid Abigail and Rachel. Even so, I refused to listen because I believed they could be taught and properly informed. 'Tis a challenge to deny feelings of guilt and responsibility for all that has happened. Thoughts of Abigail learning from Reverend Thomas and enacting all this chaos to get revenge for my rejection are also reasonable to assume.

  "We are here," I tell Henry in nothing more than a whisper. The barn sits desolate in the darkness with no signs of damage or tampering. Though I notice that the doors are now secure, which was not the case earlier today. Instincts tell me that

Abigail and Rachel are certainly inside. I let out a deep breath and rub my chest as it throbs in pain. Surely I am in no condition to fight if need be, though for Thomasin, I will certainly try.

Each passing moment is a rendition of Reverend Thomas dragging me back to the prison. Thomasin's life was in danger, and I planned to do the impossible. Failure was never an option, as I made a promise to John and knew that my friends needed to be saved. And now, this situation is but the same. Another celebration laying the foundation for chaos and wickedness within a community. Bedfordshire suffered far too many losses at the hands of Abigail and Rachel. This place is now our home and neither Christmastime nor our family shall soon recover. Perhaps we will face exile come sunrise, but regardless I must put an end to the sisters' madness if there is to be a future for this community.

"I beg of thee not to go alone," Henry pleads as we approach the barn. I understand his concern and the obvious dangers of my plan. "You need not die for this place!"

"I must do this," I reply while stopping in my tracks and staring at Henry. "I would not die for Bedfordshire, nor did I plan to die for Warren Hollow. But when it comes to you, Thomasin, Samuel, or my brother, then certainly I would die fighting for resolution. Though I do not plan on it and I do not want these sisters to die either. I simply wish for no further violence."

"Please act with caution then. For I love you deeply, Emelie. I cannot express it enough," Henry pulls me in tightly. "We will have a life on this farm and a glorious future in Bedfordshire. Do not let these sisters take what we fought so hard for." He steps away and prepares to depart. "I will go around the back of the barn. If they threaten you in any way, then I will contain the situation. And I will not hesitate to kill either of them if they try to hurt you."

"I love you as well, Henry. And before we do this, I must thank you properly. I would not have survived my injuries back in The Hollow without you. It is because of you that I am still here."

"You need not offer gratitude for any of it. I shall be by your side forever, as that is the only place I ever wanted to be."

"Let us be done with this and save Thomasin," I whisper, struggling to find further words while trying not to get emotional. Henry moves around the back as I approach the front doors. I did not want that to feel like a final conversation or a goodbye, but I understand the danger in which I place myself and I can tell that Henry suspects my willingness to embrace the danger.

As Henry falls out of sight, I take subtle steps toward the barn doors. I reach down to confirm that the blade Henry gave me is securely hidden along my waist. 'Tis my hope that it is not needed, although I suspect it shall make an appearance.

The wind makes the doors shutter back and forth. I place my hand on the large door to calm its movement while also raising my other arm to ensure that the steel hand is fastened in place. In truth the sisters likely anticipate this as a weakness, although one blow from this hand could cause immense damage. My heartbeat intensifies and I begin to feel anxious for what awaits on the other side.

With no further hesitation, I pull the left side of the door open and stare into the barn. My arrival is met with complete silence rather than a flurry of strikes from Abigail or Rachel. Our barn is absent of all life from the previous slaughter, so there is no rustling or commotion. Even so, the air is thin and I feel a sense of danger swelling around me. I know the sisters are here, waiting patiently for the right moment. It's as though a creature has its eyes locked on me with an eagerness to pounce.

"Make thy presence known!" I shout pathetically, my voice faltering but still bold.

My request is met with silence. Carefully I take a step forward into the barn, scanning as the shuttering of the door spreads the moonlight every few moments. Wind forcefully hits the barn and leaves the door in constant movement behind me.

"Show yourself!" I shout. With another step forward my request is denied once again. I notice that the few stalls on either side are empty so the sisters must be closer to the back. As the barn door closes from the wind, I stand nervously in the bouts of darkness. Then once it opens, my steps continue as I survey the area.

I notice a faint light in the distance while moving deeper into the barn. Anxiously I squint my eyes and lower my stance, spotting what appears to be the fading light from a lantern or an oil lamp coming from a stall in the back corner. This proves that someone is present, so I carefully reach back and grab hold of the blade in my waistband. Just as I begin pulling it from behind, I am stopped in my tracks at a faint voice.

"Hello?" the voice calls out. My heart begins to race and I am frozen in place, although my grip on the handle of the blade never falters. "Who is there?"

"Come out at once!" I reply, surely now in range to be heard. Slowly the stall door creaks open, and I take a step back to prepare for battle.

"Do not hurt me!" The voice calls out pathetically. After a few moments a figure comes into view. It is Abigail. She limps from the stall and uses the wall of the barn to keep her balance. I will not fall for this deception.

"Abigail! Stop where you are!" I reply, ready to draw my blade. It is difficult to fully observe her appearance because the moonlight only shines through for a few moments when the door opens.

"Emelie! You must help me!" Abigail replies. Her plea is desperate and perhaps I would believe that she is injured if I did not hold the truth. She takes a step forward with her arms out, and I notice that she is covered in blood.

"Do not come any closer, Abigail!"

The mere sight of her makes me emotional. 'Tis hard to maintain composure while facing someone who hath done such awful things. I try to steady my breathing and fasten my grip on the knife's handle to stop the shaking.

"You do not understand, Emelie! I have been hiding here for hours. I am so very cold. But I had no other choice, Ambrose tried to kill me!"

"I do not believe you! Stop with your lies!" I reply while keeping distance and circling.

"It is true! They spoke of my name in the meetinghouse and Solomon chased me away. The two of them are behind this madness, and perhaps other people are involved as well. Ambrose followed me into the forest and sliced me with his blade. But I escaped him," Abigail explains while dropping to her knees. "Please tell me that my sister is unharmed!"

"Lies! Where is Thomasin?" My patience grows thin, though her tale is quite convincing, so I begin to question her. "Why would Ambrose care to do such a thing? Of what reason to destroy his own village and slaughter his own people?"

"He wants to reshape Bedfordshire and take it back to the times of old, before we celebrated these happenings and pushed our faith to the side. And he does not act alone. You cannot listen to them!"

The moonlight illuminates our surroundings, and I notice the massive bruise that Solomon spoke of on Abigail's face. She looks up to me, desperate and full of fear. Her eye is bloodshot within the wicked bruise that covers her face. Still, I keep my distance in anticipation of the moment she decides to attack.

"Please, Emelie. Will you help me?" Abigail asks while slowly reaching out with her hand.

I do not fall for her tricks but feel sorrow for holding Abigail in such a position. At this moment I feel no better than Reverend Thomas.

"Please," she begins tearfully, "you must help to save my sister! Ambrose and Solomon will kill us if given the chance. They hath gone mad and nobody is safe. 'Tis Ambrose who killed them all! But I need to know that Rachel is safe. Please tell me she is safe! He will strike again at the meetinghouse. He tried to poison everyone and will not stop!"

Immediately I take a step back and reveal my blade. I hold it steadily before me, which draws fear from Abigail. She fumbles backwards and raises her hands in submission.

"What are you doing, Emelie? Please, do not hurt me. I am sorry for accusing you, but I know now that it be Ambrose!" Abigail pleads desperately.

"How did you know that the meetinghouse was poisoned? If you escaped before sunrise then how would you have known?" I shout in reply.

"No," she begins in a panic. "I told thee. I saw Solomon tampering with the rations last night so he chased me away. I hid here until sunrise then went to find Rachel, but I heard shouts in the meetinghouse. So I retreated back to the barn before I could find her."

"Enough!" I shout, growing unsure of what to believe. "Tell me, Abigail, why did you do this? Slaughtering innocent people, even your own grandmother! How could you do such wicked things? Do not deceive me!"

"Emelie, I have done no such thing. I am of no threat to you. And please, can I ask thee one question?" Abigail mutters with a sudden calmness.

"Say it," I demand.

As I await her words, the barn door slams shut at the front entrance. A wave of fear jolts through my body from such a noise and I immediately direct my gaze behind me. This was far too much force to merely be the wind. The doors are secure, and I hear the locks being fastened from the outside. I am now trapped in the barn. Tearfully I stare at the door until realizing that my attention is no longer on Abigail.

"Do you still think I am pathetic?" Abigail asks maniacally.

Her words leave me stunned and validate all my suspicions. Hearing her relay the words I spoke in the prison sends a chill down my spine. I turn my attention back to her, but she is already standing and catches me by surprise. Abigail viciously attacks, knocking the weapon from my hand and slashing my stomach with a blade of her own. Her assault sends me to the ground, gasping for air and rolling in pain. She stops my movement with another vicious slash to my arm as I turn over and reach for my knife. Any attempts to fight back fail drastically as she continues to slash at my limbs and forcefully stomps on my knee. Sounds of popping and snapping echo through the barn from this devastating blow.

"Henry!" I call out desperately. "Please help me!" Abigail stops at my words and offers a subtle laugh.

"We would have done great things together, Emelie. And you must admit that I almost had you fooled!" Abigail taunts with a laugh while standing over me. I reach for my knee while Abigail retreats to the stall and retrieves an oil lamp. She reemerges and moves to the other corner of the barn and knocks at the back door. The door begins to open, though I have difficulty maintaining my gaze. Her attack left me bleeding and struggling for breath. An immense pain fills my leg, and the extent of the damage is severe. Although the slashes with the knife were not deep cuts, so I suspect she was merely trying to incapacitate me for the time being.

"Emelie!" A voice calls. Though I am in a daze, I notice this to be Henry. Carefully I raise my eyes and watch as Rachel enters with a blade at his throat. Henry appears unharmed, although Rachel is ready to slice him open and Abigail also holds her weapon to his chest. They take slow steps forward until they are practically on top of me. Abigail places the lamp on the floor before us so that both of her hands are of use. I struggle to rise from the ground but achieve a seated position after a few moments.

You are hurt, but perhaps not as bad as you look. Try to catch the sisters by surprise when the right moment presents itself.

I exaggerate my breathing to indicate that her attack left me fighting for my life. Though my appearance is deceiving and I only need a few more moments to gather myself.

"What have you done to her?" Henry shouts, wishing to break free but knowing that they would kill him.

"Join her on the ground!" Abigail demands. Rachel slashes the back of his leg and he winces in pain. Henry drops to my side and we both sit defeated, staring up helplessly at the sisters. They circle us menacingly, and taunt with their movements. As Abigail passes, I watch her twist the tip of the blade on her finger like a true psychopath. The light from the oil lamp confirms that the weapon she holds is in fact that of Reverend Thomas.

"You could not leave it alone," Rachel comments while shaking her head. "You just had to keep searching and somehow escaped death over and over."

"At first I did not want to believe it. I even refused to believe that you two could be so evil," I reply, struggling to form words and fight through my escaping breath.

"And what gave us away?" Abigail asks with a smile.

"Your ribbon was left in the journal, you idiot. And a map in thy cellar led us to you."

Abigail turns to Rachel who immediately shows signs of embarrassment. "She is right, 'tis you that be the idiot!" Abigail yells at her sister. "I asked thee to perform one simple task!"

"I am sorry, sister! We had little time and the sun was rising. I truly thought that all the supplies were accounted for," Rachel replies in a submissive tone. It is obvious who sits at the helm of this scheme.

"We were good to you both. How could you do these things?" I interject.

Abigail smiles and drops down before me, completely ignoring my question. "You know, the two of you are to blame for Amelia and Samuel's deaths. I saw you enter our home in the middle of the night when Solomon granted an easy escape. I was preparing to take some tools from the cellar and vandalize thy farm to put fear in Nicholas. But then you came wondering by. And that's when I knew you had true suspicions of us. True enough to venture through the night. You should have accused us right away; it would have saved many lives." She shakes her head as if she is disappointed in me. "I lifted this beautiful blade from our cellar and slammed the door. And just as I hoped, guards came rushing within moments. You were trapped and the farm was completely unguarded. I thank thee for making this so easy. It was to be a simple jest at first. Perhaps smashing a window or lighting a field ablaze. But then I decided that something had to be done with you drawing so close."

"Why do you hate us? Emelie was good to you both!" Henry shouts, wanting to attack.

"You were supposed to save us!" Abigail shouts, her lip quivering as she fights back tears through shifting emotions. Her true insanity begins to shine through and now it is clear how these sisters caused all this chaos. "You came to this awful village and brought tales of unimaginable greatness. Talking of a magical apothecary and godlike powers! We wanted to be your friends. Hell, we worshipped you. And my feelings were pure!" She tries to calm down and circles once more while continuing her explanation.

"We know the darkness quite well because there was no other place to turn. Mother and Father were the evil ones, not us. They would beat us mercilessly for no reason. None! We were shamed for not wanting to do chores or pray to the false god. We never had the luxuries of Christmastime that you received on this disgusting farm. So eventually," Abigail stops in her tracks. "Mother and Father left us no choice. Whispers began of something known only as witchcraft. Mother and Father were terrified, so we were fascinated. It was the answer to our prayers. An answer from a force unspoken when the one above chose to abandon us. We spent days testing recipes and concoctions that could prove as fatal. Listening outside of the meetinghouse and around the corners as this became a growing concern. Talks of hexes and flying through the night were marvelous. Mother and Father became bedridden from our secret additions to supper. Eventually, some deadly nightshade and hemlock in their meal was enough to handle them rather quickly." Abigail looks to Rachel and they both laugh, proud of the success in murdering their parents.

Rachel steps forward and offers her own input. "But things did not improve. We were left in the care of a senile embarrassment in that house, never taken to a farm or given a loving family. So we called upon Satan, and he answered with open arms. Black magic, witchcraft, whatever they shall call it;

this was the way! Although, the fear ended just as quickly as it came. They thought it couldn't be real and held no meaning, so we were lost once again without purpose. We thought of escaping and starting anew elsewhere. But then the four of you came to us. That's when we knew that this, all of this, was meant to be. This is who we are, and who we shall be forever!"

"I," I begin with a faltering breath, "I tried to tell both of you many times. You would not listen to my words. Our history is one with a Reverend gone mad, not these fantasies of witchcraft. I am no witch, 'tis simply no such thing! You should have listened to Pastor Noah and Ambrose when they ended the fear."

"At first we wanted to believe it not. A true witch would hide in the shadows and conceal such a tale, so we were patient. We got closer, waiting and hoping that you would show us the way. But now, we know that you are as false as the God above!" Abigail shouts as she pushes my head from behind. "We read that journal of yours. Watching you cower that night in the village outside of our home was pathetic. You are no witch! And you come here hoping to spread this lie that the apothecary in your homeland died for? We will not stand by and watch as you question such greatness!"

"There are other ways to find your place in this world! Why turn to such a wicked force? The others in this village were good to you! Nicholas was good to you and so were Ambrose and Pastor Noah," I fix my posture and stare directly into Abigail's eyes. "Trust me when I say that we too shared a desire for something more. But fear, murder, and darkness are not the answer," I mutter with compassion.

My attempts to reason with the sisters are useless, though it is hard not to show sympathy. Even in this moment where I may lose my life, I still feel sadness for Abigail and Rachel. They did not deserve such abuse from their parents. I know what it is like to feel alone, yearning for more and trying to make sense of this life with a meaningless future laid before you. Unfortunately, witchcraft was their answer; the only light they found in the darkness while lost in a time of need. Though this does not excuse the awful things they have done.

"Our home was torn apart by witchcraft. It is not something worthy of admiration. Witchcraft is a powerful force that has taken many, many lives. There be no witches, just madmen and lunatics who allow it to spread for personal gain like the two of you before me," I claim with dizziness as blood drips from my wounds.

"You lie! Warren Hollow was destroyed by a false prophet who used these ideas for meaningless power. But not here! None of you truly know the first thing about this magic so do not come to our home and discredit our future!" Abigail rushes over to bring the blade directly down on my head out of anger, but stops herself and steps away. I never break my gaze, and this is something she notices. My composure is beginning to bother her. "Even your pathetic Rose could not fathom the chaos we created. Call it madness or witchcraft, 'tis of little importance. But if these people believe it is real, then it is real. And this is just the beginning!" Abigail proclaims in an attempt to anger me.

"So, what is your plan?" Henry shouts. "Murder us and escape into the forest? You killed innocent people off of such an outlandish idea and ruined a time of merriment for those who care for you. Innocent people died from this evil that you glorify. And how could you murder thy own grandmother?"

Abigail and Rachel laugh at his words. "We have done no such thing. We were with you in the meetinghouse so surely it was not us. But it was wise of you not to help us on that night, Emelie. We knew you needed to be stopped the moment you spoke of Barnabas's innocence. It was a quick and messy plan, but you would have died the moment you went through those doors. And we could tell that you were wise to it. I must admit that you tested our patience and set us behind in many of our plans. Accusing you was admittedly a mistake on our end that granted you an advantage. Entering the prison to speak with Barnabas was brilliant."

The sisters circle once more, Abigail draws closer to emphasize her words. "Though Barnabas was a fool who was too stupid to make an escape, even when we let him out of the cellar or through the back of the meetinghouse. It was simply too much of a challenge for him to leave through the forest with all suspicions and accusations. You somehow convinced that drunken imbecile to try and stop me after all that this village has done to him? You are impressive. Seeing you enter our home was when I realized we underestimated you. We underestimated all of you. Even Samuel and Amelia fought for their lives until the end," Abigail explains in a taunting manner.

"Enough!" I shout, no longer wanting to hear them taunt our family.

"You are wrong, Henry. Things took an unfortunate turn, and we needed to hide because Solomon almost had us. We thought of escaping and traveling far away just like you all had done. But we decided that there is no reason to go anywhere else when we can become saviors here. Come sunrise, Abigail and I will have stopped you all from corrupting Bedfordshire. We will be the unsuspecting heroes of this place. Then they shall show us the respect that we deserve!"

Henry laughs and draws their attention. They smile at his reply with eagerness to uncover his reasoning. "There is something that you are both wrong about; my Aunt Amelia. They tend to her right now in Timothy's practice. She will live and speak the truth. Killing us will not secure your innocence!" He explains with a smirk of his own.

The sisters try not to show concern at his words, but it spreads across their faces. They look at each other with uncertainty of how to proceed. If Henry speaks the truth, then this is another massive hindrance to their plan. But I start to ponder on their words during this moment of silence. They claim that they did not murder Clara, and I remember that both of them were in eyesight that night. Thoughts swirl in my mind of their presence during much of the conflict.

"You do not act alone. It would be impossible," I state. "Who assists you?"

"It certainly took you long enough to ask. 'Tis an embarrassment that you could not figure this out, though you can solve mysteries with a piece of ribbon and a feeble map," Rachel replies tauntingly.

"Bring her forth!" Abigail shouts while looking over her shoulder. There is movement in the stall. It is none other than Chrystopher. He emerges, holding a rope in his hands with a timid composure. With a forceful pull, Thomasin falls out of the stall and hits the ground. She is restrained with rope at her wrists and has a covering over her mouth.

"Thomasin!" I shout with a burst of energy. Quickly I lunge forward but Abigail swings the blade and nearly slashes my face. She points the weapon directly at me until it is nearly touching my eye. It takes no words to explain that she shall kill me if I act impulsively again. Slowly Thomasin is pulled towards us, and I am relieved to see that she is relatively unharmed. She spots us and bursts into tears.

"Hurry thy steps, Chrystopher!" Abigail shouts to the young man. I feel foolish for not considering Chrystopher as a part of their plan. He spent much time with the sisters, but I never expected someone so young and innocent to be part of something so evil. Surely his father's absence and a lack of suspicion from anyone in Bedfordshire allowed for manipulation.

"Abigail," I begin while relaxing my posture, "I understand. Truly, I see your motivations. This desire, this hunger, for a better life. You can ask Henry or Thomasin, we all know what it is like to watch your existence slowly become that of the parents you despise. Forced into chores and beaten for questioning a faith you do not care for. But all this chaos makes you no better than the authority you aim to destroy. This does not need to go any further! Though I agree that there is plenty of darkness and blindness within most, there are still good people in this place who wish to help you! Please, do not hurt Thomasin."

My words stun everyone in the barn. Even Henry offers a smile through his pain at my plea for resolution. While Thomasin is still frightened and hurting, her gaze of approval speaks louder than words. And for the first time since our arrival, I feel back in a familiar position of control. I may be bleeding out on the cold ground, although the illusion of power sends a burst of energy through my veins. It feels as though my words hold enough weight to calm the sisters and end this chaos with no further bloodshed. We may die in the next few moments, but this plea needed to be said with confidence and reason if there is any hope of a peaceful resolution.

Abigail takes in my words, twisting her blade and nodding her head side to side in contemplation. Rachel and Chrystopher dare not to speak, for it is obvious that Abigail is the mastermind. After a few more moments of silence, Abigail slowly kneels before me. "Incredible." She pauses and draws closer until we are face to face. "Truly, Emelie, you speak a convincing tale. For a moment it crossed my mind to let the three of you walk through those doors. I recognized such power when we first laid eyes upon you. Something about you was different. You are not like the followers of blind faith and delusion around us. Even now, you found a way to make me feel trapped beneath you. Every time we visited your farm or came across you, we tried harder and harder. I would push deeper, wishing that you would reveal yourself to us and even lead us through our work. This desire led me to feelings for you. But instead, you waste such power helping people who are undeserving? Who would just as easily hang you by the neck from an accusation? Who watched as your little brother died a miserable death? No, these people must answer for their sins!" Abigail rises to her feet and turns her back to me and Henry. "So now, you only have one use for us. Though it was not in the way we intended, you will still serve your purpose come sunrise."

"No!" Henry shouts, catching me by surprise.

It seems that everything slows around me over the next few moments. My steady breathing and heartbeat drown out all other sounds. In a daze I turn to Henry who launches himself forward. He connects forcefully with my shoulder, knocking me over until I slam into the ground. At the same time, Abigail turns with a vicious strike of the blade. She moves with force and anger, rather than precision. Her eyes glaze over, and her face shows all the signs that we searched for. The taunting may be forced and the banter between the sisters is unnecessary, but at this moment, I finally see the monster revealed. Abigail is pure evil. She can try to justify this behavior with witchcraft like Reverend Thomas, but she enjoys every passing moment. Thomas was a coward who wished to hide his secrets with any means necessary, though Abigail is different. Perhaps her wickedness was born as a means to protect her sister, but she is too far gone and must be stopped.

 God certainly whispered in Henry's ear at that moment and told him what was coming. That strike would have ended my life, and Henry was wise to it. Though the attack was still executed successfully by Abigail. Helplessly I lay and watch as the blade finds Henry instead. He shouts in pain while landing directly on top of me, knife plunged deep in his side.

 Abigail stares in confusion, her eyes shooting back and forth between me and Henry. She then looks to Rachel who was too slow to stop Henry's movements.

 I shake my head to regain my composure while Henry writhes in pain.

 "Henry?" I call out with sympathy. The blade is embedded deeply while he struggles to get off of me. All the while Abigail is furiously shouting in Rachel's face for once again failing to follow orders. She belittles her and demands that Rachel give up her weapon. Rachel is reluctant so the sisters shout and get physical with each other. They pay us no mind, and I realize that this is our opportunity to act.

"Get out of here, Emelie," Henry mutters. He rolls to his side so that I am no longer pinned beneath him. I try to slide out, but it is with immense pain and difficulty to push off with my damaged knee. Eventually I pull free and try to comfort Henry rather than running off. Even if I wished to move, I could not make it far in such poor condition. A knife in my back would end this escape before I take a single step.

"Why did you do that? This was not meant for you!" I demand tearfully while sitting over him. His hands shake as he gets a grip on the handle of the blade.

"Leave this place! I need to know that you get away. Please, Emelie!" Henry demands while pushing me away. Blood trickles from his mouth. I panic at this decision I now face. Surely death awaits all of us in the coming moments if I remain, but living without Thomasin and Henry would be far worse than death. Though just like with John, I do not wish to dishonor Henry's sacrifice. I want to sit here and cradle him in my arms, thanking him for saving me once again. But if I am to obey his words then there is simply no time. "Go!" He demands with struggling breath.

The sisters are still in dispute and unaware of the escape in motion. I back away from Henry, slowly rising and grabbing at my wounds. With an injured knee, open wounds, and a pounding in my chest, I eventually stand tall. Cautiously I back away from Henry while the sisters pay me no mind. Unable to properly stand or put weight down on my knee, I turn and limp towards Thomasin. "Thomasin, we need to—"

My words are silenced at the realization that I stand a few feet from Chrystopher. Just as we have done from the beginning, I forgot to consider his involvement. We stand face to face while he stares back at me with the rope to control Thomasin still in his hands. At this moment I see nothing more than a frightened and confused child, and cannot help but to think of my brother. He is young and trying to find his place in the world like the rest of us. "Chrystopher," I begin in a whisper, "you need to let her go. You are better than this. Please, you can come with us."

He listens to my words, his eyes focusing on me and then back to the sisters. His grip never loosens on the rope, but time is drawing thin, so I start to move forward. I take a slow step, raising my hands to show that I am not a threat. Chrystopher does not react so I take another step towards him.

"Abigail!" Chrystopher shouts. I close my eyes and wish to collapse to the ground. "She is trying to escape!"

His words catch the attention of the sisters as they turn and stare in shock. They had no idea that I was nearly out of the barn. Abigail and Rachel look at each other in a panic and Rachel begins rushing in our direction. She raises the knife above her head and sprints across the barn. I am frozen in fear and unable to react. Desperately I look to Henry, Thomasin, Chrystopher, Abigail, and then Rachel who shall reach me in the next few moments.

Though Henry aims to protect me once more and selflessly acts to ensure my safety. As Rachel passes, he kicks her leg and violently trips her. She slams to the ground and her blade flies through the air. Henry is weak but they begin struggling for the weapon on the ground. At the same time Thomasin pulls the rope with enough force to send Chrystopher flailing forward. He knocks over the oil lamp into nearby hay bales as he crashes to the ground. None of them are in control of the situation any longer. I lock eyes with Abigail, who stares with an identical level of surprise and panic.

The hay is engulfed in flames before either of us can react. All corners of the barn are illuminated by the spreading inferno, and I must shield my eyes from such brightness. Within moments the fire spreads to everything in sight; dried crops, hay, and even the wood of the barn begins catching fire. Smoke fills the air and the sisters scatter in a panic. 'Tis nearly impossible to locate Henry or Thomasin through the smoke as I cough profusely and the flames grow beneath me. My surroundings fade until I am left in a daze as flames climb my legs. I did not come this far to die in a fire, though it would be a fitting end. Fire is the foundation for all that we have become. With nowhere to go, I close my eyes and welcome the burning embrace of death.

XXVI

Deliver Us

When it seems that my time has come, a force emerges from the flames and tackles me. Immediately I fight and defend myself from Abigail or Rachel, but soon realize that it is Thomasin. I wipe my tears from the smoke and quickly remove the covering over her mouth. She is in poor health, and we both spend the next few moments coughing and gasping for air.

"Chrystopher, watch that door!" Abigail shouts through struggling breath.

Thomasin and I hide in one of the empty stalls. While I can hear Abigail shouting demands across the barn, nobody else is in sight. It would be nearly impossible to see through the wave of smoke and smoldering flames. The heat burns my skin even though we are out of range. My legs ache from the moments I stood with nowhere to go.

"Thank thee, Thomasin, you saved my life!" I reply with gratitude.

"Do not thank me yet! We are trapped in this barn that is sure to collapse!" She is visibly distraught and facing immense sadness from whatever she witnessed with Samuel. But her determination to survive is clear. My breathing intensifies as I crouch below the smoke. Thomasin struggles to undo the fastenings at her wrists and I do my best to provide assistance. Suddenly I remember Henry who is likely still on the ground with a knife in his side.

"Henry is badly hurt, Thomasin. I must go find him!"

"Those sisters are waiting for you, Emelie. They are guarding the door and expecting you to show yourself. If you go out there, they will kill thee!"

"But if we sit here then we will be burned alive!" There is little time for debate. We will soon succumb to the smoke if the flames do not spread to us first. Abigail and Rachel are undoubtedly searching through the barn at this very moment but there is no time to waste.

"Thomasin," I begin, "make your way to the back door. I need to go find Henry. We will meet you there, but leave if you must. I shall do everything I can to distract Chrystopher and the sisters!"

"No!" Thomasin demands while reaching for my arm. She grabs hold with both hands, pleading for me to stay by her side.

"I must end this, Thomasin. 'Tis my time to make things right," I say emotionally. Though it is with dispute, Thomasin releases her grasp on my arm. We stare at each other until I depart through the gate of the stall. Flames span across the entirety of the barn. The few tool cabinets and shelves near the back door appear to be unharmed for the time being, so perhaps I may find a weapon to defend myself. Chrystopher is nowhere in sight, which brings me hope that Thomasin may escape. The smoke burns my eyes and the earlier wounds inflicted by Abigail are throbbing. My makeshift steel hand is also rising in temperature and causes me to gasp as I mistakenly use it to wipe my face.

"Henry! Where are you?" I shout. With each pathetic step I draw closer to the space we struggled in moments ago, but it seems that he is no longer on the ground. Only traces of blood and crumbling debris from the ceiling are present. Moving brings immense pain to the knee that Abigail targeted and the heaviness in my chest leaves me struggling to continue.

"Henry, we must leave this place!" I shout again. With another step forward I spot someone faintly through the smoke. It is none other than Rachel. She is buckled over and holding onto a nearby pillar for balance. She is in bad shape but could still overpower me in my faltering state. Rachel turns her head and notices as I approach.

"Abigail! They are over here!" Rachel shouts. Though nobody is rushing to her side and she must face me alone.

"Please, Rachel. We can help each other to safety. The others could be trapped and we have little time!" I plead. Debris continues falling around us as the flames grow with each passing moment. I never faced such a grueling heat, even on the warmest of summer days. And while Rachel is struggling as well, she pays no mind to my words. Instead of listening, a subtle grin crosses her face. She reaches beneath her torn coat and coverings, forgetting that her blade was lost because of Henry. Still, she is unbothered and starts advancing. One step at a time she draws closer while coughing and fighting the flames.

"Stop!" I plead, not wanting to fight her in the midst of this chaos. Rachel is now at arm's reach, and I have no time to react before she viciously kicks me in the stomach. Her strength has not faded in the least, and I am sent crashing into a closed stall behind me with no means of defense. The impact knocks the breath from my lungs as I collide with the gate, and Rachel begins stomping me into the ground. Each strike brings immense pain, though I find momentary comfort from such familiarity. This matches the viciousness of Reverend Thomas as he brought me back to the prison. So when the right moment presents itself, I will sweep her leg and launch an attack.

Eventually her force fades and she takes a step back. I shall react at her next strike and offer a swift offense of my own.

When she kicks you again, turn over and grab her leg.

I prepare for another kick to my body, though I fail to realize that she armed herself. A burning plank of wood crashes into the back of my head, sending me face down into the dirt. Perhaps I misjudged my own reaction speed and strength. From the moment we arrived in this barn I have been nothing but pathetic and weak. The disillusion fades and it becomes apparent that my injuries are severe and this plan to gain the upper hand was foolish.

"I am sorry. I cannot do it, for I am no savior and never was." I mutter this apology under my breath, unsure of who it is meant for. This was envisioned to be a heroic rescue of my friend, though I am becoming nothing more than another victim. They outsmarted us from the beginning, and I failed to save Bedfordshire. It was idiotic to believe I could be an unstoppable force in this new home. Perhaps miracles are only warranted once.

Rachel's vicious strike with the plank left me in a complete daze on the ground. Surely another strike of this magnitude will put an end to my existence. With blurred vision, I watch as Rachel raises the plank above her head once more.

Rather than pleading or trying to defend myself, I simply close my eyes. If this is how it ends, then John shall be waiting for me on the other side.

"Stop!" a voice calls out. A few moments pass and the fatal blow is not received. It is not Thomasin or Henry who stand above me; it is Chrystopher. He placed himself between Rachel and I with pleas for her not to continue.

"Get out of the way, you fool!" Rachel shouts.

"Rachel, you need not to do this! Let her go, let all of them go!" Chrystopher demands.

"Hath thee gone mad?" Rachel yells in his face. She tries pushing past him, but he holds his ground.

"This does not have to go any further, Emelie is right!" Chrystopher speaks with a sudden change of heart. "You heard her. We are no better than your parents and those who hurt us. I have done awful things, and I am scared."

"You made mistake after mistake and confused our grandmother with Emelie outside of the meetinghouse. 'Tis you that caused us more grief than any of them. We should've never made you a part of this. Now, get out of my way!"

While Chrystopher's desire for peace comes far too late, his words are spoken with reason and reality. I was certain that they were all beyond saving, but my earlier words resonated with him. We may never know how the sisters recruited Chrystopher as part of their madness, and it was likely a choice of free will. But something in this barn finally caused Chrystopher to see their actions as wrong.

"She speaks the truth, Rachel," Chrystopher says in a way that reminds me of my brother. This moment validates exactly why I never thought to suspect him. Chrystopher is nothing more than a child. Though he has done awful things that shall never be forgiven, his words bring me faith and justify all my efforts. There is still good in the world and the hope for a better future is one that can be shared by all. Slowly I pull myself to a seated position with my back to the stall. Rachel begins lowering her weapon, and Chrystopher turns to face me. "Get to the door. I shall find the others, and we will all—"

His words are interrupted by none other than Abigail, though she does not interrupt with an argument of her own. I let out a gasp as Abigail plunges a knife directly into his chest. She pulls back and swings the blade repeatedly, twisting it nearly in a full circle as it penetrates Chrystopher's skin. This fatal maneuver sends him to the ground, eyes open and nearly on top of me. Visions of John flash in my eyes and I am in complete shock. Abigail stares at his lifeless corpse, her face splattered with blood as she breathes heavily. Rachel steps over Chrystopher's body and tries to remain composed. She shakes off any signs of doubt and prepares to finish her attack. Though before she can properly raise her weapon, a force emerges from the fire and stops her.

It is Henry. He comes out of nowhere and collides forcefully with Rachel. They both soar through the air and fall into the flames. She lets out a yell and they begin struggling on the ground. Abigail is caught by surprise and tries to defend her sister. With all my strength I grab hold of her leg, finally making myself useful in this place. She whips her head around and stares at me like a wild animal. Rachel shouts as her and Henry struggle in the flames. They go back and forth with strikes to one another, and I notice the knife is still buried deep in Henry's side.

This is also noticed by Rachel as she grabs the handle of the blade and twists it in her hand. The sisters have mastered various techniques of brutality.

"Stop!" I yell at the top of my lungs. "Please, Rachel!"

She mounts Henry as my words catch her attention. He writhes in pain beneath her while she smiles through a face of blood, dirt, and ash. Abigail continues to pull free from my grasp and beats me from above. But rather than rushing to her sister, Abigail restrains me and forces me to watch as Rachel continues her assault. She gives her sister a nod and lets out a wicked laugh.

"Watch," Abigail mutters to me as Rachel turns her attention back to Henry. With an evil smile, Rachel places both hands around Henry's neck. She squeezes forcefully and chokes all signs of life away. He struggles and pulls at her hands, but the grip is too strong. Henry's eyes roll back and his face turns shades of red.

In one final attempt to save himself, Henry enacts a maneuver that draws shouts from me and Abigail. He reaches down to his side and forcefully pulls the blade from his body. Rachel fails to notice until he lets out a deafening scream of agony; but for her, it is already too late. Just as quickly as Henry removed the blade, he stabs it directly into Rachel's neck. It is an action that we have apparently grown fond of in desperate situations.

Rachel falls off Henry and struggles at his side. Blood immediately pours through Henry's fingers as he uses both hands to cover the wound on his body.

"No!" Abigail screams with sorrow. Her voice indicates a pain that I know all too well. She stares in total disbelief at her dying sister, watching the life fade from the only person she ever loved. But before Abigail has a moment to act, Thomasin approaches from behind with a vicious strike to her head. Abigail falls into unconsciousness or death while Thomasin pulls me to my feet. It takes all my effort not to faint, and I notice the barn is seemingly moments from collapsing. The flames swallow everything around us and the ceiling crumbles.

Thomasin supports my steps as we rush to Henry's side. He is in great pain, but still aware of the situation. His skin draws pale from the loss of blood and surely he needs attention if he is to survive. My knee buckles beneath me while I assist Thomasin in pulling Henry from the ground. Henry drops back down and a shower of blood falls beneath him.

"You must go," Henry demands.

I begin to panic and refuse to leave Henry in this barn. Surely there is something I can do to slow the bleeding. Desperately I look around the barn for any cloth and start to remove my coverings, but suddenly recall the only way that Henry slowed the bleeding and saved my life when my hand was removed. Nervously I look down to my arm and remember the unbearable burning of the pot. My makeshift hand has reached a scalding temperature from the fire all around us, but I hold it directly in the nearby flames to truly make the most of this last resort. The heat climbs my arm, but I hold it steady while I feel my own skin burning. Admittedly I know not the first thing of such a technique, but this could be the final hope of saving Henry.

"Forgive me," I beg of Henry as I pull my arm from the flame and press the steel hand to his wound. He screams in agony and I hear his skin searing beneath my pressure. Eventually he can endure the pain no longer and shoots back up to a standing position. And while Henry will display burns for the rest of his life and the underlying damage of the blade is unknown, the bleeding came to a near-instant halt and Henry may now survive long enough to reach the physician.

With each of us supporting one another, we begin hobbling our way to the back door. It shines through the smoke and fire like the gate to Heaven. Just a few more steps and this nightmare shall end. Each of us is badly wounded, but we are alive, and Thomasin is safe.

"Just hold on, Henry. We are almost to the door. They will see the smoke in the village and arrive any moment. We did it, we are safe," I explain through struggling breath.

"Emelie, I fear that you are worse off than you believe," Thomasin replies, showing fear as she studies my appearance. My body is full of burns, open wounds, and surely something is damaged in my knee. The issue with my chest also troubled me since we arrived, and I will likely use it to justify my failed reactions.

I can fully admit that our success is not because of me. Henry proved himself to be the true savior and Thomasin all but saved herself while handling the sisters. They did not need my assistance, and it brings me peace to know that filling this role as the so-called leader will no longer be necessary.

Even back in The Hollow, it was never me alone who saved us as they claim. But just as Abigail mentioned, *if it is believed to be real, then it is real.* And without all that we endured and the beliefs of others, I would not be the person I am today. Instead, I would be nothing more than a child, washing clothes in the stream and carrying on with a monotonous life in Warren Hollow. It seems odd to reflect on my journey while we are trapped among flames and clinging to life, but it finally feels like all the suffering has come to an end. Perhaps it is time to move on and break free from the guilt and self-torture. There will no longer be nightmares of John's death or pressure to tell Rose's story. I will finally focus on myself.

"There!" Thomasin shouts while pointing. The back door is wide open, and I look out to see the sun rising in the sky. I watch as it peaks over the trees and through the snow, signaling the start to the final day of Christmas.

We made it.

Though as we help Henry make his way through the door, I cannot help but look back through the smoke and flames. Boards are crumbling and the roof continues to fall. For a few moments I stare, frozen in my tracks just before crossing to the outside. Thomasin holds Henry upright as they both cough and deeply breath in the fresh air. She notices my position and reaches out to assist so I can make my way through. "My apologies, Emelie. Take my hand. We must get away from this barn."

"I," I begin, my thoughts trailing off. Thomasin lowers her hand, and her emotions begin to shift as she stares directly into my eyes.

"Emelie, no!" Thomasin shouts. But as she releases her hold on Henry and moves towards me, I take a step back.

"I love you both," I reply with a smile, shutting myself in the barn. With all my strength I lower that hatch to lock the door while Thomasin and Henry pound on the other side. They plead for me to stop, but I ignore their words. Surely Abigail is still alive, and something is calling me back to her.

Carefully I pass through the barn, retracing our steps and avoiding piles of burning hay. The heat is unbearable, and I look up to see the morning sky shining above through forming holes.

"Abigail!" I yell. "I know you are still alive! Come to me!" She does not give an answer, but surely she can hear me. "Abigail, where are–"

I halt my steps as I spot her. She does not lunge out and attack me through the flames. Instead, she sits peacefully at her sister's side. Gently she holds Rachel in her lap, just as I had done with John on that dreadful day. "Abigail," I call out while approaching from behind. Still she fails to acknowledge my presence.

Slowly Abigail lifts her head and turns to gaze over her shoulder before looking back to her sister. Blood pours from her head and she is covered in ash. "I wanted a better life for us. Our parents were so cruel, and we had no means to escape. I wanted to protect her and create something for us in this place," Abigail mutters in nothing more than a whisper. For the first time she shows her vulnerability, and I see her as nothing more than a frightened and desperate casualty to the life she has been dealt.

I feel sympathy for her, even after all that has happened. That is why I did not escape with Henry and Thomasin, and it is uncertain if I came back to save her, kill her, or so we could die together. But leaving did not seem justified. From the moment we met, I recognized a bond between us and could never comprehend why. Not on the intimate level that Abigail desired, but there is a connection that I cannot deny.

"Abigail, I understand. Truly, I know what it feels like. Please, come with me and we can escape this place. I do not know what shall happen, but there is still a way forward for you," I take another step towards her until we are nearly touching.

"That day on the farm was the best moment of our lives," Abigail quietly begins. "For the first time, things felt different for us." She smiles to herself while reminiscing. "All the merriment and laughter over supper, and spending time with you and Thomasin. Though I know it was a fantasy and something that would never be real, something we would never truly have."

"Abigail, I—"

"You know it to be true, Emelie," Abigail interrupts with growing anger. "There was only one way for us. A way to become something more; something greater. But you took that away!" She rises from the ground and her demeanor shifts back to the unrelenting force of wickedness. Abigail rips Thomas's blade from her sister's neck and turns to strike me. Though I am wise to her actions and never doubted that this encounter would end in violence. As she turns and swings the blade, I take a step back and kick her hand. This causes her pain and anger, so she charges forward as I walk backwards with my hands in front of me.

"Stop, Abigail! It does not have to end this way," I plead with my back nearly to the wall. I wince as I step through a flame and slide along the wooden wall of the barn. Abigail swings the knife with tremendous force, but thankfully I am out of range. The sound of the blade cuts through the air as it passes my face. Another swing goes above my head and collides with a wooden pillar as I crouch. Once more she pulls back and swings again. There is now little distance between us, so this strike grazes my cheek, leaving a trickle of blood flowing down my face. Her coordination is surely off from Thomasin's attack and all that occurred in this barn.

"When will you ever stop? Even now, why would you come back?" Abigail shouts. She continues advancing and wielding her blade. I fail to recognize that we reached a corner and there is nowhere left for me to go. She grabs me by the throat, pushing me into the burning wall and squeezing with all her force. "Why?"

"I ... can ... help ... you," I assure with a fading breath. Her grip is tight and ruthless.

"Yes," Abigail replies with a smile. "There is only one way you can help me now!"

She pulls back the blade with her other hand and prepares to land a fatal blow. And while I wished to end this peacefully, I recognize that I must properly defend myself. It was my final hope that this effort would make her yield and relinquish all anger. Before she can plunge the blade into my stomach, I stare into her eyes and press my hand to her face. Though it is not my actual hand; instead, it is the steel device attached to my arm that has been smoldering in the nearby flame for the past few moments.

The steel hand lands upon her eye and causes immense pain. Her skin melts and hisses as I hold my arm firmly in place. Abigail lets out a cry and falls back, releasing her grip on my throat. She reaches for her face while twisting and turning in agony. Her struggle shifts to rage as she raises her gaze back to me. With one functioning eye, bruises, and severe burn across her face, she is nearly unrecognizable. Blade still firmly in her hand, Abigail sprints towards me with no restraint. Rather than trying to stab me, she simply rushes into me with all her force. I raise my arms for defense, but it is of no use. We collide and burst through the crumbling wall to the outside.

Everything is a blur, though I am no longer trapped within the smoldering barn. Instead, my body is nearly frozen and numb. I look to my side and realize that I lie in the snow among burning planks of wood. The sun has nearly risen in the sky and smoke fills the surrounding forest. Fresh air enters my lungs with a deep inhale, and a cool wind blows across my skin. With all of my strength I turn my head. To my right I can see the path that leads to the village. Very faintly in the distance, I notice a crowd of people rushing towards us. Looking to my left, I spot Henry and Thomasin making their way around the corner of the barn. And just as they lay eyes on me, I turn a bit further and see the hole we made in the wall. Abigail and I crashed straight through.

Sure enough, Abigail is alive and struggling at my side. She grabs me and we start to battle in the snow. Though I notice that she is now much weaker than in the barn. The blade also landed nearby, and we both notice it at the same time. My reflexes are faster than hers and I successfully lift the weapon from the snow. She grabs me from behind, but I send an elbow directly into her face. This leaves her falling to her back as I maneuver and pin her to the ground. My knee pushes down on her stomach, and I hold the blade to her neck.

Through all the blood, dirt, burns, and damage, we stare at each other in submission. Neither of us possess the energy to fight any further. Blood pours from my head and mouth, though she does not react as it drops to her face. We both sit with heavy breath, maintaining our gaze and struggling to stay alive.

"Do it," Abigail whispers. She shoots her only functioning eye down to the blade at her throat and raises her chin to reveal her neck. "Please," she mutters emotionally, "do it!"

I turn to Henry and Thomasin who move closer, horrified by the sight before them. They are likely relieved to see me alive, but at the moment, it surely does not look as though I am. Abigail begins to shout and cry beneath me, pleading for me to kill her while repeating her sister's name.

"No," I reply. My consciousness begins to slip, though I hold the blade firmly and refuse to let her escape. Abigail is no longer fighting my hold in the least, so I pull the knife away from her skin and relax my grip.

The people on the path grow closer, shouting and running as fast as they can through the snow. Within a few moments everyone will crowd around us, and we shall be saved. Henry will live, Thomasin is unharmed, and Abigail has been detained.

"They ... have come to ... save us," I mutter to Abigail while watching the crowd with a smile. "We are all going to be—"

"You already saved us, Emelie."

Abigail interrupts with peaceful words of gratitude. As I look down, it is no longer the assassin of Bedfordshire beneath me. Instead, it is my awkward-but-familiar friend awaiting my gaze with a gentle smile. 'Tis the same look of adoration from our first encounter or when I told her the ribbon in her hair was beautiful. This is the Abigail that I knew was still buried deep within, behind all the pain, confusion, and darkness.

    She wraps both of her hands around mine on the handle of the blade, but does not try to attack or make an escape. Before I can react, Abigail uses all her strength to plunge the knife into her own throat. It pierces under her chin until all that is exposed is the handle. I let out a fearful cry and pull my hand from her grasp. Thomasin and Henry drag me away and hold me tightly. The three of us embrace each other in the snow, understanding that the madness has reached its end.

XXVII

A Christmas Tale

Abigail's words echo in my mind. I recount everything that unraveled in the barn, from our arrival until our rescue. It can be said that the sisters almost succeeded with their plan. Yet, a series of mistakes and an overpowering desire for chaos ultimately took them to the grave. Chrystopher did not deserve such an ending in his young age and still wished to seek redemption after all they had done. A lifetime of imprisonment awaited, but Abigail ended his tale before he could speak it to the court and answer for his crimes.

And as for Abigail, she had a choice until the very end. Not once did I wish to kill her; that was never my intention. Though she was wise to the potentially short life that awaited and chose to reunite with her sister, wherever that shall be. It is with sorrow that I reflect on their existence, understanding the cruelties of their parents and the burning obsession for freedom. A yearning to break free and create a better life for each other and their young friend led to irrational decisions. They never had a guiding figure like Rose to calm their desires, so they found their own way by pursuing a dark force. While it was malevolent and unjust, to them it seemed to be the only way to bring purpose to their lives.

Bedfordshire lost many vital members and celebrations shall never be the same. It is my hope that each of the deceased, the sisters and Chrystopher included, rest peacefully in the afterlife. And for the victims who are still living like Giles's children or Thomasin, I pray that they can somehow find a way forward.

"He knew, Thomasin," I reveal, drawing Thomasin's attention in my direction. "Samuel was well aware that you are expecting a child."

"I see," Thomasin replies, looking to the ground. Tearfully she attempts to speak but is unable to continue. A subtle smile forms but is washed away by sadness. It seems that the weight of the situation has yet to fully hit Thomasin and she is attempting to conceal all the pain from Samuel's demise. 'Twas a similar situation I endured with John. I felt a deep sadness in the moment, although it quickly turned to numbness. It was impossible to process something so devastating, so in order to save the others, I fought any form of acceptance until everything was resolved. Admittedly I shall never fully accept such a tragedy and will struggle with his absence until we meet again. Surely Thomasin will find difficulty moving forward without Samuel by her side, as will I and everyone else on the farm.

"Was he happy?" Thomasin asks timidly.

I nod at her words and grab her hand. "Yes. He was overwhelmed, and reasonably so, but the idea of being a father brought a smile to his face. In that very moment, it seemed that all the darkness vanished from within him. This was his way forward."

Thomasin smiles at my words and moves closer. She rests her head on my shoulder as we sit peacefully in the front row of the meetinghouse. "The past was haunting him," I explain, "and he saw right through my false smiles. He recognized that we shared a similar pain and wished for the both of us to find peace in this place."

"Peace, in this place," Thomasin whispers to herself. She does not elaborate or question my words. Instead, she likely ponders on what the future holds. And while I have not informed the others, I see only one way that Henry, Thomasin, Nicholas, Amelia, and all of Bedfordshire shall heal.

A few hours passed since our encounter in the barn. Ambrose and the others reached us within seconds of Abigail's suicide. We were rushed to Timothy's practice and treated with the finest of care. I was in a panic when they separated me and Thomasin from Henry, though he needed much more attention in order to survive. Timothy assured us countless times that Henry will live, likely because of my desperate act. His wounds were deep and he lost a tremendous amount of blood, but a full recovery is possible. Henry and Amelia survived this nightmare, and their family is finally safe.

Thomasin walked away from the barn miraculously well, aside from minor bruises and a lingering cough from the smoke. And most importantly, Timothy sees no indications of the child being harmed. It will become certain as the days move forward, but all is well and our rescue was a success. I unfortunately did not walk away from the barn completely unscathed, although I am still breathing. There is a throbbing in my knee, a weakness in my chest, and I must endure proper treatment for my knee in the days and weeks ahead. The burns and wounds shall turn to scars and become nothing more than a memory.

Ambrose has taken our account of the situation in disbelief that Abigail and Rachel were capable of such cruelties. Chrystopher's involvement is believed to stem from his place in a motherless home with a struggling father. I never put much thought into his family, as Chrystopher was but a ghost who could appear or disappear at any moment. He was always at the side of Abigail and Rachel, so it never occurred to think of him separately.

Chrystopher's father would be on the water for days, sometimes weeks at a time, leaving him to fend for himself. The responsibility and pressure he must have felt in his young age also brings me sadness. And while Ambrose urged us to remain under care with Timothy, Thomasin and I felt a responsibility to visit the meetinghouse. We wanted this explanation to come directly from our mouths and Bedfordshire deserves to finally rest on this final day of Christmas.

The meetinghouse is full of onlookers who came to see for themselves if the tale of our battle was true. Commotion grows around us, but Ambrose does not let anyone get close. We sit alone while those in the rows behind are in distress.

"Once this is over, we shall return to the others and disappear from the attention," Thomasin nervously explains. The crowd is making her anxious, though I care little for their banter as another burden weighs heavy on my mind.

All the familiar faces of Bedfordshire pile into the meetinghouse. From Phillip to Solomon, this space is packed and eager for resolve.

"Are you ready?" Ambrose turns and asks us. We nod, and he prepares to address the crowd. "Please, everyone find thy seats so we can be done with this."

I take a deep breath and close my eyes, unprepared to explain our tragic story to the crowd. And while the next few moments will not be easy, everyone deserves to know the truth so they can begin to heal as well. The noise around us fades as the crowd complies with Ambrose's request. He clears his throat and climbs the steps to the pulpit so that everyone can see him.

"Thank you for coming on this final Christmas morning. Though our celebrations ceased and we faced unimaginable loss, I stand before you today with hopes of moving forward as one." Ambrose takes a moment before continuing. "And this will be possible because the wicked ones amongst us have been identified and brought to justice!"

People cry out with tears of joy, no longer having to live in fear and worry for the next murder or attack. It brings a smile to my face to experience the relief and happiness that unfolds. People eventually start shouting at Ambrose for more information, so I recognize that it is our time to act. Ambrose does not even have to ask before me and Thomasin rise. Together we make our way to the pulpit and ascend, turning to face the packed meetinghouse. Some whisper of my limp and make comments of the bandages across my body. All eyes land upon us, hopefully for the final time in our lives.

"I will handle this," I whisper to Thomasin, who is relieved at my offer. We make our way to Ambrose, and the crowd can hardly contain their anticipation.

"Hello," I mutter, clearing my throat with a cough before raising my voice and trying again. "Hello, everyone. Once again, I am Emelie, and this is Thomasin. Ambrose speaks the truth, and all this suffering is over. It pains me to verify that all this evil was conducted by not one individual, but three." Those in attendance look at each other with confusion, never suspecting that this was the work of more than one madman.

"Tell us who!"

"Why did they do it?"

"We must know!"

Ambrose signals for everyone to remain silent as I continue. I grab hold of the lectern to maintain my balance. Thomasin holds my arm upon recognizing my weakness. "Abigail, Rachel, and Young Chrystopher," I say boldly.

"I knew it! I told thee and you refused to listen!" Solomon yells out, pointing to Ambrose and erupting with anger as his suspicions are confirmed.

"Though the details matter not, they made some mistakes during yesterday's attack on our farm. We became wise to their actions and found them hiding in our barn. And when we confronted them, they confessed to everything before trying to murder us. I found no doubt in their words," I explain.

"And to what end did they commit these atrocities? How could they do such things to their home, to their own family?" Pastor Noah asks while gently approaching the pulpit. He seems to be just as devastated as me and Thomasin, and we know that he wanted to redeem the person responsible for these wicked crimes. Everyone agrees with his words and begins shouting for an explanation. This is the moment of our conversation that I dreaded because I know what must be done.

"They took a liking to our past. Henry, Samuel, Thomasin, and I came from the village of Warren Hollow, as you all know. We spent months in prison, watching as our friends died under claims of witchcraft. After leaving that place, my goal was to share knowledge and explain this nonsense for what it truly is. What this so-called witchcraft truly entails must be set aside from the darkness that most believe it to be. But Abigail and Rachel did not see it that way." I begin pacing the pulpit as I continue my explanation. "They were obsessing over dark magic, rituals, and all the evilness that false witchcraft entails long before our arrival. They wanted to use it as a means to destroy Bedfordshire from the inside, and then gain the recognition as the saviors who stopped it. Our arrival set their plans in motion. They called us an *answer to their prayers*."

"Why, Emelie? Why did they favor such cruelty?" Pastor Noah asks with immense sadness.

"They spoke of a hatred for this place. Abigail and Rachel confessed to poisoning their parents. But things did not change for them. Even without the parents they despised, and reasonably so if their claims of abuse and torment are true, things did not get better for them. No amount of faith could save them and eventually they recruited Chrystopher because he was but a lost soul as well."

Some people in the crowd are left in disgust and immediately break into prayer. Hearing of lost faith is perhaps the worst detail that I revealed so far.

"They slowly learned all that they could about witchcraft until they could act with perfection. But our past allowed us to see through their deceit, and we confronted them in our barn. They wished for us to join them in terrorizing Bedfordshire. But when it became apparent that we would not do so, they tried to kill us. We would be known as the outsiders who tried to corrupt your wonderful home, and they would receive the attention they desired so deeply. But they took a liking to the chaos and got lost in their wickedness. It was thrilling and became sport to them."

"But they failed," Thomasin adds, stepping forward and speaking with anger. "Henry and Emelie had no other choice than to stop them from further destruction. Abigail, Rachel, and Chrystopher are dead. It is over."

The meetinghouse echoes with celebratory chants once more, though it does not feel right to cheer for their deaths. These sisters had troubles that nobody else shall ever know. While I do not sympathize with their deaths, I do understand their existence for all that it was. And for that, I do feel sorrow.

"I am sorry," I announce, drawing a halt to the cheers and happiness. "Though the sisters were wicked and deceitful, they spoke a truth. Rather than leaving our past behind us, I came to Bedfordshire with a dark knowledge that I wished to share. While it was never my intention, my actions influenced these sisters. I only ask one thing of all of you; do not blame Nicholas, Amelia, Thomasin, or Henry for these occurrences. It is a fault of mine and I take responsibility. And for that, I will leave this place before the day's end."

The crowd goes silent at my words, and I shoot my gaze down to the lectern. I am ashamed and do not wish to face them any longer. Thomasin takes a step back and I turn to see her visibly emotional and unpleased with my words. "No," she whispers.

"I am sorry, Thomasin. I cannot stay here." I turn and raise my voice so that all of the meetinghouse can hear me once more. "It is with immense gratitude that I was accepted into your beautiful village. But it cannot be denied that my presence brought this misfortune upon you all. I do not deserve to be here."

"Nonsense!" Solomon shouts while marching forward. He stands just below the pulpit in dispute. "All of this made one thing evidently clear; Bedfordshire needs you! These fools around you failed to resolve anything. But because of you outsiders and this knowledge you speak of, our home is safe once more!"

Solomon's words take me by surprise. I look to Thomasin, Ambrose, Solomon, and then across the entire meetinghouse. People nod their heads in agreement and whisper among one another. Before I can reply, I notice someone standing in the back row and moving forward. As they approach, I recognize it to be Nicholas. His presence was not expected and makes me emotional. He passes through the many rows of people and eventually stands below the pulpit next to Solomon.

"This place is your home, and we are your family," Nicholas claims generously.

'Tis difficult to process such an unexpected welcome. I anticipated this confession to bring hatred and banishment, so I wished to exit on my own terms for the sake of the others. But this could not be further from the truth. Ambrose steps forward to share his thoughts on the situation.

"Look at all that you have done to end this madness," Ambrose expresses, scanning my wounds and all the damage from our encounter in the barn. "You fought to save a place that asked nothing of you. And for that, we are eternally grateful."

This praise is cherished deeply, but difficult to take in. I struggle to accept such gratitude on all sides, but for the first time since we left Warren Hollow, I allow myself to feel happiness. Bedfordshire is my home, and I may have finally found my purpose. Though to validate their claims, I must make one request.

"If I am to be welcome here, then there is something I must do. I wish to move forth with apothecary practices. There is much that I need to learn first, though I would be honored to hold such a position among you and properly share this knowledge," I state to those around me. Everyone is pleased by the idea.

"We can surely make a space for you to practice on the farm. We shall see to it come spring," Nicholas ensures.

"No," Ambrose says in respectful dispute, "you will need a proper place for such a service. Somewhere in the village where this can flourish."

"Abigail and Rachel's home now sits vacant. That could be most fitting for a practice," Thomasin adds, further building upon the conversation to prevent my departure. At first her suggestion seems odd, but then I begin to ponder and agree. This could be a fine opportunity to breathe life into such a dreadful place. People will pass by this home with disgust if it sits uninhabited. Though I could turn this into a space of happiness and function. I can already see the decorations, flowers, and shelves of tools and herbs, just like in Rose's home.

"That would be lovely," I reply with a smile. Nicholas and Ambrose nod to each other in agreement and it appears that this could soon be a reality. This idea of becoming an apothecary has been presented to me in surplus since we departed The Hollow, but it grows within me as well. My desire to share knowledge and help others can be achieved in this role. And rather than telling a dismal recollection of Rose's story, I can bring it to life and make it my own. She would be prouder than words can explain.

"We will look further into this come spring. It would be wise for us to inform Timothy, as you will need to work closely with him and perhaps become his apprentice for some time,"

Ambrose explains. I nod at his words and show appreciation for his willingness to grant such a position. The idea is overwhelming and does not yet seem real, though the future shall tell of its success.

Nicholas reaches out to signal for me and Thomasin to descend because our presence on the pulpit is no longer needed. He helps us to stay balanced and composed as we traverse down the few steps. Ambrose now stands alone in front of the crowd and begins to offer departing words to all of Bedfordshire.

"We were plagued by a series of misfortunes that shall never be forgotten. Many undeserving members of our community were lost, and Bedfordshire has been weakened immensely. Though like we have done in the past, we will prevail. This will be a Christmastime remembered only with sadness and fear. We shall mourn, but it will not last." Ambrose steps out from behind the lectern and stands at the edge of the pulpit. "And while it may not seem justified to speak of happiness and celebration, it is still the final day of Christmas. To honor those like Giles who made this year's celebrations possible, Samuel who held our faith, or Simon who kept us well-fed, it seems most fitting to celebrate in their honor!"

Thomasin grabs my hand, and we watch with a smile as cheer fills the meetinghouse. It is difficult to say that we are joyful at this moment but the sight before us cannot be denied. Through all the tragedy and loss, these people still hold their faith and merriment. This is the magical place that John and I dreamed of.

Some people break into chants and festive songs for the holiday while others rush to enjoy the snowfall outside. The meetinghouse quickly empties, though Thomasin, Nicholas, and

I stand near the pulpit and watch patiently. He seems to be in high spirits and likely feels guilt for not believing in our assumptions of the sisters. Though he holds great power in this community and only aimed to help the less fortunate, which is exactly as I intended as well. Nicholas's claim of me as *family* brings a warmness to my heart. We are still finding our place in this life and have only been present in Bedfordshire for a few months, but Nicholas and Amelia's generosity is something I can only wish to repay over a lifetime.

  Our time to depart has come so the three of us begin our journey out of the meetinghouse and back to Timothy's practice. Amelia and Henry have a difficult recovery ahead of them, though the rest of us shall be by their side. Thomasin is set to birth a child in the near future, and it pains me to think that Samuel will not be present. This is something that will be difficult for her, though I will do everything in my power to provide support. I also cannot deny the prominent absence of Abigail, Rachel, and Chrystopher. Nicholas will also need some time to recover from the truth of their evil, and Chrystopher's father must learn of his son's involvement and demise upon his return from the sea. How their story came to an end is truly a tale of sorrow. Perhaps this apothecary role would have given them purpose and a positive way forward. Unfortunately, we shall never know.

  Pastor Noah greets us with a smile as we reach the outside. He bids farewell to everyone who was in attendance, and it seems that most people listened to Ambrose's words. Children are rushing around and frolicking in the snow while parents clear space to start fires near their homes. The bells toll above us, and snow falls gently while the sun emerges from behind the clouds.

Thomasin and I continue holding hands as we walk down the stairs of the meetinghouse. I notice the tears in her eyes, so I hold her tighter. People rush around us and Nicholas smiles at all who pass. He guides our way as we continue through the growing celebration. All the merriment around us is lovely, though the only thing I want is to return to Henry. It is difficult not to run at full speed until I reach his side. One pained and unbalanced step at a time will lead me back to him.

Timothy's practice is close to the meetinghouse, so our walk is relatively short. I smile as we pass through the door and venture away from the joyous pandemonium into this quiet, peaceful space. We close the door to block the sounds of the outside, though it is still noticeable through the walls. It matters not, as Amelia and Henry are both in a deep sleep. They spent many hours being tended to by Timothy and his group of saviors, so this rest is more than earned. Linen bandages line Amelia's neck in many layers and Henry also has a large bandage covering his side. It is still uncertain how he did not succumb to his wounds even after my involvement, though I truly believe it to be a miracle. He wished to save us, to save me, and that is exactly what he did. And I shall spend the rest of my life by his side with love and gratitude.

Nicholas drags a chair over to sit at Amelia's side, and I do the same for Henry. Slowly I drop down until I am directly beside him. While pulling his hand into mine, I whisper gently in his ear. "Thank you for saving me, again. You give so much more than I deserve, and I am alive because of you. I am ready, Henry. Ready to accept this place as our home and to embrace the future that we sought to find. No longer will I torture myself or push you and everyone else away so that I can suffer alone.

We all need each other, and I need you more than you could ever know."

Carefully I adjust Henry on the mattress and check his bandages. I see Thomasin sitting tearfully in the corner alone, so while it pains me to leave Henry's side, I understand that Thomasin needs me as well. She notices as I approach and does her best to conceal all signs of sadness. We sit together for what feels like hours, watching the snowfall and merriment through the window and staring attentively as Nicholas and Timothy take turns observing Amelia and Henry.

"How did you move forward after losing John?" Thomasin asks in a timid manner. It pains me to see her seeking answers so desperately, rather than displaying her usual tone of teasing and jest.

"I," I begin with uncertainty, "in complete honesty, I am not sure that I ever did. Perhaps I am still figuring out how. While I tried as hard as I could, it was impossible to fully accept Henry's love or this wonderful place as our home. It was something I refused because it felt undeserved. And rather than addressing the pain, I became fixated on the distraction of telling our story and spreading the truth. Finding happiness after losing the one thing that mattered to me did not seem fair. So I hid my struggles, or at least tried until this madness sent me spiraling into bouts of nightmares, panic, and insanity. But for the first time, I feel no need to continue hiding. It is frightening to accept happiness because I felt despair since we departed Warren Hollow. But I knew from the very beginning that this is what John would want for me, and I believe that Samuel would want the same for you."

Thomasin nods at my words, appreciating my truthfulness and pondering on the future ahead. It is my only wish that she does not succumb to this inner turmoil that burned within me since John's passing. Surely it will take time and may never properly heal, but we will support each other and ensure that this child shall never face the cruelties of our past. I place my hand on her stomach as I continue. "You will be a wonderful mother to this child, and I will be by your side forever."

"We failed to establish a plan for the future, so I have no doubt of being stuck with you *forever*. Will we stay with Amelia and Nicholas on their farm like a group of vagrants, eating their rations and crowding their space?" Thomasin asks, returning to her playful nature.

"It seems they would not have it any other way," I reply with a smile.

And with that promise to each other, we go back to our peaceful silence. Nicholas and Amelia are forever grateful that Henry returned and still accept Thomasin and I into their family. If Ambrose is true to his word and Timothy is willing to teach me, then the future is bright and my potential in Bedfordshire shall be limitless.

XXVIII

Purpose

The festivities in Bedfordshire lasted well beyond that final day of Christmas. Many wished to recapture the merriment of this sacred celebration to honor the friends and family that were lost. And though it was glorious to see everyone coming together and healing, the weeks that followed were full of inevitable struggle and hardship. When the decorations were stripped from the village and the snow began to melt, the reality of this situation hung overhead like a never-ending storm cloud. Winter turned to spring and spring turned to summer in an instant.

Simon's crew at the port try to fill his role day after day. And while Simon was a drunk, his fishing skills have yet to be matched. Giles's wife and children often spend their days in the meetinghouse while struggling to survive in his absence. Some required weeks of treatment following the poisoning on that horrific morning, but this event claimed not a single life. All the families of victims receive ongoing support, although nothing can replace what was stolen from them.

Whispers of negativity surrounding Abigail, Rachel, and Chrystopher swirl through the village. There was much debate regarding a proper burial in the cemetery or leaving what was left of them in a shallow grave; Ambrose and Pastor Noah agreed on a burial with their families, but this was not well-received. Chrystopher's father succumbed to his guilt and ignorance, drowning in the open water after falling from his fishing vessel not long into the spring. Perhaps his son's involvement was an excuse to end the existence he found so dreadful, or perhaps manning his vessel while heavily intoxicated in the midst of the night led to an entirely accidental demise. The sisters' reign of terror will burden this place for many years. Their desires have come true, as they are known by all and regarded alongside the likes of Griffin Osmund, forever staining the history of Bedfordshire. I think about those sisters often and sometimes visit their graves.

Samuel was given a proper funeral service, which was one of the most difficult moments of my life. Though it was a beautiful memorial, just as Pastor Noah ensured through his wholesome efforts. Farming also suffers while Nicholas spends his every moment tending to Amelia. She is well, though she may never properly walk or speak again. A large scar shines across her neck, but she is in good spirits and grateful to be alive. Henry also grows stronger by the day while returning to his duties on the farm with restrictions. Thomasin carries tremendous pain in the absence of Samuel, but is improving faster than expected with a newfound reason to endure. And as for me, I carry nothing more than scars, horrific memories, and walk with the slightest limp.

It is a beautiful midsummer's morning in Bedfordshire. The birds sing while the wind carries scents from the coast. This is our first summer here and it is undoubtedly the most beautiful time of year. Sunshine beams down upon me in the early morning hours as the flowers bloom. Like most days, I strayed from my path and ventured into the cemetery for a brief visit. I enjoy tending to Samuel's grave and keeping the area maintained while Thomasin is occupied on the farm. Watching the shallops come and go from the port is mesmerizing as I sit in the grass and converse with Samuel. My words may be lost in the wind, but I believe that he hears my endless tales of Thomasin and descriptions of current events on the farm. And while things are a bit uncertain in this place, I assure Samuel that Bedfordshire will prevail, as will Thomasin. It brings me joy to tell Samuel how my nightmares vanished and that I no longer suffer from bouts of panic. I too have changed with the seasons. While there is still much progress to be made, I am living for myself without the restraints of the past. He believed in me, and I shall never forget his efforts.

Oftentimes I find myself visiting the graves of Abigail and Rachel upon my departure, subtly leaving flowers or staring at their side-by-side burial. And while I was not as familiar with Chrystopher, I make sure to occasionally tend to his grave or leave a plaything. He reminded me of John, and I hope that his afterlife is one of peace. Though I have no clouding of judgement for their guilt or wickedness. The three of them were pure evil. They took Samuel from us, and enacted a terror that shall last a lifetime. It is not sympathy for their deaths; rather, it is sorrow for their existence. After much contemplation throughout the winter and spring, I understand that no amount of knowledge or effort on my side could have saved them. And while I regret ignoring the pleas to avoid Abigail and Rachel, I know that Rose would be proud of my dedication.

"Farewell, Samuel. I shall return tomorrow and the day after if Thomasin be occupied," I whisper while rising from the grass and touching his gravestone. I fold the journal that I was studying and prepare to depart. Today is expected to be one of great warmth and the sun is already beaming down in the early hours. While the winds are vicious among the graves with such little distance to the port, it is a wonderful rejuvenation to start the day. The cemetery takes me back to my past in The Hollow and provides a brief escape to nature. That child who enjoyed wondering through the forest and spending time in isolation has officially returned. Whether it be in the cemetery or the surrounding forest, I make time to enjoy these private moments of solitude on most days.

But today is of great importance and there is little time to waste. I spent months expanding my knowledge by reading every scroll I could obtain and scouring over each of Rose's writings. And when my head was not buried deep in those pages, I was learning from Timothy as an apprentice. He took me in almost immediately. There is still much to learn, but the past few months prepared me to become the apothecary of Bedfordshire. It is uncertain what this role shall entail, though I am ready to hold the position with honor. Timothy will handle most matters in his practice, and I will be responsible for distributing healing remedies or soliciting treatments outside of normalcy. My willingness to share knowledge on ideas of witchcraft, dark magic, and other oddities will surely draw a crowd.

Pastor Noah also worked closely with me to build upon my faith and never found my position to be wicked or troublesome. There is a solid understanding across all facets of leadership and faith in Bedfordshire, and it haunts me to know that this was not the case for Rose back in The Hollow when she accepted this role. Nonetheless, I depart from the cemetery and make my way to the sisters' home, which is now the place I call my practice.

The finest craftsmen in Bedfordshire worked tirelessly for months to turn that dreary home into a pharmacy. They redesigned the inside, from the cellar to the roof. Everyone at the farm helped to stock the shelves full of herbs, medicines, scrolls, and anything else that you could expect to find in a mystical apothecary's lair. The result is breathtaking, and I am eternally grateful for their efforts. I begged Thomasin to join me on this venture, though she does not share my level of enthusiasm for such a role. Perhaps she will assist from time to time, but I believe that she is shaping her own destiny. Without any doubt we all succeed through our own merit.

I walk down the path with eagerness. Today my practice officially opens, and I do not know what to expect. Though the uncertainty is exciting, so I increase my speed while rushing to my destination. As I move forward, I offer smiles and greetings to the other members who also rise with the sun. These paths grow full of noise and hassle throughout the day but the moments alongside the sunrise are tranquil and cherished.

Sounds of the port fade and the winds calm as I traverse deeper into the village. My steps are quite uneven, and I do not expect my knee to ever fully heal. Treatment has done wonders throughout the winter and spring, but it is far from perfect. I am also missing a hand, so my steps draw little attention when there be a steel boulder attached to my arm.

"I see someone is eager this morning," Timothy claims as I round the corner and nearly run him over. He greets me with a smile just outside of the sisters' home; or should I say, my practice. His early visit catches me by surprise, though he understands my urgency. Timothy playfully spins the key in his hand with his back resting on the door. "You are more than ready, Emelie. You hath done well and this service will greatly benefit Bedfordshire. I see many glorious years ahead of you in this practice."

Timothy tosses me the key and steps away from the door. "I truly cannot thank thee enough," I tell him with a smile. "This all happened rather quickly and with efforts from everyone. You especially, Timothy. I will lead with all that you have shown me, to the best of my ability."

He laughs at my words and begins to step away. "You hold a lifetime of knowledge that even I do not understand. Perhaps I polished your thinking but the teachings of a physician, or the church for that matter, can only reach so far. What you endured here and in your homeland is monumental. This role is thy calling. We will continue training and work hand-in-hand for remedies and other healing purposes; though this practice is yours to operate as you see fit."

With kind words and reassurance, Timothy pats me on the shoulder and departs from the entryway. I now stand alone in front of the door, looking down at the key in my hand. There is still much uncertainty that led to this moment, and I am unsure if this be how I wish to settle myself in this life. But my aim is to spread knowledge and help those around me so this role could not be more fitting. Surely this is how it felt for Samuel while joining the church at his own free will or for Nicholas while building the farm. It is difficult not to laugh at my doubts, especially after being handed the key to my dreams and desires.

"Does this bring more justice than sharing your story in a journal?" I whisper aloud, hoping that Rose can hear my words.

My destiny lies just beyond this door. It took many years and two unfortunate circumstances of tragedy, but this is the future I dreamed of; the one I promised John and envisioned with Thomasin. Today, I shall make something of myself and become a figure of great importance. And while it is daunting, I push through the door and waste no further time.

The practice is quiet; nothing more than my own heartbeat and nervous breathing fills the room. I look across the space with gratitude at the fully transformed home. Shelves and cabinets are lined with herbs, plants, ointments, and ingredients for remedies. And most importantly, a shelf stands full of scrolls, writings, tablets, and journals for all to read. What was once a mundane living space is now a beautiful shop that smells of flowers and greenery. Sunshine beams through alongside a gentle breeze as I open the windows. A counter has been situated across from the door so that I can greet whoever visits with a smile. Nicholas even configured a bell to the top of the door so I will be alerted if I am preoccupied upstairs. Both bedrooms have been converted to private quarters for care in anticipation of visitors needing a rest or treatment in a secluded space. As for the cellar, it was not easy to travel back down to a place so wicked. Though it got easier when Thomasin assisted with clearing the space for storage. We even made an effort to add some decorations and lighten the atmosphere.

In the days ahead I will continue to decorate and make this place a notable structure in Bedfordshire. And come winter, a fire will stay lit in the hearth to bring gentle smells of smoke and perfumes to the village. Rose always had a fire burning in her hearth and you could smell the smoke through the trees on most winter days when passing through Warren Hollow's gates.

Rose was a role model to all of us and it is an honor to follow in her footsteps. Though I make no effort to become her, rather, I aim to pursue that spark that she ignited within me at a young age. This village, this practice, and this precise state of mind is where I am meant to be at this very moment. I pass through the front room, nervously adjusting jars on the shelves and fixing the flowers so they stand tall. Cautiously I take my position behind the counter and practice my smile for visitors.

What am I to say? Do I hold the knowledge to help those in need? Am I only as wise as the writings on the shelf?

Thoughts of uncertainty and doubt begin to swirl in my mind. My nerves continue to worsen so I start adjusting the decorations on the counter. I fail to realize that I raised my makeshift hand to fix a pot of flowers at the edge. The decoration topples over and crashes to the ground, sending dirt across the floor behind the counter. With a gasp of frustration and embarrassment, I bend over to fix the mess of potted shrubbery.

Suddenly the bell chimes and I hear the door swing open. Someone requires my assistance while I nervously crouch behind the counter. Thoughts race through my mind of who visits and what they shall ask of me. Self-doubt persists until I force myself to rise. Quickly I brush the dirt from my clothes and form an exaggerated smile. "We are not yet open, but if this be urgent then Timothy can assist—"

My greeting trails off at the very sight of my visitor. The nerves calm and I let out an exhale of relief at the realization that it be Thomasin who stands before me. She waits near one of the many shelves of herbs, pretending to aggressively search in a panic.

"I fear that I am cursed, or even bewitched! I was told that you could help me?" Thomasin says playfully.

"There be not enough remedies in the entire colony to save thee," I reply while matching her energy.

"This place looks wonderful, Emelie. Can you imagine what Rose would say if she saw all of this?"

"I think of her often. She would love such a place, and it is my hope that this venture would make her proud." Once more I ponder on the validation and desire for pride that Rose would grant for our efforts. Rose's support meant much more to me than Mother and Father's ever did in my childhood. They would be disgusted by this role. But Rose would walk into this place with a smile, perhaps in tears, and give all the love she had.

"Without any doubt," Thomasin replies. She makes her way to the counter and leans over, noticing the mess I made and looking at me with a smirk. I shake my head and throw my arms up without a good excuse.

"I have been gone but an hour and you already miss me on the farm? Have things fallen apart so quickly in my absence?"

"Actually," she begins playfully, "I am afraid that we moved on. None of us even speak thy name anymore."

I laugh at her words, knowing for certain that everyone would be lost without my presence, as would I without them. Her visit brings me joy on this morning of uncertainty, and my panic begins to fade.

A noise outside steals my attention, and I look past Thomasin to the doorway. It sounds as though someone is near, so I walk around the counter and make my way to the door. I am nearly halfway through the room when Henry, Amelia, and Nicholas emerge. My eyes light up at the realization that Nicholas and Amelia are carrying Thomasin's twins. A smile spreads across my face as I make my way over and give Henry a tight embrace. I step away and direct my attention to the infants. Per usual, Little Sam is crying while his sister, Eliza, sleeps soundly through the tantrum. Gently I steal Sam from Nicholas and sway side to side. For reasons we cannot explain, I am often the only one who can calm Sam when he begins to fuss. And true to my ability, he settles in my arms as I sway and hum in his ear.

"It must be sorcery," Nicholas claims, shaking his head in disbelief. He likely struggled all morning with failing efforts to calm Sam.

It was quite a surprise for Thomasin to birth twins on the cusp of summer. Neither Timothy nor Thomasin ever expected this to be a possibility. Though they are both healthy and beautiful infants nonetheless. The remainder of Thomasin's pregnancy went quite well through the winter and spring. Little Sam takes after his father and displays a shocking resemblance. Eliza already holds a beauty that will flourish through time, so we make jest of how she mustn't inherit her mother's chaotic sensibilities. Their birth brought a newfound happiness to the farm and helped to carry all of us out of the darkness. Thomasin genuinely appears joyful and in good spirits.

"And for what do I have the honor of such a visit?" I ask with a smile.

"It is your first day of trade," Henry says enthusiastically. "We wished to congratulate you once more and be thy first of many customers."

"Well," I begin with gratitude, "I am glad that you did. Truly, this was exactly what I needed this morning."

I look down to Sam, and he has fallen into a deep sleep in my arms. Visions of John after his birth flood my mind when Thomasin's children are in my grasp. John was often in constant pain, wailing through the night without any relief from remedies or medicines. Oftentimes all I needed to do was lie with him in my arms. It seems that I still hold this ability, and while I do not necessarily feel prepared to be a mother at the moment, it is surely an adventure that Henry and I await with glee.

"We do not wish to intrude any further, so perhaps we should be on our way," Thomasin explains while retrieving her son. "Aunt Emelie has much to do," she whispers to Little Sam while carefully taking him from my arms.

"Indeed," Nicholas agrees. "Henry and I must gather some supplies and return to the farm if we are to handle the barn before winter. I can already feel an autumn chill in the air."

Henry laughs at his uncle's words. "Uncle, it is but the middle of summer. And the crew has the barn nearly complete. As we tell you each day, the barn will stand tall before winter."

Amelia rolls her eyes at Nicholas's playful distress with a smile as they make their way to the door. Her and Thomasin are likely planning to visit Samuel's grave and gather provisions for the feast that was promised to me in celebration.

Nicholas continues his panic as Amelia moves him along to the outside with her walking cane. Thomasin also reaches the door and offers a farewell as she departs. "We love you deeply, Auntie Emelie! Best of luck on your first day of practicing witchery!"

Henry is still lingering in the practice. His eyes scan across the many shelves and decorations until he meets my gaze. "We are so proud of you, Emelie. And all of Bedfordshire eagerly awaits your services. Nicholas and I heard many words of gratitude in recent days. But how do you feel, Emelie, standing in this place?" Henry asks.

"I am not sure. We spent so long pondering on the future, all the way back to our days of chores in The Hollow. So if this is to be my purpose, or what I am meant to become, then it is overwhelming."

"I understand," Henry replies while moving closer, "it is difficult to predict the things you will encounter. And surely it will not all be pleasant. But if anyone is meant to do this, then it is certainly you. The way you protect those around you and take the lead in the worst of situations is remarkable. This community will benefit greatly from what you are doing."

"And what if I bring more corruption to this place? Perhaps this practice is a bad idea," I claim with swelling panic.

Henry pulls me in and holds me tightly. "Think of what shall happen if you do not follow through. Without someone to guide and educate on this darkness, it shall sneak up and bring Bedfordshire down from within. We saw how easily Abigail and Rachel brought madness to this place. But you can be the reason that something so awful never happens again."

"Perhaps you are right, Henry. I apologize for holding such doubt on this beautiful morning. 'Tis something I care so deeply for. I will do all that I can for these people," I reply with calming nerves.

"You have come such a long way since that night in the barn. Or even further back to our childhood in The Hollow. We have all been through enough in our lives. After all that we faced, I believe it is time for us to rest. Each of us deserves to do as we please and live a normal life. This opportunity could be everything you searched for. And for the first time, we truly belong somewhere. The future can be whatever we wish it to be," Henry explains. We share a kiss, and Henry offers one final bout of reassurance before departing to find his uncle. "I will wait for you on the farm until the moment you return. Be sure to come with an appetite and the desire to share all that the day entails!"

The urge to become emotional nearly prevails as I wave to Henry. I share a deep love for every person back on that farm. They have been nothing but patient and caring through my struggles, and for that, I am forever indebted. Because of Henry and Thomasin, I am still alive and slowly making something of myself in this life. And because of Nicholas and Amelia, we have a place to call our home.

We traveled far and wide together, the few survivors of two horrific events that we did not deserve. None of us expected to carry these burdens as we departed Warren Hollow. And while these feelings of sorrow and trauma may never fully pass, we will heal together. Many of our friends and those we love will never have this opportunity, which still brings me guilt and resentment for my survival. The likes of John, Ezekiel, Rose, Samuel or even Reverend Thomas, Abigail, Rachel, and Chrystopher shall never truly die. Through a cherished memory or a scar across my skin, those that were lost along the journey are simply part of me.

A future of happiness and peace presents more fear than being locked in a cell or trapped in a barn engulfed in flames. Death is true and absolute, while living is something that I was never prepared to do. Not just surviving and making it from sunrise to sundown, but to truly live our lives the way we intend and to make a difference.

Each of us felt lost upon our arrival to Bedfordshire, unable to accept this place or any bout of happiness. But through all the suffering, each of us is answering the long-awaited call of our destiny. Henry reunited with his family and Thomasin will be a wonderful mother. Bedfordshire will gather itself and prosper once more, and it is my honor to take part in the revival. Our lives are just beginning and the possibilities in this place are endless.

The others are long out of sight, so I stand alone in the doorway of my practice. Bedfordshire is starting to awaken, and I suspect that visitors will soon gather to discover this idiosyncrasy of service that Timothy and I devised. Perhaps they will experience the same level of amazement that I held every time I crossed through the threshold to Rose's home. Some will be fearful and less receptive, thinking of me as a witch or sorceress, though this is an expected response that accompanies such a role.

With one final adjustment of the shelf near the door, I make my way behind the counter with a genuine smile. No longer do I feel doubtful or panicked. After the visit from my loved ones, I am more than ready to fill this role to the best of my ability.

It's as if I can sense Rose's presence at my side. She is here, and has been with us since the start of our journey. While death shall keep us separated for the time being, I know that she watches over me through the veil of eternity. She lives on through the memories, writings, and atmosphere with an empowering force. The wild children who visited her home for bonfires and defied authority in Warren Hollow are children no longer. We broke free from the confines and forged a resistance to the life that was laid before us. And while Rose is well aware, I feel there is one last declaration to be spoken.

"I made it, John."

A Word from the Author

Thank you for supporting the Watch Over Me series. "A Witch's Tale" (2024) was written and anticipated to be a standalone novel from the very beginning. And while an ambiguous ending was the intended conclusion of this narrative, I immediately believed that there was much more depth, emotion, and adventure to explore beyond those final pages while staying true to this concept. It was a rewarding experience to revisit Emelie and envision what came next for these characters, all while relying heavily on research of the traditions, controversies, and contention surrounding Christmas to create a historically accurate depiction of colonial America during another holiday. "A Christmas Tale" (2025) serves as the unexpected but fittingly brutal, intense, and rewarding continuation of this tragic tale.

Discover More from Ajay Bell

Join the official *Watch Over Me* community on TikTok for access to exclusive content, updates, and more:

@ajaybellauthor

About the Author

Ajay Bell revisits the *Watch Over Me* series with **Watch Over Me II: A Christmas Tale**. Born and raised in Pittsburgh, Pennsylvania, Ajay graduated from La Roche University in 2022. Holding a lifelong passion for the horror genre, alongside the gained knowledge and respect for literature through his education, Ajay found inspiration and published his debut novel in 2024. Ajay presents a unique writing style, honoring the darker side of literature with an articulate focus on the grim and gothic nature of the world. When Ajay is not obsessing over all-things horror, he can be found practicing martial arts.

www.ingramcontent.com/pod-product-compliance
Lightning Source LLC
LaVergne TN
LVHW091658070526
838199LV00050B/2193